# Praise for Timothy S. Johnston

## *The War Beneath*

"If you're looking for a techno-thriller combining Ian Fleming, Tom Clancy and John Le Carré, *The War Beneath* will satisfy . . . I really enjoyed reading this book. It's what I call a ripping good yarn, a genuine page-turner. If you like action spy thrillers with lots of high tech in a science fiction setting this book will definitely please. It's loads of fun. And fast-paced. Did I mention fast-paced? 'Cause it is."—*Amazing Stories*

" . . . sit back, start reading and enjoy a deep sea dive into the future . . . One very riveting, intelligent read!"—Five Stars at *Readers' Favorite*

## *The Savage Deeps*

"*The Savage Deeps* is like a futuristic Das Boot with a lot of intense action and some interesting technology . . . I give *The Savage Deeps* a five star rating."—*A-Thrill-A-Week*

## *Fatal Depth*

" . . . heart-stopping action! Timothy S. Johnston is an incredible writer, word perfect, and so imaginatively creative . . . There's a reason Johnston was the winner of the 2018 Global Thriller Award."—Five Stars at *Readers' Favorite*

## *An Island of Light*

" . . . Brilliant, stylistically flawless writing again, Mr. Johnston. It's a pleasure to read your books for so many different reasons!"—Five Stars at *Readers' Favorite*

"Take a murder mystery, combine it with a futuristic setting, and add elements of psychological and social reflection for a sense of the action and focus of *An Island of Light*, which requires no prior familiarity with its predecessors in order to prove thoroughly engrossing on many different levels.

"Thriller, sci-fi and mystery audiences alike will find it crosses these genres with high-octane action and appeal."—*Midwest Book Review*, D. Donovan, Senior Reviewer

"As author Johnston explores the morality of torture, murder, and retribution, he manages to keep Mac's moral compass pointing north but only just. It's this aspect of the book that will stay with the reader. Mac has always been a very real character. One the reader can empathise with and one we're willing to follow into the depths. So it's very fitting that he should struggle so mightily before pulling off the most inventive and daring rescue yet.

"*An Island Of Light* is a worthy instalment in the Rise Of Oceania series and I look forward to the next book."—*SFcrowsnest*

## *The Shadow of War*

"Johnston presents readers with a diverse set of characters, along with a complicated world for them to navigate. The novel shines when describing the technology, as when the characters discuss the beam weapon, nicknamed 'The Water Pick' . . . Fans of high-tech SF will enjoy the concepts and world-building here . . . "—*Kirkus Reviews*

"*The Shadow of War* is a slambang thriller set in an all-too-plausible future. Fans of Tom Clancy and Michael Crichton will be spellbound."—Robert J. Sawyer, Hugo Award-winning author of *The Oppenheimer Alternative*

Zoey!

# A BLANKET OF STEEL

Published in Canada by
Fitzhenry & Whiteside Limited
209 Wicksteed Avenue, Unit 51, East York, ON M4G 0BB1

Published in the United States by
Fitzhenry & Whiteside Limited
60 Leo M Birmingham Pkwy Ste 107, Brighton, MA 02135

Fitzhenry & Whiteside acknowledges with thanks the Canada Council for the Arts and the Ontario Arts Council for their support of our publishing program. We acknowledge the financial support of the Government of Canada through the Canada Book Fund (BF) for our publishing activities.

Canada Council for the Arts Conseil des arts du Canada

ONTARIO ARTS COUNCIL
CONSEIL DES ARTS DE L'ONTARIO
an Ontario government agency
un organisme du gouvernement de l'Ontario

Library and Archives Canada Cataloguing in Publication

Title: A blanket of steel / Timothy S. Johnston.
Names: Johnston, Timothy S., 1970- author.
Description: Series statement: The rise of Oceania ; book 6
Identifiers: Canadiana 20230487289 | ISBN 9781554556281 (softcover)
Classification: LCC PS8619.O488 B53 2023 | DDC C813/.6—dc23
Publisher Cataloging-in-Publishing Data (U.S.)

Names: Johnston, Timothy S., 1970-, author.
Title: A Blanket of Steel / Timothy S. Johnston.
Description: Toronto, Ontario : Fitzhenry & Whiteside, 2023. | Series: Rise of Oceania, Book 6. | Summary: "Truman McClusky has led the underwater colonies in their fight against the world's superpowers. Climate change has devastated the surface; nations suffer famine, drought, rebellion, rising waters, and apocalyptic coastal flooding. But now, as Mac leads the underwater colonies to freedom and independence, he is faced with the gravest threat of his life: a Russian assassin, hell-bent on killing Mac and everyone he cares for. Now Mac must uncover the identity of the killer, face him in combat, and at the same time lead people in battle against the largest underwater force ever assembled"– Provided by publisher.

Identifiers: ISBN 978-1-55455-628-1 (paperback)
Subjects: LCSH: Submarines (Ships) – Juvenile fiction. | Espionage -- Juvenile fiction. Assassins – Juvenile fiction. | Fantasy fiction. | BISAC: JUVENILE FICTION / Science Fiction. | JUVENILE FICTION / Action & Adventure / General.
Classification: LCC PZ7.1J646Bl |DDC 813.6 – dc23

Cover and text design by Ken Geniza
Printed in Canada by Copywell

fitzhenry.ca

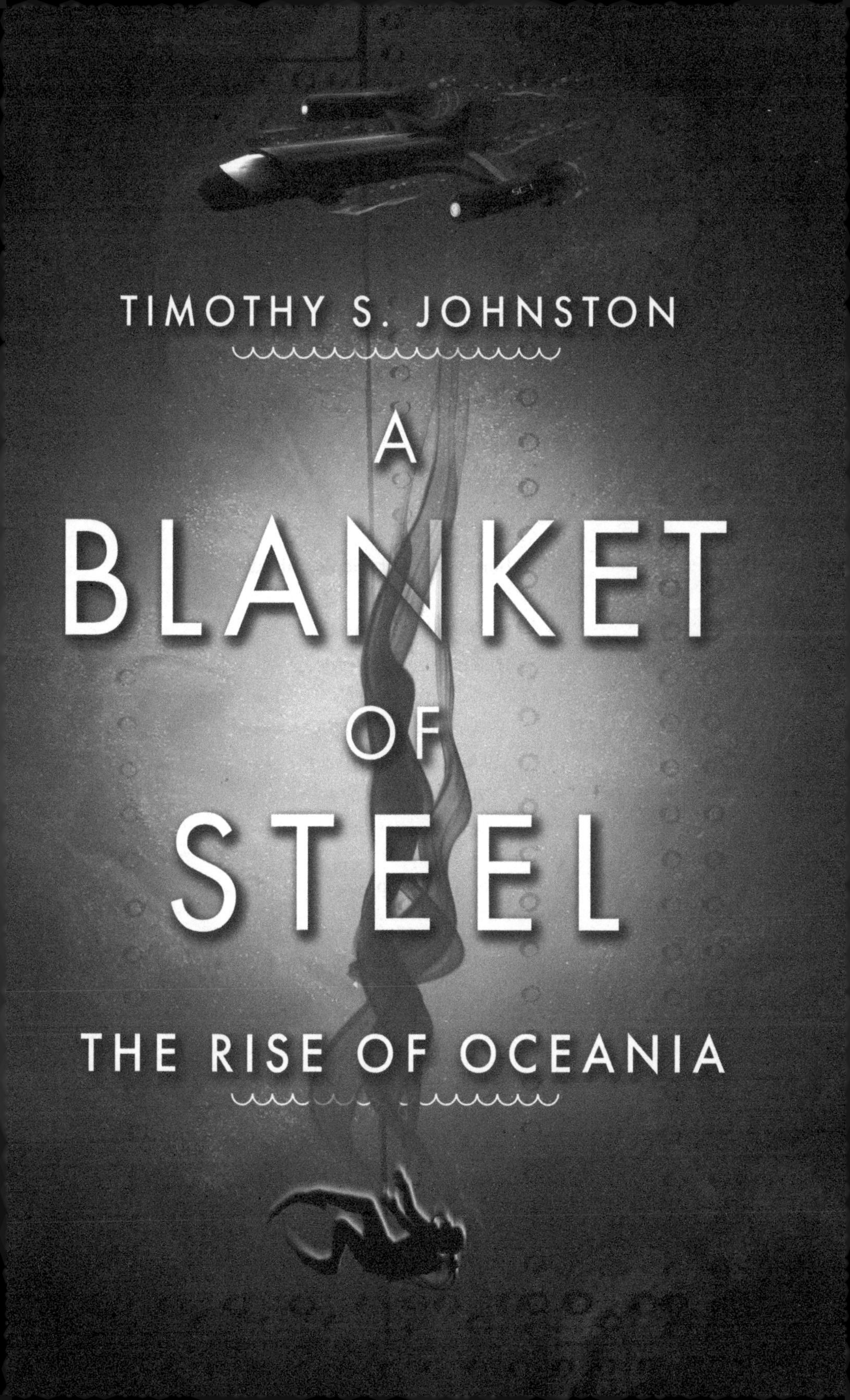
TIMOTHY S. JOHNSTON
A BLANKET OF STEEL
THE RISE OF OCEANIA

## Books by Timothy S. Johnston

Fitzhenry & Whiteside Limited

*The War Beneath*
*The Savage Deeps*
*Fatal Depth*
*An Island Of Light*
*The Shadow Of War*
*A Blanket Of Steel*

Carina Press

*The Furnace*
*The Freezer*
*The Void*

## Timeline of Events

### 2020
Despite the fact that global warming is the primary concern for the majority of the planet's population, still little is being done.

### 2055
Shipping begins to experience interruptions due to flooded docks and crane facilities. World markets fluctuate wildly.

### 2061
Rising ocean levels swamp Manhattan shore defenses and disrupt Gulf Coast oil shipping; financial markets in North America become increasingly unstable due to flooding.

### 2062-2065
Encroaching water pounds major cities such as Mumbai, London, Miami, Jakarta, Tokyo, and Shanghai. The Marshall Islands, Tuvalu, and the Maldives disappear. Refugee problem escalates in Bangladesh; millions die.

### 2069
Shore defenses everywhere are abandoned; massive

numbers of people move inland. Inundated coastal cities become major disaster areas.

## 2071-2072

Market crash affects entire world; economic depression looms. Famine and desertification intensifies.

## 2073

Led by China, governments begin establishing settlements on continental shelves. The shallow water environment proves ideal for displaced populations, aquaculture, and as jump-off sites for mining ventures on the deep ocean abyssal plains.

## 2080

The number of people living on the ocean floor reaches 100,000.

## 2088

Flooding continues on land; the pressure to establish undersea colonies increases.

## 2090

Continental shelves are now home to twenty-three major cities and hundreds of deep-sea mining and research facilities. Resources harvested by the ocean inhabitants are now integral to national economies.

## 2093

Led by the American undersea cities of Trieste, Seascape, and Ballard, an independence movement begins.

## 2099

The CIA crushes the independence movement.

## 2128

Over ten million now populate the ocean floor in twenty-nine cities.

## 2129

Tensions between China and the United States, fueled by competition over The Iron Plains and a new Triestrian submarine propulsion system, skyrockets. The USSF occupies Trieste following The Second Battle of Trieste.

## Winter, 2130

Trieste Mayor Truman McClusky begins a new fight for independence against the United States. With new deep-diving technology, he defeats French and US warsubs in battle in the Mid-Atlantic ridge, killing Captain Franklin P. Heller.

## Spring, 2130

Russia launches dreadnought *Drakon*, a new terror in the oceans. She is 414 metres long, can travel 467 kph underwater, and possesses a new weapon: The Tsunami Plow. *Drakon* sinks many vessels and destroys the Australian underwater colony, Blue Downs. McClusky leads a raid to infiltrate and destroy the submarine.

## June–August, 2130

Meagan McClusky, captured for murdering a USSF Admiral, is imprisoned at Seascape, the Fleet's new HQ. Truman McClusky, Mayor of Trieste, embarks on a perilous journey to rescue her using stolen German Submarine Fleet warsubs to draw Germany into the conflict. Seascape is destroyed with a new category of weapon, the Isomer Bomb.

## January, 2131

Aided by the magnetic and personable Mayor Sahar Noor, Mac and the team steal the most unique weapon for use underwater ever invented, the Neutral Particle Beam. During the heist, Mac discovers that one of his oldest friends is not all he appears to be. Churchill Sands, the UK colony on the shallow seafloor in the English Channel, joins Mac's struggle for independence, bringing Oceania's numbers to fifteen underwater cities.

## June, 2131

Present day.

“Vengeance is in my heart, death in my hand,
Blood and revenge are hammering in my head.”
—William Shakespeare, *Titus Andronicus*

“Ah, God! what trances of torments does that man endure who is consumed with one unachieved revengeful desire. He sleeps with clenched hands; and wakes with his own bloody nails in his palms.”
—Herman Melville, *Moby Dick*

# Prologue

## Somewhere in the Pacific Ocean

**3 June 2131 AD**

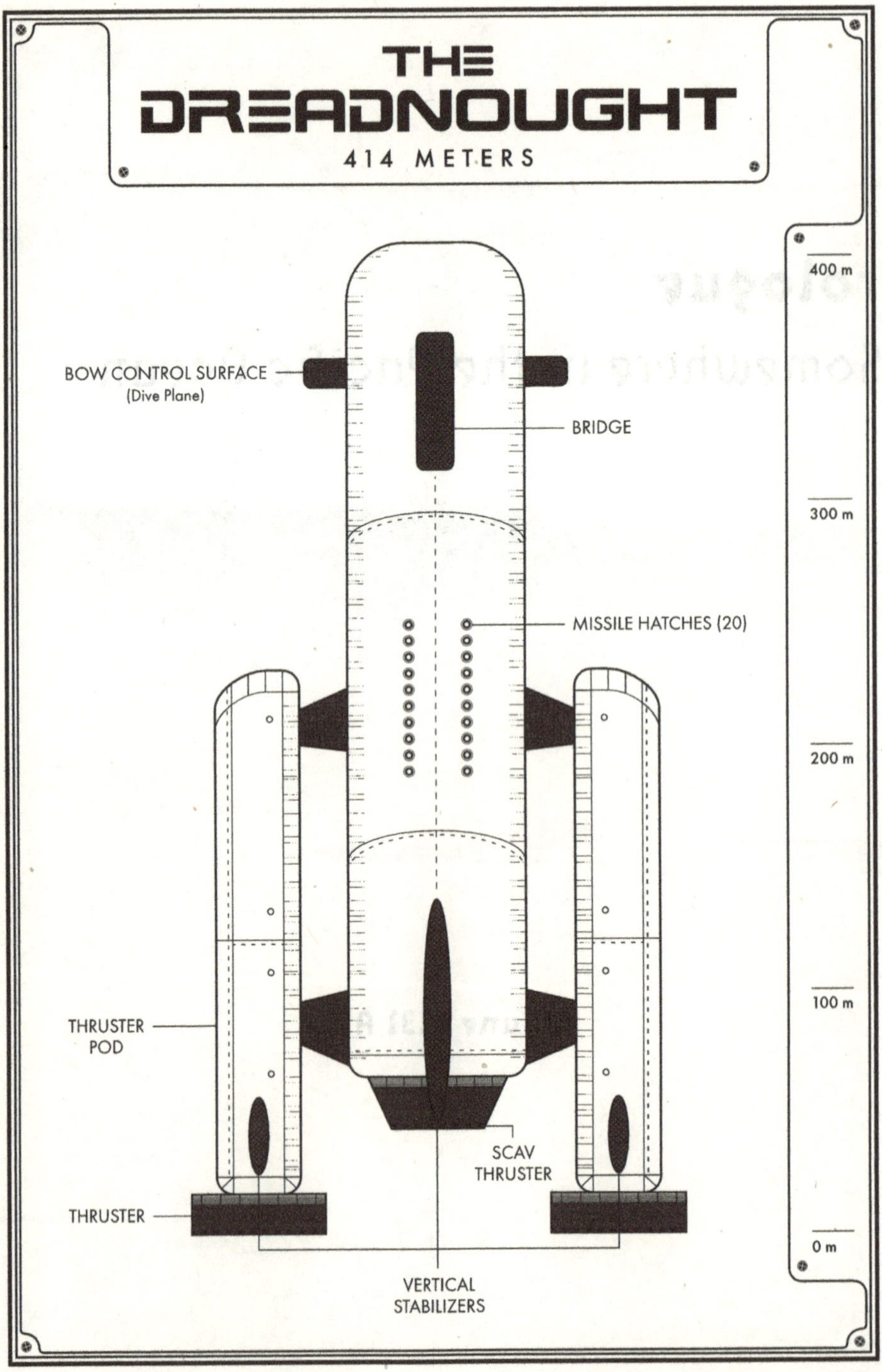
THE
DREADNOUGHT
414 METERS
BOW CONTROL SURFACE
(Dive Plane)
BRIDGE
MISSILE HATCHES (20)
THRUSTER POD
SCAV THRUSTER
THRUSTER
VERTICAL STABILIZERS
400 m
300 m
200 m
100 m
0 m

| | |
|---|---|
| Vessel: | Russian Submarine Fleet *Dreadnought* Class *Voskhod–The Rise* |
| Location: | Latitude: Unknown<br>Longitude: Unknown<br>North of The Iron Plains |
| Depth: | 100 metres |
| Date: | 3 June 2131 |
| Time: | 2058 hours |

HE WAS THINKING OF REVENGE.

The coldest and hottest revenge one could imagine.

A revenge that would strip the skin from its victims, peel away muscle and bone, drain the blood entirely, and fill a chamber with screams.

A revenge that would linger for generations.

The Russian Captain stood on the expansive bridge of the massive *Dreadnought* Class vessel and stared into nothingness. A vein traced across his temple and disappeared into his thinning hair.

It pulsed with each beat of his angry heart.

The canopy above the bridge was a tremendous sixty metres long, and nearby, men and women sat at consoles and monitoring equipment, ensuring that the vessel *Voskhod* operated at peak performance. The hum of machinery lay like a comforting blanket over the crew; the lights from displays shone up at stern faces with fixed expressions. The Captain didn't like emotion. He wanted his people to operate like computers . . . *Do your jobs*, he'd say. People depend on your actions. *Do your tasks promptly and efficiently, and the rest will fall into place.*

Strange that he had ordered his crew to perform their tasks without emotion, when deep within him a darkness churned endlessly.

—••—

LIEUTENANT MILA SIDOROV EYED THE Captain as she approached from behind. She took a moment to glance around the bridge—a magnificent achievement by Russian engineers. True, the first dreadnought had suffered defeat over the Kermadec Trench nearly a year before, but it had proven itself again and again before it had succumbed to flooding. Hundreds of enemy subs had gone down with it during the tremendous battle.

And the Captain of that vessel—*Drakon*—had been the same person who stood before her now.

Captain Ivan Arkady Ventinov of the RSF.

No wonder rage consumed him, she thought. He'd been in command of the first vessel of its type in the oceans, and had engaged in the largest underwater naval battle in history against multiple nations. *Drakon* had gone down, but somehow Ventinov had survived.

But more surprising than that, he had *prospered*.

His superiors hadn't executed him for dismal failure.

Instead, they had awarded him another vessel, another command, and a new task.

The *Dreadnought* Class *Drakon* had been the largest sub ever put to sea, at over 400 metres long and with a crew of over 600. It had two fission reactors and a SCAV drive to hammer it through the waters in a nearly frictionless bubble at over 400 kilometres per hour. Its greatest weapon, the *Tsunami Plow*, had destroyed *two* USSF shore headquarters, a Chinese Submarine Fleet force of sixty-three heavily armed warsubs, and the underwater colony, *Blue Downs*. The Australians had since rebuilt that colony, but it had been a glorious victory.

But its reign of terror in the waters only lasted a few months before its enemies destroyed it. But rather than punish her Captain, the RSF had awarded him with a new command of another dreadnought.

*Voskhod.*

Identical to the previous vessel, this was one of three new ones that had all now put to sea. Their mission was to destroy the enemy: Trieste City.

And Mila Sidorov, the ship's XO, knew that Captain Ventinov would not fail this time.

His thirst for revenge was obvious.

A child could see it.

She halted smartly, saluted, and cleared her throat.

Ventinov turned to her.

—••—

HE STARED AT HIS EXECUTIVE Officer. She had a severe look in her eyes and her expression was icy. She exuded professionalism and strict military protocol at all times. She knew what she was doing, knew the RSF procedures, and expected all crew on the vessel to behave appropriately. Ventinov appreciated this. To achieve his goals, he demanded competence from his crew. He needed strong leadership and harsh punishment on the ship. He needed his officers to funnel his intensity downward into the lower ranks, and Sidorov did this well. She was cold, and he liked this about her.

She was staring at him, and other than the brief clearing of her throat, said nothing.

Her salute was rigid and frozen in place. The lines around her eyes spoke of a life around the sea, wind, and saltwater, but the RSF had only put the warsub to sea weeks ago.

And now that they were at four atmospheres, they would not be surfacing any time soon.

Outside, the cold, deep water sighed past the thick titanium hull. Deep within the warsub, echoing and vibrating in her core, distant machinery droned on to keep the Russian crew alive and well. Atmospheric processors removed carbon dioxide, recyclers cleansed water for later use, desalinators created new freshwater for the massive requirements of a crew of over 600, and maintenance on all the machinery occurred daily, even though the vessel was brand new. The fission core was always a beast to maintain.

He finally nodded to her. "Sidorov."

She relaxed and stood easily before him. "The latest drill reports look good. Response time is down even further."

"Drills are one thing. Reality is different."

She frowned. "But without drills—"

"Yes, it's a starting point. You're right." There was a moment of hesitation. Ventinov was staring at the sea over their heads. The gargantuan canopy held back enormous pressure, and the distant sunlight glowed dimly over their heads, like burning ash in an alien planet's sky.

"Sir?" she said.

He brought his gaze back to her. "I've been in battle." His voice was gravel. "The crew can train endlessly. But we can't simulate how they'll respond under *real* pressure. As people die. As water fills their lungs and pressure cracks hulls." He thought of the events of that battle and his insides felt hollow. He knew that he wasn't the same man he'd been then. He'd been overconfident, cocky, arrogant. He'd learned lessons from it, and he knew that RSF leadership could see it within him too.

"Did your crew break?"

He opened his mouth to speak, then closed it. The abrupt nature of the question startled him. It was tactless, but he also enjoyed this about Sidorov. Niceties didn't occupy her.

He glanced around to see if the bridge crew were listening. The chamber was so huge, however, there was no one near to hear. "They performed well. But we came up against something we hadn't trained for."

"Sabotage."

The single word ripped through him like a bullet. In a moment he had composed himself. "We'd trained for intruders. Our security knew their jobs. The crew had prepared." He sighed. "But we weren't ready for a forced meltdown in our fission plant. That's what took us down." His face grew tight and the lines around his eyes deepened. "It was unexpected." No doubt she had heard the stories the crew told each other in their bunks and in the corridors and at their stations. They stopped whenever an officer came near, but they all spoke of it.

And likely blamed Ventinov for the deaths of their comrades.

Sidorov glanced down at his hands. They had tightened into fists. She said, "No one expected it. Not even RSF leadership. There's no way to train for something like that."

*But they blame me*, Ventinov wanted to say. He clenched his teeth.

"And you took down hundreds of their ships."

"Yes," he growled. "*That* was easy. Easy prey for us." He thought of the man responsible for the loss of *Drakon*. A chill went through him, and his heart started to pound.

A shiver traced down his spine.

"What is it, sir?" Sidorov asked.

Ventinov swore inwardly. Damn. She'd noticed his rage. "The person responsible. Truman McClusky."

"Of Trieste."

"The Mayor of the underwater colony in the Gulf of Mexico. Yes."

Sidorov pursed her lips. "There are three dreadnoughts now in the oceans. Surely we can—"

Ventinov took a step toward her. "Oh, we will." He pushed his face toward her. "And I'm going to kill him."

—••—

MILA SIDOROV RESISTED THE URGE to take a step back. Barely. The Captain's breath was hot on her face, and it was putrid, like three days of stale coffee and rotting meat. She'd heard all the stories, of course. She knew what had happened, and had overheard it from the crew. She couldn't know the full truth though. *Drakon*'s crew was gone, as were their stories.

"Surely we can just attack Trieste and be done with it. We have the Tsunami Plow. There are three dreadnoughts. They can't withstand—"

"He's smart. He's prepared."

"How could he prepare—"

"He has defences around his colony. He's had a lot of time."

"But three dreadnoughts are—"

"That doesn't matter." Ventinov sighed and turned to look at the bridge around him. The dim sunlight barely illuminated the area; the rest of the light came from the console displays. "I know about his defences. Even their secrets. To get McClusky, I can't go blasting in like a maniac. I've learned . . . *lessons*, Sidorov. I've learned about my enemy."

Sidorov snorted. "You make it sound like he's invincible."

"No. He's just . . . *clever*."

"So what's your plan?" She gestured at the water over their heads. "Why are we in the Pacific?"

They were north of The Iron Plains, an area the size of Brazil rich in polymetallic nodules littering the ocean floor. China, Russia, and the United States were all in competition for mineral rights to the area; there had been skirmishes and fighting already, and each month, more and more ships came into contact.

*Violent* contact.

Many ended up below Crush Depth, imploding and sinking to the smothering depths.

The conflict was growing more poisonous with each passing day.

Ventinov paused. The whisper of ventilation fans and the murmur of soft commands floated over them. He said in his coarse voice, "I've set a trap, Sidorov, and it's already begun. Like I said, I've learned from my mistakes. I'm not going to use a hammer on him." He turned to her and his lips peeled back into a cruel smile. "I'm going to use a *blade*."

```
Location:       Latitude:  Unknown
                Longitude: Unknown
                On the seafloor in The Iron
                Plains; Chinese Manufacturing
                Plant—The Facility
Depth:          1,618 metres
Date:           3 June 2131
Time:           2217 hours
```

CLIFF SIM HAD FOLLOWED THE trail diligently.

He'd tracked down the leads, and the clues had directed his movements.

And he'd ended up in hell.

Truman McClusky had assigned him the mission a week earlier. *Find out how they're doing it,* he'd said. *Get me the secret. Bring it back.* And then he'd sent Cliff on his way.

Cliff was the Chief Security Officer of Trieste City, but he was also an agent of Trieste City Intelligence. And when Mac gave a mission, there was no refusing. There was only the desire to achieve total success for the man. Cliff knew the task, knew the threats, and had given himself to the dangers. There was no fear, no hesitation. He was fully on side with Mac and his plans, and had willingly taken the assignment.

And now, here he was, at a Chinese facility on the seafloor in the Pacific, midway between the Philippines and Hawaii, wondering exactly what had happened and how he'd gotten himself into this mess.

The lights were dim. The corridors were narrow and the smells were foreign to him. The sound of machinery echoed in the distance, the *thunk thunk thunk* of heavy hammers pounding metal, and the scream of powerful tools grinding titanium. He was wearing a black wetsuit and a tinted mask to obscure his appearance.

He stood in the middle of the corridor and stared at the figure before him, also wearing black with a full helmet.

The other said, "You've come for the secret."

Cliff frowned behind his own mask. A computer had altered the voice; it sounded robotic and alien. "Who are you?"

"I'm the person who is going to end your journey." The electronic voice hissed and echoed off the metal walls and deck.

Cliff considered the statement, but only for an instant. It had taken a long investigation to find The Facility. He'd traveled thousands of kilometres, sometimes backtracking and in a circuitous route, questioning those who had information and tracking others, peering through data files, tracing email messages through the common fiber optic networks. When he had finally found the facility, the depth had immediately concerned him. He'd had to go outside, bypass the exterior controls in the hull—infiltrate through an emergency airlock—and once in the corridor, had met up with this security officer almost immediately upon entry.

He'd been waiting, just standing there.

*Security*?

A sentry?

Or something else?

"You think so?" Cliff took a step forward.

The figure matched his movement; the two moved together slowly.

They crept carefully, crouched low.

Cliff eyed his opponent. The figure was slight, standing about five and a half feet, but toned muscles flexed under the black wetsuit. The other's stance was competent, and spoke of years of training.

This person knew how to fight.

But Cliff knew how to handle such situations. He was a mountain of a man. He was all muscle, over six feet tall, bald, and nearly as wide as the corridor. He'd trained and toned his muscle, and he was *fast*. He'd been training a lifetime and fought with partners regularly. He sparred as part of the training, with orders not to pull punches. Cliff sometimes showed bruises or black eyes, but it was rare. More often than not, his training partners were bloodied and battered, and they had to explain themselves as they worked at Trieste hauling kelp or working the fish farms.

Fighting was a natural way of life for Cliff, and he wasn't scared of this little man.

But something made him take notice.

The other moved toward him with agile steps. The bent knees, the low stance. The taut forearms; sinews rippling beneath black material.

Cliff made a sudden decision and reached to his side. He drew a gun.

His opponent stopped and straightened immediately. "Fire that and alarms will sound. The entire facility will know you're here."

"And you'll be dead."

"But you won't get the secret." The electronic syllables died on his lips.

Cliff's heart pounded. The other was right.

And then, in a flash, there was a gun facing him as well.

*He'd pulled that fast,* Cliff thought. "What do you propose?"

"Let's finish it the way our training intended."

"Why are you disguising your voice?"

There was no answer. Instead, his opponent lowered his weapon.

Cliff frowned. He could fire and end it right there . . .

But his adversary was correct. There would be no choice but to run, and Mac wanted the secret. Cliff couldn't leave without it.

He lowered the gun and took a breath.

He had to fight.

Both weapons skittered across the deck as the two surged toward each other. Cliff blocked a kick with his right forearm and then swung his left elbow toward the other's jaw, hoping to end this quickly. The other was so much smaller than Cliff that it should be—

And he received a thunderous kick to his sternum that hurled him backward.

Cliff's elbow missed widely and he barely caught his balance before he fell. His breath was wheezing from his lungs. He stared at his opponent, and somehow—he didn't understand how—*knew* there was a smile behind that mask.

Cliff shot a look to the gun on the deck. The figure stared at him, following his gaze, then looked back. "It's too late for that now," he said in his robot voice.

"How'd you know I would be here?" Cliff growled as he got to his feet.

There was no response.

Cliff thought back to his movements. He'd arrived at the Triestrian mining facility, The Complex, and followed the clues that led him to this confrontation. Surely they couldn't have been set up . . . it had been too intricate a path. It had taken too much detective work to locate this place. Mac needed new technologies to keep Trieste ahead of the superpowers in the oceans. He needed the best weapons, the newest deep-diving tech, the greatest inventions to make extracting resources more efficient. It kept them at the forefront of ocean exploitation, and had given their city the advantage in the colonization efforts.

But this made Cliff's scalp tingle.

Something here was not right.

This was not an ordinary agent, and, he realized, this was not an ordinary fight.

He might actually be in trouble here.

He straightened and took a deep breath. The two circled each other warily, watching. Cliff feinted and the other responded. Cliff feinted again, with a different response.

He pretended to punch but switched to a kick.

He kicked but switched to the other leg at the last moment.

No matter what he did, the other had a response.

And each was unexpected.

The other blocked with an elbow. He stepped back easily from a kick. He ducked a feint and avoided another kick. He locked Cliff's arm in a wrist lock suddenly, and Cliff darted out of it before his opponent could snap the bones.

He was as fast as lightning.

And then he chuckled softly; the electronic filter struggled to make sense of the noise, and it sounded like a mechanical rattle.

Cliff had had enough. He had to end this and get the secret so he could escape back to Trieste. He pretended to sag, to give up, and then as the other moved in, he jumped like a coiled snake.

He grabbed his adversary around his neck and twisted into a sleeper hold.

Cliff tensed his muscles and poured on the pressure.

No one could withstand this, he thought. Cliff's strength was remarkable; at times he thought he could bend steel.

He crouched slightly and continued to squeeze. He bent backward to pull the other off balance and destroy any leverage he might have.

Only a few seconds left, he knew, and then—

Something interesting happened, and it occurred so quickly that

Cliff didn't fully realize what the other had done until it was too late.

He stepped forward then back, throwing Cliff slightly off balance. Cliff corrected, to maintain control, and the other bent with the force of a hydraulic press. His abdominal strength was phenomenal, Cliff thought dimly, and his grip snapped and his opponent twisted away easily. A foot swung up into his peripheral vision—

And it cracked into the side of Cliff's jaw.

He stumbled back, dazed, as the world suddenly dissolved into a series of blows and strikes that he could barely handle. He attempted to block, but the other was too fast. He'd raise his arms to deflect one strike, but too slow; a fist tore under the block to impact his face. Then another, from the other side, and Cliff thought he had time to block that too . . .

But too late, for an instant later that one struck home as well.

Then another.

And another.

And there were kicks too. Spinning, crescent, and more front kicks, like that first one that had knocked the breath from him.

He still hadn't recovered from it, and there had now been at least ten more of equal or greater intensity.

Blood trickled from cuts, and his face throbbed.

His sight was growing dim.

*Who the hell was this?*

In all his years, in the USSF and working for Mac in TCI, he'd never encountered an opponent like this before. He'd fought French, Russian, Chinese, and German special forces. He'd fought in facilities and underwater in scuba gear. He'd endured weeks of torture by the CIA and had never cracked. He'd infiltrated facilities and warsubs and had handled every opponent easily.

But this was . . .

Cliff took three steps back and, chest heaving, watched his opponent, who didn't even seem to be breathing hard.

Cliff knew there was no other choice.

He turned and ran.

# 7 June 2131 AD
## Four Days Later

# Part One

## Oceania Rising

At Trieste City
In the Gulf of Mexico,
30 Kilometres West of Florida

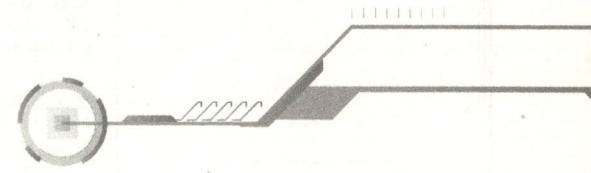

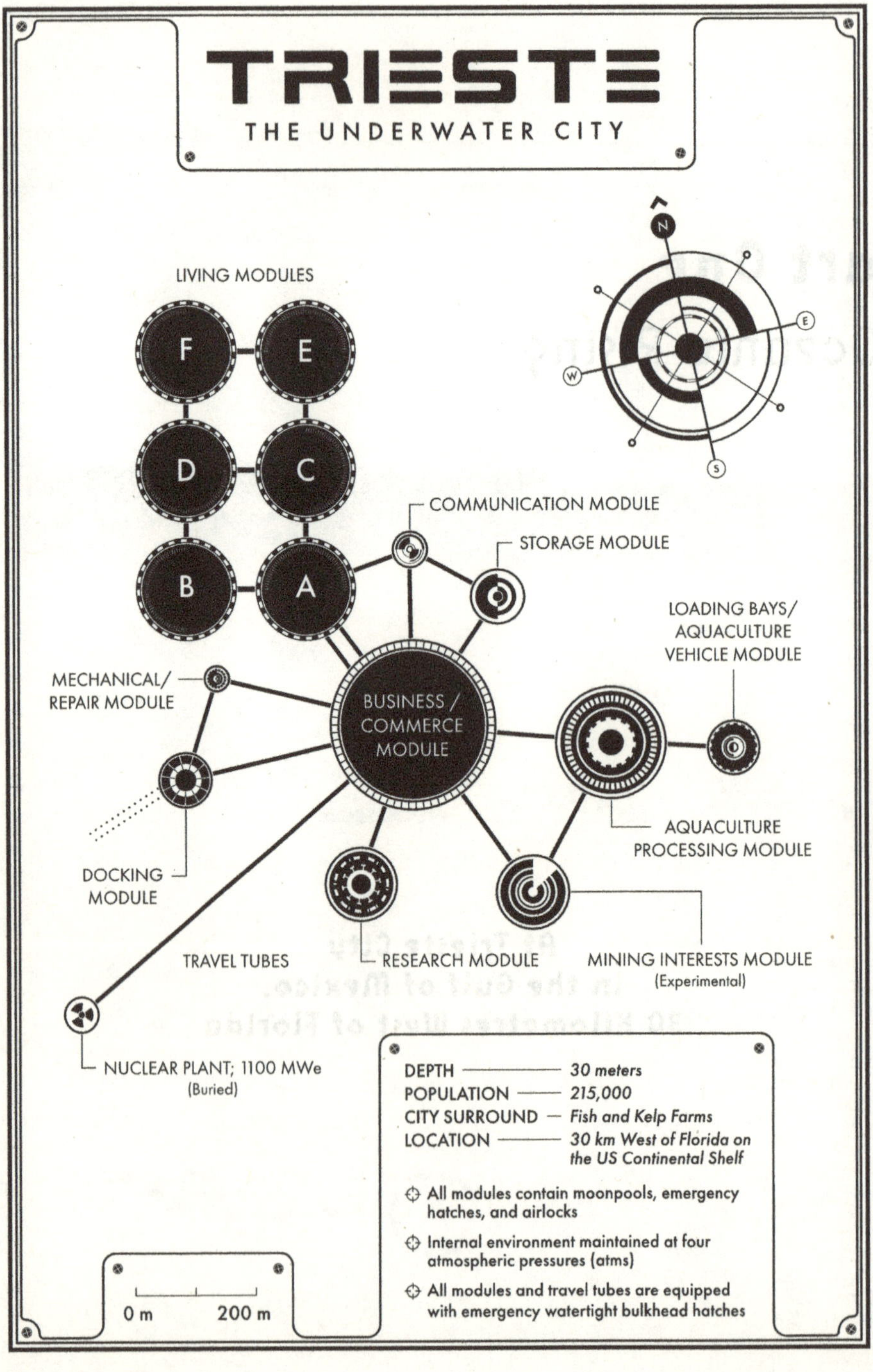
TRIESTE
THE UNDERWATER CITY
N
E
S
W
LIVING MODULES
F
E
D
C
B
A
COMMUNICATION MODULE
STORAGE MODULE
LOADING BAYS/
AQUACULTURE
VEHICLE MODULE
MECHANICAL/
REPAIR MODULE
BUSINESS /
COMMERCE
MODULE
AQUACULTURE
PROCESSING MODULE
DOCKING
MODULE
TRAVEL TUBES
RESEARCH MODULE
MINING INTERESTS MODULE
(Experimental)
NUCLEAR PLANT; 1100 MWe
(Buried)
DEPTH — 30 meters
POPULATION — 215,000
CITY SURROUND — Fish and Kelp Farms
LOCATION — 30 km West of Florida on the US Continental Shelf
All modules contain moonpools, emergency hatches, and airlocks
Internal environment maintained at four atmospheric pressures (atms)
All modules and travel tubes are equipped with emergency watertight bulkhead hatches
0 m
200 m

# Chapter One

"YOU HAVE A LOT OF enemies, Mac."

I glanced at Johnny Chang, Deputy Mayor of Trieste City. I was at my desk, in my cramped office, staring at my clenched fists on the steel before me. He stood, watching silently. The office had practically been my home for more than two years now, after the people had elected me Mayor following the battle with the United States Submarine Fleet over control of the colony. Following that had been an intense period of subterfuge, spycraft, *statecraft*, administration, politicking, and outright war in hand-to-hand combat as well as massive naval battles.

It was surreal, really, but it had all happened.

And the people living in Trieste, our burgeoning undersea colony, depended on me.

I was taking them to the promised land, following in my father's footsteps, and they were a hundred percent behind me. Sometimes I couldn't believe it, because what we were about to do was so dangerous, but they believed in the fight. They believed in my dad and his passion that had consumed him before his death.

Now, they believed in me—in Truman McClusky, Mayor of Trieste City, the underwater colony thirty metres down on the shallow and rich continental shelf off the coast of Florida.

The office had a small viewport, and outside, the crystal blue waters of the Gulf of Mexico shimmered brightly. I could see the nearby fish farm pens—walls of bubbles rising to the surface above—the kelp farms, scuba divers, scooters, and larger seacars and subs powering past our modules.

The sun was at its zenith, shining down on the city.

Beams of light sparkled and cut toward us.

Today the ocean was silent and still; there was not much in the way of weather today.

But that would change very, very soon.

I motioned to a chair and Johnny lowered himself to it. "I do have a lot of enemies, you're right," I finally muttered.

"The Germans, Chinese, Russians, English, French, and of course—"

"America. The USSF."

"They all hate us, for the things we've done."

It was an understatement, and it made my heart pound. For years we'd competed with the superpowers, underwater. We'd stolen technologies, battled warsubs, destroyed entire fleets. We'd killed many people, some face to face and others at the blunt end of a detonating torpedo. There was no limit to what we'd done. Nothing to keep me in check, except for my new friend, Sahar Noor, who refused to let me kill anyone. But now it had all come to a head, and we'd picked this week—*today*—to finally make the announcement.

"They do hate us, with good reason," I said in a soft tone. Accepting.

"But today they're going to hate us with an intensity they've never had before. We're stealing something *big* from them today."

I stared at my Deputy Mayor. He was my best friend, and he'd been my long-time partner in TCI. We'd been on many missions together, had fought many battles. We knew each other's thoughts, almost. Could work together on intricate missions with multiple decisions to make on the fly, and we could make them knowing exactly what the other was going to do, even if we were separated with no comms capability.

Like the time we'd stolen the weapon from the research facility, The Vault, in the Indian Ocean. Or the time we'd sunk the RSF dreadnought in the Pacific. Or when we'd destroyed the French Submarine Fleet in the Mid-Atlantic Ridge.

We'd been in *that many* fights, and I practically knew what was going through his head at all times. Except now. "Are you trying to make me feel better, Johnny? Because you're not."

"Just stating the obvious, I guess. I'm nervous too."

Outside, the water was so clear, so calm. It was counterpoint to what things had been building to, for years now.

"Is everyone else ready?"

He nodded. "They know what's happening. They're waiting. All fourteen of them."

"Which makes fifteen in total."

"Fifteen. *The Fifteen*."

"And we were the first."

"We were. Your dad was, at least."

I took a deep breath. For many years I'd resented Dad for what he'd done. His actions had destroyed the family. He'd been cold around us—me and Meg, my twin sister—and his focus was always solely on Trieste. We knew it; he never hid that fact from us. Hell, on the day he'd died—*on the day they'd killed him*—he hadn't even hugged us goodbye.

And the thing that pissed me off was that he *knew* he was going to die that day.

I've been through some hard shit in my life, but that was about the worst. When your own father puts something else ahead of family . . .

It tears worlds apart.

There was a knock at the hatch and it ground aside.

"Meg," I said, startled.

*What incredible timing*, I thought.

She stared at me from the hatchway. My forty-six-year-old twin sister held herself with an assured confidence and a carefree attitude that sometimes I thought I also exuded. Her eyes were blue and piercing—like mine—and she was tall, blond, broad-shouldered, with a toned and athletic physique. She was wearing coveralls at the moment, splattered with grease following a shift in the Repair Module.

It was nice to see her smile. Her eyes danced; there were small wrinkles at their corners. "Are you ready for this?"

"Not really."

She blinked. "But for years we've been waiting for it. Dad had—"

I waved her off. "I know, I know. I'm just nervous. It's going to cause a firestorm."

"We're ready."

"Are we?" I snorted. There were thousands living at Trieste. Men, women, children. I was about to put them in grave danger.

"The people voted you in. They *want* this. They want what Dad wanted." She paused and then finally marched in the rest of the way and sat in the other chair before my desk. Her occupation was aquanautic engineer; she didn't just repair seacars, she designed and built them, too. She'd been essential to the city and our efforts in TCI. Her beauty and occupation could be considered a contradiction, but men and women adored her. Sometimes she seemed aloof to potential lovers—I'd heard—but she was just focused on other things.

Like today.

"I know that, Meg. But we're about to cause more than just a minor irritation. Today means *war.* Their fleets are a lot more powerful than ours."

She raised a finger. "No. No."

"How's that?"

"They're not more powerful, Tru. You *know* that. We're the most powerful force in the oceans. They have more warsubs, more troops, more people than we do. But that's it. *We're* the most powerful in the oceans."

I snorted. It was funny that she was the one now trying to convince me. Years ago, it had been the other way around. Hell, and years before *that*, I'd wanted nothing to do with all this. I'd been working the kelp fields, hauling the harvest into the city for processing and shipment out to the mainland. But events had pulled me back to the fold. Brought me back to politics, back to espionage, and back to spycraft.

I eyed Johnny again. He was nodding. I said, "You agree with that?"

"Hell yes. It's what we've been working for. New weapons, new technologies. It's all been for today."

I exhaled, but my breath rattled out. Shit, even my body was trembling. I had to stay calm, for what I was about to do. I had to remain still.

Cold.

Calculating.

I had to appear like I knew what I was doing, and I had to exude *power.*

Could I do it?

—••—

"IS THE NEUTRAL BEAM FINISHED?" I asked quietly.

"The delivery tube is done. On the seafloor, pressurized and camouflaged."

It was our most incredible defensive weapon. We'd stolen it only months earlier from the British Submarine Fleet. It was a particle beam for use underwater. When activated, a ten-terawatt laser vaporized a channel in the water, creating a vacuum. And down that vacuum, a stream of neutral particles blasted at enemy hulls. It was essentially a neutron beam used to obliterate hulls and use the ocean pressure itself against the enemy. Once the beam had weakened the hull, implosion was inevitable. It had a short range—only two hundred metres—but we'd positioned the weapon on the seafloor to fire *upward* at the enemy. As a ship passed over, we'd fire into its underbelly, slitting the warsub open from snout to stern. The water around us was shallow. Geography was our ally.

Hopefully.

We hadn't tested our new system yet on a real opponent.

But that was coming soon.

I said, "I hope it works."

"We know it works," Meg said. "You used it already to escape the BSF."

"True." I shrugged. "But the delivery tube is new. The weapon has to slide quickly to position under the attacking fleet."

Meg eyed me, then tilted her head.

Shit, I knew what that meant.

"Truman," she said. "Why are you thinking about the Neutral Beam when something much bigger is about to happen?"

I ground my teeth. "Maybe I'm trying to distract myself. Because I'm having a hard time bringing myself to actually do this."

"The broadcast is in just a few minutes. The cabin is prepared. The cameras are on." She looked at Johnny. "Are the other fourteen ready?"

"Yeah. They're all just as nervous as he is," he replied, gesturing at me.

"But they're ready to go through with it?"

He nodded, but his face was grim.

Even Johnny knew how dangerous this was going to be.

Meg glanced out the port and looked up. "It seems nice up top. Are we sure about tonight and tomorrow?"

"Totally," Johnny replied. "It's happening."

My pounding heart suddenly went still. A calm settled over me, as if something supernatural had assured me that everything was all right, that things would be fine. That there was no better time to do this, and it was now or never. Everything in my entire life had been building toward this; the path my dad had started me on had led to *now*. This was the reason I was even alive. It was my purpose, and it was time for self-realization.

Time to announce it to the world.

I pushed the steel chair back and rose slowly to my feet. "Let's go."

—••—

"WHERE'S CLIFF?" MEG ASKED AS we marched from my office. City Control was at the apex of the Commerce Module. Crew sat at the consoles, monitoring all aspects of the city, from pressure readings to electrical distribution, to communications, to kelp and fish farm maintenance and production, to sea traffic around us. The traffic in particular was trouble, because in recent years it had grown exponentially. I waved at the crew there as we moved to the hatch.

High on the bulkhead was a map of the Gulf region and all the sea traffic in the area. I noted the locations of the USSF warsubs as we passed under it and out to the corridor. I knew Grant Bell was monitoring that, and in just a few minutes he'd be giving me a report about it.

A very important report.

The hatch shut behind us.

"Cliff is on a mission," I muttered.

Her eyes widened. "Today of all days, he won't be here?"

"He left just over a week ago. He's been hunting something for us."

"What is it?"

"Something someone else has that we need. That's the way it works, Meg."

"But *now*, of all times?"

"Other nations don't wait for us to do our business. But it's important he does it now and gets back before—" I couldn't finish the sentence, and I choked the words off tightly.

"Still," she said. "He is our Chief Security Officer."

"I know."

"We're going to need security."

"I know."

"It's going to get nasty here."

"Meg. *I know.*"

She flashed me a grin. "Just checking. Where's Renée?"

The name brought butterflies. Usually, Meg called her *Frenchie*. "Nearby, I'm sure. With the others." They'd all be watching this.

We continued to stalk through the corridors, on our way to the studio. It was a few levels down, and the ladders rang with our footsteps as we descended. The hatch slid aside and we moved back into the corridor. A few metres more, and the comm studio hatch hung open for us. The crew was already there, and inside, the lights were up and waiting.

There was a desk there, and behind it, a simulated image of the ocean around us like the one I'd just been looking at from my office, but this one was expansive and would stretch across the entire background as I addressed the world.

The other fourteen would appear behind me as I spoke.

They would speak when I had finished, and behind each of them, in their broadcasts, I'd be one of the fourteen.

We represented fifteen cities in total.

The Fifteen.

I swore to myself and sat down.

Meg and Johnny were standing off camera, watching. A member of the communications staff handed me a folder and I placed it on the desk. I didn't think there was anything in it; it was just to make me look official.

I folded my arms on the desk and sat up straight. I knew my facial expression was grim.

The clock display on the bulkhead indicated that it was nearly noon, Eastern Standard Time.

My nerves had largely dissipated, and I felt confident about what I was about to do, despite my earlier conversation with Johnny and Meg. For years I'd been Mayor of the city, increasing production of our fish and kelp and mined ores. We truly had prospered here, under my leadership. The city had proven itself, especially as the surface nations suffered under the relentless heat and famine and flooding above us.

Climate change had punished nations. The coastal ones dealt with the onslaught of rising water, and the landlocked nations dealt with famine, food scarcity, and refugees. Nations had fallen to rebellion, and everywhere, people suffered. Bangladesh was now gone, and flooding had squeezed tens of millions of people into Europe's core like toothpaste through a tube. Millions migrated through Europe, searching for homes. More were swarming from Central America, moving north toward the United States.

Rising water was as effective as a bulldozer.

Especially when there were families and children involved.

People would do anything to protect their children.

And the surface was a cauldron of war, rebellion, catastrophe, and suffering.

The colonies on the ocean floors, on the other hand, were calm, prosperous, and *growing*. The produce we sent to the mainland was now a necessary component of our mother nations' economies.

There were twenty-nine major underwater cities, with more under construction or planned, and the ocean floors were rich in resources. Kelp, fish, ore . . . seventy percent of the world was under water, and the shallow continental shelves—where the cities were—comprised a total area of over thirty million square kilometres—*three times the size of Canada*. And those shallow shelves were host to fertile soils, fish-breeding areas, and vast mineral deposits, including hydrocarbons like oil and gas.

On the shelves, there was an incalculable wealth.

Combined, they essentially made up one of the biggest continents on the planet, but hidden from view. People generally didn't give them—*or us*—much thought, but the time of us sneaking around silently was over. I was about to make it official.

"Mac," Johnny said, tearing his eyes from the clock. "It's time."

I steeled myself and took another breath.

In just a few hours, a hurricane would hit the Gulf of Mexico.

And in just a few seconds, I was about to announce our independence to the world.

And start a world war.

# Chapter Two

THE CONFLUENCE OF BOTH EVENTS would distract the United States. As the Category Six hurricane pounded the coastline, and already-weakened shore defences crumbled under the storm surge and punishing waves, the nation would learn that their three colonies were declaring independence and striking off on their own.

It might cause an immediate official government response, but hopefully the storm would significantly delay the military one. I was hoping Cliff would be back by then, but we had to move forward without him.

The fourteen were behind me, on the vidscreen. We'd announced the broadcast to the major news networks thirty minutes in advance, and it was airing to the bulk of the United States' viewers. The other fourteen had done the same with their respective countries, and the majority of the planet was now watching.

I swallowed.

Just off camera, Meg and Johnny stood silently. My sister nodded, encouraging me.

Strange, how she had come so far in two short years. I seemed to be the hesitant one now, and not her.

But I'd seen the most death, I knew, although she'd witnessed her share as well.

"Good afternoon," I said. "Behind me are fourteen Mayors of major underwater colonies around the world. We represent over half of the undersea colonists in the oceans—over twenty million people. In a few minutes, I'll be done here and they will be available to speak to their mother nations and their news networks to answer any questions you might have." I took a breath and steeled myself. "For many years, the colonies have struggled with undersea life. Nations established us with the purpose of extracting resources, farming, fishing, and shipping the produce back to the mainland. We were an experiment, you could say, to test if life underwater could work. This began in the 2070s. Since that time—for sixty years now—we have proven ourselves a thousand times over. Our fish products have skyrocketed in recent years. The minerals we mine are essential to topside industries. The kelp we grow is now a required component of diets around the world. While on land the sun bakes the soil and the rain moves to more northerly areas, we continue to provide a stable supply of food and other resources to you."

I took another breath, and tried not to make it look like a gulp. "But despite this, you have continued to take advantage of us. You treat us as slave labor. You don't pay fair market value for the exports we send. Your troops patrolling the seas harass our citizens. They arrive here for R&R, but it's a euphemism for drunken louts who ransack, abuse, and even engage in criminal activities for which there is no punishment." I had complained about this fact to numerous military figures over the years: Captain Heller, Admiral Benning, and Commodore Clarke. None of them showed much interest.

And, most curious, all three were now dead.

I gestured behind me, at the other fourteen Mayors. "The same happens at the other cities. At Ballard, at Churchill Sands, at Cousteau, New Berlin, Blue Downs, Sheng City and the others. We are more than an experiment. We've proven it. We're now self-sufficient and highly profitable. At Trieste, we have over two hundred thousand people. Churchill Sands has the best university in the seas. Sheng City mines more minerals than some topside countries. And despite this, we remain second-class citizens to you all. We've asked for more from you, like fair payment and treatment, but it hasn't helped. Last year, the USSF raised quotas on us, they occupied us, and their troops treated our men, women, and children like garbage."

I was gaining confidence now, and speaking clearly and forcefully. I'd memorized the speech, and even though it was on a teleprompter before me, I didn't even have to read the words.

I *knew* them.

I'd been practicing this for years now, going over it in my mind, again and again.

In my mind, however, war usually followed the words.

I knew this would be no different.

After I finished the proclamation, our mother nations would land troops, occupy us, and take over. They would not allow us to go off on our own.

They would try, at least.

So we were going to have to fight.

I leaned forward. "Listen to me now, and pay attention to my words. We fifteen cities are no longer yours. We are acting now as one. If you try to occupy or attack just one of us, we'll collectively view it as an act of war against all of us. If you harass one of us, you do so to all of us. We have built up strong militaries, and we've proven it many times to you, although you may not yet realize it. We have the fastest armed seacars in the oceans. We can dive deeper than you. We only ask that you treat us fairly. Citizens can continue to visit us—with passports and proper customs papers—and we will continue to take immigrants and even refugees." I paused. "We also extend an invitation to your governments to establish embassies here, on the ocean floor, in our colonies. We will provide space for you in our modules, but we will expect the same in your capital cities."

I knew this speech was causing an uproar topside. Government leaders were likely watching in horror. They were probably already ordering militaries into action, yelling at their cabinet ministers to act before I even signed off, screaming about occupations and putting their own people in control of *their* cities. Asking how this had caught their intelligence agencies off guard.

I pressed on, "This is inevitable. Our economies are strong, our technologies have surpassed yours. Our militaries are powerful. I'm going to say it again before I pass this broadcast off to the other fourteen Mayors to speak to their countries: *Do not test us*. That would cause bloodshed and death. Embrace us as peaceful allies. Trade with us equitably. You'll see that it's the best way to move forward. There has been too much death in the oceans and it's time to stop. You can use us for resources—especially food and iron—but *pay* for it, as you would other countries. You can focus on the stars, using our minerals . . . but the seas are ours, and don't forget it. We are hereby enacting a *Do Not Approach* policy around our territories for a three-month period.

"We will defend our territory with our lives."

The broadcast continued for nearly two more hours. Each Mayor spoke, and I remained on the screen. I understood most of it, except the French and German—I could speak and understand Mandarin, so I caught all of the Chinese. I was most worried about the six Chinese cities, for their mother nation was not forgiving. They might just kill everyone and start over again.

My friend, Sahar Noor, was the Mayor of Churchill Sands. She, in particular, fielded questions expertly, expounding on the needs for an independent nation on the seafloor to mitigate effects of climate change on the surface. Colonies, she said, did not produce as much as capitalist entities working to improve their own economic situation. She'd been promoting that line of reasoning for months now, and had been a frequent guest on topside media shows.

Afterward, I leaned back and gasped. Inwardly, I was trembling again. Sweat beaded my forehead. Johnny and Meg were at my side in an instant, praising me, pounding my back and hugging me.

A noise began from outside, and we stopped, cocked our heads, listening to it.

Cheering.

*There was cheering in the city.*

In the modules and corridors of Trieste, a celebration had begun. The noise drifted on the air currents into the conference room.

When I realized, it brought a massive smile to my face. I turned to my assistant, Kristen Canvel. "Can you capture video of this and send it to the mainland?" We wanted them to understand our peoples' enthusiasm. This was not a case of a rogue government doing something their people didn't want. This was an entire population electing Mayors to declare independence. They'd been asking for it for years now, in all of the cities.

Sahar Noor was an excellent example. Her people had elected her with this in mind. She was completely against violence and would refuse to fight if it came to it, and I'd asked her why she was doing it if she wasn't willing to fight. She'd told me that it didn't matter what she wanted; what mattered was what the people who had voted wanted. She was *their* voice, and her own opinions didn't matter.

I respected her for that. It was refreshing.

The celebrations continued for the rest of the day and well into the evening and the early morning hours the next day. I spent the time wandering the modules and travel tubes of Trieste, experiencing it firsthand. Children, families, workers . . . they were all the same. Smiling, cheering, parading in victory. For decades they'd felt used by the USSF; now they were free. If they had fireworks, they'd be lighting them off inside, I thought with an inward laugh. Instead, they were using noisemakers and had dressed in colourful clothes and formed impromptu parades with loud music. Some ventured outdoors in scuba gear and moved the party to the shallow, warm waters, where they danced to music in headsets and swayed in the currents in slow motion, relishing this day.

June 7, 2131 was now our Independence Day, and I wondered with a cold dread if it would last.

—••—

OCEANIA WAS NOW AN OFFICIAL nation, consisting of fifteen underwater colonies. We'd formed economic and military ties already—secretly, of course—and Johnny had played a massive role in it. He'd promised incredible technologies to the other Mayors, and I had delivered. The best propulsion system—SCAV drive—and our deep-diving technologies too, including the Acoustic Pulse and our syntactic foam. We all had similar navies, and if pressed, we would fight and defend each other.

In the span of my speech, the world order had changed. A new nation now existed, and we'd turned the underwater Cold War upside down.

The world would now decide what happened next.

—••—

IN THE EARLY MORNING HOURS, I was still awake and enjoying the celebrations. There was no sign of them tapering off. Music pounded through the city and everywhere people were grinning, laughing, and throwing themselves at me. The jubilation was clear. All agriculture and industrial activities had ceased.

I walked with Renée Féroce, my girlfriend, hand in hand. She had been at my side for months, and in fact had at one time been in the FSF and desperate to kill me. I'd turned her to our side, once she lived in the cities and saw what we were capable of and how the superpowers treated us. Now, as we journeyed from party to party and celebrated with the thousands of Triestrians, she hugged our people, high-fived the children, and kissed me again and again.

Meg had accepted her into the family, and Renée was an important part of the team. She'd been on multiple missions with us already, and had proven herself many times.

Johnny and Meg were with us too, as were the others in our team who had collectively fought for this over the years: Max Hyland, the inventor of the hafnium bomb. Chalam Kaashif, the geologist who had helped us steal the Neutral Particle Beam; along with its inventor, Alyssna Sonstraall; Manesh Lazlow, inventor of the Acoustic Pulse Drive; Doctor Stacy Reynolds and Laura Sukovski and Josh Miller and Kristen Canvel and Grant Bell and more.

All were celebrating with us, enjoying the moment.

Inside, I knew they were scared too.

They knew what the superpowers were capable of, and how they would not allow us to just walk away.

Grant Bell sauntered past, barely balancing as he moved. He was drunk and there was no hiding it.

It made me grin. "Any response from the announcement?" I asked him.

He leaned in to yell over the music, "None! The USSF ships are still on their previous courses. They're all getting ready for the storm."

As predicted. They were worried about the coming Cat Six storm; they'd have to deal with us later.

"I'm going to Blue Downs, Mac!"

I frowned. "What do you mean? The three-month quarantine—"

"Remember? We have to coordinate Sea Traffic Control procedures. We're part of the same nation now, have to use the same systems. Also, I need a vacation . . . it's been a long time coming. I've wanted to visit there forever! I have family there!"

And then the crowd swept him up in its embrace and pulled him from sight. I considered what he'd said, but only for an instant. He'd been working hard for years now, without any time off. If anyone deserved it, surely he did. He'd been in charge of Sea Traffic Control, and there were others who could take over while he was gone. I just hoped he'd be back before the USSF showed their cards.

Another reveler passed us, smiling and drinking a mug of kelp beer. It was Chanta Newel. She was in security and we'd spent a great deal of time lately with her preparing for an upcoming operation. She was as tough as titanium, a great pilot, and everybody respected her. Cliff Sim had even selected her as his backup in times of his absence. She grinned as she passed, and I returned the smile.

And then, in the Research Module, while celebrating and dancing and people shoving drinks into my hands to try and down before the next one appeared, a quake hit the colony.

—••—

It only lasted a few seconds, but the rumble through the decks and bulkheads was clear.

The power flickered and died.

Chalam was at my side in a second. The young geologist was glancing around, processing the vibrations as they coursed through the city and from the deck plates up his legs. "It's not a quake," he said. "The wavelength is wrong."

The lights were off, the music had stopped, and even the ventilation fans had ceased.

Emergency illumination snapped on, casting a glow over the crowd in the corridor.

At least there were no blue flashing pressure emergency lights, I thought.

Outside the nearby viewport, a current swept past. It was thick and murky; sand swirled and bits of seaweed and debris churned by.

Renée gasped and pointed outside. "It's an explosion."

Someone had cut our power. I desperately hoped it hadn't damaged the fusion plant.

# Chapter Three

I BOLTED INTO THE NEARBY travel tube to see more clearly. The bulkhead was transparent and the scene outside made me swear. Johnny, Meg, Renée, and Kristen crowded around me. The light was dim, but the flowering sand blossom southwest of the city was easy to see. An explosion, between us and the plant, had cut the power lines. The plant was underground and likely undamaged, though someone would have to get out there to check to be sure.

But someone had cut the city's power.

"I need a SitRep," I snapped at Johnny. There was always a military perimeter around the city, in our powerful seacars. "Find out if there's an enemy vessel nearby." I looked at Grant, now with a serious expression and drinks discarded. He was standing just behind me, also looking out the transparent bulkhead. "I thought you said there were no USSF warsubs nearby."

"None is close, Mac. Surely not close enough to have acted so quickly."

"They have the SCAV drive now."

"We would have noticed. STC didn't report anything."

"Who's on duty right now?"

"Claude Lemont. I've been in constant contact with him."

I nodded. Good. Despite the celebrations, he'd been keeping track of things, as I'd asked. I said to Renée, "Check with the patrols, get more info for us. Also, get more *Swords* out there. I want a near-solid perimeter now that we've made the declaration." To Meg: "Get repair crews out to the damage; get it fixed." Then to everyone, I said, "Meet back in my office in an hour."

—••—

AN HOUR LATER, THEY'D GATHERED in my office. We'd declared independence, and within the day someone had sabotaged our power supply. There had to be a connection between the two events, and yet . . .

And yet, the USSF was nowhere near at the moment. Still, we all knew they had operatives everywhere. Working in the city even, who could mobilize at a moment's notice.

Suddenly, I wished for Cliff Sim at my side. Our security officer offered a sense of calm and stability. He was off on his mission though, and I'd have to wait for him to return with his prize.

The storm was coming. The news broadcasts topside were showing nonstop footage of our proclamation, over stock footage of the underwater colonies, but the US government hadn't yet made an official response.

Grant was in my office too. "Still nothing, Mac."

"*Nothing?*"

"They haven't moved."

"No SCAV signatures?" There was no hiding the SCAV drive. It used a fusion reactor to flash-boil seawater, which shoved the steam out the aft, propelling the vessel to incredible velocities, within a frictionless bubble—but it was *loud*. I knew the USSF had developed the drive, copying our own invention from two years earlier. They had numerous warsubs and other vessels now equipped with it, most notably their *Hunter-Killers*, the *Houston* Class warsubs.

"No, Mac. The USSF isn't doing *anything* right now."

I glanced out the viewport and looked upward. The sky was dark; it was still early.

"The storm is brewing up there," he said. "It's building. It's going to give us a buffer of several days."

*That was the plan*, I thought. "It doesn't make sense then. Who did this?"

Johnny and Meg entered the office. Johnny said, "The blast

destroyed the lines. Meg has crews already out there."

"Repairable?"

"Yes," Meg said. "Of course." My question had nearly offended her, and it made me snort. "It'll be a day or two though. The damage is extensive."

"What about the plant?"

"No damage. Everyone there was celebrating, but there were no security breaches. The reactor is functioning."

I sat back and breathed a sigh of relief. We'd buried the reactor in 2129, after the USSF destroyed it. It was now heavily fortified under sand and entombed in bedrock. Still, someone knew where we'd buried the lines, and that made us vulnerable. "Is the travel tube to the plant okay?"

"No," Johnny said. "It's destroyed. I had to swim out there."

"Crews are on it," Meg added.

"In the meantime, the plant crew is okay?"

"They'll be on their own for the duration, but they're fine. I've been in contact with them."

It seemed like everything was happening all at once. I knew our announcement would unleash hell. My dad had wanted this for his entire life, and I'd finally achieved his dreams. It had taken years of brokering agreements with the other underwater colonies and building up our own military technologies, but we'd finally done it.

The celebration hadn't lasted long, though.

But now the danger from the announcement, the Cat Six storm, and the explosion had merged into a dilemma that spelled potential doom.

Kristen Canvel signaled me at that moment. She was in City Control, just outside my office, monitoring the situation from her consoles.

"Go ahead," I said into the comm.

"Mac, we've got a seacar requesting to dock."

"We've declared the three-month quarantine. No one enters without—"

"—without permission from you. Right?"

"Yes."

"So what do you think I'm doing? I'm relaying the request to you."

I grimaced. I could hear the tension in her voice. "I'm sorry, Kristen.

Things are . . . *tense* right now."

"I'm feeling it too."

I deflated. I had to be more understanding of the pressures others were under too. This wasn't all just on my shoulders, and Kristen was in charge of City Systems Control, and no doubt her role as my assistant created stresses that I wasn't even aware of. "Yes, I should have known." I sighed and said, "What is the seacar's point of departure?"

"Sheng City."

That made me sit up and take notice. That was China's first and most important underwater colony, and they had just thrown in their lot with us. It was also the city Johnny had worked at for nine years earlier when he had defected from Trieste. He'd ended up back with us, at my side, but the coincidence here was notable.

I continued, "The seacar came straight here?"

"According to the logs. Used the passthrough at Panama."

"Who's at the controls?"

"A woman named Min Lee."

There was a sudden gasp in the cabin and I stared at Johnny. His face had gone pale. He'd even taken a step back and was staring at me in shock. I frowned. "What is it, Johnny? Who is this?"

He didn't answer.

—••—

I GAVE PERMISSION FOR THE seacar to dock, but made sure security swept the vessel first. The last thing we needed was a bomb detonating in a module during a dispute with the superpowers, and just hours after someone had cut our main power. Within minutes, the seacar's lone operator was on her way to City Control and my office, under escort.

Johnny's reaction motivated me to allow the entry, though he still hadn't said much to us. He'd only nodded when I asked him if he wanted her here.

Meg was whispering to him as I made the arrangements over the comm. Soon she was at my side, and Johnny was in a chair, still pale, but looking slightly improved.

"You remember when Johnny was living at Sheng City, nine years ago, give or take?"

I grunted. I did indeed. Johnny had discovered that the Director of TCI, George Shanks, had been holding Chinese prisoners at Trieste, and treating them badly. He'd been torturing them for information. Johnny had switched sides in protest, but it had been during a mission that he and I had both been on at the time, to Sheng City.

I didn't know much of what Johnny had been up to during that period, in Sheng City, though he'd lived there for seven years. I knew he'd had a difficult life there; he'd never felt as though he'd belonged. But he'd worked for their intelligence agency, conducting missions, and had even stolen valuable secrets from us, before he and I had reconnected and he'd returned to Trieste, the only place he really felt was *home*.

And now this woman had arrived . . .

*Min Lee.*

I stared at Johnny. He glanced up and our eyes met, but he still didn't say anything.

—••—

Events had thrown me off guard. A thought suddenly occurred to me, and I called Grant Bell back into the office. He said he'd arrive shortly.

The backup generators had kicked in, though they didn't deliver nearly the same power the plant did. The ventilation fans barely functioned, only the emergency lighting was on, and there were long and sharp shadows falling across the decks and bulkheads. I could hear the pressure monitors clicking, which told me that they had enough power to maintain the four-atmosphere constant in the modules.

If they didn't, then the ocean would crush us.

It was an immutable law of seafloor colonization, and the world had standardized internal air pressures across the oceans, including seacars, warsubs, submersibles, colonies and outposts.

The hatch ground aside and our visitor walked in.

She was slim and about five foot seven inches in height. Her hair was shoulder length—odd, for an ocean dweller, for we generally kept it short to speed up drying—and she appeared athletic. Her shoulders were broad and she was clearly fit, and her stride and stance spoke of someone who was confident, secure, and in fact, *deadly*.

I snapped a glance at Johnny.

This wasn't an ordinary person. This was an *agent*.

I had a practiced eye; I could tell immediately.

Johnny glanced at me and nodded. She was a spy, all right.

A figure appeared in the hatch behind her, and before Min Lee could speak, I gestured to Grant. He stepped in and I said, "Can you trace where her seacar has been?"

"Kristen reported it to—"

"What about STC? What does it say?"

He looked puzzled. "The track? Her vessel came straight from the passthrough."

"Did she stop outside our city?"

Realization settled across his face. "She came straight here and only just arrived. I can see the entire track, with timestamps, as she approached from Panama. There's no evidence that she arrived, waited outside our limits, and planted the bomb."

She'd been watching me, silently, during the exchange. Her eyes were serious, but they were probing for information.

She was studying me.

"Thanks," I said, still staring at her. "Are you still planning on going to Blue Downs, after all this?"

"Have to," he muttered. "We need to coordinate our STC systems." He backed away and departed.

I continued to study Min Lee. Her cheekbones were high and her hair shiny. With her physique, in addition to being a fighter, I had the impression that she could also have been a model. But there was a quality to her that was hard to describe. She seemed aloof, in a way, or *hard*, as if she protected herself from hurt by making herself unapproachable. Even that didn't quite explain it, though.

She finally spoke, "Bomb?"

Meg finally stepped forward to introduce herself. I sensed that she was giving Johnny a moment to compose himself; there was a history between these two, and Min's arrival had totally thrown him. Meg gestured at the ceiling. "The lights are off. Power's out. We've suffered an . . . *incident*."

"I saw the broadcast, and know what you're doing." She turned to me. "I'm a member of Sheng City Intelligence. I know that we've made the same announcement, that we're all on the same team."

*Maybe*, I wanted to say. I glanced again at Johnny. I still wasn't sure what was going on. "I just want to make sure you didn't play a role in the sabotage."

She offered me a slight smile. "I can understand that, but I only just arrived." She turned to Johnny. "Hi, Johnny."

He looked like he wanted to pass out.

At that point, my comm beeped and I stared at it for a moment. I'd had to tear my eyes from Johnny and Min Lee. They were not speaking, perhaps because of the awkward nature of a reunion with the rest of us standing around, but looked as though they wanted to explain.

I stared at the device on my desk, and a shock that felt like another explosion passed through me. It was the USSF, with a single, brief, text-only announcement.

Renée said, "Mac, what is it?"

ATTENTION U.S. COLONIES TRIESTE, SEASCAPE, BALLARD. WE DO NOT ACCEPT YOUR THREAT OF INDEPENDENCE. YOU HAVE SEVEN DAYS TO COMPLY. AT THAT POINT, WE WILL LAND TROOPS TO OCCUPY AND REORGANIZE YOUR CITY COUNCILS. DO NOT TEST US.

I snorted at the message. The *Do Not Test Us* ending was clearly a response to my own statement hours earlier, and the seven-day deadline was no doubt due to the hurricane above, which would hit any hour. Conditions up there were worsening quickly.

"Well," I muttered. "We have their response. We know when the attack will come."

Meg said, "And it's going to be unlike anything we've ever experienced."

Renée said, "We're prepared. They've shown their hand now, and we know what we're up against."

"Unless it's a ploy," I said, "and they attack earlier."

"We'll monitor their warsub movements . . . we'll know soon."

Then my comm buzzed again.

This signal originated from the British underwater colony, Churchill Sands. It was their Mayor, Sahar Noor. They were now with us officially—part of *Oceania*—and I wondered if they were under attack or threat by the mainland BSF military.

I stabbed at the ACCEPT button and Sahar appeared on the screen. "Go ahead, Sahar. Is everything okay? Did you receive a message from the BSF?" I wondered if the superpowers had sent all their colonies the exact same message.

She wore a topaz hijab and a pale yellow scarf. Her face was soft and appeared young, but there was a clear penetrating intelligence in her eyes. She had strong convictions, was a proponent of peace, and never wanted war. Inside, my heart pounded. If her city was under attack . . .

"Mac," she said. "Sorry to bother you, now of all times."

"The Fifteen need to remain in close contact, should anyone threaten us. It's not a problem."

She nodded. "My call isn't about Oceania, although let me say that you did a fantastic job. Your speech was magnificent; I couldn't have said it better."

"Thanks. What have you been up to?"

"Planting seeds, you could say."

"I beg your pardon?"

"I've been speaking with media around the world. Speaking of the need to colonize the ocean floors as a free nation. I'm sure you've seen some of the interviews."

"Yes, for sure."

"I'm hoping it grows into something that might help us, when the time comes." Then she paused, and there was a look in her eyes. "My call is about your Chief Security Officer, Cliff Sim."

My heart nearly exploded and I rose to my feet. "What are you—"

"I've recently come across some information. I think you should come to Churchill, immediately."

"Can you tell me—"

"It's too sensitive."

"Where's Cliff?" I shot a look at Meg and Johnny. Both were staring at me; they could hear the entire call with Sahar. They knew I'd sent Cliff on an important mission a few weeks earlier, to a facility in the Pacific.

"Mac," Sahar sighed. "I'm sorry to say this, but I think he's dead. Killed, to be precise."

# Interlude
## Somewhere in the Pacific Ocean

**3 June 2131**
**Five Days Earlier**

| | |
|---|---|
| Vessel: | Russian Submarine Fleet<br>*Dreadnought* Class *Voskhod–The Rise* |
| Location: | Latitude: Unknown<br>Longitude: Unknown<br>North of The Iron Plains |
| Depth: | 100 metres |
| Date: | 3 June 2131 |
| Time: | 2113 hours |

LIEUTENANT MILA SIDOROV STUDIED THE older man's lined face. Captain Ventinov had scowled when he said the last words, and something violent had passed through him as he'd said it. "A *blade*," Sidorov said. "What do you mean?"

They were standing on the dreadnought's expansive bridge. The light was dim; it filtered down through the ocean from far above. Surface light only made it to a depth of 200 metres. They were above that threshold, but the ocean had scattered and diffused most of it by the time it hit them at their current depth. It cast a shadow over his face, making the lines deeper. He seemed laser focused and intent on the person he was speaking about killing.

Ventinov's rage was intense.

He shook himself from his reverie and said, "McClusky of Trieste is very smart. He's had a lot of experience, in both espionage and politics. He's a good fighter, highly trained. He led the team that sunk—" He choked off the words, but then drew a breath and tried again. "That sunk *Drakon*."

"By sabotaging the reactor."

"It melted down. Then he . . . " he trailed off.

"Yes?" she prodded.

He took a breath. "Then—then, he inverted the boat. It destroyed the vessel's compartmentalization."

Sidorov gasped. She'd heard the crew speak about it, but wasn't precisely sure of the exact details. The melted core must have burned a path right through *Drakon*.

"But now I have *Voskhod*," he said, his voice firm once more. "*The Rise*. It will be our rise from the ashes of defeat. He won the battle, but now I'm going to win the war."

"But that's what I'm saying, sir. We have three dreadnoughts. *Voskhod* is just one. We can attack together, finish him."

"They have a remarkable defense network, Sidorov."

"Against our Tsunami Plow—"

"It's not enough. He has countermeasures. Torpedoes. SCAV torpedoes too, that travel a thousand kph under water."

"But compartmentalization will prevent the dreadnoughts from sinking."

"That's what I thought last time. He worked around the dilemma. So I'm giving him a new one. I'm throwing him off balance."

"With a blade."

He nodded. "Yes."

Her brow crinkled. "What does that mean?"

He sighed and moved forward, heading toward the bow. "Walk with me." They walked slowly, leisurely, under the canopy. The bridge was so large that a walk around its perimeter felt like a stroll through a park. "I also know about their newest weapons. They have acquired a Neutral Particle Beam which will keep all attacking vessels at bay. We can't approach too close, or the beam will slice us open. It's five kilometres from the city."

Sidorov gasped. "An energy weapon? Underwater?"

"Yes. You'd think it wouldn't work, but it does. We have intelligence reports from the Indian Ocean, where he stole it. But I've set up a trap for the man. To defeat Trieste, we have to first cut off its head. If we eliminate McClusky, the others will fall into place. Their command structure will collapse. I've laid the breadcrumbs. I've spent the last year arranging it. It'll lead him to a place of my choosing."

"What place?"

"A facility in The Iron Plains, south of us, but much deeper."

"What facility?"

"It's a manufacturing plant, operated by the CSF."

Sidorov blinked. "Are we allied with the Chinese now?"

"No. But my blade is."

—••—

VENTINOV HAD SPENT LONG NIGHTS following his defeat coming up with the plan. He had the perfect weapon to do it, and in the period following the disaster, he'd devised the path that his quarry would follow. Russian leadership had listened to the story of his dreadnought's defeat at Trieste's hand. He explained how he intended to beat them now. It was a long path, a circuitous one that hopefully would seem intricate enough so as to be real and not a trap.

And it ended at a Chinese facility in the Pacific Ocean.

Where the real weapon would be waiting.

A person.

His *blade*, as he explained to Sidorov:

"The Chinese base will throw the scent off us. He won't suspect an RSF Captain as the one who's after him. The Chinese make a nice diversion, and my blade is aligned with them. But it's not a knife I'm referring to," he said. "My blade is not industrial in nature, but just as sharp. It's a handmade blade, one that we created, over many years. One that we moulded and sharpened and scraped and viciously bent into shape. We took a person and created a weapon. And that blade will slice through McClusky, and end him. And then—and *only then*—will we be ready to take Trieste."

Sidorov's confusion was clear. Ventinov stopped and turned to her. "What do you call a handmade knife? Made from other materials?"

A series of expressions passed across her face as she processed his question. Confused—perplexed—wonderment—and then . . . and then, *realization*.

"A shiv," she said. "A weapon made from some other material."

He smiled. "Yes. But this one is steel. It is a steel blade, forged by people, by our military, by experts, Sidorov. But it's been forged over many, many years, so it's a *shiv*. Or, more precisely, it's *The* Steel Shiv."

—••—

MILA SIDOROV CURSED OUT LOUD. She had heard of The Steel Shiv. He was one of Russia's finest assassins. No one knew if The Shiv worked for RSF intelligence, or if he was a paid assassin who had previously been in intelligence or the military. No one knew if The Shiv was even Russian. But the stories were intense. They were almost mythic in nature. Over the decades, they'd become fairy tales to tell children, to warn them to behave or The Shiv would get them in the night.

And lives would end with the pierce of a steel blade in their spines and a hand clutched over their mouths so they couldn't scream for help.

No one even knew if The Steel Shiv was a man or a woman.

*The Shiv was helping Ventinov kill McClusky?*

On a path that led to a Chinese manufacturing facility?

She stared at Ventinov in silence, but inside, she trembled. His need for vengeance would consume him. She'd seen it before, and she knew what might happen. It could backfire on *Voskhod*, and then scratch yet another dreadnought. Still, the thought of being carved up by a Neutral Particle Beam did not appeal to her. She still couldn't quite believe such a weapon could exist underwater, but according to the Captain it did, albeit with a short range.

She stared at Ventinov again, as he studied the bridge crew around them as they conducted their tasks. His eyes were hard, his face like iron.

*He really is obsessed with this*, she thought.

| | |
|---|---|
| Location: | Latitude: Unknown |
| | Longitude: Unknown |
| | On the seafloor in The Iron Plains; Chinese Manufacturing Plant—*The Facility* |
| Depth: | 1,618 metres |
| Date: | 3 June 2131 |
| Time: | 2344 hours |

CLIFF SPRINTED DOWN THE CORRIDOR as fast as he could move. The fight had dazed him. His vision was blurry and he felt sure that one or more of the strikes had concussed him.

A vision of his opponent flashed through his mind. Slight, wiry, *fast. Too* fast.

Cliff had trained for decades in intelligence and combat. He'd stood toe to toe with countless opponents and had beat them all.

Perhaps he'd grown overconfident, especially when facing such a small opponent. He wouldn't underestimate this person again. The blows had felt like metal clubs hitting his forearms and face.

They *stung*.

And that electronic voice . . . *why*? For what purpose?

He blinked to clear his cloudy vision; before him, the corridor spun crazily.

He risked a quick glance backward; the figure in black was marching toward him, stalking.

And Cliff had left his weapon behind.

He ducked through a side passage and into a small cabin. He leaned against the bulkhead, chest heaving, sucking in gulps of air. He considered his options. Mac had sent him to find this place and steal its secrets. He'd accomplished half his task, but hadn't yet transmitted the coordinates back to Trieste. The other part—locating and downloading the process—he'd yet to achieve. Now, it seemed impossible.

Not with the figure in black hunting him.

Cliff swore. He'd been through a lot in his time, but he'd never been beaten so easily.

And, he knew, it wasn't over yet.

There were footsteps in the corridor outside.

There was a control pad next to the hatch inside the cabin and Cliff pushed the LOCK button. It didn't help, for the hatch ground open an instant later.

He stepped back.

His opponent marched in.

Cliff took a moment to size the other up again. Just over five and a half feet tall. Slim with a practiced fighting style that was more fluid than brute strength. Toned muscles concealed under a black wetsuit. The tinted helmet hid all facial features, and that voice—

"You can't escape me," it said. The electronic syllables drifted on the air currents.

Cliff frowned. "What country do you represent? China?"

"Whoever pays the most."

"You're a hired gun. A mercenary?" He snorted. "Figures. You have no allegiance to anything or anyone."

"I work for one country mostly. But sometimes I sell my services."

"Have I heard of you?" Cliff continued to step away, but suddenly there was a bulkhead at his back. He fell into a fighting stance.

The other stopped and matched his position. Sideways, left leg forward, slightly crouched, practically vibrating on that back leg. Hell, the guy looked like Bruce Lee! The stance was so similar.

"You may have," droned that voice. "But not a name." A knife had appeared in a gloved hand. It wasn't long; it was stubby with a hilt that surrounded the entire fist, much like a set of brass knuckles. It appeared worn and used. "They call me The Steel Shiv."

A tremor coursed through Cliff's body. He had indeed heard of him. "You work for Russia."

"Usually. Sometimes not."

"Why hide your face?"

"You work in intelligence and security, Cliff Sim. At Trieste and before that, for the USSF. Have you ever seen my face? Any images, videos? Have any witnesses ever told a tale about escaping from me and describing what I looked like?"

He grunted. "I see your point. But that means you expect me to live through this and escape." He took a quick look around, but it was a featureless cabin, likely used for storage at one point, but it was currently empty. There was nothing in there to help. "And you won't even remove it to fight?"

"It's how I've protected my identity for all these years. And you're not getting out of this."

"Why are you here?"

"Because *you're* here."

"What does that mean?"

Another laugh, and those odd vibrations echoed in the chamber. "You haven't figured it out yet? Come on, Sim."

"Because you followed me here."

A pause. "I *led* you here. You followed the trail I left."

Cliff gasped inwardly. He couldn't let the other know his surprise. "All those clues . . . all the information . . . *planted*?"

"It wasn't you I had hoped for. That part didn't quite work the way I wanted."

Cliff pondered that statement as he wondered what to do. There was a knife on his left thigh, and he wondered how fast he could pull it. Could he throw it and hit, chest or neck, before The Shiv could move?

He doubted it.

The other option was to pull it and engage in a knife fight. He'd trained for it, but, he wondered if The Shiv had matched or exceeded his training. He assumed he had. "You didn't want me. Who did you expect?"

"Truman McClusky, of course. Though once you're gone, and news gets back to him, I'm sure he'll follow. And I'll be waiting."

Cliff knew it was true. Mac was loyal, and he'd come next. He might even bring Renée, Johnny, or Meg . . . and Cliff couldn't stomach the thought of any of them dying.

He steeled himself and pulled the knife from his thigh holster.

He held it out, toward The Shiv.

He knew that smile was there again, hidden behind the helmet.

"So be it," the electronic voice droned.

The steel blades flashed before the two. Their edges glanced off one another and the sound pierced the cabin. Sparks flew. Their motions were a blur, as the two practiced fighters struck and blocked, circled each other warily, feinted and sliced again. Within minutes, The Shiv's knife had painted Cliff's arms with multiple slices, blood dripped to the deck, and his grip strength faded.

He knew it was only a matter of time.

He feinted with a hooking slice and decided on the fly to try an elbow with his left arm—

The Shiv ducked under the knife and blocked the elbow with right forearm.

Then, a shin soared through Cliff's line of sight. It ratcheted through his skull, crushing against his temple and rocked his head back against the bulkhead.

He slumped to the deck, the knife fell from his hand and slid away, clinking against the cold plates under his hands.

Cliff's chest heaved.

He was going under.

He could only run. He'd left his seacar outside the facility. He hadn't connected via umbilical; he'd descended nearby and left it behind a rock outcropping. He'd swum to the airlock to enter, and the depth had required a decompression. That was likely what had alerted The Shiv to his presence.

He could escape the same way—*maybe*—but he'd have to suit up. He was still in his wetsuit and mask; the tank and regulator were in the nearby airlock.

Cliff raised his head and stared at the hatch.

The Shiv stood between him and escape.

He took another breath, then another.

"Think you can run?" the other said with a snort. "You can try. You have no hope."

"I won't give up. Not to a piece of shit like you."

The other laughed again. "Your reputation preceded you. I knew you'd be good. You're confident, that's for sure." There was a pause, and then, "I heard you withstood CIA interrogation a few months back. In Seascape, before it blew up. Is that true?"

"Fuck you." He continued to suck in air, trying to regain his strength. He was on his knees, and he pulled one leg behind him to help him get up quickly.

"Did you destroy Seascape, Sim? Or did McClusky? People generally believe Germany did it, but I don't think it's true. They used a hafnium bomb. Does Trieste have that technology?"

Cliff took another gulping breath. Three more, then he'd go.

One.

Two.

Three—

He jerked forward and rammed into the smaller figure. The Shiv nearly twisted away successfully, but at the last moment slipped on a puddle of Cliff's blood. The slight figure hit the bulkhead hard. He grunted, the electronic tones blurting out in surprise.

Cliff spun, the hatch opened, and he lurched out into the corridor, limping away.

He was going to run.

There were footsteps behind him again. His chest was heaving, and it felt like his blood was boiling in his veins, and his head was throbbing. No matter what happened, he couldn't allow Mac to walk into this same trap.

The airlock was a few metres away, and Cliff hauled himself toward it. Strange, there was no one else around. No workers, no staff, no administrators. This was a Chinese manufacturing facility on the seafloor in The Iron Plains. Perhaps The Shiv was working with them . . . maybe they were hiding, letting The Shiv do his work.

On the deck were large yellow arrows directing people to emergency exits in case of catastrophe. This facility was no different from any other in the oceans. The airlock was highly visible, and the bulkhead and deck markings were clear, even though he didn't understand the language.

The airlock hatch swung into view before him. He could barely make out the control pad on the bulkhead, but he hit the CYCLE button and the hatch ground aside. Inside, his tank and regulator were in the corner, still glistening wet. Cliff turned to the hatch and—

The Shiv was on him.

Cliff fell off balance and crashed to the deck. Blood from his forearms splattered across the steel. A searing pain flared in his left side as a blade entered his flesh and pushed upward into his kidney. He gritted his teeth and nearly screamed from pain. Spinning around, he reached up and wrapped his meaty arms around the other's neck and pulled him close. If it was a grappling match, Cliff would win, based on his sheer size.

He wrapped his legs around The Shiv's and hauled him into a bear hug—

The knife entered again.

And again.

Again.

It was a staccato attack, the knife plunging in over and over.

Blood covered the bulkhead and the deck, and the pain was beyond intense.

With the final thrust, The Shiv twisted and ground it as deep as it would go, to the hilt and beyond.

It felt as though the tip of the blade penetrated Cliff's heart, and his breath stuttered as he struggled to gasp. His back arched off the deck as his arms continued to pull the other closer, to lessen the gap, to try and keep the other from striking . . .

But it was no use, Cliff knew.

It was over, now.

Locked in that embrace, on the cold deck of the airlock, his means of escape on the other side of the bulkhead and out in the water of the Pacific, Cliff struggled to keep his eyes from shutting forever. He grabbed The Shiv's helmet and twisted savagely, trying to dislodge it.

His sight was growing dim, his pounding heart fading quickly—

And the helmet came loose and rolled across the floor.

Cliff stared up, into the assassin's eyes.

Into The Shiv's eyes.

And Cliff gasped in surprise as life poured from his body onto the deck and into the drain in the center of the airlock.

The Shiv's face was the last thing he saw.

But he'd seen it. He'd looked into the eyes. He'd never forget that glassy, cold stare, and it surprised him.

Cliff's last breath rattled out, and he lay limp on the deck, dead.

# Part Two

## A Confluence of Predicaments

**Five Days Later**
**8 June 2131 AD**

# Chapter Four

In my office were Meg, Johnny, Renée, and the visitor, Min Lee, who had thrown Johnny so off balance. On my comm vidscreen, Sahar Noor, calling from Churchill Sands, had just shocked us all. She refused to provide any more information; the comms weren't safe, especially after the announcement. I agreed to meet her, at her city, and we made the arrangements before signing off.

I stared at the group before me. My insides felt hollow.

Cliff had been by my side for ages, it seemed. He'd been an essential member of TCI, and his abilities were unsurpassed. Just a few weeks ago, he'd helped us steal the Neutral Particle Beam from The Vault in the Indian Ocean, and the previous year he'd helped Meg escape from Seascape and the CIA. He'd been completely, absolutely loyal to us.

And I'd been the one to send him on this mission to the Pacific.

To steal a technology that now didn't seem so important.

I didn't know what I'd do without him at Trieste, heading up security.

"It might not be true," Renée said, her hand on my arm. "Are you able to reach him? Can you try?"

"I sent him on a mission. I can't contact him."

"What was he doing?"

I glanced up, then noticed that Min Lee was studying me intently. I shook my head. I said to Johnny, "Can you confirm her identity?"

He was also watching me, in silence. I could see the pain in his eyes, for Cliff had been his friend too. He'd largely recovered from the appearance of the woman, but we still didn't know why it had affected him so.

He responded, "It's her. She's a Sheng City operative."

"Why are you here?" I asked her.

She remained tight-lipped, glanced at Johnny, then back to me.

"Where did you come from?" I asked.

"The Panama passthrough. Your man, Grant, confirmed—"

"Before that. Where were you?"

"I'm from Sheng City, off the coast of China. Or, I was on a mission." She offered a coy smile. "I can't really tell you. But you know the city—you've been there."

I snorted. "Yeah. Tortured for four months."

"We're on the same side now, McClusky. We made the announcement too. We have to watch for a Chinese attack on our cities. And we don't have a hurricane to protect us."

"Did your city get the same message we did? With the seven-day deadline?"

"I don't know. It's possible." A pause, and then, "I wonder if Sahar Noor received it too. It would make sense for all the superpowers to act as one, rather than try to take each city back on their own."

"Because they know the rest of us would act," I muttered. We were an alliance now, after all. I watched Min Lee carefully. Something was not right here. Her appearance at this particular time was odd. I noticed absently that there were a series of bruises on her right forearm, but I didn't mention them. "And why are you here?"

She glanced at Johnny again, but didn't respond.

I sighed and turned to my Deputy Mayor. "What about it? Do you know?" I gestured to Min Lee. "She's a Sheng City spy. She's arrived here at Trieste but won't say why."

"We're on the same side now, Mac. You declared Oceania. Maybe she's here to coordinate military efforts."

I turned back to her. "Is that it? Why won't you—"

"That's part of it. But not all."

"How did you know I was going to declare independence right now? Only The Fifteen knew."

"I can't say." Her voice was soft, yet forceful, as if telling me not to ask about it again.

To Johnny, I said, "Anything else?" I peered at him. The way he had responded earlier to news of her arrival had been unlike him. He'd lived in Sheng City. He'd had a life there that I knew very little about, other than the fact that he hadn't appreciated how his superiors had treated him. "Come on, Johnny. There's something—"

"She's my wife, Mac."

My mouth fell open.

The others were just as shocked.

All this time, Johnny had been married to a Sheng City spy, and he hadn't told us.

I leaned back in my chair. I couldn't speak. Johnny had always kept to himself at Trieste. He'd had a hard time finding a place that felt like home to him, I knew that. He'd been at Sheng for a while, but had returned to Trieste when we started the push for independence. I hadn't seen him socializing with anyone other than our own group of operatives and administrators who ran Trieste. I hadn't known him to date anyone at all, but hadn't really thought too much about it. My own work had always absorbed me. *Consumed* me. In running TCI, in pushing for our superior position in the oceans.

On sending our operatives out on missions to steal secrets, like—

I choked off the thought savagely.

I would have to deal with it later, when Sahar could provide a little more detail.

Hopefully.

Johnny was standing before me, watching, but he said no more.

"And you vouch for her?" I said, not knowing what else to say.

"Yes. She's safe. Trustworthy."

"Why haven't you ever said anything about her?"

He sighed. "Until we formally allied with the Chinese colonies, Mac, it could have caused complications. Politically, as well as with you and TCI."

"You mean, because you're Deputy Mayor?" I pondered that. "You thought it might bother people here?"

"Perhaps."

"Surely not me?"

He shrugged. "Perhaps. But she doesn't work for Trieste."

"But Sheng is an ally. Part of Oceania."

"*Now* it is."

"We've been working with them for a year. Lau was with us on the mission to sink *Drakon*." I was referring to another Sheng City spy who had helped us take the RSF dreadnought down over the Kermadec Trench. He'd died on the mission, but he'd sacrificed himself for us.

"Working with them is one thing. But we've all been competing in the oceans, Mac. Now that it's official, we felt that we could . . ." He trailed off.

I studied the couple. Now that we'd made the announcement, he felt they could tell me the truth. And The Fifteen had only signed the official treaties the day before.

But still, he hadn't expected her to arrive today. Of that, I was sure. I thought about asking him, but decided to wait. He seemed hesitant to tell me everything, yet.

I could wait.

—••—

KRISTEN HAD CALLED THE DOCKING Module to request that the crew prep my seacar, *SC-1*, for travel. It wouldn't take long, and in the meantime, I'd collect a few things from my cubicle. Churchill Sands was in the English Channel, but with the speed I could travel, the journey would only take a day. I expected to return before anything major happened with the USSF and their response to our proclamation of independence. Besides, they'd given us seven days before any attack . . . *if* they stuck to their word, that is, and it wasn't some kind of false deadline to distract from a real threat, much earlier.

But the storm gave us a buffer as well.

I decided to wander the corridors of the city before leaving, and Renée and I went for a short walk to clear our heads. She let me lead the way, and I marched through the city in the early morning hours, studying the people and the celebrations still underway. It made me happy to see it finally, after all these years. My dad had struggled so much for this—it's all he had ever dreamed about—but he had failed miserably, and the rest of our family had viewed him as a blight or a black mark on our name. At first, anyway. Now, Triestrians worshipped him—*he was the Frank*

*McClusky*—and we memorialized the day he'd been assassinated. His dreams of ocean floor colonization and independence had finally come true, thanks to me and Meg and the rest of the team.

And now it had come to fruition.

We'd made the announcement; we were finally free.

For the next seven days, anyway. We had one chance at this, but we needed to win the looming battle.

People we passed in the modules and travel tubes cheered when they saw us. Renée gripped my hand tighter in joy and we shared hugs, handshakes, and high fives with Triestrians. Everyone was thrilled to be at the forefront of ocean colonization. It was hard work, but we did it with the knowledge that we were pushing the boundaries as the surface nations struggled under climate change that industrialization and ignorance had caused. Now we were providing for them, and they wanted us to do it freely, and not under the pressures of maniacal USSF officers, bent on personal fame and wealth, which we'd seen happen before.

For the moment, I had to suppress my feelings about Cliff, to remain positive and optimistic in front of our people.

For now, anyway.

Soon we found ourselves in the travel tube in the southeast quadrant of the city. The travel tubes were three metres high with curving, transparent bulkheads. Opposing conveyers were constantly moving along the centers of the tubes, getting Triestrians from module to module quickly. We worked three eight-hour shifts in the city, so two-thirds of the population was awake at any time, and there were plenty of people still around and celebrating the news. Topside, above the waves, the sun was rising, and the ocean around us grew lighter.

I stepped off the conveyer, leaned against the bulkhead, and stared up.

The waves up there were massive.

They churned the surface, shadows plunging downward and engulfing the colony in a cascading strobe light. Sand was churning and the visibility had worsened noticeably since the previous evening.

"Is everyone prepared for the storm?" I asked.

"The metaphorical one, or the actual one?" Renée answered with a grim smile.

"Both, I guess."

"We've scratched all scuba excursions for the next several days. Mining, fishing, and farming operations are on hold except for the work they can do inside."

"Which means equipment maintenance."

"Yes."

I peered toward the fish farm pens, where the bubble walls were swaying in the waves. The fish perceived the bubbles as solid, and wouldn't pass through them. Waves from the storm would likely disrupt them, however.

Renée said, "We've processed all stocks for now, some a bit earlier than usual. The young ones are still here, but nets are up around them."

We didn't focus as much on fish as we did on kelp, but I was happy that we were prepared for the storm. The waves would grow even larger, and their currents would make it down to thirty metres, or a hundred feet, with ease. Our structures were strong, however; we could handle it.

"Regarding the superpowers, they will try to occupy us, eventually."

The Fifteen had gone over the dilemma many times. What would they do first? Attack us all, simultaneously?

Or . . .

They'd pick one city, and all attack together. Cut off the leadership's head, and pick off the rest of the colonies one at a time.

That's what they'd do. They'd attack Trieste in seven days, then target the others.

They'd want to kill me and Meg, before any of the others.

The question was, could we withstand that onslaught? The storm was one thing. This was another matter entirely, and it meant blood and bones and water-choked lungs.

There were civilians and families and children here. We'd built shelters for them, under the modules and carved into bedrock. That project had taken over a year, but it was finally done. Our defences were extensive, but countermeasures and torpedoes wouldn't last forever. Our Neutral Particle Beam, on the other hand, was our crown jewel. Our enemies didn't know about it yet, and if any ship came near, we'd carve them apart.

I shivered as a cold tide washed over me.

Renée glanced at me. "You okay?"

"I guess."

"Things are mostly proceeding as we expected."

"Johnny has thrown me off a bit. And of course, Cliff . . ." I trailed off.

"You think it's true?"

"I am scared. Sahar wouldn't have called without hard evidence." I looked outside again; the kelp was pressed nearly to the seafloor as currents tore at it. And the waves would grow far worse, over the next few days. "This was where it happened."

Renée looked startled, but only for a moment. She knew what I referred to.

My dad's murder. They'd trapped him in that travel tube. Shot him in the head, then flooded the tube for good measure.

Taurus T. Benning had done it, but he was now dead and gone, a victim to the path he'd helped start. The deck plates here were the same as everywhere else. Cold steel. Hard. Unforgiving. Grates to allow water to pass through.

And blood.

My dad had fallen here, bleeding.

I wondered if anyone could truly understand that feeling. To stand in the exact spot . . .

To live so close to it, and to remember it, every single day.

Every.

Single.

Day.

It wore you down.

I turned to Renée. "Let's go. Let's find out what Sahar wants to tell us."

—••—

*SC-1* WAS MY SEACAR. It had once belonged to Katherine Wells, brilliant scientist and engineer—and my former lover—now also dead in the fighting. So much pain and suffering, I thought. We needed to end it now, and the next seven days would tell the tale. Our cities would either survive the onslaught, or we'd fall victim to servitude once again.

Until the next person tried.

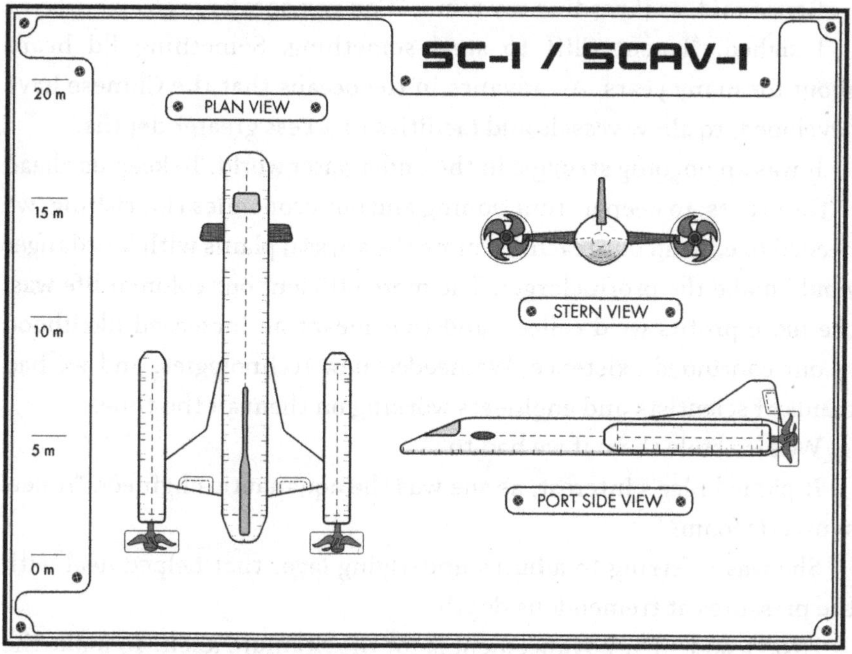


The vessel was sleek and fast, with two thrusters on either side. They were battery powered and could accelerate the seacar to a top speed of seventy kph. It had a long, narrow fuselage. The control cabin had two pilot seats. Behind that, recessed in the bulkheads, were two sleeping bunks. Then came the living space, with couches facing each other, the moonpool hatch in the deck, the lavatory, the single airlock, and then engineering. Finally, in the aft compartment, was the SCAV equipment, which housed our fusion reactor.

Renée and Meg were with me in *SC-1*. I piloted downward, through the module's moonpool, and out into the rough waters surrounding the city. Accelerating gave us some stability, but the waves pushed us about more than usual, and the ride was rough. The belt around my shoulders held me to the chair as I forged out into deeper waters, where the weather topside wouldn't bother us so much.

Soon I was rounding the tip of Florida, I pushed the SCAV reactor button, and acceleration shoved me to the seat.

The trip to Churchill would take eighteen hours at top speed.

Renée said, as if reading my mind, "Can you speak now?"

I sighed. "I sent Cliff to steal something. Something I'd heard about for many years. An advance in the oceans that the Chinese have developed, to allow vessels and facilities to access greater depths."

It was an ongoing struggle in the underwater world. To keep us ahead of the others, to keep us functioning and our economies flourishing, we needed to expand our reach. To mine the abyssal plains with less danger would make the profits larger. The more efficient our colonial life was, the more profits we'd collect, and that meant an increased likelihood of our continued existence. We needed new technologies, and we had teams of scientists and engineers working on them all the time.

We also stole them if we had to.

It piqued Meg's interest, as she was the aquanautic engineer. "A new syntactic foam?"

She was referring to a hull's underlying layer that helped deal with the pressures at tremendous depth.

"No," I said. "The advancement is for the titanium itself. To make the metal stronger."

Meg frowned. "A new alloy or manufacturing process?"

"In a way." I turned to her. "The Chinese have finally perfected graphene layering."

She swore.

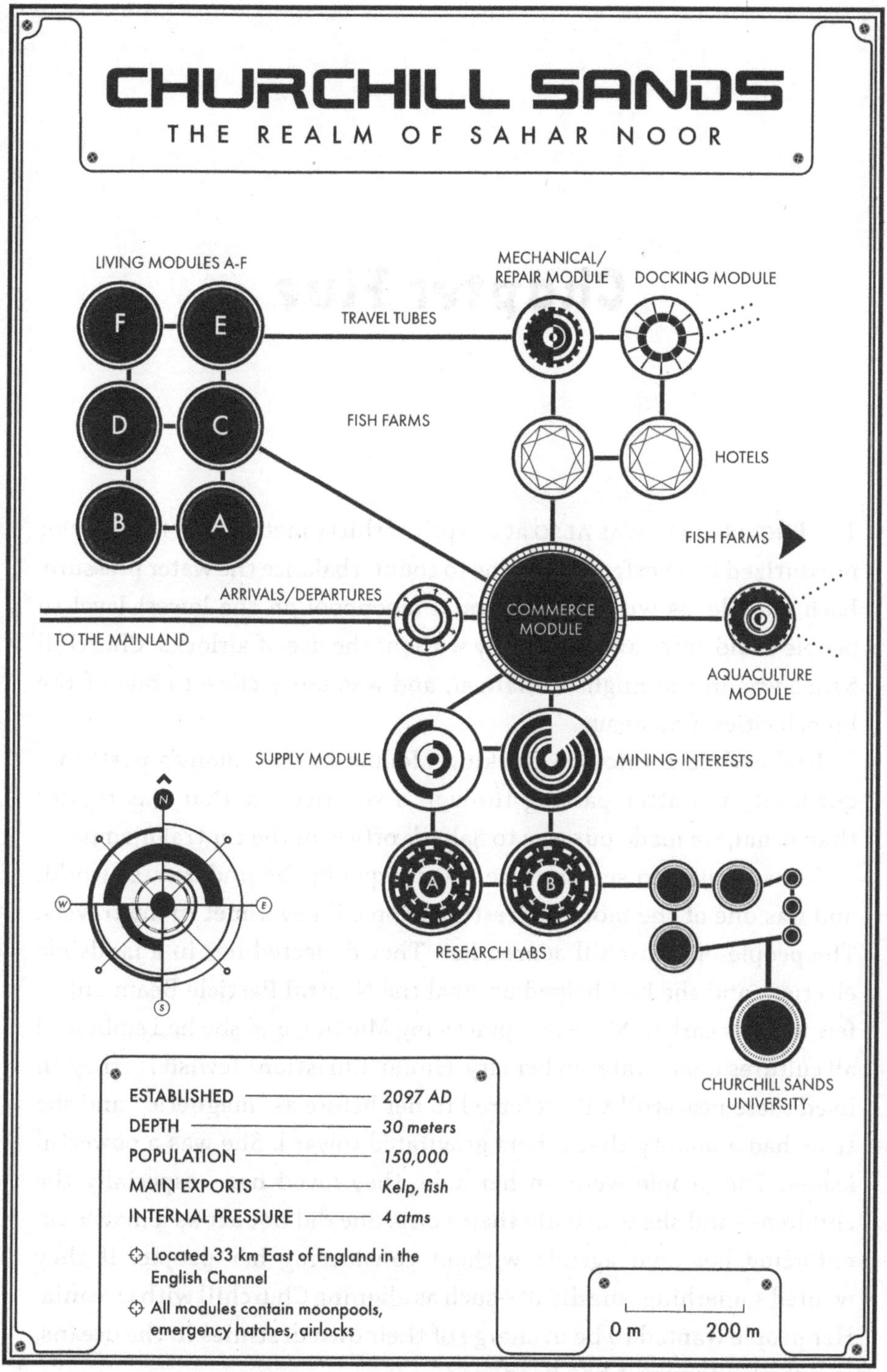
CHURCHILL SANDS
THE REALM OF SAHAR NOOR
LIVING MODULES A-F
F
E
D
C
B
A
TRAVEL TUBES
MECHANICAL/
REPAIR MODULE
DOCKING MODULE
FISH FARMS
HOTELS
FISH FARMS
ARRIVALS/DEPARTURES
TO THE MAINLAND
COMMERCE
MODULE
AQUACULTURE
MODULE
SUPPLY MODULE
MINING INTERESTS
N
W
E
S
A
B
RESEARCH LABS
CHURCHILL SANDS
UNIVERSITY
ESTABLISHED 2097 AD
DEPTH 30 meters
POPULATION 150,000
MAIN EXPORTS Kelp, fish
INTERNAL PRESSURE 4 atms
Located 33 km East of England in the English Channel
All modules contain moonpools, emergency hatches, airlocks
0 m
200 m

# Chapter Five

THE ENGLISH CITY WAS ALSO at a depth of thirty metres, and the interior pressurized to a perfect four atms to counterbalance the water pressure. Each module, as with Trieste, had a moonpool on the lowest level so people could enter and exit easily without the use of airlocks. Churchill Sands was in the English Channel, and was fairly close to one of the French cities, Cousteau.

I piloted *SC-1* into the Docking Module in the colony's northeast quadrant, and after passing through a security net that was tighter than usual, we made our way to Sahar's office, in the central module.

I was excited to see her. She was unique in the underwater world, and was one of the more interesting people I'd ever met in my travels. The people of Churchill adored her. They'd elected her in a landslide election, and she had helped us steal the Neutral Particle Beam only a few months earlier. She was a practicing Muslim, and she had embraced all cultures underwater in her city. Hindu, Christian, Jewish . . . they all lived there peacefully. I'd referred to her before as "magnetic," and she truly had a quality that others gravitated toward. She was a powerful leader. The people were on her side, they loved her—especially the children—and she was truly their voice. She did not act as a maverick, enforcing her own agenda without considering her people. If they wanted something, she did it—such as aligning Churchill with Oceania. Her people wanted to be in charge of their own destinies in the oceans, and she made sure it had happened.

She was also a pacifist, and was very much against killing or bloodshed. I wondered what would happen when the superpowers attacked all of us in just a few days.

It was coming . . . and she would have to accept a war and fight, or surrender her city without firing a shot.

She appeared before us and embraced Meg and Renée instantly. She wore a colourful hijab with an even brighter scarf. She wore makeup, her eyelashes were dark and long, and she even wore lipstick. She was English by birth, but had adopted strong elements of her own culture, and had adapted to Western ways. It was something some people struggled with—trapped between cultures—but she made it look easy, as with everything else in her life.

"Sahar," I said. "You called, and here we are."

"Mac. I'm so sorry to give you that bad news. Especially now, of all times."

"I'm the one to blame, not you." I glanced around. Her office was sparse, like mine, but the viewport was much larger, giving a wider view of the ocean floor beyond. The furniture was utilitarian, and on her desk was a single flower that was always there. The last I'd seen had been a red rose. This one was purple.

There was someone else in the office with her. He had dark hair and light eyes, thin lips, and chiseled features. He stretched out his hand to me and said in a British accent, "Hello Mac, nice to meet you. I'm William Windsor. Bill."

His grip was strong and I could tell immediately that he was a highly trained individual. There was even a small scar on his neck, near his collarbone. It was old, yet it spoke of violence in his past. His shoulders were broad, but his body was more compact than massive. He had a thin yet toned physique. Too much muscle likely slowed him down. I'd known many people before to hold that philosophy.

Then there were others, like Cliff, who felt sheer musculature and size could dominate in a fight.

"Nice to meet you," I finally said.

"I'm sorry about this news."

I blinked, then glanced at Sahar. "Who is this, exactly?"

She said, "He's one of our operatives, which I'm sure you guessed,

Mac. He works for Churchill Intelligence."

"Ah. I kind of figured."

Meg chuckled. "Truman has this superpower. He can tell who's in espionage just by looking at them."

I shrugged. "It's a skill, not a supernatural power."

"From a practiced eye, no doubt," Windsor said in a clipped, precise accent. The pronunciation was perfect and educated. He had likely studied on the mainland, in an upper-tier university.

"Cambridge?" I asked. "Or Oxford?"

He smiled, and it was charming and disarming at the same time. "Cambridge. Good job, chap. You got it on your first try."

I glanced at Meg, and she was trying to contain a smile. I frowned, for I had not known her to like too many men. But there was something about Windsor that she clearly appreciated. I made introductions, and he paid particular attention to her.

He said, "Of course I have heard all about Mac and Meg McClusky of Trieste. It's a pleasure to finally meet you."

"Likewise," Meg muttered, still staring at him.

Renée shook hands and glanced at me. She clearly had something to say about this man, too. The name *James Bond* came to mind, though he was a folk hero now of years gone by. And Windsor was just a little too short to have been him, I thought.

Sahar said, "The news about Cliff came from our intelligence sources in the South Pacific. From Windsor here."

He said, "I came straight here when I heard. I didn't transmit it. It happened about five or six days ago now."

I exhaled and didn't know what to say. I moved to the seating area in the office and glanced at Sahar. She gestured and we all sat, facing each other in a circle. "What exactly did you hear?" I asked him. I was beginning to dread this. He had the general location correct, already, and the chance that it was all a sick lie was slipping away.

He leaned forward and put his elbows on his knees. "I was in the Pacific, on a mission."

I stared at Sahar. She wouldn't be sending people out to perform violent acts, but I knew she'd engage in fact-finding or intelligence gathering. A look from her confirmed it.

Windsor continued, "Our network picked up a mention of a Triestrian citizen in Blue Downs. He was poking around. Our people there identified him as Chief Sim. He stayed there a few days before moving out in a private seacar toward The Iron Plains. He was following something or going to a location he'd discovered."

"Do you have coordinates or know his track?"

"Just a general heading. The next transmission we intercepted from the area was Chinese. They had a body at a manufacturing facility. They didn't know who it was or what he was doing there. The description matched Cliff Sim. They buried the man at sea."

My guts clenched at that. *Buried at sea* meant they'd dumped him out an airlock.

Meg said, "But you don't know it's him. It could be anyone. Was there a description? Was there a—"

"There was a picture. We intercepted it. I passed it over to Sahar, and she identified him."

I stared at Sahar, horror clear in my face. "Is it true?" I hissed.

She locked eyes with me. "Mac, I'm so sorry. It's him."

"I have to see it, Sahar. I have to know."

She brought her PCD into view and her finger hovered over a button. She glanced up at us. "Are you sure?"

"We're in intelligence," Renée said. "We can handle it."

"Still. It's more than an acquaintance here."

Her desire to stay away from violence must have made this difficult for her. "It's okay. We want to see it," I said. *I need to see it*, I thought.

The holographic image appeared before us, slowly rotating in space.

Renée gasped. Meg swore.

I ground my teeth.

*Dammit.*

Cliff Sim was on his back in an airlock, limbs splayed out. He was in a wetsuit and his mask was askew on his face, the glass faceplate shattered. There were bruises all over his face, along with splatters of blood, presumably his own. His nose was broken, and based on the facial wounds, so were his cheekbones and eye orbitals. There were slices all over his forearms, painted with dried blood—defensive wounds?—and there was a pool of blood under his left side, dripping through deck plates to the drain.

It was horrible.

He'd been through hell.

Someone had absolutely *destroyed* this mountain of a man.

But worse, I thought, was his position on the deck.

On the cold steel deck.

Just as my dad had likely crumpled to the deck, before his killers flooded the tube and made sure he was dead.

Strange, I connected the two like this. Then again, Cliff had been like a father figure. He wasn't as old, but as Chief of Security, he'd always held a protector role over us. He wanted to keep us safe, at all times. Me, Meg, Renée, Johnny.

He wanted us to achieve our ultimate goals, and he'd been intent on keeping us safe.

Until he'd died doing something *I'd* ordered.

There was a bench in the airlock, stretching around the chamber against the bulkheads. The deck had an odd cross-hatched grating. It was all gray steel—the bulkheads, walls, bench, grating, and ceiling.

He'd died in a cold room, enclosed by steel.

"A bullet wound?" Meg asked, staring at Cliff's side, near his kidney.

"Multiple stab wounds," Windsor said in a soft tone. "You can zoom in . . . " He did so, and the area filled the image. There were over ten entry wounds there.

"Ah, shit," I mumbled.

Sahar snapped a look at me, but she didn't say anything. Instead there was compassion in her eyes.

"I'm sorry," I said. "We were hoping it wasn't true."

"I feel the same. It's terrible."

I stared at William Windsor. "Who got this information?"

"Our network, in the South Pacific."

"You have many people there?"

He glanced at Sahar. "A few," he said, hesitant. "There's a large British contingent down there, in the islands. Many nations were once the King's colonies, and there are many people who are . . ." He pursed his lips. "Let's just say they agree with what we're doing."

"Because of climate change?" Meg asked, staring at Windsor.

He nodded. "Many islands are struggling with the rising waters. Some are completely gone. Many people side with Oceania."

To Windsor I said, "You were there."

"In Blue Downs, yes. Watching, waiting."

"For what?"

"We knew your announcement was coming. We've been preparing, keeping our eyes on the area. On China and Russia, mostly. Then Cliff Sim showed up, and we really took notice of that. Watched him closely."

I leaned back and sighed. And now Cliff was gone.

"There's more, Mac," Sahar said, glancing at her PCD.

I felt like swearing again. What more could there be after learning about Cliff?

The hatch slid aside, and a man entered.

Then I did swear, again, because once more, for the third time in only a day, yet another operative entered my life.

# Chapter Six

HE WAS MIDDLE-EASTERN, ATHLETIC, TONED, and agile. He entered the cabin and marched straight to where we were sitting. I rose to my feet to greet him. He had a darker complexion, with matching hair and eyes. There was an intelligence there, behind his gaze, a probing and curious look that William Windsor didn't possess.

While Windsor was prim and proper with a clipped British accent, this new man's eyes gave the impression of a carefree, easy-going person, who seemed curious about me. There were lines in his face, though not from age. They were dimples that stretched downward toward a strong jaw, though facial hair partially obscured them.

He stretched his hand out to me, and I took it.

Sahar said, "This is my brother, Mac. Sidra Noor."

His grip was firm and his eyes continued to study mine as we shook. I cocked my head as I stared at him, and I heard laughter.

"What's funny, Meg?" Sahar asked.

"It's Mac's superpower, again."

"You must have it too," I grunted. I glanced at Sahar. "Your brother. He's in intelligence too, I gather?"

She smiled. "I'm going to have to make sure our operatives are less physically capable."

Returning to my seat, I pondered what had happened in the last day. Three people had now come into my life—Min Lee, William Windsor, and Sidra Noor—and all three were operatives working in the intelligence field. I shot a glance at Renée; she was thinking the same thing.

Her lips were pursed and she was watching the two men.

I turned to Sidra. "It's so nice to meet you. I have to confess, I don't know much about Sahar's family."

"She has spoken a great deal about you." His voice was soft and disarming, and he also sported the British accent, though it was not nearly as formal as Windsor's. "I also know about your recent mission. I'm glad you watched over Sahar for the family."

I snorted. "You have it wrong, I'm afraid, Sidra. It was the other way around. She watched over us. She saved all our lives."

"Please, call me Sid. Everyone else does. And let me say how great it is to finally meet you and Meg."

I suppressed a grimace at that. I didn't particularly enjoy the fame that my father's death brought to our family. It was something we had to endure, because it was never going to go away.

He continued, "My sister is my boss. She sends me on missions for Churchill."

"And you were in the Pacific during, during—" I stopped abruptly.

"Actually," he replied, noting my difficulty, "I have been in the Atlantic, monitoring events. I have news for you on that front."

"I see." I sighed and stared at the group before me. Than to Sahar, "I didn't realize you had more to tell me. I thought it was just news about Cliff."

"No, there's more, Mac. A lot more. And you're not going to like it."

Sidra leaned forward as he spoke. His voice remained soft, melodious, almost musical, but there was a seriousness that laced every syllable. He was all business now. "I've been watching the enemy forces collect, especially since your announcement. Everyone is worried about what's going to happen."

"What has the UK done about it?"

"We received a single statement, giving us seven days to retract our decision. Then . . . then, all hell's going to break loose."

"An attack."

"Yes, but not here."

"How do you know?" Renée asked.

"The military buildup isn't near us. It's not on the nearby shore. It's not in the Channel, or the North Sea. It's farther south. Much farther."

"Let me guess," I said. "Near the Gulf."

"You got it. And it's not a small attack force."

"Go on."

"Every country involved has warsubs on the way now. German, French, American, Chinese."

Just as I'd suspected. They were going to focus on me, first. On Trieste. Hell, I'd made us enough of a target. I just hoped our defences could hold. What they didn't know, however, was that I'd expected this, and I had made plans for it.

"Maybe we can talk them out of it," Sahar said.

I studied her. "We've spoken about this before. I know what your intent is, and it's admirable. But eventually, torpedoes and mines are going to start exploding, and we'll need to defend ourselves."

"I know. And defence is fine. But we need to talk our way out of it, or at least try."

I turned to Sidra. "What do you think?"

A look of confusion passed over his features. He glanced at Sahar, then back to me. "I agree with my sister. We need to try. It's Allah's way. We can't intentionally hurt people. It's utterly against our beliefs. There's no way we can agree to that."

I knew this about Sahar, and clearly her brother had the same ideas. Nevertheless, Churchill Sands was our ally, and we'd have to count on them in an emergency. Sahar and Sidra would likely face a test, and soon.

And if they didn't help, I hoped Trieste didn't pay the price for it.

"We've tried to negotiate," I said. "I made the announcement. How they respond is up to them."

"But we can also talk to them, over the next seven days, Mac," Sahar said. "We don't have to sit back and just wait for them to attack."

I chewed the inside of my cheek as I thought that over.

Renée said, "If they find out we know they're building up a strike force, they might attack sooner."

"It's a risk," Sidra said with a nod. "Everything is a risk."

"How many warsubs?" I asked.

"More than I care to say." He exhaled. "There are hundreds on their way now. I've got the coordinates. But Mac, that's not the worst of it."

Another cloud passed over his features and he clamped his mouth shut over what he'd been about to say.

"Go ahead," Meg prodded. "Tell us."

His breath blew out in a rush. "It's Russia."

We'd known for months that the RSF was getting ready to put three more dreadnoughts to sea. And now—

Now, it had finally happened.

Last year, it had taken everything we had to defeat just one. We'd had to infiltrate it and sabotage it from within while a fleet of vessels attacked it from outside as a distraction. We'd planned the attack for weeks before carrying it out.

"How many are there?" I hissed.

"Many of their classes. Dozens of warsubs. But there are two in particular that you need to be aware of. Dreadnoughts, Mac. The *Vechno Medved* and *Soprotivlenive*."

"What does that mean?"

"The first is the *Forever Bear*. The second, *Resistance*."

"Where's the third?" I asked, with a frown.

"We're not entirely sure. The name is the *Voskhod—The Rise*. We don't know the exact coordinates, but we know the general area."

Windsor said, "Mac, it's in the Pacific right now. Near The Iron Plains."

Near where Cliff had just died.

I sighed and shook my head. "I'm not sure what that—"

"There's more, Mac," Sahar said.

"Dammit Sahar!" I snapped. "I'm under just a little bit of pressure right now!" I regretted the outburst instantly. She was watching me, silent, but there was compassion in her eyes, not anger. "I'm sorry. Again."

"I understand what you're going through. We all are. We just declared independence and we're watching the greatest buildup of undersea forces we've ever seen just outside your territory. And on top of it, Cliff Sim and the Russian dreadnoughts add to the dilemma."

"But what else could there be? I don't understand."

She sighed, then, "It's the Captain of the *Voskhod*."

I frowned. "But who—"

"It's Ventinov. Captain Ventinov."

I rose to my feet and stared at the others. Then I turned and walked to the viewport. Outside, the water was murky and dark. It swirled around the city modules like a snowstorm in slow motion. Light from the modules and the sky above created a glow around us, and fish and sediment drifted through the scene before disappearing at the edges of light.

Ventinov had Captained *Drakon*, the vessel I'd taken down. We thought we'd killed him, but there had been a chance. We'd worried about this exact situation. The ship had gone down in the Kermadec Trench, but it had been shedding debris and equipment and sections of hull as it plunged to Crush Depth. There were likely escape pods, too.

And now, not only was I facing a firestorm of imminent attack, but three dreadnoughts commanded by a man who was probably hellbent on revenge.

The weather was strong in the Channel. The waves were usually high, and the currents flowing to the North Sea were always powerful. The sand swirled around the city as if caught in a perpetual storm. It gave the city its name—Churchill *Sands*.

Ventinov.

The name sent shudders through me.

Not because he was such a terrifying figure in world politics or in global naval power, but because of what I'd done to him. He and his ship had harassed the world for a period of several weeks. He had crushed the USSF bases at Norfolk and San Diego, then had easily destroyed a CSF force of sixty-three warsubs. Then he took out Blue Downs before setting his sights on Trieste.

Ventinov had never really scared me, but now . . .

Now, he was no doubt full of rage, and it was all directed at me and Trieste. And revenge is one of the most powerful emotions. It clouded people's minds. It *consumed* them. It made them do things they normally wouldn't. A man driven by revenge would do anything to get what he wanted, and he had *three* dreadnoughts under his control.

"Are you sure?" I said.

"Yes."

"How?" Meg asked.

"Monitoring activity in The Iron Plains. The dreadnought is there. Ventinov is too."

"They gave him another command," I muttered, still staring out at the ocean.

"Apparently."

"There's likely only one reason for that."

My statement hung in the silence.

I considered the situation, but I knew we didn't have much time. I also knew what we had to do, and there was no choice. Time was the issue here, because the attack was approaching quickly.

"Can I use your comm, Sahar?"

"Sure Mac, it's on my desk."

I pushed the keys and called Trieste. Within minutes, Johnny was on the line.

"How are things there?" I asked.

"Power is back up. We're still investigating who might have done it. The reactor is fine; we've increased security there. Everyone is keeping an eye out."

"The people?"

"Triestrians are totally on side. They're still celebrating."

That made me smile, at least. "Great. Listen, I need you to do something for me." I steeled myself, then, "Get your *Sword—Destiny*. Meet us in The Iron Plains, at The Complex. Be there as soon as possible."

Total silence met my statement. The others in the office with me were shocked; their expressions were flat and faces pale. Renée was frowning, wondering where I was going with this.

"Mac," Johnny said. "It'll take you days to get there. We only have six more—"

I'd already done the math. "We can go through the Mediterranean, through the Suez Passthrough, around Indonesia and east of the Philippines. It'll take us two days at full speed."

"But what are we going to do at The Complex?"

I paused before saying anything. The line was secure, but still, the information was so sensitive that I didn't want to say it. "Johnny, do you remember who I sent out in that direction, two weeks ago?"

He paused. "Yes, I know. I remember what Sahar told us earlier."

"We need to go there, now."

There was another long, tortured break. "Is it true, Mac? It can't be—"

I hesitated. "It's true. He's dead."

The connection was so clean and clear of static that I thought he had signed off. Then, "You're serious?"

I sighed. "There's more, Johnny, but I need you out there with me. At The Complex."

"Got it." He had responded without hesitation now and was likely already marching toward the Docking Module at Trieste.

"One more thing, Johnny."

"Go ahead."

"Bring your wife. Bring Min Lee."

After signing off, I turned back to the group in the office. They were collectively staring at me, perplexed.

"What's going on, Mac?" Meg asked.

"It's simple, really. We have to go out to the site. We have to follow Cliff's trail, find out what happened to him."

"We?" Meg said. She looked around. "Obviously Renée and I are with you, but what do you—"

"We all have to go." I stared at Windsor. "You have contacts there. You've just come from the region. You know where Cliff was at Blue Downs." Then I turned to Sidra. "You know about the gathering forces. You're an operative, like Windsor, and right now, I need all the help I can get. I also have someone else going to the area—Grant Bell." Then to Sahar, "And I need you in this too. To keep me . . ."

"Grounded?" she asked with a twinkle in her eye.

"Perhaps." I shrugged. "I appreciate your—your sensibilities. You can keep me focused and on track."

She cocked her head. "And perhaps prevent you from doing what you really want, correct?"

"And that is?" I asked.

She rose to her feet, and her face was simultaneously solemn and serene. "Revenge is a terrible emotion, Mac. It makes people do crazy things."

Exactly what I'd been thinking. And revenge for Cliff's death was something I most definitely wanted.

More than anything else.

# Chapter Seven

Renée said, "Mac. Why did you really ask Sahar, Sidra, and Windsor to come?"

We were on our way to the Docking Module in the northeast quadrant. The British contingent was in their cabins, collecting their supplies for the trip.

"And Min Lee," I said. "Don't forget her."

"And Min Lee." She sighed in frustration. "I wish you'd fill us in sometimes on the things going on in your head."

I snorted. "Look, Cliff is dead. Suddenly in the span of a day we meet three operatives, all of whom have a connection to the Pacific, to The Iron Plains, or to me and Cliff. Coincidence? Or more?"

Horror laced her features as my words sunk in.

"At the same time," I continued, "We declare independence and now Ventinov and three dreadnoughts are on the horizon. I need to know what he's up to."

"He means to destroy Trieste. It's clear."

"Is it?" I stopped in the corridor and stared at her. The bulkheads were bare steel with exposed pipes and wiring, and deck plate grating for water to drain in an emergency. The city was largely utilitarian and meant for fish farming, except in the southern quadrant, where the university was located and the personnel were more academic instead of laborers. "Then why is he in the Pacific while the other two dreadnoughts are gathering in the Atlantic?"

She frowned for an instant, then a look of shock exploded across her features. "You think he played a role in Cliff's death."

"Seems connected, yes."

"But what for?"

"For me, Renée. He wants me, and he's laid a trap that caught Cliff instead."

Her eyes flashed. She was French and had spent part of her life hating me. She'd wanted to kill me for a time, for revenge, until I'd convinced her that the path I was on was the only option for the undersea colonies. She eventually turned to my side, and now we were involved romantically, but sometimes that flush of resentment and anger appeared. It was simmering underneath her psyche, all the time, as the need for vengeance often does.

I'd learned to just accept it.

"And now you're going to walk right into it! What are you thinking?"

I hesitated and stared at her for a moment. Then I looked away. "I need to put this to rest before the attack. I need to deal with it."

Meg said, "But you're cutting it close, Tru. The forces are building. They'll attack in seven days, or when the hurricane lets up. They might strike earlier."

I had indeed considered that. "If we can go to The Iron Plains, maybe we can deal with Ventinov and scratch him from the fight. That would take care of his dreadnought and maybe the other two as well."

"But it took a team of us and weeks—"

"I know, I know. I don't mean to infiltrate and sabotage it. But if I can get Ventinov face to face, maybe I can take care of him."

"Kill him. With Sahar standing right over your shoulder."

"If it's him or me, Sahar would understand."

"But even so, killing Ventinov wouldn't mean a thing! The dreadnought is still at sea. It's the most powerful vessel in the oceans. The Tsunami Plow would wipe us out—and there's *three of them*, Mac."

Renée touched my arm, and her eyes showed compassion. "She's right. Ventinov isn't going to make much difference here."

"Don't look at me like I'm a basket case."

"I'm not. But Cliff's death has really hurt all of us, not just you. I understand that you want to face Ventinov—"

It was the wrong thing to say. "It's not revenge I'm after," I snapped.

"Cliff knew the dangers of TCI. Every mission he went out on, he knew he might not come back."

"But he didn't come back from this one. And it's on us."

"It's not *on us*," I retorted. "I already said that. But Ventinov is trying to get me over there—"

"To kill you!"

"—and I'm going to go there and find out what happened to Cliff. How he got tricked."

"By offering yourself up on a platter? That's madness, Mac."

I sighed and turned to the two of them. They likely felt they were dealing with a crazy man. "Look. I'm also going to have Johnny at my side, as well as three other trained operatives."

"We don't know anything about them," Meg hissed.

"We'll also have Sahar. *And* Sidra. Surely we can trust them of all people."

Meg glared but didn't reply to that.

Renée said, "Yes, we trust Sahar completely. But we don't know Sidra, Mac. *Or* Min Lee and Windsor."

I thought about the three agents. They were mysterious, for sure. I said, "Look, we'll go to The Complex. We'll check in with our people there. We'll find out where Cliff went. *Maybe* we'll come across Ventinov. Maybe we won't. But whatever happens, we'll be back to Trieste before the countdown ends. We'll be there. We're ready, anyway . . . we're just waiting out the storm."

They glanced at each other, then back to me. They realized they couldn't change my mind. No one could.

Except *maybe* Kat. She could have done it, before she'd died fighting for our cause, that is, and she was long gone now.

I watched as Renée and Meg turned and began walking along the travel tube toward the Docking Module. They looked back and Renée said, "Well, come on then. We don't have much time. Full power all the way, right?"

"To make the deadline."

"Then let's go."

I marched forward and grabbed her outstretched hand.

We were on our way.

And maybe, just *maybe*, we'd come across the person who had murdered Cliff Sim.

Because despite what I told Meg and Renée, revenge consumed me.

I didn't really care about Ventinov.

I was going to kill Cliff's killer.

—••—

I KNEW THAT I COULDN'T let it overwhelm me. Cliff was just one man, and at Trieste there were over two hundred thousand people depending on me. There were also twenty million ocean dwellers who had joined us in Oceania, and I wouldn't sacrifice everything for my need for revenge.

A squeeze of Renée's hand reassured her, and I flashed her a quick smile as we walked. Meg looked at me and shook her head. "You do seem obsessed, sometimes. You're stubborn, like Dad."

"You're calling *me* obsessed? Meg, come on." Only a year ago, she had murdered the man who'd killed our father, and ended up in prison at Seascape. She'd ignored all the consequences. Renée, Johnny, and I had rescued her, along with Cliff.

In *SC-1*, we prepared for the long voyage. There were only two bunks, both recessed into the bulkheads on opposite sides of the lone corridor. Renée and I slept in one—though it was cramped and really only large enough for one person—and Meg had the other. The couches in the seating area were a good alternative. I guessed Sahar would set up a place in the aft SCAV compartment, where on the previous mission she had stayed. It was also a good location for her and Sidra to pray, which they did five times each day.

The seacar could handle our passengers easily. We'd had ten or more on some occasions; people had been forced to sleep on the deck or on makeshift bunks on those missions.

In the pilot cabin, I admired the controls as I almost always did. Kat had designed and built this seacar. She'd passed it to me after her death. It was fast, sleek, maneuverable, and dependable. We'd been to great depths with it, for it also had the Acoustic Pulse Drive, which used sound waves to force the ocean pressure back on itself. It only worked if the vessel was moving though; it couldn't sit still and keep the pressures at bay.

The seacar had also been in countless battles. We had conventional and SCAV torpedoes aboard, as well as countermeasures. Kat had poured herself into this vessel, and had even died while in the pilot seat. I felt close to her when I sat there now, though sometimes it seemed as though her ghost were with me wherever I went. But I knew I had to continue to press forward through life, form relationships, and try to keep myself as sane as possible.

Meg had practically adopted Renée into the family. She and Johnny were all we really had now. There was no mom and dad anymore, no extended relatives, no one other than those we interacted with every day at Trieste.

A few minutes later, the top hatch opened and Sahar, Sidra, and William Windsor descended the ladder and entered *SC-1*. They looked around in appreciation, and Sahar in particular had a smile on her face. "It's good to be back," she said.

She had changed her hijab and was also wearing a more comfortable set of coveralls, though she still wore a colourful scarf—this one crimson. They were her trademark, and the children in Churchill actually looked for her in the corridors and travel tubes to see if they could spot her, and to see what colour she was wearing on any particular day. The scarves coordinated with cultural holidays, and there were even websites and online groups dedicated to Sahar, *including* her scarves.

I knew Sahar's need to avoid bloodshed was not from fear, that much was certain. It was ingrained in her upbringing and in her culture.

Sidra would likely be the same. They'd been born on the mainland, but historically the family had migrated from the Middle-East.

William Windsor was another matter entirely. While Sahar and Sidra were polite, quiet, and demure, Bill was chattering away with Renée and Meg and wandering freely around *SC-1*, looking in every nook and cranny. I noted absently that Meg had taken it upon herself to show him around, and there was a slight lopsided smile on her face as she spoke with him about some of the missions we'd been on together in the vessel. It was a look I hadn't seen on her face before.

He'd captured her attention, there was no doubt of it. But I did find it odd. Men were always approaching her, but she usually brushed them off.

Maybe it was the accent, I thought. It could be attractive, especially when it was a spy speaking.

Eventually we were ready to go, and Renée and I piloted the seacar out of the Docking Module and began the journey southward, toward the Mediterranean and the Suez Passthrough—the tunnel that paralleled the surface canal and opened into the Gulf of Suez and the Red Sea.

Then Meg approached from behind and said, "So, Mac. Don't you think it's time to explain what's really going on here?"

I turned with a frown on my face. We were under SCAV drive, at 450 kph, and powering toward the Med at a depth of 200 metres. Outside, it was nearly completely black, except for the churning maelstrom of cavitation where the SCAV bubble and water collided in a near-frictionless membrane. "What do you mean?"

"The reason Cliff left Trieste. His mission. What was he *really* after?"

# Chapter Eight

I STUDIED THE COLLECTION OF eyes that met mine. The passengers were in the living area of *SC-1*, just a few metres aft of the pilot cabin. I sighed. They deserved to know.

Renée said, "I've got the controls." She gestured aft with her chin as she held the yoke. "You can go."

I moved to the back and sat on a couch. Sahar, Meg, Sidra, and Windsor were still watching me. "I told you, Meg."

She snorted. "Graphene has been around for years. Graphite even longer. But you haven't really told me what exactly Cliff was doing in The Iron Plains. What was he after?"

Outside, the water whipped past the viewport, held away from our hull by the bubble. Air churned out from the water due to cavitation at the low-pressure zone that the bow created, and the bubble stretched back and enveloped the entire seacar, reducing friction to nearly zero. Our fusion drive was rumbling as it vaporized seawater and pumped the steam out the rear nozzles, hammering us along. The Suez was only hours away, where normally it would have taken days.

"Pressure is the biggest issue in underwater colonization," I said. "Getting deeper, safely, is the key to our survival."

"We're doing okay now," Sidra said.

"Our major colonies are only at thirty metres down, because we all live at four atms and that perfectly balances the depth. We keep *SC-1* at four atms too, so we can dock with any other facility and move easily to it. Meanwhile, kelp and fish farms are shallow too. They're no problem. But deeper outposts have to exist where the minerals are, and they have to be inexpensive enough to open up those areas for us."

"The Iron Plains are pretty deep. Nations are mining those easily enough."

"Yes, but manned outposts stick to areas that are less than 4,000 metres. The abyssal plains, from eight or ten kilometres, are where the *real* riches are. We need to be able to get to those to truly unlock our potential. Once we do, *all* the oceans will be open to us."

"We have strong hulls now," Windsor said in his crisp tone. "We have syntactic foam that allows deeper outposts."

That had been a marvellous invention from the Twentieth Century. It was foam that consisted of microscopic glass or ceramic spheres. The viscous conglomerate hardened after application. The spheres withstood pressures well, and allowed greater strength in submarine hulls. Engineers sprayed it on titanium hulls, or, more commonly, between hull layers.

We'd discovered that another nation had developed a better type of syntactic foam, and we'd worked hard to steal a sample. Turned out that the new process had used water at the center of each microscopic sphere.

And since water can't be compressed . . .

It had been a most effective new technology in the quest to further expand our reach into the ocean. It allowed hulls to be lighter, thinner, and stronger. As a result, ships could go deeper and faster in the ocean realm.

The thing that made this all so ironic, is that the person who had stolen that invention for us had been Cliff Sim.

Now I had sent him out to get yet another secret that would allow us to go deeper, but this one had been a different mission, and obviously one far more dangerous.

Hell, he'd been up against a threat that he wasn't even aware of. It wasn't just a simple invention or process in a Chinese facility in the Pacific.

He'd been up against Captain Ventinov, and hadn't even known it.

Because of me.

"Mac?" Sahar asked. "Are you okay?"

"Yes, why?"

"Your expression, it suddenly changed."

I brushed it off. "Just thinking about—about *everything*, I guess."

"You show great concern for your team. It's clear."

"I want to keep people safe."

"Yes. You do."

"I keep people safe? Or I *want* to keep people safe."

"Both."

"Clearly not."

She sighed. "Sometimes this happens. To me, too."

"You're a pacifist, Sahar. You don't send operatives out on dangerous—"

"Not true I'm afraid, Mac," Windsor interjected. "She sends us out frequently. Myself, Sidra—" Then he stopped short. "There are others, too."

"I'm sure."

"Some of the missions are dangerous. Most are reconnaissance, to gather intel to give Churchill the upper hand in treaty or economic negotiations. But we have lost operatives."

Sahar grimaced. "And I have had to bear that pain, Mac. I know how it feels."

She seemed to handle the guilt and pressure, especially for someone who was so against violence. "I didn't know that, Sahar."

A silence settled over us as *SC-1* plowed through the cold, deep water. The thrum of the reactor and drive vibrated everything, but it eventually faded into a white noise, which our brains tuned out.

"Go on, Mac," my sister said. "What was Cliff after?"

"We heard a tip about a new process to strengthen hulls. The Chinese are using it in The Iron Plains. Their facility to manufacture the titanium used in seacar or warsub construction is there too."

"Who gave you the tip?"

"Someone sent it to the commander of our mining facility in the region. To The Complex."

"Anonymous?" Sidra asked.

"That should have been the first red flag. But there have been so many tips over the years that panned out. The Neutral Particle Beam, the Acoustic Pulse Drive, the Hafnium Bomb that Dr. Hyland created for us."

"That was Trieste?" Sidra gasped.

I nodded. "We blew up Seascape last year."

He shook his head. "I had no idea."

"I thought Sahar would have told you. We used the bombs in the Indian Ocean recently too, when we stole the beam."

He snapped a look at her. "No, I had no idea."

"I keep secrets, Mac," Sahar said.

"It's not such a secret anymore," I said with a sigh. "We have to share everything with The Fifteen now." Then I steeled myself and pressed on, "Commander Coda Rose at The Complex received the tip. He told me about it. I sent Cliff a couple of weeks ago."

"What was his mission?" Sidra asked.

"To track the message. Find out if it was legit. And if it was . . . "

"Follow up on it and steal the invention."

I raised a finger. "Only if he felt it possible. I left him in charge. I knew it was about graphene. I researched to learn more about it. I spoke with Doctor Lazlow and Hyland to find out more. It seemed important. I sent him." I exhaled. "The Chinese have thrown themselves into mining in the region."

"Iron is crucial right now," Windsor said. "Nations are pushing into outer space."

"They've given up on Earth," Meg muttered. "Destroy the climate, destroy the planet, and move on. The superpowers are worse than alien invaders."

"They're pressing outward, that's true," I said. "And iron is more important that any other mineral right now. And Cliff must have thought the tip was believable."

"And now you want to follow the same path?" Meg asked, her expression one of disgust. "Follow the trail and die like Cliff? Is that it?"

"We've been over this," I sighed. "We have help." I gestured at the others. "Johnny and Min Lee are going to meet us too. Besides, the process is too important to pass up."

Sahar frowned. "What does that mean?"

Meg said, "It's why Cliff went in the first place." She stared at me. "*I think*, anyway. Care to explain?"

"It's graphene. Commander Coda Rose at The Complex told me about it."

Meg said, "People had theorized about it for decades during the 20th Century. It's basically a single layer of carbon, only an atom thick, laid in a two-dimensional honeycomb lattice. It's the strongest material ever tested."

The others were staring at Meg with blank looks. Then, as one, their gaze shifted to me. "Is this true?" Sidra asked.

"Yes. Engineers discovered graphite long ago. That's a three-dimensional structure though. The dilemma for many years was how to get it to just a single layer. So it had been a theory only. For many years people actually forgot about it. It left science's collective consciousness, you could say. Electron microscopes possibly observed it in 1962, but scientists only studied it—they hadn't laid the graphene down intentionally. Then, in 2004, at the University of Manchester, Andre Geim and Konstantin Novoselov isolated and investigated it. They successfully produced a single, atom-thick layer."

"How?"

I snorted. "It seems ridiculous, but they used scotch tape to peel it away from graphite. They won the Nobel Prize for it."

Silence met my statement, along with more blank stares.

I continued, "I assure you, it's true. It was very low tech. But they proved it could be done, and the material existed. In a honeycomb lattice, a two-dimensional material."

"And this is useful because it's so strong?"

"Absolutely." I sighed. "That's what we're all doing here, all the time."

"In the Mediterranean?" Windsor asked.

"In the oceans. Period." I gestured outside the window. "The easier we can get to great depths, the more material we can mine."

Sahar said, "So you're suggesting that it's a strong material for use as a warsub or seacar hull?"

I said, "The material is stronger than you can imagine. It also has really interesting properties that have captivated engineers since 2004."

"Such as?" Sahar asked.

"It's conductive, so you can pass an electric current through it. It's transparent at that thickness, or even thicker. And it's flexible too. But its strength is what appeals to us in the colonies."

"But scotch tape, Mac?"

I managed a grin. "I admit, it sounds crazy. Hyland called the process *micromechanical cleavage*. Engineers also eventually used a single crystal diamond wedge blade to slice an atom-thin layer. But the two inventors who isolated and discovered it won the Nobel in 2010 and started the Graphene Gold Rush."

"For engineers."

I shrugged. "For anyone who could use it. Industrialists. Scientists. A single layer with remarkable properties that's only .000001 inches thick!"

"But with scotch tape!" Sidra blurted. "That doesn't seem very useful, in a commercial sense."

"You're right. The problem was how to create single layers in a stable, commercial manner. You could imagine how engineers threw themselves at the dilemma." And when the scientific community tackled a problem, the solutions and innovations were more than a "rush," they were a flood. "Imagine this material coating our seacars. On our *Swords* or on *SC-1*." I shrugged. "It would continue to open the oceans for us. And China is *doing it*, right now, in The Iron Plains."

"According to the tip the Commander received."

I nodded. "We had to investigate."

Sahar was pondering it. "But Mac, how strong is this material, exactly? It's only carbon, you said."

"This is how Lazlow and Hyland explained it to me, back at Trieste. If you created a hammock of the material one square metre in area, it would support a four-kilogram cat, but would only weigh as much as one of the cat's whiskers."

"Like a spider web?" Sidra asked.

"Far lighter. And also invisible to the naked eye. You'd need a very powerful microscope to see it." I paused. "There are also some *extremely* interesting characteristics which are commercially useful to us."

"Such as?"

"It is self repairing."

"What does that mean?" Sidra pressed.

"If there's a break or a tear in the material, engineers can bombard it with carbon atoms. These align into the hexagonal structure, bonding with the graphene layer, perfectly filling any holes."

His face was pale, as was Meg's. "No welding? No rivets? No laser sealing or pressure fixing hulls?"

"Exactly." I forced another smile. "It's a miracle substance, more or less."

"But if we've known about it since 2004, and earlier, then . . . " Sidra trailed off. "What is the process?"

"That's the difficulty," I replied. "Creating it in single sheets, each an atom thick. Obviously the Chinese aren't using scotch tape. It has taken many, many years to perfect it. It turns out it needed a substrate, or another substance that engineers lay down first, then the carbon on top of it, in a chemical form. It's called CVD, or chemical vapor deposition, to produce it on a large enough scale to coat entire warsub hulls."

"And laying it down on titanium hulls?"

"Exactly, but many layers of graphene. Not just one. Hundreds of thousands. One on top of the other, until it's collectively strong enough to withstand pressures at the ocean floor."

"What's the substrate?"

I paused. "That's the problem. We don't know."

Realization lit Sahar's features. "But the tip to Commodore Coda Rose . . . "

"Exactly. That's what it was. The Chinese are doing it at some secret facility in The Iron Plains." I clenched a fist. "Cliff found it. He discovered the location *and* maybe the process itself. We have to follow the trail and figure it out.

"And get back to Trieste before the world attacks us."

# Interlude

## Somewhere in the Pacific Ocean

**3 June 2131**
**Six Days Earlier**

| | |
|---|---|
| Vessel: | Russian Submarine Fleet *Dreadnought* Class *Voskhod–The Rise* |
| Location: | Latitude: Unknown<br>Longitude: Unknown<br>North of The Iron Plains |
| Depth: | 100 metres |
| Date: | 3 June 2131 |
| Time: | 2218 hours |

LIEUTENANT MILA SIDOROV WAS IN the bowels of the dreadnought. She'd left Ventinov on the bridge, where he could continue to plan the destruction of Truman McClusky, a desire that clearly now consumed him. Now she was doing a routine inspection of the torpedo launchers on the warsub's port side. There were so many, however, that it would take days to finish. She'd been trying to do a number of them each shift, so she could plan and manage when the task would be finished: *five days from now*, she thought. Perhaps by then they'd be finished in the Pacific and *Voskhod* could make its way to the Atlantic, where the others were waiting.

The prospect of three dreadnoughts destroying a single underwater colony was simultaneously exciting and embarrassing. It was a tiny settlement, in the grand scheme. The warsub was over four hundred metres long and could obliterate entire fleets. Surely they could take out a single, fragile, lone, and exposed collection of modules on the shallow seafloor.

Still, Ventinov's warnings rang through her.

A Neutral Particle Beam underwater was nothing to scoff at.

If it were true.

She wondered what would happen to crew if they were standing near the outer hull, against the bulkhead perhaps. What if the beam hit them? What would happen to human flesh?

In a few days, after Ventinov was done with his games—his traps—they would embark on the journey.

Then the real attack could begin, and they could finish Trieste once and for all.

CAPTAIN VENTINOV WAS STILL ON the bridge. He was waiting for word from his assassin, the mercenary, The Steel Shiv, that the Triestrian was dead.

Truman McClusky.

All the pieces were falling into place. They'd planted the clues. The path was clear.

And The Shiv was waiting.

Thankfully, Ventinov had backup after backup, just in case, not the least of which was two more dreadnoughts, waiting in the Atlantic for his word to attack.

Ventinov also had another surprise waiting for McClusky and the people of Trieste.

He had taken a page from the Triestrian book, and was going to also try to take the underwater colony *from within*. He had a Russian spy in the city, embedded there. When the shit hit the fan, his operative would begin to work his magic, and throw the city off balance.

Ventinov wanted to kill Truman McClusky and destroy Trieste.

There was no other way this would end.

| | | |
|---|---|---|
| Location: | Latitude: Unknown | |
| | Longitude: Unknown | |
| | On the seafloor in The Iron Plains; Chinese Manufacturing Plant—*The Facility* | |
| Depth: | 1,618 metres | |
| Date: | 3 June 2131 | |
| Time: | 2358 hours | |

THE STEEL SHIV STARED DOWN at the body. Cliff Sim was bloodied, battered, broken, and finally dead. It had been a tough fight, despite what the security officer may have thought, for Sim was large, muscular, fast, agile, and he had great technique. It had caught The Shiv off guard at first. The man had fallen into the trap and traveled to The Facility. He'd discovered the clues the Russian Captain had planted at Blue Downs, and had come straight to the location in The Iron Plains. The Shiv had tracked the seacar the entire way, waited inside the airlock, and then—

The fight had begun.

And ended, as expected.

The Shiv reached down and grabbed the black, tinted helmet from the airlock deck. Sim had torn it away during his death throes, and had looked into the mercenary's eyes at the very end.

It was satisfying, in a way, to study a victim as life leaked out. As blood spilled, as the last lungful of air escaped, as the very soul departed the body. The eyes dilated open fully and all life seeped out.

But Sim had seen The Shiv, at the very end. Once that happened, Sim had to die, although that had been a foregone conclusion the second he'd entered the facility.

The Shiv was careful not to glance backward, or up at the ceiling, for there were likely cameras there, studying and recording. No one knew The Shiv's identity.

Some secrets would *never* get out.

It was the best way to survive in the world of espionage.

The Shiv took a series of photographs of CSO Cliff Sim, on the deck, dead. It was humiliating, and The Shiv appreciated that. He often took photos of victims and distributed them. It enhanced The Shiv's reputation and spread fear through the intelligence community. Truman McClusky would be furious, and that's what the Russian Captain would want. A touch of another key and the comm device signaled the Russian dreadnought, *Voskhod.*

A voice answered. "Go ahead."

"It's done. He's dead."

"I need a photograph."

"Sending now."

A moment passed, then, "That's not him!" The Russian, Captain Ventinov, was furious. "I ordered you to kill Truman McClusky."

"We laid the trap. This is who it ensnared. We're not done yet. It works. We'll just try again. We wait."

"I paid you to find McClusky! Not some nameless—"

"That's Trieste's CSO. It'll have an impact."

"I don't care! I want the Mayor!"

The Steel Shiv paused and let Ventinov fume to himself. Then he continued screaming about the plan, how the Triestrian had destroyed him, had humiliated Russia, and more. Finally The Shiv said in the electronic voice, "He will come. Especially now that we have given him more incentive."

"And what's that!?" Ventinov screamed.

"I killed one of his best people. Maybe even a *friend.* You have to understand what that does to people, Ivan."

"Don't call me that," he snapped.

"I'll call you whatever I want. I'm doing a job. I didn't provide you a timeline."

"The understanding—"

"Understand *this, Captain.* I'll kill him when I face him. Until then, we have to wait. I have another idea. But the trail that we planted *works.* It'll work again."

There was a pause. "What do you suggest?"

"The pictures I just sent you."

"Yes?" He was still breathing hard, but his tone was lighter.

"Send them to your superiors. Let them get out into the world. Leak them."

"Why? How will that help?"

The Shiv paused. "Of all people, I thought you'd know what the hunt for revenge does to people, Captain."

"What does that mean?"

The sigh was mechanical and drawn out. "It eats you away, from the inside. Like *Drakon*'s reactor when it melted down. It tears your insides apart. I'm sure you can understand that, at least. This will draw McClusky here, I promise."

The PCD went silent as Ventinov processed that. Inside the helmet, The Shiv grinned. The intentional insult would drive the Captain mad.

It was insanely satisfying.

"How dare you say that to me," Ventinov said. "I have dreadnoughts at my hands. *Three* of them!"

"The dreadnought didn't help you before, and I don't care about your feelings. I only care about finishing the job, and this is going to do it. Your need for revenge will make you unstable. You have to control it. Now do what I say, and send the photos."

"And what are you going to do?"

"My job, Ventinov. I'm going to do my job. Now leave me alone and let me finish it."

# Part Three:
## The Complex

# Chapter Nine

THE JOURNEY THROUGH THE MEDITERRANEAN and the Suez Passthrough was uneventful, which I appreciated. The high speed meant we attracted a lot of attention, but we ignored all comm signals, most of which were from curious ocean travelers who had detected our drive on their sonar screens. It was so loud it appeared as a brilliant white flare. Glowing, pulsating, the maelstrom of steam was so loud that *stealth* was not an option. At first, when we'd started using *SC-1* and the SCAV drive, we'd had to maintain a semblance of secrecy. We'd had to travel deep, or in trenches, or far away from other vessels. Now, however, other nations had the drive, and it was becoming more common in the oceans.

Soon we were beyond the Passthrough and into the Red Sea. It had been an easy voyage up until then, but we were going to have to start threading between the island archipelagos of Southeast Asia, including Indonesia and Malaysia.

On board *SC-1*, the mood was tense and quiet. Meg and William Windsor—or *Bill*, as he asked us to call him—were spending more and more time together. There was something about him that captivated her, and I could understand what she saw in him. He was friendly, charming, and his smile and the twinkle in his eye was disarming. He was easy-going and laid back. He would sit in the couch with his arm outstretched on its back, and talk about his missions and life working in the under-sea world. Sahar watched him, usually silently, but sometimes she would shush him with a casual glance or a glare. She smiled at him too though, for she found him likeable as well.

"How much do you know about him?" I asked her while he was somewhere in the back, exploring the SCAV equipment with Meg and Sidra.

"He's worked for Churchill Intelligence for many, many years. Even before I started."

"He was there when you were elected?"

She nodded. "My predecessor spoke highly of him."

"Where is he from?"

She watched me silently, and there was a smirk on her face. "Why are you curious? Is it because of Meg?"

I frowned. "Meg is an adult. She can do what she wants."

"You're her brother though."

"She's a strong, independent person. We've spent most of our lives apart. She had her own life, in Blue Downs."

"And as a result, you treat her as a grown up. I understand."

Something about the way she said it . . . "Ah. The way Sidra treats you?"

Sahar grinned. "He's my brother. He wants to protect me. Sometimes he's *too* protective."

"Does he know what you did on our mission to steal the Beam?"

"Not all the details. But some."

"He was mad?"

She frowned at me. "No. He was proud!"

"Then he doesn't know the full truth about what you did. How you almost died to save us. To save the movement." Had she not performed that final act, jumping into the moonpool and swimming downward to plant the bomb, the other warsub would have destroyed *SC-1*. I was on board, along with Meg, Johnny, Cliff, Renée, and others. The *entire* independence movement at Trieste was in one place, at one time, and we'd been seconds from destruction.

"I don't know if I'd put it that way, Mac."

"I would."

She laughed. "You have twisted it in your memories. Glorified it maybe."

"Not at all."

"Let's just say it was a team effort."

"I'm happy you're with us on this."

She studied my expression as I piloted the vessel. "Cliff's death is tough. But don't let it affect you *too* much. Focus on the graphene."

"Have you had to deal with things like this?"

She paused and stared ahead at the out-of-focus, swirling, pulsating bubble; at the blunt bow where the low-pressure zone caused air to boil from the water, the tiny bubbles collecting and growing into the single large cavity that enveloped the entire seacar. She said in a quiet voice, "You think I don't do the things you do? I don't send people to die?"

I hesitated. Offending her was the very last thing I wanted in this world. "I know you don't engage in fighting or battles the way I have. Sahar, we *destroyed* Seascape with a hafnium bomb last year. I *know* you wouldn't have done that."

"You were saving Meg's life."

"Are you saying you'd have done the same for Sidra, had the CIA captured him?"

She paused. "No one can truly say until they're in that position, but no, I likely would not have. But that's an extreme example."

"But you've sent people to die?"

"No, absolutely not. I couldn't do that. But I have sent agents on dangerous assignments. The threat is always there, and sometimes, rarely . . . there's been death."

Laughter echoed from behind us, from the living area. It was Meg and Windsor.

Sahar said, "She seems happy."

"She likes him."

"That's good."

"She doesn't show a romantic interest in many people, to be honest. I've never seen her like this."

Sahar appeared surprised. "Really? She's so pretty . . . she seems that she'd have no problems in that department."

I sighed. "I guess you have to understand our lives. What happened to our family. It's been in turmoil since . . . "

"Since your dad's murder?"

"Meg and I only recently reconnected. Two years ago. We're the only family we've got, except for others very close to us, like Renée and Johnny."

"And Cliff."

"Yes. And Cliff."

"Renée is your lover and Johnny your best friend. Cliff was also one of your best friends. But who does Meg have?"

I couldn't answer that at first. It was an astute observation. Then, "Her work is important to her. She's the best at it. People highly respect her."

Sahar looked forward again but didn't respond immediately. I knew what she was thinking. "But she needs someone in her life, Mac. Love."

"To make her whole?"

"No, I don't mean that. I just mean that humans need humans. Love is important. I don't think Meg needs it to survive or be happy. I'm just saying that after what you two have been through, she might like some companionship."

I didn't appreciate the notion that we needed someone in our lives, otherwise we could never be happy. I also didn't believe that it applied to every single person. I'd spent seven years as a loner, after my capture and torture at Sheng City. I'd had lovers during that period, though I had to admit that I'd felt as though something were missing, but I didn't exactly know what. The partners had just been for sex, nothing more.

I had felt lonely, during those years.

Reconnecting with the independence movement had really given me some drive, and a goal, and of course I fell in love with Kat first, and then Renée. Those two had really filled holes in my life.

But did Meg need the same thing? She'd never mentioned it to me. Hell, men were always looking at her, studying her, gauging whether they should ask her out. Meg almost always shut them down, either by her words or a look in her eyes, or blatantly ignoring them and sending them on their way. Why did she do that, still, after all these years since Dad's death? We'd been fourteen years old when he'd died, and we were now forty-six.

Meg laughed again, and the sound floated on the air currents into the control cabin.

I stared at Sahar. "Can you tell me about him? Or is it secret?" He *was* an operative, after all.

She said, without hesitation, "He's from the mainland. A place south-west of London called Ripley. Formally educated at private school and then at Cambridge, which you guessed correctly."

"I try."

"He came to Churchill before I ran for office."

Each undersea colony had an intelligence agency with operatives who went out on assignments to monitor other nations' troop buildups, navies, to steal inventions to reverse engineer, and more. Even assassinate threatening political or military figures, though I doubted Sahar took part in those activities. We tried to keep our espionage activities as secret as possible; I remembered when we'd thought Trieste's had been absolutely covert and unknown, and then had discovered the USSF had known all about it for years. That knowledge had thrown us into a crisis.

"Is he a good spy?"

"Never had a problem."

"His specialty?"

She looked at me. "Are you doing the work of TCI right now, or are you asking for your sister?"

I shrugged. "I want to make sure he's a good guy."

After a moment she said, "He works a lot in the Pacific. He knows our network there, and he's made strong connections in Blue Downs and the New Zealand colony too."

"And was he born in Ripley?"

"Yes. It's smallish, a nice town."

I glanced back at them; they were sitting on the couch, talking and laughing. Sidra was nowhere in sight now; he was likely still back in engineering. I said in a soft tone, "He doesn't seem to have the killer instinct. He *looks* like an operative, but he's . . ." I trailed off.

"Easy going, softer. Polite?" She shrugged. "It's the English way. I've seen him in action before. Some of it on video after missions. He can definitely handle himself. I've seen him take out many enemies. In self-defence, mind you, but he knows what he's doing. I never worry about him."

The two were still talking, though there seemed to be a lot of flirting going on as well.

"And Sidra? Are those two friends?"

"Yes. They sometimes work together. They're usually in the same theater—the Pacific—so they cross paths a lot."

"And is Sidra good in a fight?"

She was staring at me. "What are you fishing for, Mac?"

"Just curious if he's capable."

"Or if he's just in intelligence because his sister is the Mayor?"

"Something like that, I guess."

She exhaled and considered it. "Sid has been training since he was a boy. He's highly skilled. My parents didn't enjoy all the fighting when he was young, but it was more of a sport for him. He wasn't getting in fights at school."

"It was all in a dojo or gym?"

"Yes."

Meg laughed again, and I turned to look at them.

—••—

LATER THAT NIGHT, WHILE MEG had the controls, Renée and I were in our bunk together with the curtain drawn tight. We'd already navigated the Passthrough, had dinner as a group, and were now getting some sleep before the voyage through the island archipelagos of Southeast Asia. We were still at full power, intending to arrive at The Complex as soon as possible. Time was tight, and we couldn't let up. We had one more day of travel before we'd arrive and could investigate in more detail what Cliff had discovered and where he had gone. The Chinese manufacturing facility would be an important location. I couldn't underestimate the importance of graphene in our underwater quest for dominance. It would open up so much more of the ocean to us, possibly the entire ocean floor. The substance was *that* strong, and if China had really perfected a process to apply layers to warsub hulls, then they'd use that against us.

Against Oceania.

We needed it too, in order to compete with them.

Renée said in a soft voice, "What are you thinking about?"

She had a French accent, and Meg affectionately called her *Frenchie*. We were naked and next to each other; it was too warm to have a sheet over us. Her hand was on my chest, her finger tracing lines, following muscle ridges and the odd scar.

I said, "What's coming, I guess."

"Do you have a plan?"

"We need to follow Cliff's path."

"And if you do? Where does it lead?"

"To the manufacturing plant."

"The graphene?"

"Yes." I hesitated, then, "When we get to The Complex, watch the others for me."

"Who, exactly?"

"Windsor, Sidra, and Min Lee. I have something in mind, but I need you to watch my back."

"Don't put yourself in unnecessary danger." She eyed me in the darkness; I could just barely make out the shape of her face, her nose, her lips. I glanced down; her breasts were small and firm, and they were pressed to my body. Her legs were taut and lean. "Mac?"

"Yes?"

"What are you looking at?"

"You."

Her fingers traced lower, and within a few minutes we were making love in the bunk, her on top, riding me in rhythm to the rocking of the vessel as it forged through water and our ultimate destination.

After we were done, spent and sweaty and lying next to each other again, panting hard, she said, "Where else does it lead?"

"What?"

"Cliff's path. Where does it lead?"

"To the graphene plant. I said that."

"But where else?"

I stared at her for a minute, not understanding. Then suddenly, "Ah. I get it."

"You want to go to where he died?"

"In a way."

"You're hoping for your revenge."

"Maybe, Renée. To find out who did it, for sure."

"But it might lead you straight to him."

"I'm hoping."

"He beat Cliff, Mac. That's no small feat."

I didn't answer.

"I don't know anyone who could beat Cliff in a fight."

"Me neither," I finally said. "Not even I could beat him. At least, not easily." I could barely hear myself speak.

"And you want to go face the same person. An assassin."

"Some have called me that before, too."

"This isn't the same, Mac."

I didn't respond.

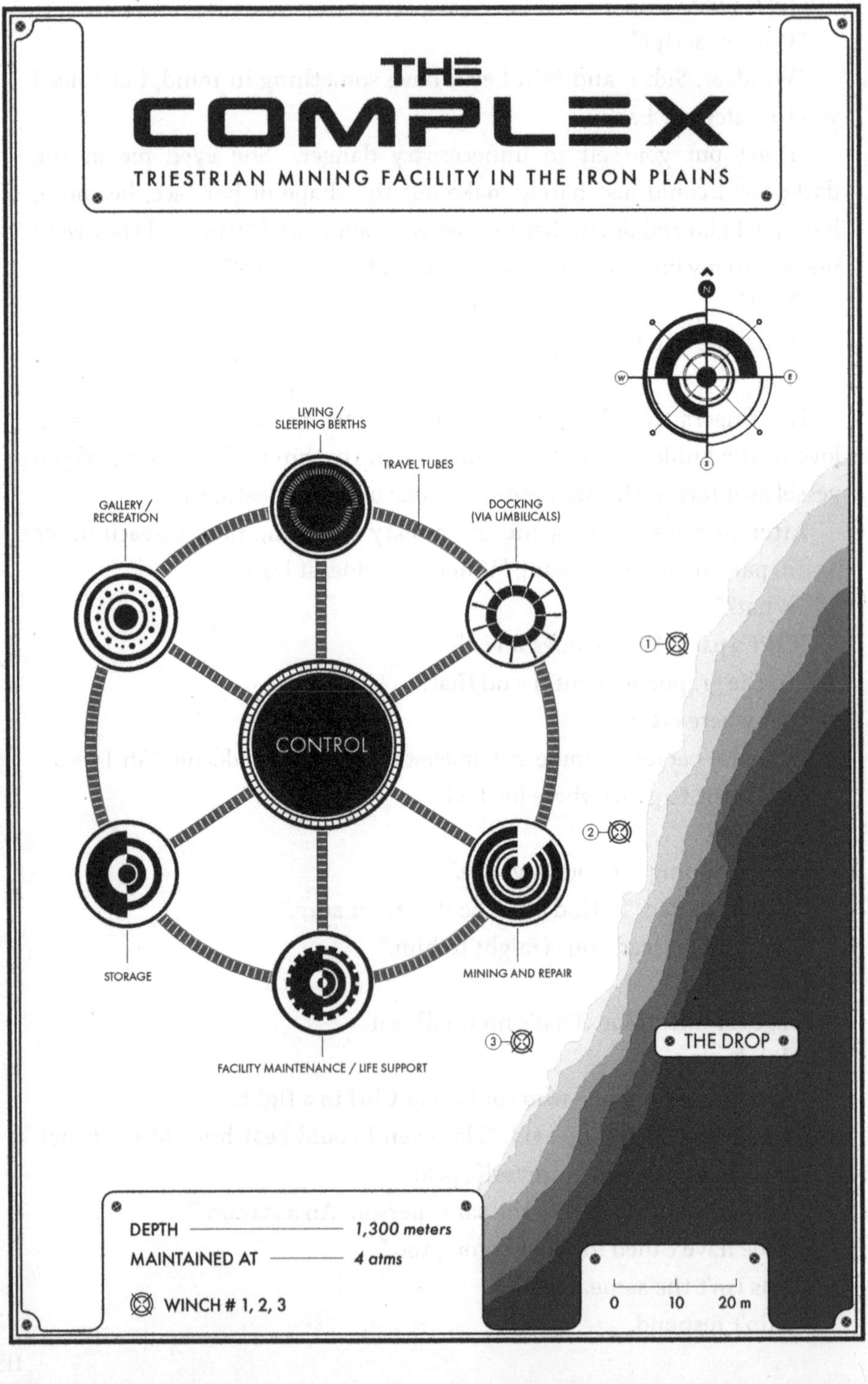
THE COMPLEX
TRIESTRIAN MINING FACILITY IN THE IRON PLAINS
N
W
E
S
LIVING / SLEEPING BERTHS
TRAVEL TUBES
GALLERY / RECREATION
DOCKING (VIA UMBILICALS)
CONTROL
STORAGE
MINING AND REPAIR
FACILITY MAINTENANCE / LIFE SUPPORT
1
2
3
THE DROP
DEPTH 1,300 meters
MAINTAINED AT 4 atms
WINCH # 1, 2, 3
0 10 20 m

# Chapter Ten

The Complex was our mining facility in The Iron Plains. We'd established it for one purpose only—there was a zircon deposit nearby, and hafnium is often associated with that element—but we hadn't had great success at first. It was supposed to be secret, but within a few weeks of operations, it had fallen silent, victim to a CSF attack. Most of the crew had died in the incident. We'd rebuilt it in recent months, and Commander Coda Rose had been running it smoothly ever since, though quietly so as not to attract unwanted notice. The Russians, Chinese, and Americans were all operating patrols and mining operations in The Iron Plains now, east of the Philippines and West of Hawaii, and the dangers there were very real. We still didn't know all the details of how or why the CSF had destroyed the base, but our security and defences were tighter now.

Six small domes, each fifteen metres in diameter, surrounded a larger Control Dome thirty metres across. Travel tubes connected all the domes. The Complex was at a depth of 1,300 metres on the edge of a trench that led down in a series of steps or tiers to an abyssal plain. The hafnium deposit was on one of the flat tiers. We called the cliff *The Drop*, because of its sudden plunge to Crush Depths far below.

It was a dangerous location, but our need for hafnium was crucial. We needed it for our unique bombs which were nuclear in nature but skirted the non-proliferation treaties because they did not involve fission or fusion. And besides, one could argue that *anywhere* on the ocean floor was dangerous, regardless of depth.

The Docking Dome was on the east side, near The Drop. It was too deep to have a moonpool, and it was too small to have an airlock large enough for vessels, so we had to use an umbilical to connect. There was already a seacar there—a *Sword*—likely Johnny's, from Trieste. I peered closer; sure enough, it was indeed *Destiny*.

I piloted *SC-1* over The Drop and brought ballast to negative. It was daunting, for the depth finder was blinking red numerals and a soft alarm was chiming. It said 8,308 as we drifted over the abyss. *Way* below Crush Depth, and the computer was reminding me of this fact.

I swallowed.

Then we powered slowly over the ledge where The Complex rested, and the depth finder abruptly flickered in quick jumps to a green 1,300. I pulled back on the throttle, extended the landing skids, and brought us down.

Johnny and Min Lee were just inside, waiting. They had wide smiles on their faces, and I had to admit, Johnny looked happy. We hugged and I introduced him to the others. He knew Sahar, but Sidra and William Windsor were new to him, and he met each with a handshake and grin.

The Complex was a remote outpost and very different from the city in which we lived. The corridors and travel tubes were shorter and tighter. Pipes, wiring, fiber optics, and air vents lined the bulkheads. Colour denoted the function or contents of each. Red for flammables, yellow for dirty water, blue for clean water, and so on. The decks were grates and there were puddles on the black metal, water dripping to the sump collectors hidden below. There was moisture dripping from the ceiling, though it wasn't leaking—it was condensation. It was simultaneously humid and cold.

Johnny grimaced as we marched toward the Control Dome. "It's a problem they're working on. Life support can't keep up with the needs. There are thirty-eight people living here. Now there are—" he looked back and counted "—forty-six, with the eight of us. The Complex was only meant for twenty-five, so it's operating way over capacity."

And the ventilators were struggling to remove the moisture from the air. I just hoped the carbon monoxide scrubbers could keep up, as well as the pressure monitors.

I had to duck going through the hatchways, but the tube opened into the Control Dome where the air seemed fresher. It was a wide space with consoles to monitor mining operations and all the base's engineering needs. There were people within, and two turned to us as we approached.

The first was the commander, Coda Rose. He was African American, highly skilled at mining and leadership, with round glasses and a receding hairline. The second was the First Officer, Melinda Sinora, a Japanese American. Both had been Triestrians in the mining operations division. Following the destruction of the base, they had volunteered to come and restart operations.

Both greeted us joyfully. They didn't get many visitors here. The thirty-eight spent all their time with each other, and after months, now craved the company of outsiders.

I said to Coda, "You need a better life support system, I hear."

"The one we have is just fine. The problem is we have too many people." He smiled again.

The thinking was that the miners were usually gone anyway, in The Drop collecting zircon/hafnium, so the base complement should actually be lower than twenty-five. We'd done all we could for The Complex, at the time anyway. We'd had to get it up and running quickly, after its destruction. "I'll see what I can do. For now, it'll have to work."

"We're managing, Mac. All is good here."

There were puddles at our feet, and I glanced down at them. "Still, I do see the issue." This is where they lived *and* worked—24/7—so a more comfortable living situation would have been better. "We'll try to send a better system when we're done here."

Melinda Sinora cleared her throat. "We're a bit confused, Mac. The Mayor and Deputy Mayor of Trieste have just arrived at our tiny mining outpost in The Iron Plains. Meanwhile—"

"Meanwhile," Coda added, "you've just declared independence—marvellous speech, by the way, we were all watching and cheering you on—there's a coalition fleet gathering in the Atlantic, and Trieste has an imminent battle on her hands."

"You know about the fleet?" I asked.

"It's in the reports from Trieste. And it's not so secret anymore. The global news is reporting on it too. German, English, American, French, Russian, Australian, and Chinese warsubs are preparing." He chuckled. "You do have a way of pissing people off, Mac. Could you have angered *any more* countries?"

"There's still Canada." His mention of Australia surprised me. I hadn't heard that yet.

"Well, there's still time I guess."

I glanced at the control consoles. "Can you show me the operation? The mine?"

—••—

IT WAS A FASCINATING SETUP. The mine was at a depth close to 4,000 metres. The miners were in vessels connected to the ledge with tethers moored to rods driven deep into bedrock. The zircon deposit was in the exposed basalt ledge jutting out from The Drop. Miners were drilling and using explosives to remove the ore, which they loaded into their vehicles and lifted back to The Complex. There was a pile of it nearby, on the seafloor west of the base, which our cargo subs would pick up for shipment back to Trieste. I could see the mounds on a schematic. I stared at it for a moment, and then noted a red X north of the outpost.

"What's that?" I asked, pointing.

"Unexploded ordinance," Melinda answered. "From the CSF attack."

I blinked. "A torpedo? A mine?"

"A mine. It landed about a hundred metres away. We're staying away from it in case it blows. It's too far to cause any real damage, but under this pressure, you never know. And our life support is struggling anyway, we wouldn't want it to go down, even temporarily."

I frowned. "Can you push it off the edge, into the abyss?"

"We're still debating. We'd prefer an ammunitions expert to look at it, to be frank."

I could understand that.

He stared at me for a long moment. Then he said, "So. Is this visit about Cliff Sim?"

I sighed. "It is, Coda. Can you tell me what he did when he was here?"

"And perhaps show us any communications he may have had?"

Johnny added.

"I can tell you what he did when he was here. I'm not sure about the communications." He glanced at his XO, Melinda Sinora, who gestured at a console.

She said, "I can dig into his digital movements. Give me a few minutes on it. Maybe an hour."

"Fair enough," I said. "We also need to see the original communication you received that started this whole thing."

Coda's brow wrinkled. "You mean the tip I sent you."

"It's why Cliff came here." I looked around at the interior of the Control Dome, at the many panels and stations and readouts.

I think he could interpret the pain in my tone, but his eyes showed confusion. "I'm sorry, Mac, I don't fully understand."

"Cliff's dead. We're here to find out why. And how."

—••—

THE OTHERS WENT ON A tour of the facility—more self-guided than anything else—while Johnny and I stayed with Coda and Melinda. The commander brought the original communication up on the vidscreen, while Melinda sat at a comm panel and studied the readouts and tapped at a keyboard. She was diving into Cliff's computer use while at The Complex. Codes and logs scrolled across her screen, too fast for me to make sense of.

"I don't suppose you have his PCD? It would make this a lot easier."

"No," I mumbled. "It is gone."

A look passed across her face and she turned away. "Understood."

"Here it is," Coda murmured. "I gave this to Cliff the moment he arrived." The message appeared on the holoscreen.

```
Triestrian,

I came across information that may interest
you. I want to help with independence and your
goals in the oceans. I'm on your side. There is
a Chinese facility in the Pacific, somewhere
```

west of Hawaii, that has perfected graphene layering. I don't have the precise location, but it's nearby, I think. The facility is manufacturing titanium coated with layers of graphene. They're starting to use it on their warsubs and mining equipment. If they possess sole knowledge of this and the process, then The Iron Plains belong to them. I don't want that, and neither do you.

There's a man at Blue Downs who has more information. He's a Chinese national. On the outside he's apparently an innocent businessman who's invested his own finances into rebuilding the colony, though really it's a front for the CSF. There's a connection to the graphene-layering plant, though I'm not sure what, precisely. I'm convinced that more information about him will help you find the plant. He goes by the name Tsim Liu, though it's likely an alias.

Good luck.

I exhaled. "It's not where he died, but it's likely the path he took. From here to Blue Downs." I considered the tip. There was no explanation about graphene or its importance—he'd left that up to me to figure out. He'd given a general area—west of Hawaii—but nothing nearly specific enough to track down the exact location. It was in The Iron Plains, but that's it. Hell, it could be a few kilometres just to the west of where we currently were, and no one would ever know.

But the information about the financier, Tsim Liu, was important.

I knew Cliff would have followed it.

"Did he leave immediately after seeing this?" I asked.

"No," Coda answered. "He was here for more than a day. He was researching, I guess."

"Did he sleep here?"

"Yes. For one shift, though not very long at all. I can take you to the bunks. It's where your people will stay as well."

"Sounds good." I straightened and said to the XO, "Sinora, keep working on tracking his digital signature. Let me know when you have something."

—••—

THE LIVING DOME WAS THE same size as the others surrounding the central Control Dome—fifteen metres across. It was small, especially for so many people. There were bunks stacked on top of each other, lining the perimeter. In the center were lockers for personal items and clothing. There was water pooled on the deck plates here as well; it was humid and cold, the same as in the other locations at The Complex.

Coda led the way to some bunks with plain mattresses and some rolled sheets on the footlockers before each.

He said, "These will be your bunks, for as long as you're here. This one here was Cliff's."

I studied the surroundings. There was no privacy and it was apparently co-ed. I knew Sahar would not be living here for the duration; she would stay in *SC-1*. Johnny and I looked around, but it was hopeless.

There was nothing there.

# Chapter Eleven

I SAT ON THE EDGE of Cliff's bunk and continued to study the dome where the crew lived. Thirteen hundred metres down, on the ocean floor at the edge of a trench straight to hell, nestled quietly between circling superpowers and in the middle of a cold war. Most surface nations didn't even know what was going on in the oceans, beneath the waves. They were focused on their own struggles and their own failures under the baking sun.

It was cozy though, I had to admit, despite the cold, clammy air and the puddles on the deck. There was a poker table set up, along with strings of lights across the dome's apex. Beer bottles and whiskey glasses were scattered across the deck near the table. Some of the bunks had sheets across them, likely for sex.

I'd known places like this. We had many people around the world, doing Trieste's work: building weaponized seacars, mining rare mineral deposits, spying on other nations. The people worked hard and were always under the threat of imminent death. It's very human how our defences lowered and we became open to almost anything with colleagues.

But Cliff had been here only one night. There'd been little opportunity for him to interact with many people.

Coda left to check on his XO, and Johnny sat nearby. "What happened, exactly, Mac?"

"I'm not sure, but I saw the body. Pictures that Sahar obtained."

"How?"

"Leaked somehow to her network here in the Pacific."

"That sounds odd."

I stared at him. "It does."

"And then Windsor and Sidra show up."

I hesitated before, "And one more too, Johnny."

It took him a moment before understanding flashed across his features. "You mean Min Lee?"

"Your wife. Yes." I snorted. "How come you never mentioned her? All this time, and after everything we've been through?"

"Are you offended?"

"You're my best friend. One of my only friends, and the oldest one for sure. Yes, I am, slightly."

He sighed. "I guess you have to understand what I've been through."

"I know the basics. The time you spent at Sheng City was tough."

"I'd betrayed Trieste. I'd betrayed you. I thought you'd forgiven me though." His eyes grew hard.

The truth was that I *had* forgiven him, long ago. We'd moved on. I told him so, in no uncertain terms. "You don't have anything to worry about, Johnny. I'm just curious why you kept Min Lee a secret."

He frowned and stared at the deck. Then his eyes shot back to me. "Is that why you wanted her here?" He bolted to his feet. "To confirm your suspicions? That's she's going to double cross us?"

"Not to confirm them. Just to keep our eyes on her." I sighed. "Don't get upset. Be objective."

"But you can trust me! Of all people—"

"Johnny, I'm referring to the bomb that cut our power at Trieste. The nuclear plant. Remember?"

"I remember. But she said she didn't have anything to do with it. Grant Bell confirmed her seacar track."

"That doesn't prove anything. I'm just keeping her close, that's all, until we know for sure." I snorted. "Hell, I thought you'd be happy! You just traveled here together in a *Sword* in total privacy."

He didn't reply; he was chewing his lip.

"Come on, Johnny. I'm asking for some objectivity here. Tell me about her."

He studied me for a moment before he deflated. "All right. I see where you're coming from." He paused and sat back on the bunk.

"Go ahead . . . "

"What do you want to know?"

"How'd you meet? Why keep her secret? Why didn't you know she was arriving at Trieste?"

"You know why I kept her a secret. We're in a Cold War against China. She's a Sheng City agent."

"Sheng City is not CSF. Not mainland."

"Do you think the average Triestrian would understand that? No. They'd think I was a traitor too, especially after my history."

"I don't blame you at all. I just want the truth."

He sighed again. "We fell in love. Went on a few missions together, too. She understood my dilemma."

"Did she agree with your decision to come back to Trieste after you defected? To make amends with me?"

"She knows all about it. She knows about you. She agreed with me. The plan was always for her to come to Trieste, once we declared independence. But—"

"But what?"

"I didn't know when she would be coming. She had to tell her superiors in Sheng City Intelligence. I wasn't aware that she was going to do it so soon."

"She knew the announcement was coming?"

"I guess. I never told her."

"She found out from her bosses?"

"Had to have." He shrugged. "She's in intelligence, Mac."

"And you love her." It was a statement.

He glanced up at me. "I needed someone, Mac. All that time at Sheng. I was lonely. And she understood."

And now she wanted to come to Trieste, to stay. Of course it was fine with me, I had no issues with it. It was just the timing . . . we had to be careful. But I wished he'd have trusted me more, and trusted Triestrians too. We would have understood and accepted her with open arms, just as we had with Renée—a French Submarine Fleet officer who'd tried to kill me multiple times! Now Renée was a Triestrian, and people had never questioned her motives.

"Min didn't plant the bomb, Mac."

"Who did?"

"We haven't figured it out yet."

"Did surveillance show anything?"

"Nothing on the cameras, though that location wasn't close to the city modules, so it's hard to see."

"Someone knew the location to hit." It had happened in the dark, during the festivities after the proclamation. Still, Johnny was correct: Grant had cleared her. "What was the explosive?"

"Crews are still investigating, last I heard. Looking for pieces of wiring, and so on."

I hesitated for a heartbeat. And then, "Is she nice to you, Johnny? Does she make you happy?"

His face flattened for a moment before a smile exploded across his features. "Of course. It's why we're together."

That was all I could ask for. "That's a good thing. She's welcome at Trieste. In TCI too."

"After we get this all figured out, I'm sure." But he was still smiling.

"Cliff's death is only a part of it. There's a battle on the horizon."

I studied the dome around me. I needed to know more about this place, while the base's XO was gathering Cliff's digital footprint for us. "What's she like in a fight, Johnny?"

He exhaled. "Insanely good. Fast. She's well trained and has studied multiple forms of fighting."

"Have you ever seen it?"

"Yes."

"Could you beat her, if it came down to it?"

He frowned. "What are you asking? You want me to beat her?"

"Not at all. I'm just curious."

"Strange question, Mac."

"I'm wondering what Sheng City agents are like, that's all," I deflected. He seemed to accept that and didn't say any more. "Care to look around, Johnny?"

He frowned. "What do you mean?"

"Outside. The Complex. They have a mine in The Drop."

"You want to go there?"

I shrugged. It was a Triestrian base, and I was the Mayor. I needed to know how our people were living. "What else is there to do right now?"

He grinned.

—••—

As we suited up to go outside, I contacted Trieste. Sinora transferred my signal through the base's comm panel, and to the nearest fiber optic junction out on the ocean floor. Within seconds, Kristen Canvel was on my PCD. Johnny and I were in the airlock, prepping for the journey outside, sitting on a steel bench. Kristen's image floated in front of us as she replied to my questions.

"How's the situation there?" I asked.

"Things are quiet, I guess. The storm is really pounding the mainland."

I peered at the viewport behind her, in City Control. It was murky with swirling sand as the waves thirty metres above churned across the Gulf. Usually the scene was crystal clear. "How are the Modules handling it?"

"No issues. No scuba diving or going outside right now though. The currents would rip people away."

"But the investigators . . . ?" I trailed off.

"They're doing their best under the conditions. Tethered to their scooters and seacars."

"Have they discovered anything?"

"Not yet, sorry to say."

"No other issues?"

"None. Except the gathering fleet in the Atlantic. The newscasts have been reporting on it nonstop. Time is counting down, Mac."

"I know." I paused, and then, "Listen, Kristen. I want you to know that there's still a danger. Make sure security is aware. Step up patrols and monitor sensitive areas, like the reactor, our launchers, and countermeasure stations."

She nodded. "Because whoever planted that bomb is still here."

I glanced at Johnny. "Likely, yes. Be on the lookout."

She frowned. "Mac, when are you coming back? There's a lot

happening here, and you, Johnny, and Cliff are not around right now. We could really use—"

"You're in charge right now. I trust your instincts. Find someone to take care of security and lead our efforts out in the Atlantic. Can you think of someone?"

She considered my request for an instant. "Chanta Newel comes to mind. She's already a part of the plan. She's in security and she's fully aware of developments."

"Sounds good." I knew Chanta; she was a great choice. "Take care of Trieste." And then I flashed her a grin. "And good luck, Kristen. You've got this."

—••—

IT WAS A DEEP DIVE, at 1,300 metres down. The pressure was immense, but we were going to conduct the excursion protected in a bathysphere designed to descend The Drop and return safely with ore. They maintained an internal pressure of four atms and could handle three or four crew each. We found a mining crew in the Repair Dome, and they practically exploded in glee when they realized who we were.

They'd turned from a workbench and stared at us, not understanding at first, as the hatch opened and we marched in. Then realization appeared on their faces. One said, "Mac? Johnny? What the fuck?"

I grinned. "Didn't Commander Rose tell you we were here?"

"Hell no!" He was a swarthy man, literally *built* for mining, and his hands were thick, beefy, and covered in grease. He wiped them on his overalls before he shook our hands with great enthusiasm. He was with two women, also clearly miners, who also showed incredible surprise and joy at seeing us.

I gestured at the vehicle in the dome that they'd been working on. "We want to see the mine while we're here. I don't suppose you could take us down to it?"

"Of course!" the man bellowed. "We've just finished maintenance on this ore collector. I'll take you down myself."

The Complex was on the edge of an abyss. There were three stations dug into solid rock at the rim of The Drop. Each had a winch that could raise and lower the ore collectors to the mine, far below. I wanted to take a look at the system and see how it worked. There was a chance to gather some other intel, as well.

Johnny and I boarded the vehicle, along with the man, Vinnie, who couldn't stop grinning. I'd seen him around Trieste on occasion, before he volunteered to come to The Complex and mine hafnium. He was talking nonstop about the work, about their living conditions, about independence, and more. Johnny and I let him talk as he lowered us down The Drop.

There was no natural light outside the airlock, once the ore collector emerged from the dome. The mining vehicle was essentially a bubble of titanium with a single large screw on its stern, and manipulator arms at its "bow." There was a large viewport, which occupied nearly a third of the sphere. Below the vessel was a cage attached to load the ore and carry it to the base, where they'd dump it on the west side of The Complex.

"Why do we need to stay attached to the tether, if this vessel can move by itself?"

"The ore is unpredictable. There's no telling how heavy any load is, and usually it exceeds our positive buoyancy." He pointed at the panel in front of him, which indicated the depth, pressure, speed, atmosphere, load weight, and more. "If we're negative, even with ballast purged, we need extra help to get back up from The Drop."

Johnny swore. "Sounds dangerous."

He nodded. "If you've got a full load, the tether is pulling you up, and it's straining, it can be. Especially with unstable loads. Add in the pressure outside, and you can sometimes dump a load in your pants, too." He laughed at the joke and pointed at the rock wall as we descended under our own power, but above, I could see the tether trailing upward to the winch. "It's solid basalt. Millions of years old. But within it, there's a vein of zircon, from an old magma intrusion we think. At least, that's what Chubs thinks."

"Chubs?"

"Our geologist. The vein is almost three thousand metres lower, so we're pushing four kilometres down. It's dangerous, for sure. Parts of the vein seem to stretch down to five kilometres and more."

"And the hafnium?"

"Oh, there's some there. Not much, but where there's zircon, there's usually hafnium." He frowned. "What's that used for, anyway?"

I didn't want to tell him the truth—that Doctor Max Hyland used a metastable nuclear isomer of it for our new Isomer Bomb—so I deflected and continued to ask about the mine and how the operation was progressing.

Outside, the layers of basalt slid by quickly as the ore collector lowered into The Drop. It was completely black outside, the only illumination coming from our intense radon lights which lit a sphere around us; long, sharp shadows stretched sideways across the rock wall, and angular daggers fell across shattered, broken basalt. There were traces of brighter colours in the wall, glinting in the night.

"You can see the minerals all right," Vinnie practically yelled. "There's all sorts of stuff in there, but not in great quantities. Not like the zircon."

"How much deeper?"

He peered at the readout. "We're nearly there. Four kilometres down."

The tether disappeared above us, through the sphere of light and far up toward the winch on the edge of The Drop. It was just a safety feature at the moment, for we hadn't picked up any ore. Finally we came to a stop, and Vinnie pointed at the operation. It was a wide step, or ledge, with loaders scratching at the rock, scooping crumbled boulders and gravel and moving toward the edge, where the ore collectors waited. There were only three winch lines, meaning there were only three collectors, of which we were now one. The ledge was roughly forty metres across. "It's a tight space," I muttered. "Has anyone fallen from this?"

"To the abyssal plain? No, but there have been some close calls."

"Is everyone anchored to the rock?"

"Yes, sir. Our safety rules demand it. Some prick back at Trieste insisted on it." Then he laughed as he stared at me. "Just joking, Mac. I know you're trying to protect lives."

I was really starting to like this guy. "And you use explosives to break up the ore?"

"We have to. It's hard rock here, and we have to break it up. The rock above the vein collapses too, so the more we remove, the safer we have to be."

"What do you do with the rock above the vein that you remove?"

"Dump it over the edge. Into the abyss."

The vessel bounced roughly as a loader deposited a mound of ore in our cage, attached to our underside. We received a few more loads before we were ready.

Then Vinnie pointed at the display; our weight had far exceeded positive buoyancy. "The winch comes in handy just about now."

Johnny swore. The tether grew taut and began to haul us up.

"Next stop, The Complex," Vinnie said.

The cable ground slowly along as it pulled us straight up. The winch motor above on the cliff edge was loud, the cable itself transferring its sustained whine into the ore collector's cab. I peered through the wide viewport at the area around us and the sheer rock wall as it glided past. My heart was in my stomach, and my breath was short, but eventually we hit the edge at 1,300 metres below sea level, and the lights of The Complex glowed around us. We couldn't achieve any buoyancy, but the vehicle had skids that it could use to glide along the sand, and Vinnie thumbed the screw on and pushed the power to full. We clattered along the rocks littering the sandy bottom, and powered toward the ore pile, west of the base. He dumped the load and the vehicle bounced upward, suddenly free from the extra weight.

"Gotta be careful here," he muttered as he adjusted the ballast. "We don't want to suddenly shoot to the surface . . ."

The ore collector bobbed so dramatically that it shook us around the interior, and we had to fight not to bump into any controls or switches. We should have put our shoulder straps on, but Vinnie hadn't suggested it.

I checked the time on the PCD. Only a few minutes had passed; it hadn't taken very long to make one round trip.

"Want to try another?" he asked.

I glanced at Johnny, who shrugged. "Why not?"

We did three more trips in thirty minutes. The ore collectors moved in constant rhythm, up and down the winch lines, before dragging their loads to the far side of The Complex. Then they'd reconnect to the line and go down for more. The only way to increase ore operations here would be to add more winch lines, or have more ore collectors on a single line. I didn't know if that were possible though.

We were on our fourth and final trip up when my PCD pinged. I glanced at it—Renée. "Go ahead," I said.

"Mac. Are you alone?"

I hesitated. "No. Johnny and a miner, Vinnie, are with me. You can switch to text if you want."

"There's no time. Look, I can't find the others. I've been searching. They're all gone."

My brow crinkled. She was referring to William Windsor, Sidra Noor, and Min Lee. I'd asked her to keep an eye on them. "What do you mean, *all gone*?"

"I just can't find them."

"The Complex isn't big."

"I know that! I just want you to be aware—"

At that instant, a loud *twang* reverberated through the vessel and it jerked suddenly to the side. It shoved Johnny and me into the bulkhead and knocked the breath from my lungs. Then a scraping as the vehicle ground against a rock outcropping—

We swung outward and then crashed back into the wall. Lights flashed red on the control panel and alarms blared. Vinnie swore and clutched at the yoke.

Then our stomachs jumped abruptly into our throats.

The cable had snapped, and we were falling into the abyss.

# Chapter Twelve

WE WERE PLUMMETING STRAIGHT DOWN into the chasm, nearly seven kilometres below us. Crush Depth was only just beyond the mine on the ledge at 4,000 metres; if we couldn't stop by then, surely at around 5,000 metres we'd be pulp. The flashing readout indicated we were falling at twenty metres per second. The alarm was piercing the cabin and we were grinding past the rock wall as we fell, a staccato scraping as we chipped and scratched basalt from its face. Soon it was falling in a cascade around us, as if we were in the center of a rockfall.

"Purge ballast," I snapped, falling instantly into command mode, even though Vinnie knew the vessel better.

"It is!"

"Dump the ore."

He peeled open the emergency shield protecting a large red button and slammed his fist on it.

Nothing.

He did it again.

His face flattened and paled instantly. "Oh my god," he hissed.

"Shut those alarms off," I rasped. Peering down, I could only see the murky water and bits of rock falling with us. We were swaying in the current, oscillating in the intense fall. My stomach was in my throat, and my heart was pounding.

We couldn't dump the basket that held tons of ore. There was a single, large screw on the vehicle though. We didn't use it much until reaching

The Complex, when we had to lug the ore to the pile. But it might be useful now. "Make the top tank negative!" I bellowed. "Bring us horizontal!"

"What the fuck?" He was staring at me. "We're trying to lose weight, not gain—"

I reached out and slammed the ballast to negative. The pumps whined as water churned into the upper tank. The descent readout abruptly increased: forty metres per second.

More alarms pierced the small space, drilling into my brain.

Not much time left. The enclosure was tiny and I reached above my head and hauled myself up to the ceiling. Johnny followed suit and we held ourselves out of center mass and as close to the bathysphere's top as we could.

The vessel began tilting backward—

We had thrown it off balance by changing its center of gravity.

"Get your ass up here!" Johnny yelled at Vinnie. He realized what we were doing, and he unsnapped himself and leapt up.

We tilted farther back, but the mine ledge was approaching fast now. We'd collide with it and implode at any second.

"Mac!" Renée cried from my PCD. "What's happening! I hear alarms!"

We were nearly on our backs now, with the screw facing the abyss below. I screamed, "Full power to the screw, *now*! And trim the ballast, keep us angled like this! Make us as light as you can."

The vessel *groaned* as the screw churned the water and pieces of falling rock fell through its protective cage and slammed into the blades. Then the screw hit high gear and screamed as it attempted to slow our fall. We weren't perfectly level, though; we'd angled toward the rock cliff face. The propulsion slammed us into the rock and we ground and scraped past it.

"The viewport!" Vinnie cried.

It had cracked. A spiderweb had appeared and it was snaking across the entire length.

"Push us against the rock," I grated. "Friction will slow us."

"It'll also shatter the—"

"It's either that or Crush Depth."

The vessel plowed and grated against the rock. Pieces broke off and shattered and cascaded around us. We were falling in a ball of plummeting rock pieces, shards and gravel, like a comet falling to its doom. The friction had slowed us though, but not enough.

The rate of fall was still too high.

—••—

"DUMP THE ORE!" I SHOUTED.

"Still not working." Vinnie was pressing the key again and again, struggling against the fact that we were lying on our backs, now looking *up* at the cliff towering above our heads.

"Johnny, see if you can cut power to it."

"On it." He dove toward the electronics panel, ripped it open and searched frantically for the ore cage controls.

"What about the manipulator arms?" I asked.

Vinnie frowned. "I can try, but what do I grab?"

"The rock? An outcropping? Anything—*try it*!"

He shoved his hands into the manipulator arm controls and brought them forward. They slammed into the rock whipping past our viewport, and immediately bent and snapped from multiple impacts.

Something was on fire in the vessel now; acrid smoke was drifting around us, burning our nostrils and lungs.

"Keep the thruster on full," I said. "Keep the ship grinding against the wall."

The spherical ore collector was colliding with the sheer face, bouncing along, knocking pieces from it. The manipulator arms were merely stubs, but they were still pressed into the wall, grinding shorter and shorter, and friction was working its magic. There were sparks shooting from the protrusions, either from scraping the rock or severed wires, I couldn't tell.

But it was working.

We were slowing.

We were still going to collide with the mine ledge below us, however, and it was going to be catastrophic.

Johnny yelled, "Got something!" He grabbed a bundle of wire and tore them from the housing.

An instant later, the vessel bounced upward as if freed from its deadly plunge.

The ore cage fell free—

And we leapt up, now positively buoyant.

And then we collided with the rock ledge, and the impact hurled us against the rear bulkhead with a vicious *snap*, knocking the wind from our collective lungs.

I nearly blacked out, but I forced my eyes to stay open and stared through the cracked viewport at the sheer rock face, stretching upward into blackness far, far above.

A blurry cloud immediately caught my gaze. It was shifting and growing in size—

Shaking my head to clear my vision, I fought to understand what I was seeing. It seemed to be morphing its size and shape . . .

*Shit.* It was an avalanche of rock.

Plummeting into the abyss.

There was a shower of boulders headed downward, straight for us.

"What the fuck!" Vinnie cried.

The rock peppered us with blows and slammed into the already-broken viewport, but none bigger than a fist hit us. A few larger ones the size of basketballs and buckets landed close, but luckily missed us by a few metres.

Finally, I lay back, chest heaving, swearing profusely and trying to breathe in the ore collector's smoke-filled tiny cabin. "Tell me it's not like this every day," Johnny said.

—••—

"I LOST THEM, MAC," RENÉE said. "I have no idea what happened, how they got out of my sight."

We were back in The Complex, in the Control Dome, and Johnny and I were nursing our wounds, bandaging lacerations. He had a nasty cut on his forehead, and slices and welts crisscrossed my arms. The other miners had heard the entire incident over their comms and watched in horror as our ore collector had plummeted to the ledge far below. They couldn't believe how close we'd cut it; Johnny had finally dropped the ore with only ten metres to spare. The sudden buoyancy had slammed the three of us to the rear bulkhead, only a millisecond before final impact.

"Where are they now?" I asked Renée.

"I still don't know."

I shook my head. "Sahar? Meg?"

"They're in *SC-1* doing maintenance. I've asked them, but they don't know either."

I swore. Our three mysterious operatives, all missing. Sidra, Windsor, and Min Lee.

Johnny was staring at me. "Surely you don't suspect all of them."

"Someone tried to kill us. They cut the hoist cable. The winch."

"Or it failed."

"*Come on*, Johnny."

He stared at me, as if pleading, for another instant. Then he deflated. "Yeah, you're right." One side of his face was swollen. "But who?"

Coda Rose was with us. He was coordinating efforts to clear the wreckage and get the mining operation back up and running. They had other ore collectors, and were working to get one out of the Repair Dome and into The Drop. "What happened?" I asked him.

"The cable snapped."

A prickle worked its way up my scalp. "The winch is fine?"

"Yes. It's just the cable."

"How did it happen?"

He shrugged. "Stress, over the last few months. Bad timing maybe?"

"It's more than bad timing."

His face was drawn. "I know what you want to believe. But look at it from where I'm sitting. That cable has been under enormous stress for a long time now."

"But the ore cage wouldn't drop either."

"You think someone sabotaged *both*? Your tether *and* the ore?"

"For two to go at the same time? What are the chances?"

There was a pause as he stared at me. I understood his thinking. He didn't want to deal with the knowledge that his operation had almost caused the simultaneous death of both Trieste's Mayor *and* Deputy Mayor.

"Did anyone go outside? Through an airlock?"

He scowled. "We're 1,300 metres down here. If they did, then they'd still have to be decompressing right now." He gestured at the control panel. "No airlock is in operation."

"They could still be outside." I considered the dilemma. We needed to locate everyone, immediately. "Do you have an all-call system here?"

"Yes."

"Show me."

—••—

"ATTENTION ALL BASE PERSONNEL, INCLUDING visitors from Churchill and Trieste. Report to the Control Dome immediately." I repeated the message and set the microphone down. Then we stared at the entry hatches.

My gun was at my side, and my fingers hovered over it.

Within minutes, there were numerous personnel there, residents of The Complex.

Then Sahar and Meg entered with quizzical expressions on their faces.

And then the hatch opened again—

And in walked Min Lee and William Windsor.

"Where's Sidra—" I started.

And then a different hatch opened, and Sidra Noor entered.

I stared at them, perplexed. They were all there, inside the facility. No one decompressing in an airlock. No one wet from being outside.

Shit.

—••—

SIDRA HAD BEEN WORKING OUT and having a run around The Complex. One circuit through the travel tubes and all six domes was two hundred metres. Video surveillance confirmed this.

Meg and Sahar were in *SC-1* conducting routine maintenance on the SCAV drive and charging batteries for the conventional drive. Video surveillance confirmed it.

Min Lee was in the Recreation Dome, preparing a dinner for herself and, presumably, Johnny. Confirmed by video.

William Windsor was in the Life Support Dome, working on the equipment to see if he could improve the system and get some of the moisture out of the air. Also confirmed by video.

And of course that left one, Renée Féroce, who was in the Control Dome, trying to locate everyone and watch my back.

It hadn't worked.

—••—

LATER, IN OUR BUNK IN *SC-1*, Renée scolded me as she stared at the bruises and cuts on my body. "That must have been some fall!"

"It was about two thousand metres. It happened fast."

"You jerk!"

I stared at her. "What are you talking about? I almost died."

Her eyes narrowed. "You knew it was going happen, prick!"

The way she said it in her French accent made me chuckle. I couldn't help it, and it only made things worse. "Shut up!"

"Renée, what are you going on about?" I reached out and pulled her closer to me.

"You suspected one of them was going to kill you."

"One of whom?"

"Windsor, Min Lee, or Sidra! That's why you wanted me to watch your back for you. You asked me to, before we arrived here. Am I right? You said you 'had something in mind.' Tell me I'm wrong! I dare you!"

I exhaled and stared at the ceiling, only a few inches over my head. We were in my seacar with the hatch sealed and locked. Sahar was in the SCAV compartment, where her bunk and supplies were. The others were in The Complex's Living Dome, where Coda Rose had set up bunks for them. "Yes," I muttered finally. "You're right. It's why I went to the mine."

Her expression turned to one of horror. "You wanted to *test* them? To see if they'd kill you?"

I tried to shrug while lying down. "It was the perfect opportunity. We had some time before Melinda Sinora's report about Cliff's activities here . . . "

"You absolute—"

I smiled. "It almost worked."

"You mean, you almost died."

"I didn't."

"You don't even know if one of them is after you."

"Still," I muttered. "It seems likely."

She was glaring at me. "So why keep them with us?"

An image of Cliff came to me. Lying on the deck, bleeding and broken. I didn't answer.

# Chapter Thirteen

MELINDA SINORA WAS IN THE Control Dome, sitting at a console and staring at the vidscreen. She'd been there for hours, digging through codes and records in the base's computer servers of events that had occurred during a very short period of time—specifically, Cliff Sim's visit to investigate the anonymous tip regarding graphene. While this had happened, I'd been at Trieste coordinating the other colonies for the announcement to the superpowers, as well as preparing our defences for the inevitable attack and attempted occupation. Cliff had been here, at The Complex, following the clues to determine whether graphene layering was actually a possibility, and it wasn't just a pipe dream or a wild goose chase.

Renée and I were standing over Sinora, peering at her screen. She'd called us in the middle of the night, dragging us from our bunk in *SC-1*.

"Cliff has a higher security clearance than I do," she said. Her voice was sharper than I'd expected, after working on the problem for so long, and her eyes were even clearer than mine. Then I noticed the coffee cup at her side; she'd been downing it since I'd arrived. She was artificially chipper and aware. "It's taken longer than I first thought it would, but I've traced some of his actions." She pointed at a log on her screen.

I stared at it. "That's it?"

"I can't read the contents of his messages. Like I said, he's the security chief. There's no way I can penetrate the system to see what he sent others, or listen to his messages, and so on."

"But that's why we're here. Surely my clearance is higher."

"Try convincing the computer of that," she replied. She shrugged. "I've never encountered an issue like this before. I think it's because of his rank."

"Explain."

"I've been able to identify his communications by studying our incoming and outgoing logs. I've had to search through *all* of them. We have thirty-eight people here too, all sending and receiving messages. Some are private and personal, others are work related. Asking Laura Sukovski at Trieste for more supplies, updating her about our mining activities, calculating the cost per ton, and more. There are *hundreds* of messages during the period he was here."

"But he was only here for a few hours," Renée said.

"Exactly. That's a *long* time, in terms of an entire base's communications. On top of it, the automated computer system is in constant contact with Trieste. Also, the mining officer is communicating with the global network of trade, to calculate zircon prices—"

"Sukovski takes care of—"

She stared at me. "We send you the ore for hafnium, Mac. The States takes the zircon from us, at a reduced price, remember. But it's all related to the global market value."

I sighed. "Okay. I get it. You've had to dig through all the records, and you're not able to read individual messages."

She frowned. "There's some sort of worm in the system. It's removing the text from his messages. At first I thought it was a virus, or something planted, but it's actually part of the system. That took me a few hours to—"

"What do you mean, 'part of the system'?"

"Because he's CSO. It automatically protects his movements. It must happen at any Triestrian outpost or base or module he visits. It protects his investigations and activities."

"He's dead now," I reminded her.

Her face went blank. "I know, Mac. Sorry."

I waved it off. "Not your fault. But it's the reason we're here. I'm not thrilled to hear that we can't even see his communications."

"Well, I've identified things he sent and received. Just not the actual contents."

Renée looked at me. "It might help. You never know."

"Maybe," I said to Sinora, "Can you show us what you've got?"

She gestured at the log. "I've compiled it into one chart. Calls and emails."

| Date | Time | Type | I or O | Destination | Recipient | Duration |
|---|---|---|---|---|---|---|
| 05302131 | 1414 | Call | O | BD-245462 | Unknown | :56 |
| 05302131 | 1439 | Message | O | ? | | |
| 05302131 | 1538 | Call | O | BD-648594 | Unknown | 2:32 |
| 05302131 | 1558 | Call | O | BD-457892 | Unknown | 1:30 |
| 05302131 | 1745 | Message | O | ? | | |
| 05302131 | 1834 | Call | O | BD-002154 | Rec Dome 2334 | :34 |
| 05302131 | 1835 | Call | O | BD-645328 | Agri-Dome 28 | :23 |
| 05302131 | 1910 | Message | O | ? | | |
| 05302131 | 2239 | Call | O | BD-648594 | Unknown | 1:13 |
| 05302131 | 2245 | Message | I | Unknown PCD | ? | |

"That's interesting," I said. "But it's not much."

She seemed slightly offended. "I scrounged and searched every database we have. The interesting thing is that the messages weren't with the usual comms chatter."

"Where were they?"

"Buried in the AI comms. The computer is always communicating with Trieste's servers. Cliff's comms were with those." She took a sip of coffee, then added, "Except for one, that is." She gestured at the chart. "You can probably guess which."

I stared at it. They were all from the same day, when Cliff had arrived at The Complex, on 30 May. All the calls or emails were from mid-afternoon until nearly midnight. I knew he'd stayed in a bunk there, so he likely spent one night before he departed. We didn't know where he went or how he'd ended up dead.

Renée said, "What does BD mean?"

"Blue Downs," I said. "He arrived here and read the tip that Coda Rose received."

Her features flattened. "The tip referred to Blue Downs. To a Chinese investor."

"And it looks like he called a series of places at the colony. Likely tracking this person down. Then he went there." It wouldn't have been hard for him. He had contacts in most underwater colonies.

He'd been the perfect CSO, I thought absently.

Sinora said, "Have you figured out which message is unique and not disguised with the computer chatter?"

I pointed at the fourth column. "One or zero. It's the only one that's different. Is that binary?"

She blinked. "It's not binary. I should have been more specific—it's *I* or *O*. Incoming or Outgoing. Not numbers."

"Ah. Makes sense." I studied it. "He sent a number of messages and made calls. Then one response, and—"

"He finished immediately. He went to sleep, woke up, and left."

"And we can't see the message? He didn't write that one, though."

"His clearance, Mac," she reminded me. "Higher than all of ours. The worm deleted it."

Inwardly, I shrugged. At least it made me confident that my communications with him had been well protected during all these years.

Renée said, "What do we do now, Mac?"

"We go to Blue Downs." I pointed at the chart. "That's who we need to speak to."

She looked puzzled. "Who?"

"BD-648594."

"But how—"

"It's the only call he made twice. There's a reason for that." I studied the log again. "We also need to investigate that dome."

"Which?"

"The agriculture dome. Number twenty-eight. There's something odd about that too." I frowned. Why the hell would he be communicating with someone in a dome growing crops? We were searching for graphene, after all. Not pineapples.

—••—

WE LEFT THE COMPLEX IN the morning. We said our goodbyes to the crew, who were sad to see us go, but likely happy that we would take some of the stress off their environmental systems. Vinnie smiled broadly and pumped my hand vigorously; we were standing outside the umbilical to *SC-1*. His hand practically swallowed mine, and I thought that many of the workers here were larger than the normal human. *That* likely put more pressure on the life support systems, too.

He said, "It was an adventure, Mac! I'm going to miss you."

"We nearly died, Vinnie."

"You saved us. Barely." He grinned again and it made me question his sanity.

"It wasn't fun."

"It was more adventure than we see here."

"That mine is for risk takers and daredevils. It's dangerous." I grabbed his shoulder and squeezed. "We really appreciate what you are all doing here." I looked at Coda, who stood next to the large miner. "We need the ore you're bringing up. It's helping our independence efforts more than you can know."

Vinnie frowned. "But how? Water and air purification uses zircon. That's important, but we sell most of it back to the USA."

I glanced at Meg and Johnny, who were standing with me, and made a sudden decision. It didn't matter now, after we'd declared our independence. "It's not the zircon. It's the hafnium. It's important."

He frowned. Coda squinted and cocked his head at me. He'd never heard this either.

I continued, "The zircon is going to make us money, now that we can sell it at fair market prices. But the hafnium, we keep for ourselves. Our weapons division can make good use of it."

"But how?"

"Remember Seascape, last year?"

"Blew up in an isomer explosion, Mac," Coda said. "The Germans—"

"It wasn't the Germans." I stopped and said no more.

Realization detonated on their features. "Oh my God . . ." Sinora whispered.

"Keep working, keep mining. You're crucial to our independence."

Vinnie swore. "I wish we'd known earlier. It would have really helped with morale."

I knew how he felt. Isolated, alone, and cut off from the rest of the colonies, working in such a place could be a challenge, and that was an understatement. It wore crews down. It could even end careers.

But now they knew they were doing something important . . .

I shook Coda Rose's hand as well as Melinda Sinora's. "Keep up the great work here. We'll be back to pick up Johnny's seacar, soon. We'll cross paths again."

—••—

BACK IN *SC-1*, WE SET course for Blue Downs and quickly reached 450 kph. It was due south, but we'd have to navigate around the coast of Australia. The colony was in the Bass Strait, sometimes now called the Tasmanian Strait, on the border with the Tasman Sea. The RSF dreadnought had destroyed it, but the country had quickly rebuilt it in the original footprint because its resources—fish and kelp—were just too important for the topside nations.

The others were all on board, but had quickly relocated to their bunks and sleeping areas. We'd left as soon as we knew about Cliff's communications, and had dragged the others from their sleep. Sahar was already in the aft compartment, but the SCAV drive had likely awakened her too. Johnny and Min Lee were also with us, now.

Sidra was in the living area, sitting on the couch, reviewing something on his PCD. He motioned to me and I sat across from him.

He said, "Did you discover what you were looking for?"

"Clues only. Not the answer."

"Your man, Cliff?"

"He went to Blue Downs. We're following in his footsteps."

Sidra frowned. "I hope not all the way."

"I hope not," I muttered.

He glanced at me, interpreting my tone, and his expression turned instantly remorseful. "Mac, I didn't mean to sound callous."

I waved him off. "No, no. It's okay."

"Still, I'm sorry. I know you were close."

Sidra was Sahar's brother, and I trusted him because of that. Still, I knew to keep my guard up. He was one of the three operatives who had entered my life unexpectedly, neatly coinciding with Cliff's murder. Sidra was a spy, and according to Sahar, very good in a fight and an excellent agent. He was athletic and lithe, and I'd seen him working out in the seacar and in The Complex. He would definitely be a strong adversary, should it come to that.

He noticed my expression. "You are wondering about me."

"Maybe."

"I would too, after what happened to your CSO."

"Why's that?"

He shrugged. "I'd want to know the truth about what happened. Especially with the fighting about to break out."

"Are you someone I need to worry about?"

"Not at all. Sahar and I are totally on side with you. With Oceania."

"I know Sahar is. She's proven it a thousand times over."

He looked surprised. "And not me?"

"You're her brother, but I don't know you, Sidra."

"In our culture, each is a representation of the entire family. You need to understand that. If Sahar behaves a certain way, you can bet that the rest of her family does too."

I considered that. "Have you had difficulty in Churchill? As a practicing Muslim?"

"No. There are more and more Muslims in the oceans now. In Churchill. And the city is very accepting, thanks to our leader. She has embraced all of our differences, and it's brought the people together. We're all in this as one."

I recalled watching Sahar lead the St. Patrick's Day parade through the city just a few months earlier. It had been one of the more remarkable sights in my life. Sahar was an extraordinary person, and I knew why the people had elected her. I wanted to believe that Sidra was the same.

But still . . .

I had to be careful, and not let my guard down.

He continued, "Look, Mac. Before we met, I'd been in the Atlantic, monitoring the buildup of forces. The attack is going to hit Trieste in only a few days."

"I know."

"But there's more." He gestured at his PCD. "I've been in touch with my network there. Other operatives. The two RSF dreadnoughts are there. It's causing quite a ruckus."

"What do you mean?"

"The rest of the fleets are not exactly friendly with the Russians. Especially after what Ventinov and *Drakon* did last year."

I nodded. They had destroyed two USSF bases, sunk sixty-three CSF warsubs, and destroyed Blue Downs. Then the battle over the Kermadec Trench. And Australian, Chinese, and American forces were gathering now, in the Atlantic.

"You can imagine how much animosity exists there right now."

"It might be useful, actually," I mumbled, considering it.

"They're keeping their distance from the dreadnoughts, but they're studying them, intercepting communications, learning everything they can from them. My colleagues have intercepted something that you need to know."

I leaned forward, curious. "Go ahead."

He sighed. "Do you know much about Russian folklore? Stories about spies. Their versions of James Bond, and so on?"

"Not a lot. I don't pay much attention to Russia, to be honest." The truth was, before Ventinov appeared on the scene, Russia was not a player in the oceans. They'd been on the decline since the 20th Century, and only recently had re-emerged with territorial and military ambitions in the world's oceans. The dreadnought's first appearances had shocked us, in fact.

"What about The Steel Shiv?" he asked in a soft tone.

That made me sit up straighter. A prickle worked its way up my scalp. I *had* heard of The Shiv. It was a real person—a spy—but also a story parents told their children, like the Boogey Man or some other sort of supernatural villain. "They say The Shiv is unbeatable. Insane fighting skills. But almost like a ghost. Can get in anywhere, kill anybody, and get out without being seen. There's not much known about him." I hesitated and stumbled over the pronoun. "They don't even know if it's a man or a woman." I frowned as I stared at Sidra. "What are you—"

"Mac, we intercepted comms about this. The crew of the dreadnoughts are in an uproar, believing they're helping bring Russia back to global prominence and restore their former glory. They also want others to know that whoever messes with them will die horrible deaths. Their morale is very high right now, because of this news."

"Why's that?"

"The person who killed Cliff . . . they're saying it was The Steel Shiv."

# Interlude
## Somewhere in the Pacific Ocean

**11 June 2131 AD**

| | |
|---|---|
| Vessel: | Russian Submarine Fleet |
| | *Dreadnought* Class *Voskhod–The Rise* |
| Location: | Latitude: Unknown |
| | Longitude: Unknown |
| | North of The Iron Plains |
| Depth: | 2,458 metres |
| Date: | 11 June 2131 |
| Time: | 0708 hours |

CAPTAIN VENTINOV STARED AT THE sonar display. The technician—an ensign on his first tour of duty, barely out of the academy and barely out of diapers, Ventinov thought—was pointing at the screen. He was saying, "You can see the trail here."

There was a bright white signal moving across the image. The callout label noted that the velocity was 450 kilometres per hour.

*SC-1.*

McClusky.

He was here.

Ventinov's insides quivered. It had worked. The man himself was in the region, following the clues.

"What is the course?" he growled. "Where are they going?"

"They just appeared on the screens. I'm not sure where they were, although the computer indicates there is diffused noise somewhere in the lower depths in that area. In a trench perhaps, where it's protected—"

"Is there a base there?"

The ensign paused. "I can't tell—"

"Then find me someone who can!" he bellowed. He straightened and took a deep breath. He knew he couldn't let McClusky affect him so. He stared about him, at the majesty of the bridge, at the enormous canopy overhead—sixty metres long!—and the ocean far above. It was black now; they were too deep to see anything but the odd fish or plankton or plastic floating by, caught up in currents and eddies, some natural, some not. The vessel's thrusters were on low power though, to maintain position only, and were quiet. Stealthy.

"Our distance is too great, sir. If we go closer, we'll learn more, but it might give away our location and identity."

Ventinov sighed. The child was correct.

"But I can see the seacar is going south. Toward Australia."

The Captain barely suppressed a grin. McClusky was indeed following the path.

There was a noise behind him, and he turned. "Hello, Sidorov." His XO approached slowly. She'd heard his explosion, and there was a look of concern on her features.

"Captain," she said in a soft voice. She watched him for a moment, and then, "It's come to my attention that you have mentioned The Steel Shiv to some of the crew."

He frowned, taken aback. Surely his XO wasn't criticizing her Captain. That would be political and career suicide. "What of it?"

Her response was quiet, and the sonar technician had turned away to give them privacy. "The crew is talking, sir."

"So?"

"The Shiv is all anyone is speaking of. They're communicating with their comrades about it. I just wanted to extend a warning."

"What do you mean? And how dare—"

"Sir. Stop. Listen to me for a moment." She paused and glanced around. Then she stepped away from the sonar station.

Ventinov followed, though his anger was rising.

She continued, "The crew has contacted other warsubs about this. They're referring to The Steel Shiv openly."

"Your point? I want people to know how serious it is to go against the Party, our system. Russia is rising again. The very name of this dreadnought—"

She cut him off. "Until you achieve your goal, it's not a good idea. We can't let McClusky know what's coming for him. He already knows that his man is dead. If he knows too much about his enemy, it'll give him valuable information."

"It's my decision, not yours." His voice was ice.

"Don't give in to your base emotions. That's all I'm saying. Sending him a warning might scare him away, not bring him closer."

He was glaring at her. "That's for me to decide. Not you. And don't interrupt me ever again."

"I'm doing my job as your Executive Officer." She took a breath and seemed to collect her thoughts. "My apologies, sir, but I thought you'd like to know this."

He gestured at the sonar station. "He's here, Sidorov. He's in the region. The trap worked!"

—••—

LIEUTENANT MILA SIDOROV WAS STUDYING the Captain. He seemed full of rage. His façade was cracking, she thought. He'd kept it together for many days, many weeks, but now things were falling apart. She had completed her checks of the torpedo stations on the immense warsub. Four days of work. Now she was done, and she expected to depart for the Atlantic soon, so they could rendezvous with the coalition strike force before the attack on Trieste.

But Ventinov . . .

He insisted on remaining in the area. In The Iron Plains. And there didn't seem to be a reason, other than his obsession. And not only that, he was *telling people* about The Shiv and his plans to kill McClusky. Word was out, and it had been unnecessary.

Then again, she thought as the Captain stormed back to the sonar screen to study the seacar's track, if this went bad for Ventinov, then it might go *well* for her.

Perhaps she could prosper from this situation.

Maybe even emerge from the coming events as Captain of *Voskhod*.

Now *that* would make her family proud. For years, she'd trained for a future in the water. She'd sailed with her grandmother on Lake Baikal growing up. She missed the sun and wind on her face. It had left its mark on her, without much question, physically and emotionally, and she knew that her grandmother was proud of her.

Still, if she could *command* a vessel like *Voskhod*, it would cement her position in her family, for generations.

Her great-great grandchildren would speak of her.

She watched Ventinov as he yelled at the young ensign currently overseeing the sonar station.

*He's losing it*, she thought again.

DATA PROCESSING

| | |
|---|---|
| Location: | Latitude: Unknown<br>Longitude: Unknown<br>Somewhere in the Pacific Ocean |
| Depth: | Unknown |
| Date: | 11 June 2131 |
| Time: | 0748 hours |

THE STEEL SHIV HAD WATCHED events unfolding over the course of the last week. First the killing of Cliff Sim, who had followed Ventinov's planted clues and ended up dead. Then McClusky had entered the picture, and The Shiv followed the man closely, waiting for an opportunity to kill him without giving up any knowledge about The Shiv's identity. There was a lot to hide, though. The birthplace, the upbringing, the family.

Everything.

The last name itself was a monumental clue.

Stali.

*Steel.*

If McClusky even learned this minor detail, everything would fall apart in an instant.

The Steel Shiv's last name was *Steel*?

And the fight would be immediate.

The Shiv didn't think *everyone* in McClusky's sphere—collectively, that is—could be beaten. But one on one, The Shiv knew the result would be victory, and McClusky would die. It would please Ventinov.

The Shiv might even bring McClusky's head to the Russian Captain.

Now *that* would be something. Present an enemy's severed head to Ventinov . . .

Maybe the Captain would pay more.

The explosive was the first attempt on McClusky, but it hadn't worked. A small bomb, on the wire tether to the ore collector. It had been remotely controlled, so The Shiv didn't have to get too close. Didn't even have to get wet.

But it hadn't worked.

No matter.

There'd be more chances.

The Shiv could wait.

Even now, McClusky was within reach, but The Shiv would wait until there was a clear escape path, and a clear opportunity.

Then McClusky would be in the deadliest fight of his life.

And he might even lose his head, after all.

# Part Four:
## At Blue Downs

# Chapter Fourteen

We were in *SC-1*. Johnny was at the controls, Sidra Noor and I were in the living area, and the rest of the group was sleeping in their respective bunks—Meg in the one recessed in the bulkhead, Renée in our usual spot, Sahar in the SCAV compartment, and William Windsor and Min Lee somewhere aft, in the engineering spaces.

Sidra's news had sent shockwaves rocketing through my body. I was trembling in anger and—

And there was something more, I realized dully.

Trepidation? Anxiety?

*Fear*?

I had indeed heard of The Steel Shiv—*every* spy in the oceans had, everyone who was working for an intelligence organization, and everyone involved in the cold war currently underway between opposing superpowers. He did exist—he was real—and his exploits were legendary. He'd once infiltrated an entire Chinese facility and killed everyone in their sleep. As the story went, the bodies had remained there, rotting, until their superiors finally sent a rescue patrol to find out why the facility had gone dark. The Shiv had left his calling card: he'd sliced each throat with the knife he'd supposedly made himself. He'd sabotaged the computer and removed all video evidence of the assault before leaving.

I'd never known anyone to have crossed paths with him. There were only victims, but even the victims had been among the best. If

The Shiv had beaten them, I knew he was good. And since Cliff had been a victim . . .

Then The Shiv was *the best*.

There were even stories that The Shiv was not actually a man. Some stories said she was tall for a woman, but just as capable as any man. That she wore a suit that obscured her figure, a helmet that covered her face and changed her voice, and that when most men encountered her, they immediately underestimated her because she was smaller than they. But when the fighting started, it became immediately apparent that The Shiv outclassed them in every regard.

Cliff had known the stories too. So had Johnny.

I wondered what had gone through Cliff's mind when he'd realized what he was up against. If it was really The Shiv. Had he tried to pull his gun? His knife?

Sidra was watching the thoughts churn through my mind. "Do you believe it, Mac?"

"It's possible." I sighed. "The Shiv is Russian, apparently. If Ventinov is really still alive and after me, then . . ." I trailed off. He was pulling out all the stops. The Shiv notoriously sold to the highest bidder, because of his—*her?*—reputation, but favoured Russian contracts because of allegiance to his country.

I considered my situation, on *SC-1*. The three agents who were with me, in close proximity.

Min Lee, Sidra Noor, William Windsor.

None was Russian. I didn't think one could be The Shiv.

But still . . .

The Shiv was apparently a master of disguise. A ghost, even.

"Do you think it's just a story?"

I glanced up at the man. "You've been in intelligence for years. You know The Shiv is real."

"But no one has ever seen the guy."

"No one who's lived. It's how he's kept his identity secret."

"His bosses must know."

"All interactions are by comm or video. There's been no face-to-face contact, as far as anyone is aware." I hesitated. "And now the Russians are saying The Shiv is working for them on this. And you're telling me that he killed Cliff."

Sidra watched my face for a long, pregnant pause. "Was Cliff *that* good?"

"What?"

"It's got you scared. Has it occurred to you that that's what Ventinov wants?"

I frowned. "Cliff was that good. He was big too, which some might think would slow him down, but if he got his hands on you, it was over very, very fast." I considered what Sidra was saying. "And yes, I know that's what Ventinov wants. It's why he's spreading the story now."

"To scare you."

I pursed my lips. While it had thrown me off guard, I wouldn't say I was scared. At least, not *paralyzed* with fear. I just didn't want anything to happen to Renée, Johnny, or Meg.

I'd sacrifice myself for any one of them.

—••—

BACK IN THE PILOT CABIN, I sat next to Johnny and stared through the canopy at the churning bubble surrounding *SCAV-1*. The fleet was still collecting in the Atlantic, the deadline was looming, and I needed more information. I keyed Trieste into the comm, and a few moments later Kristen Canvel was on screen. She was in City Control; I could see others from the team behind her, like Joey Zen, Claude Lemont, and Zira Miller. "Hi, Kristen."

"Mac!" she exclaimed. "How are things going?"

I sighed. "Just trying to figure a few things out. I'm wondering about you and the colony, though. What's happening there?"

She shrugged. "The explosion that cut power is a mystery. The storm has churned everything up. There's no evidence left. No wires, circuit boards, nothing. The currents and waves have taken it all away."

"Shit," I muttered. "I hope security is still on the lookout."

"Of course. The fleets are collecting still. The news reports are—"

"Don't worry about them."

She paled. "I think we need to be *just a bit* concerned. We have two hundred thousand people here."

"We'll hold them off. We have the upper hand."

She blinked at that, but didn't respond.

"What's happening with the storm?"

"It's powerful. The shoreline defences in Texas have largely failed. The topside military is evacuating millions from the coastlines."

It wasn't a new story. We'd been hearing it for decades, and the stories had been around for centuries. Since Galveston in 1900, when 8,000 people died. A storm surge had hit the beaches, and there hadn't been satellite weather-tracking technology at the time.

No one had known what was coming.

"Where's Grant Bell?" I asked.

"He's in Blue Downs, remember? I thought he told you."

"I remember now." He had been planning on coordinating Sea Traffic Control procedures with the other colonies, to standardize practices. Now that we were all part of the same nation, though not connected by geography, we had to all use the same systems.

"Look, Kristen. I need some information. I want you to contact security for me. I need some background information, some research."

"Go ahead." She grabbed a pen and waited for the names.

"Sidra Noor. William Windsor. And—" I paused and glanced at Johnny. "Min Lee."

He shot a look at me, but didn't interrupt.

"The woman who just arrived? I don't think she's here—"

"She's not. But I want some information on all three. Where they come from, their backgrounds, their military histories, and so on."

"Will do."

"Can you transfer me to Doctor Hyland please?"

"Yes, but it's not his shift."

We operated on a three-shift system at Trieste, so the city ran for twenty-four hours with one third of the population asleep at any time, and working or volunteering or taking care of family for the other two-thirds.

"I'll wait," I said.

The call went silent and dark, but we remained connected.

I turned to my friend. "I'm just covering all bases, Johnny."

Funny, how baseball terms applied to situations when few of us had ever played before. Not topside, anyway. We had a version, underwater, but instead of a bat we used—

"You think Min Lee is going to double cross us?"

"It's worse than that, actually."

He shook his head savagely. "She's better than that. I *know* her. She's my wife, dammit!"

"You haven't seen her much in two years. You didn't know her for the first couple of decades of her life. You don't know—"

His eyes grew hard. "Don't tell me I don't know my own wife! You're not—"

I waved him off. Angering my best friend was the last thing I wanted. "I'm just digging up some information on all three. I have to include Min Lee." I took a deep breath. "Besides, you don't know what I just learned."

"What?" he snapped. "You think my wife set the bomb that blew the reactor lines? You think she would put her own husband in danger?"

"The Steel Shiv killed Cliff."

The statement stopped him cold. His mouth snapped shut, and his wild-eyed look turned instantly to one of confusion and shock. "That's—that's not—"

He couldn't even get the words out.

"My thoughts exactly." I leaned back. "Look, Johnny, I know what you're thinking. You want to defend her. But I just want to learn more about the three of them. Something odd is going on, and Cliff is *dead*. This is no joke. I can't ignore one person just because you say I shouldn't look into her past. Let me study it a bit, but I'll take your word for her too. I know you trust her. That goes a long, long way with me." I gestured behind us. "But Meg is here, Renée is here, and you're here too. I can't let anything happen to any of you. Cliff was enough. No more." My voice was a rasp.

The comm beeped and Kristen said, "Got him, Mac. He's actually working during his sleep shift. Transferring you now."

Johnny was watching me, and he finally relented and looked away. "Okay, Mac. I understand. But I question your sanity."

"Why's that?"

"The Shiv? Really?"

I stared at him for a moment. "Could *you* beat Cliff in a fight, Johnny?"

He considered that. "I don't think so."

"I saw his body. He was *broken*."

"How'd you see him?"

"A picture. The killer took photos and sent them to his superiors."

Johnny blinked at that. He knew The Shiv did such things, and not just for proof. He took graphic photos of death to enhance his reputation.

Then Max's voice echoed from the speaker. "Mac, how are you?"

"Hiya, Doc," I said.

"Where are you?" He was in his lab; I could see charts and displays plastering the bulkhead behind him.

"Somewhere in the South Pacific. Do you remember I asked you about graphene earlier?"

"Yeah. The miracle nanomaterial. It'll change life in the oceans as we know it. Do you recall the story about the ping pong ball made of graphene? People could stand on it—"

"I have a few more questions."

"Shoot."

I considered the topic for a moment. "It's about the process of layering it."

"It's been a challenge, because the honeycomb matrix is only two-dimensional, and it needs something to support it while producing the layers. It needs a substrate to support and insulate it during production."

"Isn't a ship's hull enough support?"

"In a way. But not really. It has to remain a two-dimensional structure. Doing what you're suggesting causes its growth into the third dimension."

"But we want thick layers, don't we? That's three dimensional."

"It has to consist of two-dimensional layers, all laid in a honeycomb or with hexagonal bonds. One on top of the other."

"Why haven't we achieved this yet?"

"We will soon. It just takes time. Hell, maybe someone already has. We're using nanotubes now, in power transmission and communications. We're using graphene in transistors. Also nanoribbons and quantum dots made of graphene. Chemical Vapor Deposition has allowed tech companies to produce layers effectively."

"Just dumping it on titanium hulls?"

"No, no. It will actually grow on some elements, like nickel and copper and iridium. But not titanium, because there are so many different elements in those alloys. They can include molybdenum, palladium, oxygen, niobium, chromium, and more. The problem is the 2D crystallites bend too easily. The proposed solution is to have it bond with a substrate like an organic monomer and grow 'bottom up' as opposed to 'top down.'"

I sighed. "It's all gibberish, now."

He grinned and his dimples deepened. He was in his forties, with dark hair and a near perpetual smile. "I get it. But engineers are still working on it."

"I think they've figured it out, Max. There's a Chinese facility apparently doing it."

There was a long, long pause. Then, "Truman. You've got to get information on it. You need to find out more for us. If another nation has cracked the code, so to speak, they'll be the winners in this war."

He was referring to the war for the ocean's resources, the riches on the seafloors, deeper colonies, and more. "I'm working on it, Max."

—••—

THE CONVERSATION WITH KRISTEN AND Max Hyland was still ringing in my brain. Johnny was silent, just staring ahead as he piloted us toward Australia and Blue Downs. I knew he wasn't angry with me. I felt he understood my concerns, especially since Cliff was dead, The Steel Shiv was now in the picture, and the graphene layering process was the target.

Johnny was likely mulling over the news about The Shiv.

That would stun anyone into silence, I thought.

I pushed myself up and marched back through *SC-1*. At the bunks, immediately aft of the pilot cabin, I could hear Renée breathing softly. Only a curtain gave privacy; one-by-two-metre recesses in the bulkheads barely gave one person any room, let alone two.

It was the other bunk, on the opposite bulkhead on the other side of the corridor, that caught my attention. Turning, I stared at the thick curtain. It was the bunk Meg was using, but there was noise coming from within.

There was a man in there with her, I thought with a sudden shock.

William Windsor and Meg were inside, having sex.

—••—

I CONTINUED TO MOVE AFTWARD, to give them some space and privacy. This would no doubt cause a wrinkle in my investigation, I thought, swearing silently to myself. Both Johnny and Meg were now involved with these people, and I didn't want to damage my relationship with either of them.

And the third was Sahar's brother! I didn't want to hurt her, either.

Meg was a grown woman and she could do what she wanted. She had needs too, which she'd likely ignored for many, many years now. In a way I was very happy for her. Windsor seemed like a decent guy, though too prim and proper for a roughneck like Meg who lived and worked on seacars in the underwater world. Still, if she was happy, then so was I.

In the engineering compartment, I found a bunk tucked into a corner, nestled among ballast pipes and ventilation ducts. Min Lee was there, sitting on the edge.

She smiled. She'd been on her PCD, scrolling through pages, studying something, or maybe communicating with someone. We were close to her base of operations, and there was a chance that she'd been in contact with her Sheng City bosses. She was quite attractive. Tall, athletic, long black and shiny hair, with broad shoulders. She was wearing a tank top, and I noted her forearms again.

"Are you on a mission right now?" I asked.

She chuckled. "You're as blunt as I've heard. Johnny speaks about you a lot."

"He's my best friend," I said. "And partner."

"In politics as well as spycraft. I get it. There are few relationships closer."

"Just one, I guess," I said.

She tilted her head. "Jealous, Mac?"

That took me aback. "Not at all. I'm happy for him, after all these years." Just like Meg, I wanted to add.

"Why do you ask if I'm on a mission?"

"You're on your device, reading something. And the bruises on your arms."

She pulled her arms up, as if ashamed of them. "Ah, I forgot. I'd hoped they'd be healed by now."

"What are they from?"

"Training. Full force. We don't pull punches in Sheng City."

"I remember," I said, thinking back to my time there.

She was studying my expression, and then realization lit her features. "Johnny told me all about it. All about Agent Lau." She glanced around the cramped space, but it wasn't in derision. "The seacar is incredible, Mac. The speed we're going, it's unbelievable."

"First time on a SCAV vessel?"

"No, we've had some in Sheng for a while. Thanks to you and Johnny giving us the SCAV tech."

The roar of the fusion reactor flash boiling seawater permeated the chamber; it was extremely loud in that cabin. I opened my mouth to apologize about it and she cut me off.

"Thanks for bringing me on the mission with you."

"Why?"

"So I can finally spend more time with Johnny. It's been a while."

"Things are going to be tough, after proclaiming independence. You're welcome at Trieste for as long as you want."

She smiled. "Thanks." She continued to eye me. Then, "You don't trust me."

I decided to be frank. "Nope."

"It's okay. I understand. I'm a foreign spy."

"We're allies. It's not that. It's just that you shocked Johnny when you arrived. He's . . . " I stopped and considered what to say. Then I made a sudden decision. "He hasn't mentioned you, to be honest. I think your arrival put him on the spot with the rest of us."

"I know he hadn't said anything."

"Why didn't you tell him you were coming?"

"I think he would have told me not to come. So, I forced his hand."

"Didn't give him a choice. I get it."

She smiled again. "Exactly. Asking forgiveness is better than asking for permission."

"Something tells me you don't ask for permission. Ever."

"It helps, in life, Mac, which I'm sure you know."

I looked around her makeshift bunk. She and Johnny were using some ducts for shelves, and there were clothes on them. There were a lot of black clothes there.

She noted my gaze. "We've turned engineering into a bedroom, until we're back at Trieste. I hope it's okay with you."

"Absolutely. Not an issue at all." I made another decision. "What mission were you on before you came to Trieste?"

Her expression went flat. "I can't talk about missions, Mac. Not Sheng City ones, anyway." Her eyes were cold now, like ice.

It had been an abrupt transformation.

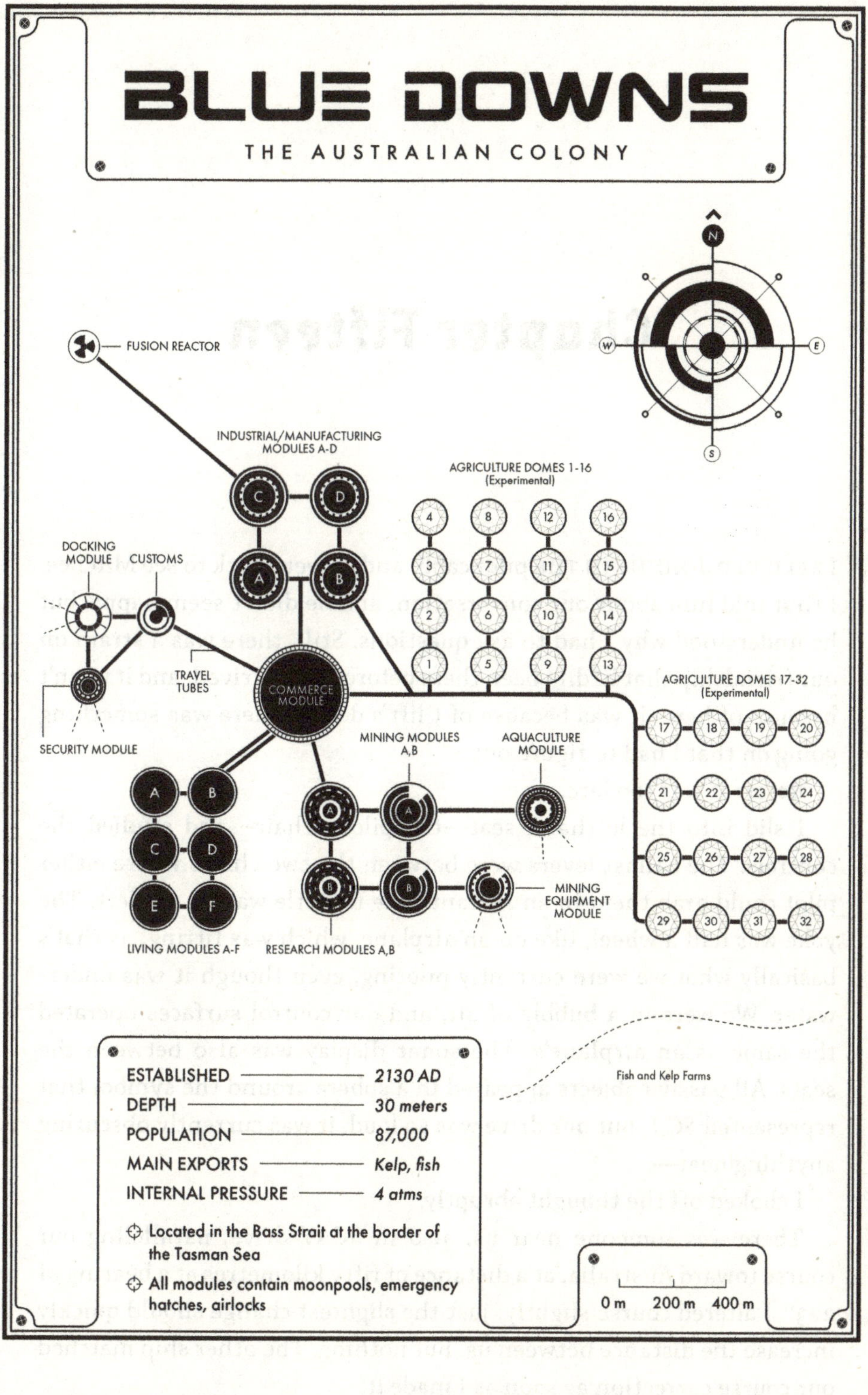
BLUE DOWNS
THE AUSTRALIAN COLONY
N
W
E
S
FUSION REACTOR
INDUSTRIAL/MANUFACTURING MODULES A-D
C
D
A
B
DOCKING MODULE
CUSTOMS
TRAVEL TUBES
COMMERCE MODULE
SECURITY MODULE
AGRICULTURE DOMES 1-16 (Experimental)
4 8 12 16
3 7 11 15
2 6 10 14
1 5 9 13
AGRICULTURE DOMES 17-32 (Experimental)
17 18 19 20
21 22 23 24
25 26 27 28
29 30 31 32
MINING MODULES A,B
AQUACULTURE MODULE
MINING EQUIPMENT MODULE
A B C D E F
LIVING MODULES A-F
RESEARCH MODULES A,B
Fish and Kelp Farms
ESTABLISHED 2130 AD
DEPTH 30 meters
POPULATION 87,000
MAIN EXPORTS Kelp, fish
INTERNAL PRESSURE 4 atms
Located in the Bass Strait at the border of the Tasman Sea
All modules contain moonpools, emergency hatches, airlocks
0 m 200 m 400 m

# Chapter Fifteen

I RELIEVED JOHNNY IN THE pilot cabin and he went back to see Min Lee. I first told him about our conversation, and he didn't seem happy, but he understood why I had to ask questions. Still, there was a strain on our friendship that hadn't been there before she'd arrived, and it wasn't because of her—it was because of Cliff's death. There was something going on that I had to figure out.

Before it was too late.

I slid into the lefthand seat—the pilot's chair—and studied the controls. The ballast levers were between the two chairs where either pilot could grab them in an instant. The throttle was on my left. The yoke was half a wheel, like on an airplane, which was fitting, as that's basically what we were currently piloting, even though it was underwater. We were in a bubble of air, and our control surfaces operated the same as an airplane's. The sonar display was also between the seats. All passive objects appeared in a sphere around the symbol that represented *SC-1*, but our drive was so loud, it was currently obscuring anything near—

I choked off the thought abruptly.

There *was* someone near us, also in SCAV drive, paralleling our course toward Australia, at a distance of fifty kilometres at a bearing of 223°. I altered course slightly; just the slightest change should quickly increase the distance between us. But nothing. The other ship matched our course correction as soon as I made it.

They were following, without much question.

And they were matching our velocity too, at 450 kph.

A SCAV ship that could match our speed.

It was something new in the oceans.

The computer had no idea what it was. The callout label said UNKNOWN CONTACT next to the speed and bearing. I could key in an ID, when I knew, and in the future our computer would remember. It could be Russian, US, or Chinese, as well as any other nation, for that matter.

The map was on the nav screen, and I made sure we were on course for Blue Downs. I'd watch our companion, make sure he didn't get too much closer.

I wondered absently if it was The Steel Shiv . . . or, if he was already on *SC-1* with me.

—••—

BLUE DOWNS WAS AROUND AUSTRALIA'S southern shores, in the Bass Strait on the border with the Tasman Sea. It was also shallow, at thirty metres, and maintained the standardized four atm interior environment. The currents were strong there, and I lowered speed as we made the final approach. I noted Australian Naval vessels on the surface, near the city, as well as a few smaller warsubs in a thirty kilometre perimeter. They were sending a message, no doubt, after Blue Downs had joined us in independence.

The last time I'd been here, I'd had to blow our way out with a torpedo when they tried to capture us. It hadn't been a friendly interaction, to say the least, but I had a very positive relationship with the current Mayor—Talia Tahnee—who had taken over during the rebuilding phase. Australia had first established the city in the 2070s, but after the dreadnought destroyed it, they had only just rebuilt. It was basically brand new, even though it was in the footprint of the former city. There were differences, however. While it had only had three Living Modules before, now it had six—a sign that Australian officials recognized the importance of the colony for a sustained source of kelp and fish.

I remembered watching the city's destruction via video feed, as Meg's co-worker and friend, Mason Lunwick, had struggled for survival during the attack. The Tsunami Plow had crushed the modules, causing multiple implosions and tens of thousands of deaths.

Beside me, William Windsor appeared. He slid into the co-pilot's chair and watched the city through the canopy as we approached.

He had been in Meg's bunk only minutes earlier.

I forced a smile. I was wary of our guests.

"You and Meg have hit it off," I said.

He looked abashed and charming at the same time. "She's something special, Mac. Same as you, I assume. Both from a spectacular family."

"There's not much of the family left."

"But people in the oceans know your dad. He's famous."

"For the wrong reasons."

He studied me with a sideways glance. "Now this is a side of the McCluskies I wasn't aware of. Regret?"

"Not regret. Anger. He was brash. Acted too quickly. He tried for independence before we were ready, and they killed him because of it."

"And you feel you're ready now?"

I shrugged. "The new tech. We outclass the other fleets in the oceans. Our weapons, our deep-diving ability." Then I remembered the graphene. "For the most part, anyway. If they attack, we'll be ready for them."

He pointed at the sonar. "What about *them*? Surrounding the other cities, like Blue Downs?"

"Most of their fleets are collecting in the Atlantic. These are just for show. There aren't enough ships here for an effective attack or occupation."

He stared at the contacts on the screen. "You're likely right, Mac. But don't be overconfident, like your dad."

I snorted. It was rude, but at the same time, he was correct. It was that blunt nature that so many English possessed. What I didn't tell him, however, was that I had made plans for this eventuality. The Fifteen were with me, and we'd prepared for it.

Blue Downs spread out before us, glinting in the sunlight. We'd arrived in early morning, and the colony was beautiful. There wasn't a lot of traffic around—they had the three-month quarantine, as with all other members of Oceania—and there were no scuba divers out either. I noted traces of the attack from the previous year: a few remnants of old, broken and discarded travel tubes, and piles of ruined bulkheads from crushed modules laying west of the colony. A scrap heap, more or less.

It spoke of thousands of deaths. This place, though beautiful, was also a graveyard.

"Where'd you grow up, Windsor?"

"Bill, please," he replied. "I grew up in Ripley, southwest of London, England. Went to a private school. It was an easy upbringing, actually. Had a lot of friends. The English system worked well for me. Corporal punishment kept me in line." He laughed, and it was an easy-going and friendly laugh. It made me like him more. "I got strapped once, never happened again."

"What did you do?"

"Didn't finish my lunch."

I frowned. "Really?"

"Yes. I didn't like the custard."

"You got strapped for that?"

He shrugged. "Behaviour had gone downhill for decades, from what I hear. They reinstated corporal punishment for kids. It worked." He hesitated. "Anyway, I ended up at Cambridge. I studied politics and focused on undersea history. Went to Churchill, joined intelligence."

"Were you born in Ripley?"

He eyed me. "Checking into my history, Mac?" He laughed again. "Well, I don't mind. Yes, I was. Born and raised."

"And your training?"

"There as well. BJJ. MMA. Karate. Judo. Anything I came across, really."

"You look a little small for a fighter."

"But I'm wiry. And fast." And he smiled at me. "I can hold my own."

*Just treat Meg right*, I wanted to add.

He pointed out the canopy. "Look at those."

Along the colony's northeast and east were a series of smaller domes, all with transparent exterior bulkheads. There was foliage within; they were for crops. These were also additions to the city; they must have been investing in biodome growth as well as the standard kelp and fish farms outside in the open water.

"The nations know this is the future. Especially a country as arid as Australia."

The comm squawked. "Attention, seacar on approach for the east quadrant. This is Blue Downs Sea Traffic Control. We're currently in a lockdown quarantine. Do not approach farther."

I pressed the trigger comm on the yoke and spoke into my mic. "This is *SC-1*, of Trieste. McClusky here. I'm hoping to meet with Mayor Tahnee. Can you contact her, please?"

There was a long pause. I pulled back on the throttle and floated in the currents, waiting. Then, "You have permission to enter the Docking Module. The Mayor will meet you there."

I filled the group in on what was happening as we piloted into the moonpool and ascended. *SC-1* broke the surface and we floated in the open pool. I navigated to a dock, and a work crew secured our lines.

Johnny was over my shoulder, staring out the canopy. "We should have brought *Destiny*, for a little extra firepower, Mac."

I disagreed. I'd wanted everyone on board *SC-1*, with me, where I could keep an eye on them all.

"I think Australia will welcome us," I said.

"That ship following us might not."

I grunted. "You might be right."

The others were in the living area, waiting. They were all awake after a fitful night of travel; some of them had gone to sleep at The Complex, and we'd woken them in the middle of their sleep and started on our way to Blue Downs. They looked tired. Meg too, and she shot me a half smile as I fixed my eyes on her.

I turned to the group. "Ready?"

—••—

TALIA TAHNEE WAS WAITING ON the mesh dock. The module was fifteen metres high and mostly open water with seacars, submersibles, and other vessels moored. The water splashed against the bulkheads and docks, creating a pervasive white noise. The area was well illuminated and the air was moist and salty. It felt like being outdoors again, even though we were still thirty metres under the ocean's surface.

I approached Talia with a smile on my face. "It's nice to finally meet you in person."

"You as well, Mac. Welcome!"

She was Aboriginal Australian and had taken over control of the city after the previous leaders died in the destruction. Her name meant *Near Waters* and *Sound of the Surf*. It was fitting, because she was also from Talia, on the southern coast, which the ocean had flooded years earlier. She'd followed her name to the ocean and beyond. She'd had a successful career in politics, and the survivors had elected her Mayor after reconstruction began.

"What are you doing here? I thought you'd be preparing for the attack."

I swore softly. "I know. But there are things happening which I can't ignore right now, and the hurricane has given us a bit of a buffer."

"As you'd hoped, I'm sure," she said with a smile.

"Yes. But I do have to leave quickly." I paused and then glanced back at my team. "We're here to investigate a bit. I'm hoping you can help."

At that moment, the Mayor recognized Sahar Noor, perhaps the third most famous living person in the undersea world, after Meg and myself. She gasped and stepped toward her. "Sahar Noor. I had no idea you were coming."

Sahar extended a hand. "It's a pleasure to meet a fellow Mayor of Oceania."

"What are you doing here?"

She glanced at me. "I'm helping Mac on this mission. It's important."

"I'd like to give you the red-carpet treatment, if possible." She looked abashed and turned to me. "You as well, Mac. *All* of you." Then she turned back to Sahar, still clearly shocked. "I can't believe you're here. I would *so* love to spend some time talking with you."

"It's okay," Sahar said. "I will try, but we just need some information, then we'll be on our way." She grimaced. "I don't want to be rude to you, but we're pressed for time."

Tahnee looked crestfallen, as if she wanted us to stay far longer. "My people would also love to meet you."

"Perhaps after all this is over. After the superpowers accept the inevitable."

The Australian nodded. "Very well." Then she turned to me. "I guess you can all follow me."

—••—

"THE AGRICULTURE DOMES ARE NEW. They're experimental. We're seeing how different crops work in a controlled environment."

We were walking through the city's travel tubes and modules, toward Tahnee's office. Renée said, "What kind of crops?"

"High yield ones. Soybeans, tomato, cucumbers. They produce a lot of food per square metre."

"But the domes are small. Each is only about a hundred metres in diameter."

"The plants grow upward as well, in hydroponic towers and trellises. Each dome is full, to the ceiling. I'll give you a tour."

"I'm not sure we have the time." Around us, people had noted our presence and were openly grinning at me, extending handshakes and high fives. I tried to get them all. Then, "Our CSO died. Murdered. We're tracking the killer."

Her expression turned to horror. "I'm sorry, Mac."

"I have some questions for you." I glanced behind me again. "In private, if possible."

—••—

A FEW MINUTES LATER, I was alone with Talia Tahnee in her office. The rest of the group went on a tour of the city after all, though Renée was not happy about it, but knew that I wanted her to keep an eye on the three operatives. Johnny and Meg went willingly, knowing I wanted to pry a bit without the others hearing.

"Shoot," she said, sitting at her desk.

The office was a lot like mine, though more comfortable. The viewport was wider, and the office was also larger. The scene outside was remarkable. Not only was the ocean clear and clean here, but with the sunlight cutting downward and the visibility high, the modules and domes covering the ocean floor were simply breathtaking. At night, lit up, they'd look like jewels.

"I want to know if you have a record of any of the following people visiting Blue Downs recently."

She pulled her keyboard closer. "Go ahead."

"Min Lee, from Sheng City. William Windsor and Sidra Noor, from Churchill Sands. Cliff Sim, from Trieste."

She frowned and looked up at me. "But aren't these the people you just introduced me to?"

"Most of them, yes. Cliff is dead. The others are . . . "

"Don't tell me they're suspects?"

I shrugged. "Maybe." I paused. "I also need some information about some contact numbers." I gave her the numbers Cliff had discovered. And then I realized something. "And I would like that tour, actually."

She blinked. "Of course. Of the entire city?"

"Just Agriculture Dome #28, actually."

# Chapter Sixteen

ASSISTANT MAYOR DAVID DOWLING TOOK me to Blue Downs's agricultural sector while Mayor Tahnee investigated my other requests. The city was airy and bright, with more viewports than I recalled in the previous colony. The people seemed happy, even with the looming crisis following our announcement of Oceania. Dowling droned on about the construction of the colony as we went through the long travel tube. The ocean surrounded us on all sides; the conveyer was moving us quicker than I would normally have liked, for it was so beautiful. The colourful fish, the bright blue waters . . . when people topside imagined life under water, this is what they pictured.

We were headed for Dome #28; it was the final dome in the second-last series, and practically the farthest one from the Commerce Module.

It was a kilometre-long journey.

*This colony is huge*, I thought.

Though its population wasn't massive; the city was just more expansive than others I'd been in. It stretched out a long way onto the sandy floors of the strait.

"Tell me about this dome," I asked as we moved.

Dowling was staring at his PCD as he recited information from its screen. "A company rented the space. Produce Traders LLC. We found it easy to rent these domes. The demand is—"

"They rent from you, or from Australia?"

"It would have gone through our commerce department. We made the decision to allow it." He shrugged. "It's just produce, though. Nothing illicit."

"Cannabis?"

"Not grown here. We stick to what's needed to survive."

"Tomatoes, soybeans, peas . . . I get it." We continued to move through the tube. It seemed like a *long* journey. "What about the company?"

"Registered with Australia."

"Is there a parent corp?"

"Give me just a minute, Mac." A minute later he said, "It's a Chinese company."

Figures. This was likely a front for something else.

He looked at my expression. "You knew it. How?"

I shrugged. "There's something off about it. I don't know how we came across the info yet, but this dome is a part of the path."

"Path?"

"The breadcrumbs," I said. "I need a name, Dowling. Can you give me the person who rented it?"

"One minute." He continued to scroll through information on his PCD.

The crowds had thinned out considerably. The only people in this area were the workers in the facility. They wore overalls and dark tunics. A few had soil-covered hands, though in hydroponics, very little soil was used, if any at all. It was likely fertilizer of some sort, or used as a method to nurse new sprouts to life.

Then Dowling said a name which I'd expected. "Tsim Lui."

The investor mentioned in the tip sent to The Complex. Of course. "Does this person live in Blue Downs? Or does he just invest from another location?"

"He's the representative of Produce Traders. He's in Living Module E."

"Perfect," I said. We were nearly at the dome now. I was desperate to find out what was in there.

Dowling led the way down a narrow travel tube that cut through three other domes. Around us, water dripped from the ceiling and plants stretched up along structures high above. The water was from humidity, which was at 100% without much question. There were workers around, tending to plants and harvesting produce. They noticed me as I walked past, and their eyes showed shock at my presence. I tried to acknowledge them, but I was in a hurry.

Finally, we reached it.

Dome #28.

I looked inside at the towering vegetation within. Taller than the normal variety, plants stretched straight up to the transparent ceiling. The sun was high above, and it pierced the water and illuminated the interior. Water dripped downward, and there were even some chirps from birds in the dome.

At my questioning glance, Dowling shrugged. "It's a contained ecosystem. They try to keep it as natural as possible."

"Insects too?"

"From what I understand, yes. No cockroaches, though. No infestations allowed."

I stared at the vegetation for long, long minutes. "Strange that topside needs this more than other crops. You said the domes were for survival."

He frowned. "You're right. But they're paying for the space, so there's no reason for us to really question it."

It made me wonder, for these were not soybeans, or tomatoes, or green beans.

They were trees.

Lemon and lime trees.

—••—

THEY HAD LARGE, SPRAWLING LIMBS. Wires supported the largest ones, stretched taut to the ceiling, and the trees strained higher than seemed natural. While the other domes had thin, fragile plants on trellises for support—or growing up columns or along plastic lattices—these trees seemed abnormally tall. Their trunks were not wide enough to maintain structure; the branches seemed like tangled masses of wire that filled the sky with artificial clouds of steel wool. The lemons and limes were *everywhere*.

I didn't have much experience seeing trees as an adult. It was usually just the rare single one you'd catch sight of in a dome somewhere, in the centre with the rest of the foliage arranged around it. But this scene was simply incredible.

"I've never seen trees like this before," I whispered.

"Bioengineered. The wires are supporting them to help them along the way."

"The crop . . . it must cost a lot. It takes time for fruit like this to grow."

Dowling paused. "You must be right. There's a need for it, obviously."

"What I'm saying is that someone's spending a lot of money on this. Cliff was investigating it for some reason." He'd called this dome from The Complex while investigating. "It's not an easy crop to grow, and it's not plentiful. The rent on this dome must be enormous." I glanced around. While the other domes all had workers tending to vegetation, there was no one here.

"Maybe it's to fend off scurvy. Like in the old days, before we had vitamins."

"They're still growing crops on the surface. The cropland isn't as stable and many areas are ruined . . . " I trailed off. It wasn't a good argument, and this still didn't make sense.

Cropland on the surface had migrated northward to cooler temperatures. The soils there weren't fertile, however, so they needed fertilizer. *Quadrillions* of tons of it. It had damaged rivers, streams, and lakes; eutrophication had killed them due to the chemicals. In areas that started getting more rain, evaporation from the heat was a menace, and the salt layers left behind had made many areas impossible to grow anything. In areas where crops *were* growing, it was for staples like wheat, corn, rice, soy and potatoes—food that could feed a lot of people.

The surface was approaching Soylent Green times, I thought, grim.

"It's a mystery," Deputy Mayor Dowling said. "But there must be profit behind it."

—••—

WE MARCHED BACK TO THE Commerce Dome, a journey that took nearly twenty minutes. I'd been reviewing the mystery over and over as we walked the conveyer; Dowling didn't mind my silence; I think I'd interrupted his pleasant life in Blue Downs and he just wanted us gone.

"Can you give me Tsim Lui's PCD contact please?" I said.

He referred to his own device and recited the number. It was the same one that Cliff had called twice from The Complex.

So. The trail was growing clearer. My CSO had received the tip, which had led him to Blue Downs. But the meaning of the lemons and limes still eluded me. I couldn't quite see the relevance, unless it was just a place that Tsim Liu tended, and it had nothing to do with the plot to kill Cliff.

As we moved through the travel tube in the Agricultural Dome sector, I noticed that someone was following us.

—••—

HE WAS SEVERAL METRES BEHIND, but very easy to spot, wearing black from head to toe, including a black helmet. It was common to see divers wearing scuba gear, lugging tanks and regulators and masks around, but this helmet covered his whole head, like a motorcyclist would wear on the surface.

With farmers and technicians surrounding him, he was obvious.

I gestured to Dowling and we made an abrupt turn toward Agricultural Dome #5, or, as the signage on the bulkhead tube stated, ADs 5-8. He looked surprised but followed my lead. I increased my stride, and he said, "What's going on, Mac?" He was starting to breathe hard; he was middle-aged with a paunch and balding head. He was obviously not in intelligence or connected to the military in any way.

"Someone's following us." He started to turn and I snapped, "Don't look." I continued through the tubes, now passing through the middle of a dome. Plants were all around, water dripped down on us, and workers turned from their tasks as we exploded through their foliage. I jerked my PCD out. "Renée," I hissed.

"Go ahead." She'd replied instantly.

"Is there anyone missing from your group?" I was wondering if Min Lee, Sidra, or Windsor had suddenly left her watch. If so, it would be an easy—

"Mayor Tahnee's assistant is showing us the research and mining sector right now."

"Are they with you?"

"I can't see everyone right now."

I turned and peered behind me. The figure in black was entering the dome, difficult to see because of all the vegetation growing high to the ceiling, but he was there.

My right hand found the gun in the holster at my side. I also had a knife on my left thigh—traditional in the undersea world—and I could always use that if I wanted to be quiet.

"Find them!" I said to Renée.

Dowling and I crouched behind a forklift and I said to him, "Stay here. I'll take care of this."

I crept toward the edge of the dome, but tried my best to keep the figure in my sights. It was difficult with the greenery, and his outfit blended in with the shadows, but the sun was high above and thankfully I could see him. My heart was pounding abnormally fast for a situation like this, and my breath kept catching in my throat. I wondered why, for it was unlike me. Then I realized with a start: *it's because this might be The Steel Shiv.*

I was about to face the fight of my life.

I wondered if I should just use the gun and be done with it, but there was no honour in that.

*There's no honour in death either,* I scolded myself.

I knew if it came to it, I'd pull my weapon.

But right now, I didn't know what to do.

I felt off balance.

I swallowed and continued to move.

There were wide plants brushing my face as I pushed forward. Birds had been squawking earlier; now, it had fallen completely silent, as if they knew what was coming. Water dripped from above, and it suddenly fell in a cascade.

A programmed rainstorm.

I looked up, momentarily stunned. The sun far above, rain falling in my face, foliage all around . . .

It made me feel as though I were on an alien planet. Memories flooded back from childhood, from before Dad had brought us to Trieste to chase his dream of undersea living and the quest for independence. It was a core memory that shocked me for a moment—

He attacked from my side, shoving me to the ground with a tackle that had followed an elbow to my temple. My head snapped around, my vision dimmed, and stars swam around me.

I struggled to my feet and shook it off as best as possible. The figure was there, directly in front, in that black helmet. He was small in stature, though muscular. I crouched before him, circling, trying to see through the shadows. His elbow had really hurt.

Feinting with my right, I swung a left which he blocked deftly. I fell immediately into a boxing routine, bobbing and weaving, throwing lefts and rights and uppercuts, and noted that his stance was off. He was not using his legs effectively; he was having issues blocking all of my strikes. Some of them even connected, though I'd had to lower my aim to the neck area because of the helmet. I tried a few kicks to the kidneys, thighs, knees, and he backed off, wary.

I watched him, feeling better now. I had easily switched to combat mode. Zoned in; nothing else mattered. We moved through the vegetation as the rain poured in a torrent around us. The leaves were soaking, and my clothes were now saturated. The sound was thunderous; the droplets were huge and fell in a cascade over the entire dome.

I lunged at him.

# Chapter Seventeen

THE FIGHT PLOWED THROUGH MORE foliage, knocking aside structures meant to hold the plants and give them stability. There were distant cries from workers, but I ignored them. The towers were fragile and splintered as elbows and legs plowed through them. Someone watching from above could have followed our fight as we drove through the plants, like an angry monster chasing its prey through a jungle. The leaves and stems parted as if they didn't exist. I struck again and again and took very few hits.

Something occurred to me, but I didn't have time to think it through just yet.

I darted behind a larger conduit of some sort—for water, I guessed—and peered around it, searching for the man in black. He was looking for me, though was slightly off balance now. I'd hurt him, the way his elbow had first hurt me, though he was worse off than I. Of that I had no doubt.

He turned away from me, still searching—

And I struck.

I attacked from behind. A kick to his right knee, and his leg buckled instantly. Before he fell, I kicked his right kidney and then immediately struck his neck with a knife-edge palm. He jerked to the side and I swung a thunderous roundhouse to his head, hitting the helmet with everything I had. The helmet clattered away, rolling through shrubs, and my opponent fell in a heap, on the deck, still and silent.

He wasn't even breathing.

I grabbed him and turned him over, wondering whose face I'd see.

—••—

DOWLING APPEARED OVER MY SHOULDER as I peered into the dead man's face.

I didn't recognize him. He was Caucasian with dark hair, soaked now from the rain and the puddle he'd landed in. There was a weapon in a holster that he hadn't had time to use. He wasn't breathing; my last kick had been too much for him. I'd either broken his neck or crushed his skull.

"Who'd you expect?" Dowling asked.

"I'm not sure," I muttered.

"Seems like you thought it would be someone you knew."

"Maybe I did."

Dowling looked around. "I think I have to call security."

More people clustered around us now, wondering what the hell was going on, who had been fighting, and who we were. They seemed surprised at Dowling's presence, but when they noticed me, their faces *exploded* into shock.

"Mac, what the hell?"

"What's going on, Mac?"

"*Truman McClusky? Here?*"

I rose to my feet and continued to stare at the corpse.

One thing was sure. This was not The Steel Shiv.

—••—

BACK IN THE MAYOR'S OFFICE, I was explaining myself and what had happened. Talia was angry. Residents had witnessed the fight, and not only that, her Deputy Mayor had even been a part of it. She wondered how she was going to explain and how it would affect her political future.

"Just explain that it had to do with independence," I said. "They saw me there. They know it was serious."

She was staring at me. "You think that'll be enough?"

"I know it will. They're on side with us. They were happy to see me." It was common in the undersea colonies. They knew my family and what we represented. They understood that I was fighting for them. If I was there, then there was a reason for it.

The hatch slid aside and the rest of the group arrived. They stared at the scene, wondering exactly what was going on.

Johnny said, "Mac, why are you wet? Did you go out?"

I sighed. "No. I've just been dealing with something here." I told them about the attack, how someone had followed Dowling and me.

"Do you know who it might have been?" Windsor asked.

"I have a few suspects," I answered slowly. "But it wasn't who I thought it could be."

"Who did you suspect, Mac?" Sidra asked.

Sahar was watching the entire exchange with a curious expression, though she seemed more concerned than anything else. Concerned about me. She was eyeing me now, and her face was lined.

"Look," Windsor continued. "This guy followed you, attacked, and you took him out. End of story."

"It's not so cut and dry," I said. "Who was he? Why did he do it? What did he want? Did he kill Cliff?"

"And?"

I exhaled. "He wasn't skilled enough. There's no way he could have beaten Cliff."

Meg said, "And you're thinking, what, Mac? That it's one of our group?"

"I didn't say that."

"You called Renée during the attack. You wanted to know who was missing."

I glanced around. She was absolutely correct. "I was checking in. I was curious."

"Is this another test, like at The Complex?"

"No, this was unexpected. I didn't know someone would attack us here."

"Someone followed us here, right? In a SCAV vessel. Could it have been him?"

"I don't know." I looked at Tahnee. "Are you allowing ships to dock?"

"Just yours."

Meg said, "He could have set down nearby and swum here. Entered through a moonpool."

"It's possible. But why are you so quick to pin the blame on others?"

"It was a ship following us! Isn't it obvious?"

Her face was growing flushed and she was breathing hard. "Meg," I said in a quiet voice. "I'm not blaming anyone here. I'm just being careful."

"You're testing them again."

"No, I didn't expect that attack."

Sidra, Min Lee, and Windsor were watching the exchange. It wasn't what I wanted. Sibling rivalry was also embarrassing. She snapped, "Yes, you did!"

"Meg, let's chat about this somewhere else."

"You're damn right we'll talk about this!" She stepped forward, facing me.

A silence descended over the room, except for Meg's breathing.

Sahar said, "Let's all just be calm. We can chat about this on *SC-1*. Go over the facts in more detail."

Mayor Tahnee scowled. "Everything has been so peaceful here since we restarted operations. Hard, yes, but no violence."

"Sorry," I said. "I am trying to figure out this mystery."

She continued without even paying attention to me. "—now there are two deaths in a day, and you all have just arrived, and—"

"Wait a minute," Meg interrupted. "*Two* dead? Who were they?"

"The one I was with looked vaguely familiar," I said. "Until I saw his face, that is."

"Who was it?" Johnny asked.

I stared at him. "He wanted me to think he was The Shiv."

"He wasn't?"

I shook my head. "Not even close."

"How do you know?"

"He wasn't a great fighter. Couldn't handle himself. Didn't have great experience."

Dowling entered the office and said, "He was a laborer from the agriculture sector. The kelp farms, to be precise."

"Likely hired to track me, then attack if a possibility arose." I turned to Tahnee. "Who's the other?"

She sighed. "A visitor from your neck of the woods, I'm sorry to say.

He was working with my people here, helping train them."

I rose to my feet slowly, a chill working its way down my spine. My guts slithered.

She continued, "His name was Grant Bell."

—••—

A COLLECTIVE GASP ECHOED IN the chamber. She stared at us. "You knew him?"

Johnny said, "He was here to review STC protocols with your controllers. He was in charge of that division at Trieste. He was going to coordinate with every colony in Oceania."

I lowered myself back to the chair and considered the developments. They were happening nearly too fast to process.

Grant Bell.

He was in charge of Sea Traffic Control in Trieste. I'd seen him on the day of the proclamation. He'd been celebrating. Later, he'd come into the office when Min Lee arrived, and told me about the track her seacar had taken from the Panama Passthrough to the colony. He'd mentioned the trip to Blue Downs on both occasions.

Min Lee was watching me, and I locked eyes with her.

Johnny said to Tahnee, "You haven't had *any* violence here since resettling?"

"None." Her voice was firm.

*Accusing.*

"And the first person killed is a Triestrian. And the second is someone who was *attacking* a Triestrian." He turned to me. "The connection is clear."

"How'd he die?" I asked Tahnee.

"We found his body this morning. In a corridor in the living module. Someone broke his neck. The clinic has his body now. Their examination is still preliminary, but they say there's also evidence of strangulation."

"What time did it happen?" I asked.

"An hour ago."

"After we arrived?"

"Yes. After." She was watching me.

I glanced at the group again. Meg was still furious, and she was staring at me too. Johnny was also beginning to look angry, probably because he knew that I suspected Min Lee.

Sahar said into the void, “What is the purpose of all this, Mac? Cliff, the attack on you, Grant’s death, the ship following us?”

*There’s even more than that,* I wanted to reply, but I could only shake my head.

Johnny said, “What did you find while you were gone?”

I pulled myself back to him. “I went to Agricultural Dome #28, to see why Cliff was interested in it.”

“And?”

I shook my head. “Nothing, really. Trees. But the investor was a name we’ve heard before. Tsim Lui.”

“From the tip to Coda Rose at The Complex? The Chinese investor?”

I didn’t answer. The others were watching in silence, wondering what was going on.

“The Steel Shiv is sending me a message,” I said. “He’s close. And he wants me to know that I’m next.”

# Chapter Eighteen

I NEEDED TO CLEAR MY head. I couldn't think clearly. Grant Bell had been a friend of mine, a *good* friend. He'd been in STC since the beginning of my journey and I couldn't process what it was going to be like without him around. He wasn't officially in TCI—wasn't actually supposed to even know about it—but he'd put two and two together over the years. He suspected what we were up to, especially in those final months, as we'd put finishing touches on our plan.

And now that we'd actually made the announcement, he was helping usher Oceania in to a new beginning for us all.

Grant was dead.

I had to keep repeating it to myself, as I walked through the colony.

*Grant was dead.*

*Grant was dead.*

*Grant was dead.*

There had to have been a reason other than sea traffic. Sure, he was standardizing procedures, and he was an ambassador of Oceania, so to speak, so other nations might feel as though there was good reason to kill the man. But really, the reason was more basic. It had to be something related to me, to warn me.

Or to scare me.

Once again, my actions had resulted in someone dying. Inside, my stomach was in my throat; I felt nauseated.

The Shiv was sending me a message.

*Another* one.

There was a noise behind me and I turned, suddenly on high alert. The sounds of the city were all around, with people moving about to their jobs or back to the living modules to catch a few hours' sleep. It was right at a shift change, and the people of Blue Downs were moving with a purpose. Most had smiles on their faces; like almost all other ocean colonists, they realized that what they were doing was for a greater good. Pushing into the oceans, expanding our realm, harvesting important resources to help humanity . . . these things made life easier, even though the work was harder.

My senses tingled as the footfalls approached—

It was Sahar, and I immediately relaxed. I exhaled, relieved.

She smiled at me. I was next to a bulkhead and an enormous viewport; the view outside was magnificent: kelp, fish farm fences, blue waters, the sparkling sun. She said, "I'm sorry about following you."

"It's okay."

"I wanted to check in on you. To see if you . . . " she trailed off.

"Feel bad about killing someone?"

She shrugged. "In a way."

"It was self-defence, Sahar. I had no choice."

"You might have pulled some punches. Or made him surrender. I'm not okay with killing people. You know that."

Her participation and involvement in Oceania depended on that fact. Alienating her was the last thing I wanted, especially because her people were so loyal. They'd elected her and followed her wholeheartedly. If she left Oceania, they'd go too. We couldn't afford to lose an entire city only a few days after declaring independence.

I sighed. "I do know that. Trust me. I thought he was the guy though. I thought the fight would be harder."

"You thought he killed Cliff." It was a statement.

"Anyone who could do that would be nearly an immovable obstacle." Back in the agri-domes . . . Hell, I'd been *scared*, I had to admit. I continued, "I didn't think I had a chance, to be honest. Cliff was . . . well, he was someone I thought would always be there for me. I didn't think anyone could ever hurt him, let alone *kill* him. It's craziness." I leaned against the bulkhead and exhaled, staring at the deck. "I'm so sorry,

Sahar. I should have brought him in." I thought of that last, final kick. I'd given it everything I had.

She was watching me. "Were you angry?"

I frowned. She was trying to gauge my motivations. "No, not at all. I was not out for revenge. I was just trying to survive." I thought about that fight, in the foliage, in the rainstorm.

"Who'd you think it was?"

"The Shiv, I mentioned—"

"No. That's not what I meant." She stepped toward me. "*Who?*"

I stared at her. Her eyes were pleading; they were no longer judgmental or angry. "There are three options," I finally muttered.

"And two are my people."

"And the other is one of mine, in a way."

She sighed and continued watching me. Then she looked away. "I do see your dilemma, Mac. Do you really think it's one of them?"

"There's a good chance."

"It's not Sidra. I know his heart. It can't be him."

"Will you let me keep investigating, without letting your emotions interfere? I promise not to guess. I'll make sure to be a hundred percent certain."

She studied the scene outside but remained quiet. Then finally, "You acted before knowing for sure. A man is dead."

"I see your point."

"Did you learn from it?"

I snorted inwardly. I didn't need a lecture, but it was hard to admit that she was absolutely correct. "Of course, Sahar."

She continued to study the water. "It's so clear outside. A lot different than in the English Channel."

"It is."

"If only life were like that."

"It can be. It just takes time."

"Until the next period of murky water comes your way."

I watched her from the corner of my eye. She always seemed so sure of herself, but now she was hinting that she was unsure about our path toward independence. Or was it—

"Sahar, do you question your brother? Do you think it could be him?"

She didn't respond immediately. "I told you, it can't be him."

"But?"

"But . . . sometimes there can be another side to people. It's difficult, living between worlds, you know?"

"You mean the mainland and the oceans?"

"No."

"Your culture and religion gives you peace, Sahar. It calms you. You've mentioned it to me before. Your prayers."

"*Me*. Yes. But sometimes I sense in him . . . frustration." She shrugged. "It's not enough to warrant killing people though, Mac. We'd never do that."

"He's an operative. He's been involved in fights like the one I just had."

"I'm confident that he would never kill in anger, or for revenge. I know him. He's my brother."

Which was reason to overlook the obvious, I knew. Family was different. We let them get away with things other people could never do.

But I didn't say it.

Mayor Talia Tahnee approached us. "Am I disturbing you?"

"Not at all," Sahar said. "We're . . . we're decompressing, you could say. Trying to figure this out."

Tahnee said to Sahar, "This is not how I wanted to spend time with you, to get to know you more."

"It's okay. We can make that happen, eventually."

"I've been wanting to learn about you. About how you captivate your people so."

It was true. It was also mysterious. There were videos of Sahar at political rallies, speaking to her voters. They adored her. There was a drive to support her. She never betrayed them, either, and they appreciated it. If they elected her to do something, then she made it happen. But there was more to her than that. She exuded confidence and peace. She was not a fighter, but she'd win in a political fight, every single time.

Sahar replied, "I am just myself, Talia. The people appreciate it. They can see through fake politicians. At least, I *think* they can, after everything we've been through. All the lies about climate change, all the trouble the surface is experiencing now. They finally realize that industries have been making the rules, and it's brought us to this point." She shrugged. "I think there's just a tipping point, and I'm here at the right time and place."

"There's more to it than that," I said. "Don't underestimate yourself."

She smiled at me. "If you say so, but I have my doubts."

"You have fan groups." I pointed at the people passing by; some had noticed her. "You can see it in their faces."

"You do too, Mac. Your whole family does."

"My history is significantly more complicated than yours. I think it turns some people away from me."

Tahnee said, "What about this? This situation seems complicated too."

"Do you regret joining Oceania now?"

"No way." She said it without hesitation. "I'm anxious to move forward. To get this over with and enter the next phase of work and cooperation with the superpowers. To end this cold war."

"But I brought death and violence to you."

"Only temporarily."

"Until I leave, is that it?"

She looked wounded. "No. Not at all. Until we figure out the mystery, that's all."

"It's a tough one, for sure."

Sahar said, "What did you find in the dome, Mac?"

I turned to her and took a deep breath. "Nothing, as far as I can tell. I think it's just the investor who's important. I have to speak to him."

"What was growing there?"

"Lemons and limes, if you can believe it."

Creases appeared on her forehead. "That's odd."

It was indeed. We used vitamins to avoid deficiencies. And space was too valuable for a crop like that.

"Mac," Tahnee said. "I have some information for you. About what you asked." Then she glanced at Sahar and back to me.

Sahar interpreted the look and began moving away. She almost glided in her long dress. People nearby had recognized her, and there were groups waiting to speak to her. Many were children, especially young girls. A smile split Sahar's face as she moved to them.

"Hello," she said, her voice practically sparkling. "How long have you lived in the colonies?" And later I heard, "What do you want to be when you grow up? A scientist? An engineer?"

It was amazing, I thought. Sahar was truly a magnet for people. They naturally respected her; no one could ever question her motives. She was the future of the oceans.

I studied Tahnee for a heartbeat. "I'm sorry to be so pushy, Talia. I would like to meet and have more of a social gathering, instead of this rushed investigation."

"But I understand, of course." She smiled.

I had read a great deal about her before. She was the only aboriginal politician in the oceans, and she was well known for bringing her people's philosophy to the colonies. She wanted to work and exploit the seafloor, the same as the other colonies, but she had pushed for the process to be more environmentally friendly. She didn't want their work in the oceans to result in devastation underwater as the Industrial Revolution had done to the surface. She had spoken of this at meetings with The Fifteen, and I agreed. She had also made reference to the SCAV drive being detrimental to wildlife—the loud noise possibly causing whale and dolphin beachings—which I was more hesitant about. The superfast drive had opened the oceans to us and given us the advantage over the superpowers. Still, she had a good point. Hurting marine life was the last thing I wanted. It occurred to me that she was bringing the aboriginal philosophy to the oceans and this was a positive for Oceania. We needed to include *everyone* in the oceans, otherwise we risked alienating our own people. Division within was the weak point that others would eventually use to their advantage.

"Thank you," I replied. "I would like to arrange something, after all this is done."

"And we can chat about protecting the oceans along with exploiting them?" She frowned and sighed. "Even the word is tough to say. *Exploit*. We should talk about *making use* of the resources, and giving back at the same time. This way we can really ensure our future underwater, instead of just for the next few centuries."

"I agree."

She shrugged. "Something to talk about, perhaps. Next time. After this is all done. Now, about those four people . . . "

I nodded. "Go ahead."

"We don't have any records of Sidra Noor, Min Lee, or William Windsor visiting."

I snorted. As expected. They were spies, after all. They'd use aliases.

"Cliff though, is another matter."

"You know he came here?" That caught my attention.

"Just a week ago or so. He arrived and then left soon after."

"What was he doing? Did you find out?"

"There were a few transactions. Food, a hotel room, supplies for his vessel, and so on. Nothing stands out."

"I see," I said. Once again, a dead end.

"He did go to Living Module E though."

I stood up straighter. "Let me guess."

"He went to see Tsim Liu."

The Chinese investor. I was sure Cliff had also visited Agricultural Dome #28. The lemon and lime trees had probably shocked him too.

"He was also digging through some industrial records. He went to the manufacturing modules as well."

I frowned. "Which ones?"

"You won't believe this, Mac."

"Go on."

Her eyes were wide and she looked down at her PCD. "According to our records, it was the facility here that processes certain harvests."

"And where does the produce come from?" I practically whispered, already knowing the answer.

"Dome #28."

# Chapter Nineteen

JOHNNY WAS NEXT ON MY list. I had a job for him. I keyed him via my PCD and he immediately appeared on the screen. He was in a travel tube somewhere, with Meg and Min Lee at his side.

I frowned.

"Johnny, where are you going?" I'd left him in Tahnee's office only an hour earlier.

"The next logical location, Mac. I brought friends, don't worry."

That made me smile. "Where are you—"

"We're going to pay a visit to the investor, Tsim Lui. Windsor told me which living module. We're going to find out what he knows."

He'd read my mind. "Great work. Keep me updated."

Trieste was my next call. Sahar was still talking to citizens, and I let her chat as I spoke into the PCD. Tahnee had left, and I could feel eyes on my back. The people here were shocked to find Sahar there, but my presence also surprised them. I knew they wanted to talk to me, but I had to keep pressing forward on this.

"Hello Kirsten," I said.

Kristen Canvel, my assistant at Trieste, was currently running the entire show. I'd even put her in charge of appointing the new CSO for the colony.

"Mac!" she cried. "How are things?"

It made me smile. "Fine. What's happening there?"

She paused. "The fleet is still building. There are tracks from all over the globe, heading for it. It's on the news. It's all they're talking about."

"Are they still on schedule to attack on 15 June?"

"It's possible."

"Any more communication from the USSF?"

"Nothing."

"And what about our plans? Are they moving forward?"

"Quietly, yes."

I couldn't say any more about it, so I switched topics. "And what about the people I asked you about?"

"I dug into it." She looked down at her notes and recited everything she had about Sidra Noor, William Windsor, and Min Lee. There was really nothing out of the ordinary, especially for operatives whose cities were protecting their pasts and identities. Sidra lived in Churchill and appeared to work for the seacar repair crews, Min Lee worked as staff for a diplomat in Sheng City, and William Windsor was indeed from Ripley and had moved to Churchill to work in the Mayor's office as an administrator following his education at Cambridge. All were dead ends, even though I knew all the information was a front to protect them.

"Nothing stands out," I muttered.

"They're all clean."

"They're all spies."

She blinked. "Really? How do you know?"

"They're with me on this mission. *I know.* But something's not right with one of them."

She looked down at her computer again. "I'll keep digging then, Mac. Maybe I can discover something."

I nodded, though I knew it would be next to impossible. They had iron-tight covers, aided by their governments and protected with proper records. Falsified but made to look authentic. "Can you put Doctor Hyland back on?" I asked.

"Will do. And I'll stay on it, don't worry."

Max Hyland appeared on the screen after a few moments. He flashed his dimpled smile at me, which always made me feel better. He had a laid-back and relaxed attitude which I appreciated. Especially with all the tension building right now. There were people out there hunting him for information about the Isomer Bombs, and he didn't seem to mind.

"Did you find what you were looking for?" he asked.

"Not yet. Not even close." *The mystery keeps building,* I wanted to say. "What else can you tell me about graphene?" I was grasping at straws here; I was hoping he could shed some light on whatever Cliff had discovered.

"Can you be more specific? There are so many different uses and applications."

"The layering problem. To make hulls stronger."

"Ah, got it." He sat down; he was in his lab; behind him, charts and graphs plastered the steel bulkhead. "I told you it's a two-dimensional substance. Very rare. Very hard to produce. But engineers eventually isolated it, and it triggered the rush."

"The graphene rush."

"That's it."

"Using scotch tape."

He smiled. "Sounds ridiculous, but it's not. Remember, scientists had theorized about it for decades before finally isolating and documenting it. It won people a Nobel prize!"

"The honeycomb lattice."

"A single atom thick. Yes. Two-d."

I sighed and leaned against the viewport. Sahar was still nearby, talking to people. The group had grown even larger. "A single sheet is too light to manipulate."

"It's strong compared to its weight, but it's hard to produce in layers. Mind you, we're talking thousands, maybe millions, of layers in order to resist the kind of pressure you're concerned with. CVD might be the answer."

"Refresh my memory."

"Chemical Vapor Deposition. It's self-repairing, did I mention that?"

"Yes. No welding, no rivets, I got it."

"The new carbon fills any holes by bonding with the rest of the lattice. It's a miracle substance."

"But the two-dimensional nature," I pressed. "You said its growth pushes into the third dimension, distorting it. How'd they perfect it?"

"That's the dilemma. That's what you're hunting for." He tilted his head and stared at me. "Have you discovered anything."

"A name. Not much more. An investor."

"Investing in what?"

"A crop."

I flashed back to the fight only a few hours earlier. We'd crashed through some structures meant to support the plants all the way up to the skylight. Lattices, trellises. Some had been larger towers, surrounded by vines and plants, which crawled upward, filling the domes with crops for topside.

Something struck me as important.

A tingle had started in the back of my mind.

"Max, you said something about a monomer and bottom-up growth."

"An organic monomer. It might allow the graphene to grow in layers from the bottom up as opposed to top down. It'd have to be something that was clean, sterile, easy to produce and handle."

"What's a monomer?"

"A compound that binds to form a substance with a large number of repeating units."

"Like the honeycomb lattice."

He nodded. "Sure. Maybe. But the point is to allow more layers to form. To create larger molecules. It's called polymerization. Organic monomers help."

I sighed and turned back to the ocean view.

He said, "What's wrong, Mac? What have you discovered?"

"Nothing, apparently. Someone's following us. Someone tried to kill me, but it looks like he was a hired gun. He wasn't very good."

"Are you okay?"

"He's dead. Anything he knew died with him."

"What else?"

I shrugged. "An agriculture dome." And then a sudden shock surged through me.

*Oh my god.*

An organic monomer.

To help with graphene growth.

"Max, give me some examples of monomers."

He frowned. "Ethylene. Terephthalic acid. Epoxide." He looked away. "We create those in a lab though."

"Any natural ones?"

"Sure. Those are easy. Isoprene. Amino acids. Monosaccharides—sugar, or glucose. Citric acid. Lactic acid is too, then there's—"

"Wait a minute." I hesitated, my heart pounding. "Citric acid? Holy shit."

He stared at me. "It's an easy one. It's used in passivation too, of some metals. They can form a hard, inert outer layer when exposed to air. This can weaken metal during manufacturing processes. A warsub hull has to be absolutely perfect, to resist all the pressure. Some substances provide a shield against corrosion. Citric acid is also an organic monomer that I guess could be useful for graphene layering. For passivation too. It depends—"

"Max," I interjected. "What do you need to create it?"

He frowned. "Any citrus fruit, though I couldn't see anyone using valuable space for it. The fruit with the highest concentration would be lemons or limes."

I clenched a fist and swore quietly.

*Agricultural Dome #28.*

The Chinese were using the crop for their graphene process.

It was another breadcrumb.

I'd found it.

# Interlude

## Somewhere in the Pacific Ocean

DATA PROCESSING

| | |
|---|---|
| Vessel: | Russian Submarine Fleet<br>*Dreadnought* Class *Voskhod–The Rise* |
| Location: | Latitude: Unknown<br>Longitude: Unknown<br>Over The Iron Plains |
| Depth: | 2,200 metres |
| Date: | 12 June 2131 |
| Time: | 1708 hours |

CAPTAIN IVAN ARKADY VENTINOV WAS in his cabin, pacing in front of his desk and staring at his comm console. It was an ornate cabin. The desk was wood, inlaid with polished obsidian and a light finish. It was unheard of in a warsub. The crew likely ridiculed it, especially after he'd forced them to move it in, but he didn't care. There were other, more important things on his mind. There was a large viewport in the bulkhead, comfortable couches, and even a wider bunk than was standard. Compared to other Captain's cabins in the RSF, it was palatial, to match the rest of the vessel. Nothing could be small on this ship, he thought.

The engineers had agreed with him.

He'd been following Truman McClusky's path over the past twenty-four hours and wanted nothing more than to throw all the planning aside to just kill the man. Surely his crew and *Voskhod* were more than capable of doing it. They had the 467 kph dreadnought, which outclassed McClusky's pitiful seacar in every way. SCAV torpedoes, mines, the Tsunami Plow . . . they could outrun, outgun, and ram the insectoid-like craft into pulverized metal and leave it sinking to the bottom in an instant.

Still . . .

Still, Ventinov understood there was a reason why he was doing things differently this time. He had plotted a revenge for the Mayor, instead of diving in headlong and hoping for an easy kill. McClusky had proven himself more than capable of avoiding death on many occasions now. Instead, the Captain had laid a trap for the man, a path which he was now on, and from which there was no escape. He'd left his mining base, The Complex, and traveled at full SCAV drive for Blue Downs, seemingly without a care in the world. Full speed, damn the sonar signature. The RSF support team had followed him without any difficulty. True, they'd had to maintain the same speed to keep up with him, and in the process revealed their own position and presence, but the team had felt it necessary.

They were an RSF kill squad, elite forces trained in underwater combat. They knew that The Steel Shiv was involved and also hunting McClusky, but they didn't know The Shiv's identity. No one did.

Not even Ventinov.

The Shiv always wore that damned helmet with the voice-distorting tech. He kept his identity a secret from everyone on the planet.

The RSF kill squad was in a Triestrian vessel that had once belonged to Cliff Sim. He'd used it on his path to The Facility in Ventinov's first attempt to trap the Mayor. Instead The Shiv had killed the American colony's CSO. It was a *Sword* Class vessel, and they'd altered the sound signature so no sonar could identify it. They'd been following McClusky, had infiltrated Blue Downs easily, and had killed yet another Triestrian at Ventinov's command.

The more angry McClusky grew, the less capable. His thinking would grow cloudy from anger. He would barrel along the path like an angry dog in a China shop, throw caution to the wind, and make himself an easy target.

At least, that was the plan.

And now he knew about the citric acid.

Ventinov had played a role in the death of two people in McClusky's life. The mayor had discovered the clues, and now he was en route to the final location.

The Facility.

The same place where Cliff Sim had died.

Now it was Truman McClusky's turn.

And Ventinov would kill as many of McClusky's family and comrades as possible.

Then, and only then, Ventinov would turn *Voskhod* to the west, meet up with the other two RSF vessels, and destroy Trieste.

The comm beeped and Ventinov bent to it. On the screen was an elderly Chinese woman, the Chief Administrator of the graphene-layering plant located in The Iron Plains. The CSF had allowed Ventinov to use it for his plans, but they had no idea for what purpose. The administrator, Zhao Lin, was not happy.

"Captain Ventinov. Please explain exactly what is going on." She spoke in Mandarin, and the built-in translator changed her words to perfect Russian.

"Your country told you to cooperate with me, did they not?"

"Yes." Her eyes were cold; she was clearly not happy about this fact. "And I have."

"I appreciate it."

She sighed. "The first body was concerning. We followed all instructions perfectly. We allowed the man to enter. We then allowed a second man to enter. We kept that area of The Facility on lockdown. But I didn't agree to murder. He left a body for us to deal with. An American, no less. Should they find out, it would cause problems between our nations, and we have enough of those already."

"Yes, I know." *I ordered it*, Ventinov felt like bragging.

"Things could have gotten far worse than they did. We dumped the body outside to let the wildlife take care of it. But this facility is not to be used for games—"

"These are hardly games," Ventinov snapped. His tone was steel.

"They *are.* We are a manufacturing facility, working to better China's position in the oceans, not just in The Iron Plains. We can't have strangers infiltrating and fighting in our corridors."

"You're helping Russia right now. You're strengthening ties—"

"With you, the man who sunk sixty-three CSF warsubs? Then more over the Kermadec Trench?" She leaned forward. Her face was stern, and her eyes had matched Ventinov's expression. "Before *Drakon* sunk into the trench, imploding and taking hundreds of RSF sailors to their deaths. Am I correct?"

Ventinov clenched a fist, just out of view of the camera. This damn woman. How dare she say such a thing? But inside he knew that he would never live it down.

And it was all Truman McClusky's fault.

But he also knew that he needed her support. McClusky was on his way. Then again, sometimes power was the way to go. Threats and violence worked, especially with a four-hundred-metre vessel backing you up.

"You are helping strengthen ties with us," he finally grated. "And you will continue to do so, or *Voskhod* will destroy your precious facility too."

Zhao Lin paused and stared at the camera. "So. This is your strategy. Threaten us into submission. But you give us nothing. Your only purpose is to use us."

"I give you your lives. Never forget that."

"You've been quite clear." She leaned back and glared at him, but said no more in response.

Ventinov took a deep breath to control his anger. "In a few hours a vessel will approach The Facility from the south. People from it will debark and enter via an airlock."

"The same one as the other man?" She had given in to the inevitable now.

Ventinov shrugged. "I don't know. Let them enter. Shut down that section and we'll take care of the rest."

She shook her head. "So, another body, is it?"

"Maybe more than one."

"For us to clean up for you. So kind."

"I told you, your reward will be more than worth it."

"Reward? You call threats a *reward*?"

"View it any way you want. Be happy you have a life."

And he slammed his fist on the disconnect call button. Her image faded to black.

—••—

CHIEF ADMINISTRATOR ZHAO LIN STARED at the blank screen. Inside, she was furious, but she tried her best to disguise her emotions. The Russian Captain, Ventinov—a national failure from all reports—was walking over them as if they didn't exist. Normally it was only her own superiors on the mainland who treated her in such a way. Their people were used to it. After all, they were producing sheets of graphene-layered titanium for the CSF, and it was their purpose on the Pacific seafloor. She expected the treatment from them. But her people had succeeded at that mission. They'd established The Facility, perfected the process—thanks to her engineers—and were churning out titanium sheets with a one-centimetre sheet of graphene coating, each made up of thirty million layers of single atom-thick honeycomb lattice. They'd spent years perfecting the technology, only to now have to deal with ridiculous demands by failed Russian Captains.

She wondered why her own superiors would give in to Russians.

Beside her sat her executive assistant, just off camera. He had viewed the entire exchange. "That was interesting," he muttered. "And annoying."

"It was." She sighed. "So. Another stranger will be arriving at The Facility. Make the arrangements. We have to protect the process."

"I don't think we have to worry much about it, if the same sequence of events happens. It's just an irritation."

She considered that. "It's dangerous. The Facility is secret. We can't allow people to discover what we're doing."

"You don't know if people are aware."

She frowned. "Think about it for a minute. Ventinov is using us to attract his victims. What do you think he's using to get them here?"

His face showed shock. "You think the Russian has told people what we're doing here?"

"To get them to come. It's possible. Our secrets are a powerful target. We're on the forefront of mineral exploitation. China will win the race to scoop the nodules from the seafloor. From the *entire* deep abyssal plains. The others won't have a hope, without the graphene layering. We can't involve ourselves in these pitiful games."

He stared at her. "What are you suggesting?"

She shrugged. "If they all died this time, what would happen?"

"You're suggesting killing them all? Even the Russian spy?"

"Why not? Flood the corridors, crush them. Protect the rest of The Facility. Ventinov will think they died in their private little war. Meanwhile, we'll keep knowledge of our location from escaping. Maybe it'll end there."

He continued to stare at Zhao. Surprise painted his face. "But you're talking about murder. And betraying Russia."

"I don't think it's Russia. I think it's one man. His superiors are likely humoring him, and he's obsessed with revenge." Then she swore. "And it's not murder, Yan! It's protecting our national secrets. It's patriotic. We're fighting a war, and I need to protect the process. We have over 300 people here, and all of them are counting on us." She stared off into the distance, mulling it over. Then she nodded to herself. "Yes. Flood them, kill them. It'll work." She jerked her gaze to Yan. "Prepare the trap. For the Russian as well as the Americans."

| | |
|---|---|
| Location: | Latitude: Unknown<br>Longitude: Unknown<br>Somewhere in the Pacific Ocean |
| Depth: | Unknown |
| Date: | 12 June 2131 |
| Time: | 1853 hours |

INSIDE *SC-1*, THE STEEL SHIV waited patiently.

They were shooting into the Pacific now, back to The Facility, where earlier The Shiv had beaten Cliff Sim in hand-to-hand combat. This would be no different. They would enter the underwater manufacturing structure the same way, and then The Steel Shiv would make an appearance.

The only issue was that there would be more than one person to beat this time. Somehow, The Shiv had to manipulate Truman McClusky to enter the structure by himself. If more than one entered, The Shiv would have to kill them all. There was no possibility of letting witnesses escape. *Maintain your identity.* Keep the secret.

Already others were talking about The Shiv. The entire Russian Submarine Fleet seemed to know. Ventinov had spread the news to increase his own reputation in the Fleet, after the debacle over the Kermadec Trench.

Figured.

The Shiv wondered if after all this was done, Ventinov could die as well.

Secrets needed to be kept, after all.

*SC-1* plowed quickly through the waters. It was amazing technology, really. McClusky had pioneered it all, thanks to his scientists and engineers at Trieste. There were also the anechoic tiles, a camouflage from sonar. And Syntactic Foam, to resist ocean pressure. The Acoustic Pulse Drive, to descend farther than five kilometres. The Isomer Bomb. The SCAV drive. The Neutral Particle Beam, stolen only a few weeks ago and already in place around Trieste. And now he had his sights on the process to stack single-atom layers of graphene, pioneered and perfected by China. But as with all the other inventions, Truman McClusky had a way of learning about them, discovering their locations, and stealing them.

It was why Trieste had prospered in the world's oceans, while the surface nations struggled to withstand climate change. They were putting their energies into mitigating the inevitable, while the ocean colonies were forging ahead and designing new technologies, for the future.

The Shiv knew McClusky was a pioneer. Perhaps the greatest one, ever. It would hurt to kill him. It would alter human history, and for that, The Shiv did feel some remorse. Still, it was a job.

The Shiv had never failed.

Events at Blue Downs had proceeded as expected. The Russian support team had infiltrated and killed the Triestrian, Grant Bell. The Shiv knew of his presence there, and simply passed along the intel. It had been a perfect distraction, and it pulled some attention away from McClusky's suspects. Still, The Shiv knew that the Mayor suspected one of the three as being the assassin. The Shiv couldn't keep the secret much longer.

The revelation was coming, and soon.

And Mac would die.

# Part Five:
## Encounter with *Sword*

# Chapter Twenty

THIS WAS IT. THE INVESTOR was using Agricultural Dome #28 to grow a crop to create citric acid. They likely used a company in the manufacturing sector to process it. Then they shipped it to the graphene-layering facility.

I only needed to find where the acid was going, and I could track it to the facility.

And find out where The Shiv killed Cliff.

Johnny signaled me at that moment. I accepted the call and said, "Tell me you found Tsim."

"He's not talking."

"Tell him you know about the citric acid."

"What?"

"It's how they're layering the graphene."

There was a long pause. "I'll try. Should I kill him?"

I glanced at Sahar and hesitated, but only for an instant. "Just threaten. If he knows that we already know, he'll talk just to get you off his back."

A minute of silence passed. Then another. I clenched a fist. We needed this information. We needed to steal the graphene . . .

Johnny came back on the line. He stumbled over his words, then swore. "How'd you know, Mac?"

I ignored it. "We need to know where he's shipping it."

"Already got that info."

Swallowing a cry of triumph, I said, "Bring everyone back to the seacar. We have to leave immediately."

I was still standing against the viewport and staring out into the waters of the Bass Strait. Behind me, Sahar Noor was speaking with citizens and talking about her life in politics and the struggles for independence. She emphasized the need to do so peacefully. Some of the citizens disagreed with her, but she spoke clearly of appealing to the good people of the world, convincing them of the colonies' needs to expand peacefully and *profitably*. It was the only way to save humanity, she said. Under the thumb of dictators, it could never happen. But peacefully, for profit, they would harvest more resources at faster rates than ever before. Cities like Blue Downs, Trieste, and Churchill Sands would be at the forefront of colonization and exploitation, and humanity would only benefit.

I watched in surprise as the people she spoke to listened calmly, raised a few objections, but eventually agreed with her. She had a special quality to her; it was obvious. She could not only lead people, she could *change* people for the better.

Lifting the PCD to my mouth, I said, "Meet at *SC-1*. We're leaving."

An hour later, we were in *SC-1* and at full speed back to The Iron Plains. We knew the location, thanks to the clues in AD #28, but there was still more to do.

We now had to prepare to infiltrate The Facility, steal the process, and expose The Shiv.

The biggest problem was that I still didn't know who it was. The three had been with Renée during their tour, when someone had killed Grant. Tahnee was looking at the video surveillance, and would contact me as soon as she knew, but The Shiv would never give himself up via video surveillance. He was too smart for that.

I knew it had likely been someone else, a third party. Hired to make me look the other way. That's what had happened in the agricultural sector, after all. A hired hand to attack. A simple distraction.

I felt bad about killing the guy, especially while explaining to Sahar, but it had been either him or me. No choice.

"Why is China using an Australian colony?" Renée asked. "They have their own cities."

I considered it. "Blue Downs was under construction. They needed a place to grow and produce the acid. The dome was easy to rent. Plus, with all the difficulties they've been having with their own colonies . . ."

Min Lee said, "They could arrange a place that was nearby and would only cost a rental fee. The problem was Tsim Lui . . . he was a weak spot in the chain."

"Maybe," I said.

Windsor said, "Seems fishy, actually."

"How so?" Min asked.

"Kind of easy. The tip to Dome #28. Then the lemons and limes." He shrugged. "Cliff would have figured it out easily too, wouldn't he?"

"We had the benefit of having his communication log," I said. "He had to do the research on his own." Still, the Brit made a good point.

We were in the seating area. I studied the three of them sitting there, together: Min Lee, Windsor, Sidra.

Things were growing more complicated, and not getting easier, I thought.

And then Kristen Canvel contacted me again. I made my way back to the pilot compartment and slid in next to Johnny. She said, "Look, Mac. You need to think about coming back here. The fleet is enormous."

"Bigger than when we last spoke?"

"Substantially. Many other nations have thrown in with the superpowers." Her face was pale and her eyes wide.

"What are you saying? How many—"

"Over a thousand now."

That stopped me. "Small craft, or—"

"Warsubs. Huge. They are not going to let this happen, Mac. They won't let Oceania split from the mother nations."

I sighed and sat back in my chair. "We've planned for this. We knew it was going to happen. What's going on in the Trench?"

"Forces are building there too."

"Numbers?"

"Hundreds. But still."

That was our plan. It was in motion, and hopefully would surprise the coalition forces.

"The others keep calling for you. They don't know why you won't respond."

"What are you telling them?"

"That you're on a mission. You'll call when you can."

"Good. That works. Are all our defences ready?"

"Yes, but Renée is in charge of them, and she's not here either!"

I swore. Things were building, and the battle was just around the corner. But I couldn't abandon our current plans just yet.

"I'll keep it in mind," I muttered.

She stared at me for a long moment. She knew I was just putting her off. I could see the disappointment in her face. Leadership was tough sometimes, and right now, she was in charge. I knew she could handle it. I also realized I was putting her in an uncomfortable situation.

"Is there anything else?" I asked.

"There is something. I've managed to get some more information about those names you sent me."

That made me perk up. "Anything important?"

"Maybe." She pursed her lips. "I'm pursuing something. I'll send it to you, marked as URGENT when I know for sure."

"Sounds good. I'll be in touch soon, and we'll return as soon as possible, I promise. I won't leave you hanging there by yourself."

"And the others?"

"I'll reach out to them too."

That seemed to placate her. For the moment, anyway. She exhaled. "Good enough. I'll let them know."

We signed off and I considered her news. Something was coming, shortly. Something that could explain this mystery we were involved in.

"Don't worry," Johnny said. "We'll get back before the battle. The storm is worse than what we expected."

"How bad?"

"I've been monitoring it. It's a Cat Six, but it's been more destructive than anything in recent history. It stalled for a bit over the coastline. It's really wreaking havoc."

"Shore defences?"

"Obliterated. The flooding is ongoing and there's no sign of it stopping. The waves have shattered coast walls in some places. The Corps of Engineers is moving equipment in, but they can't get there yet because of the storm."

And in the meantime, the flooding would continue moving inland, displacing millions of people.

Global warming was an enemy for which there was no counterattack possible. Only defence and mitigation. It was an unstoppable force.

And the result?

Flooded shorelines. Famine. Dead crops. Severe storms.

Death. Refugees. Swarms of homeless people.

Rebellion. Dictators. War.

Johnny said, "Our companion is back."

I stared at the sonar. "Matching course and speed?"

"He's catching up to us. He's on an intercept."

The mystery vessel was making a move. Inside, I was quivering. The ship was superior to ours. We were already at max velocity. I still didn't know the model or make, but there were very few nations with SCAV vessels in the oceans. I knew the USSF and CSF had some now—the *Hunter-Killers*—but this was not one of those. If they had SCAV torpedoes, we'd have to somehow avoid them while attempting to take the vessel out.

And, I realized with a thud in my chest, if we sustained damage, or lost our own drive, then we'd never get back to the Atlantic in time.

The attack on Trieste would happen without me there to coordinate and lead.

We had a full complement of torpedoes—ten—and countermeasures. Five of our torpedoes were conventional only, meaning a top speed of just eighty kph. The other five were SCAV, however, and could travel over 1,000 kph. We were in the Coral Sea and approaching the Solomon Islands. I wondered if geography could help us here. Perhaps a trench could allow us to go deeper and shoot torpedoes up at him, protected by our greater Crush Depth?

We were at full speed, but the other ship was slightly faster. They were behind us, glowing white on the sonar screen, a flare in the darkness and a warning sign of what was coming. There was no hiding that kind of noise, and there was no stealth involved in such an attack.

They meant to kill us.

The others realized what was happening. The alarm was ringing, for the computer algorithms had recognized an intercept course, and was warning us of a potential collision or perhaps worse. I thumbed it off and stared at the callout identification on the screen.

```
Class: Unknown
Speed: 460 kph
Depth: 200 m
Bearing: 193°
```

Requesting more information on the contact, the callout label expanded with columns displaying length, width, beam, Crush Depth, max speed, and so on. There was no information yet, as the computer did not recognize the signal. Not only that, the other boat's SCAV drive was so loud that nothing other than position, speed, depth, and course was available. If they slowed to conventional screws, we'd be able to determine more information about her, but not just yet.

On my canopy, the VID system projected all objects within a five-kilometre radius. I glanced back to where the enemy contact would be, but there was only a bright white glow. The system didn't yet know what the vessel looked like, even though it was within the effective range.

While I was looking backward, I noted Sahar in the living area. She was watching me, and I said, "I think they mean to fire on us."

"Then we don't have a choice."

"But Sahar, the people on that warsub will die. Are you okay with that?"

She paused, glancing at the others in the area. Everyone was there. "They are making a choice. I only ask that you don't shoot first."

Min Lee called forward to us, "Johnny, can you speak with them? Will they talk?"

"Nothing yet," he replied. "They're coming for us, though. We'll have to communicate somehow, soon."

I keyed the comm. "Attention SCAV vessel approaching from bearing 193. State your intentions."

Nothing.

I said again, "If you do not respond, we will interpret that as an act of aggression. We'll fire on you. State your intentions, immediately."

"Mac," Sahar whispered.

"I'm just trying to get him to respond."

I pulled back on the throttle to decrease speed. The thunder of the SCAV receded and our velocity fell quickly. The contact matched the change, slowing their approach. Their noise receded, and I kept my eye on the sonar.

Our speed continued to slow. The bubble surrounding *SC-1* receded. "Everyone sit down, get ready for a jolt!" I called. Falling from SCAV back to conventional drive could knock people flat on their asses.

The callout display finally started showing some details about the vessel, now that it was quieter and our computer could interpret the sonar data coming back to us. It had a double vent at the rear for steam exhaust. The horizontal stabilizers were slightly longer than ours on *SC-1*, at about four metres, the top of the hull was flatter, the bow for supercavitation that created the SCAV bubble was similar to ours, and the total length was approximately twenty metres. It was more of a seacar than a warsub, but the similarities to *SC-1* were obvious.

My throat went dry. I knew what vessel this was.

"Oh my god," I said.

"What is it?" Renée asked.

"It's not what I expected." I'd thought this was a new vessel that one of the superpowers had created and put to sea to patrol The Iron Plains or defend their claims in the ocean. But no. It was far, far worse.

The sonar should have recognized it earlier. It didn't, which meant someone had deliberately changed its acoustic signature.

It was a *Sword* Class vessel. One of ours.

Or, to be more precise, it had belonged to Cliff Sim.

This was the vessel he'd used to find the Chinese Facility.

I told the others and silence met my statement at first. Then Min Lee said, "Are you sure?"

"Yes. The sonar information is now pretty clear. Plus it's on the VID system. I can see the shape of the hull, projected on the canopy. It's a *Sword*."

"But how do you know it's Cliff's?"

That stopped me. "His was the only vessel out this way. He's dead, which means his killer—"

I choked the thought off immediately. Could The Steel Shiv be on that ship?

She said, "Don't forget the vessel Johnny and I came in. We left it at The Complex. Maybe this is it?"

"Someone has altered this vessel's signature. The sound of the SCAV is different."

"That would take engineering," Meg interjected. "To alter the shape of the exhaust vents, the intake vents, the shape of the thruster pods. It would take time."

Five days had passed since Cliff's death. More than enough time.

"But why would they change it?" Min Lee continued.

"To disguise themselves. To confuse us." I stared at Johnny. He seemed perplexed at her statements too. Was she trying to protect them?

"It's the people who killed Cliff," I snapped. "They mean to take us prisoner, or they'll shoot to kill." I pointed at the sonar. "They won't respond and they're on an intercept." They'd maintained a consistently higher speed than ours on their approach.

"But still," she said. "You can't assume they're the killer or killers. Maybe they just found the vessel."

Johnny said, "It's true, Mac. If Cliff left it at The Facility, then they'd take it. They wouldn't give that technology away." He was defending Min Lee, his wife.

"Someone murdered Cliff. That's his vessel. Put two and two together."

"I'm just saying that we can't assume."

"I won't fire unless they do first," I muttered.

The sonar rang and my eyes shot to it.

*Torpedo shutters open.*

Oh, shit.

# Chapter Twenty-One

*Sword* Class vessels exceeded our capabilities in every way. They were essentially copies of my own seacar, though improved. The double vent exhaust, for instance. The slightly wider thruster pod placement. The flatter hull. It all improved performance. Deeper, faster, and more agile.

This was going to depend on the pilot.

In my heart, I knew The Shiv was not on that vessel. He wouldn't attack like this. He preferred hand to hand, so he could take his photos and release them to the world.

There was no honour in pressing a button to fire a torpedo.

It wasn't sporting enough for him.

The alarm was still ringing and I slammed the throttle back to full power. "Hang on!" I bellowed. Behind me, I heard people scrambling into chairs or the couches. Banking the vessel to the port, I triggered our own torpedo shutter open and prepared a SCAV torpedo, set to HOMING.

On the sonar, the vessel matched my maneuver. Its speed was greater, though, and the turn even tighter.

*Fuck.*

"Get countermeasures ready," I said to Johnny.

"Do you want to just fire and escape while they're avoiding the torps?"

I hesitated. It was a good strategy, but I didn't want to do it. "They have a higher speed. They'll run us down. We have to end this, now."

"Are you sure? Torpedoes will distract them. Then we'll find a place to set down, wait it out."

"There's no time. We have to finish this and get back to Trieste."

"Then let's fire now and circle back to take him out." He reached for the FIRE button—

"No!" I snapped. "Not yet."

He stared at me in horror. "Mac, are you—"

I banked the other way—to starboard now—and pushed the nose down. Deeper was better. It would minimize any detonations; the pressure waves would be less dangerous.

It was a double-edged sword though, for while depth would confine the explosions and make them less destructive, the pressure would be greater and therefore minor flaws or cracks in a hull could result in a faster implosion.

The sonar *shrieked.*

Torpedo in the water!

"Dammit!" Johnny snapped.

"Fire back!" I screamed.

"Finally," he hissed. He pressed the button.

Our torpedo whined angrily as it soared from our bow, like an excited dog anxious for freedom. It matched our turn and angled backward, toward the *Sword*—

I banked again the opposite direction and watched the enemy torpedo on the sonar. It was red on the screen, and its speed had shot up rapidly. It was already at 800 kph and climbing.

It was a SCAV weapon, like ours.

*Shit shit shit shit!*

"Countermeasures!" I cried.

The churning devices dropped from the hull and remained in place, spinning, screeching, and attracting as much attention as possible. Bubbles soared upwards, but the neutral buoyancy of the devices kept them hovering in place. I maintained our course, keeping the countermeasures between us and the torpedo, and it headed straight for them.

The torpedo was basically an underwater missile. It burned rocket fuel and liquid oxygen together, hammering the fuselage through the water. Supercavitation at its bow generated a bubble that stretched back and encased the entire weapon. It was now at 1,000 kph and still accelerating.

Shit. It was one of our torpedoes, I realized. They were trying to kill us with our own seacar and our own torpedoes! It was infuriating.

"Fire again," I said. "Homing."

I stared at the sonar. The enemy torpedo had reached the countermeasure cloud, a frothing white mass on the screen.

It detonated. The explosion shook *SCAV-1* and I gripped the yoke tighter. My fingers were sweaty. A second concussion ripped out as the ocean fell into the collapsing void of vaporized water.

Our two torpedoes were still out there, circling.

I turned us around, headed right back to the enemy ship.

He fired again, straight for us.

The alarm pierced the cabin. Behind me, I heard cursing. They knew what was happening, and were interpreting the battle from our comments and the various alarms.

Then another alarm, overlapping the first.

There were now four torpedoes in the water: two of ours, and two of theirs. Ours were green on the display, and would not detonate near us.

"Drop more countermeasures, Johnny. We'll lead their weapons right through them."

"They're double our speed though, Mac."

"I know," I grunted. They were closing on us, falling on our tail, and I took my eyes off the enemy seacar. I began to turn *SC-1* from side to side, weaving back and forth. Each turn forced the weapons to adjust their own course, slowing them slightly. I angled toward the frothing cloud of bubbles and sound.

"Keep your eyes on them," I said.

"They're running from our torpedoes too."

"Are they dropping countermeasures?"

"No."

That made me frown. It made no sense, unless they just weren't familiar with underwater combat.

We blew right through the mass of countermeasures—there were now multiple devices in the same location, sirens calling to sonars like magnets pulling in steel filaments—and then I immediately pulled back on the throttle and brought us to a stop. The bubble receded instantly and we hit the water; friction stopped us almost like a wall. I slammed forward, the shoulder straps snapping tight on me.

Johnny grunted and there were a few cries from behind. I hoped everyone was okay. Windsor was on the deck, swearing, and Sidra was supporting his sister to keep her from falling. Meg helped Windsor up, and the two sat together, gripping each other.

The weapons closed on the countermeasures . . .

I didn't want to move far away, otherwise the weapon's onboard computers would recognize us and lock onto the seacar instead of the countermeasures. It couldn't "see" us now—since we were on the other side of the cloud—and both weapons detonated.

Simultaneously, I rammed the throttle forward and the eruption thrust *SC-1* ahead, through the water. Now the acceleration slammed us the other way, and I hurtled back, into the chair, grunting from the impact.

Our SCAV stuttered, and my heart skipped a beat. If our drive went down, it was all over for us, as well as for Trieste . . .

Searching the sonar, I located the other ship.

Our two torpedoes had detonated nearby. The concussions were visible on the screen, but fading rapidly. The *Sword*'s SCAV was down, and she was drifting, listing to the side.

She was out of commission.

—••—

We pulled up next to her. The sonar was blinking for attention. There were a variety of alerts, the most obvious of which was the sound of flooding from the *Sword*. The next was a warning of loud voices. There was yelling on board.

There was more than one person on that vessel, which told me something very important.

It was not The Shiv. He worked alone. He would not be with others.

Johnny said, eyeing our position, "It's dangerous, Mac. Should they fire again, or detonate their own vessel, it could take us with them."

"We have a chance to get some valuable information."

He looked horrified. "You want to go over there?" He pointed at the sonar. "We're at 2,300 and going down. Rate of descent is increasing. The flooding is getting worse over there. That ship is gone, Mac."

"Which means I have to do this now." I bolted to my feet, throwing the safety straps aside. "Get the umbilical connected."

Renée said, "Mac! Don't be brash."

I rushed past the group in the living compartment. The scuba gear was next to the airlock, and I threw on a tank and a full face mask over my clothes.

*No time for a wetsuit.*

The pressure was too great outside for my mix, too. It was *enormous*. But inside a flooding vessel, it'd be fine.

Until it was full of water, that is.

I had only a few minutes.

I flashed a glance at Renée and Meg. "I'll be okay. Get ready to run in case it's a trap."

"But what are you hoping—" Renée started.

I slammed my fist on the airlock's CYCLE button. "Sorry, Renée," I blurted as the hatch slammed shut. "No time!" The umbilical was stretched taut already against the other hull, but we were falling into the depths quickly, and the rate was increasing, as Johnny had promised.

I swallowed past my dry throat.

I practically fell out of the airlock into the umbilical. Once I opened the other airlock, I knew the water flooding the *Sword* would spill into our own umbilical and threaten to bring *SC-1* down too. I had no idea what was going on in the other vessel, or even how many people were there.

There was a noise behind me and I spun to look. It was Sidra, also in a mask. He flashed me a grin, and he gripped a needle gun. "Let's do this," he said.

I opened the airlock, and we lurched into the small chamber. The vessel was at a vicious list, however, and it was hard to maintain our balance. I pushed the EMERG OPEN button and the interior hatch slid aside, but only part way. Water *poured* out from the ship and immediately half-filled the airlock. The umbilical sagged under its weight, and the green saltwater churned toward *SC-1* and slammed against the inner airlock hatch.

Shit. The group inside our seacar would have felt that.

I poked my head through the hatch, into the *Sword*, and a gunshot rang out.

I jerked back, pulled my own weapon, and plunged below the surface of the water, which was at chest level. The needle gun had a square barrel and shot stainless steel needles. It was a deadly weapon, especially under water. I peered down the seacar's long cabin, toward the bow, and the direction the gunshot had come from. There were two figures there, in the living area, facing my direction. I didn't think.

I was in survival mode.

It was them or me.

Don't think, Mac—just *live*.

I fired. One series of needles at the first target, another at the second. The tiny spears lanced out, impossible to see in the dim light and due to the speed they traveled, but the shock as the water moved aside was barely perceptible. Tiny concussion waves radiated outward as the needles arrowed toward two sets of legs—

And hit their targets. The two instantly dropped into the water, writhing in pain.

Clouds of blood spurted out.

Sidra followed me, firing backup shots. The interior was more than three-quarters flooded, tilted to the side, and it was a chaotic scene. Blue pressure warning lights were flashing, the regular lighting was strobing as the power failed, alarms were piercing the cabin, and there were screams from the two who'd just gone down.

They were Russians.

They were gurgling now, their faces half submerged as they choked and drowned.

There was another in the pilot cabin, slumped in his chair and strapped in place. There was a large impact wound on his forehead; a concussion from a torpedo had slammed his head into the bulkhead at his side. There was blood there, too.

I spun quickly backward. "There might be more here," I said.

Johnny's voice fluttered in my ear. "Mac, the depth is too great, the umbilical is full. It can't handle this stress! Get back here, now! They're sinking fast!"

"You're telling me," I muttered. The water was lapping at the ceiling, and there was very little air in the cabin left. "Sidra, look at the bodies! Grab anything you can." Searching frantically, I tore through the living cabin. Underwater, I hunted for anything that might be a clue or of value.

Then I saw it.

On the deck, against the bulkhead, pushed against some pipes welded to the walls. A PCD. I grabbed it and shoved it into a pocket. The screen was cracked, so I didn't know if the damage had ruined it beyond repair, but I was sure we could retrieve some information.

Sidra appeared beside me. "There were only three on board. All dead now."

I stared at him. The two had drowned, and we had no time to drag them to our seacar.

"Let's get out of here," I said.

Water filled the tunnel and it was on a severe upward angle. Johnny was barely able to keep up with the rate of descent. We couldn't run. We swam toward *SC-1*'s airlock.

A dull pressure in my ear suddenly began amping up. Within seconds the pain had turned to a sharp, spiking agony.

The pressure was rising.

Water now completely filled the vessel, and the ocean pressure increased rapidly.

Sidra was still in the umbilical. I was in *SC-1*'s airlock and I reached back for him. "Sidra! Grab my hand!"

He reached out. The *Sword* shuddered and fell away abruptly. The umbilical split and the vessel dropped downward. Shreds of the umbilical still connected us, and Sidra swam frantically, now virtually straight up, to get back to *SC-1*. His face was a grimace of agony as the pressure hit him full on.

Behind him, the ruined vessel plummeted into the dark depths, blue lights still flashing, casting him in an ethereal glow.

I grabbed his hand and hauled him up, into the airlock, then slammed a fist on the CYCLE button.

The hatch shut. The water drained—

And we fell against the bulkhead, gasping in shock.

# Chapter Twenty-Two

THE *SWORD* PLUMMETED TO THE depths, spiraling as it sank and taking three Russian soldiers with it. The strike team had been small, but they'd likely been the ones who'd killed Grant Bell in Blue Downs. They'd been following us since we'd left The Complex, and now they were gone.

Once back in *SC-1*, I changed into dry pants and a black t-shirt and settled into the pilot cabin. Johnny watched me; his expression was curious.

"What did you find?" he asked.

"They wore the same uniforms we saw on *Drakon*."

"The dreadnought." He sighed. "So. Ventinov sent them after us. Or you."

"Along with The Shiv. Seems likely."

"Maybe more will show up. I just hope we have the balls to take them out when they do."

I studied his expression, then turned and shut the hatch between us and the living area. "Look, Johnny. I'm doing what I have to. Please back me up here."

His eyes flashed. "What if backing you up means my death? And Min Lee's? I'm not going to let us both go down with you."

He'd practically snarled his answer. This was not the Johnny I knew. He was being antagonistic and questioning my actions, even if it was just the look in his eyes. I knew him *that* well. I said, "I'm trying to figure out what's going on here. We also have to keep the alliance together."

He looked perplexed. "What's that supposed to mean? If there's a ship out there meaning to take us out, then we have to take it out first."

He was referring to my hesitation to fire. "We can't. I had to wait for them to fire."

"Why? Because of an allegiance to Sahar Noor? You're going to put us at risk for her?"

"It wasn't to put us at risk. It was to make sure they actually meant to kill us, before I killed them. There are certain things we have to protect here. Our treaty with Churchill Sands is one of them."

"Even if it means death?"

"It doesn't, though. We won the battle."

"We were lucky, Mac. That seacar was better than this one."

"With an inferior crew who weren't familiar with it. And a lucky shot that hurt the pilot."

"It's not just me I'm concerned about."

I sighed. "I realize that. I'm trying to figure out what's going on with these three on board. Something's fishy, and I can't—"

"Don't say it. You don't think Min Lee means to hurt you? Still?"

"I'm just trying to figure out the mystery. She's a part of it."

"We've had this talk before. She arrived at Trieste when everything started going down. But we'd planned it to coincide with the storm, Mac."

"So her arrival was just coincidence."

"No. She came when you declared independence. That's as simple as it gets."

"And Sidra, and Windsor?"

"I don't care about either of them. Only Min and protecting our lives here, with you."

"Johnny." I leaned back and took a breath. I had to tell him, in order for him to understand what I was doing. There was no other way. "I told you that Russia—Ventinov—is trying to kill me to get revenge for what we did. He's going to take out the entire city too."

"I know."

"And he's using The Steel Shiv to do it."

"Some people may think that. You told me this earlier. It might not be true."

I stared at him in shock. "Who could have beaten Cliff in a hand-to-hand fight? It was The Shiv."

"It might still just be myth. A rumor." He shrugged and stared at me.

"And right when it all starts, three operatives show up within hours of each other."

He frowned. "What are you saying?"

"One of them is The Shiv, Johnny."

---

HIS MOUTH FELL OPEN. "ARE you crazy? I knew you suspected them of helping the Russians, or The Shiv, but you think one of them is actually—"

"*Think* about it. Ventinov shows up with rumors of The Shiv. Someone kills Cliff and sends photos of his corpse around, in exactly the way The Shiv always does. Then those three show up. Good operatives aren't just killers. They *infiltrate*. They get inside and pick the enemy apart *from within*. They embed with the enemy to discover the best time to kill. The best method of attacking. You know the intelligence community. You've never doubted it before."

"Still."

"I know you want to protect Min Lee, but she's a suspect. I want all three with us, close by, so we can watch them."

He processed what I was saying. "You're trying to keep your enemies closer. Even if one is *The Steel Shiv*?"

"Exactly."

He shook his head. "Min Lee is not a Russian agent."

"And what about Sidra Noor and William Windsor?"

"Neither seems Russian."

"And that's the beauty of it. They have perfect disguises." I said before he could respond, "*All three of them*."

His face twisted in a flash of uncharacteristic rage. "She's a Chinese operative working in Sheng City. She's not working for Ventinov. She's not Russian."

"It would be a perfect disguise," I said. "Look at it objectively. She shows up at Trieste right as a saboteur cuts our power. She's got a mysterious past. We don't know what she was doing before she arrived. She might have killed Cliff."

"She doesn't have a mysterious past!" He was growing angry now. "She's my wife! I've known her for close to ten years!"

"You've been in Trieste for some of that time. The recent two years, anyway. Does she talk about her missions?"

He snorted. "You know what this work is like. You can't talk about your missions."

"Exactly." I stared at him. "Exactly. You *don't know what she's been doing.*"

"But I know she's not a Russian agent!"

"I'm just trying to figure out which of the three is. *One of them is.*"

"Not Min Lee."

I hesitated. "I'm just asking you—*again*—to be objective, Johnny." I gestured at the controls, more as a reminder of the battle that we'd just endured. "You heard what she was asking. She wanted us to talk. She was trying to protect the people in that *Sword.*"

"So was Sahar."

"You were angry a minute ago about Sahar. Now you're protecting Min Lee for doing the same."

"She just wanted to make sure we'd try to communicate with them. That's all."

"Even though they were on an intercept course, with torpedo shutters open?"

"You were defending pausing just a minute ago too," he said, though his protests were weaker now.

"To keep Sahar in the alliance, I had to wait until they fired first. I understand where she's coming from. It's her philosophy, her culture. Her very way of life. But Min Lee?" I shook my head. "I just don't understand what she was doing."

He leaned back and closed his eyes, considering it. "I think she was just trying to make sure, that's all."

"Possibly. But she's a suspect. I'm trying to figure this out. We're heading for a Chinese facility where The Shiv killed Cliff. The Chinese and Russians *are* working together. And Min Lee is Chinese."

He remained quiet for a while longer. "What are you planning?" He was calmer now.

I sighed. "I have to get them out of here. Into The Facility to steal the graphene-layering process. Once we're over there, one of them will make their attempt. Then we'll know."

He seemed horrified. "You're going to offer yourself up as bait? A trap?"

"That's what this entire thing is, Johnny. A trap."

He frowned. "What? You mean the graphene?"

"I think the graphene is really there. The citric acid is part of the chain. But the tip to Coda Rose, the clues at Blue Downs pointing to the location. Yes, I do."

"But—"

"It caught Cliff. The Shiv killed him. We're on the same path right now. We just have to be more clever than Ventinov, and stop it before he springs it."

"You're crazy," he whispered. "You brought all three on board when you suspect one is The Shiv? And you're walking into a Russian trap? *Knowingly*?"

"I know, it sounds insane." I grinned at him. "But what other choice did we have?"

"We could have stayed in Trieste."

"But we'd never get the graphene. That's what we need."

"And to take out Ventinov."

I shrugged. "That would be a bonus, yes."

Johnny hesitated for a moment before his expression finally cracked and the hint of a smile appeared. Then he chuckled. "You're crazy, Mac."

"I know you love Min Lee. I promise when all this is over, she'll be part of *my* family too."

He watched me for a long heartbeat. "You mean, *if* she's not The Shiv."

"That's right. We still have to find out."

He leaned back and considered that for a long while. I knew what was going through his mind. He knew I'd brought her along to keep an eye on her, but also now that I questioned her identity.

And, I'd bet he was now wondering if there was a chance I was right—if she really was a Russian agent.

—••—

THE HATCH TO THE LIVING compartment was open again, and behind us, a heated discussion was building. I turned to look; it was Sidra and Sahar. She was not happy about something. It was an argument between siblings, and I knew not to interfere with family dynamics, but because of my suspicions about Sidra, I paid attention to what they were saying.

It was about the recent attack by the Russian strike team, and the trip across the umbilical to the *Sword* for more information.

I thought briefly of the PCD that I'd discovered; it was with my gear in the airlock—where my wet clothes were hanging to dry.

Sidra was saying, "Mac needed someone to watch his back. I wasn't going to let him go alone."

"You can't put yourself at risk. You need to protect yourself."

"I'm an operative, Sahar. I'm not going to sit back and let someone else risk himself for me."

"So you put yourself in danger. What about me? What about the family?"

"I'm fine. Nothing happened."

"Have you lost your mind? They attacked you. We heard a gunshot! You barely got back through the umbilical."

She was growing angry; I'd never heard Sahar speak in anything but a pleasant tone or using a well-articulated argument.

"Mac took care of them. I was behind him. There could have been more than three there."

"Why did you go? I asked you not to."

"We're on this mission together. We're part of Oceania, right? He's our leader."

"I'm your sister. And your boss. *And* your Mayor."

There was a long pause. "You're asking me to let him risk himself for all of us, and not do anything?"

"Windsor did. He stayed here."

"He obeyed your orders, so he's in your good books, is that it?"

"I don't want unnecessary death, Sidra."

"Neither do I. But we have a job to do."

"Just don't do it again."

"What? Disobey you?"

"Correct."

The voices stopped, and I considered what I'd heard. Sahar had ordered Sidra to stay behind, but he'd gone anyway.

And William Windsor had been the one to follow her orders.

—••—

HOURS LATER, WE APPROACHED THE Iron Plains. The map was on my nav screen; our own mining settlement, The Complex, was there, clearly labeled. The Chinese graphene-layering facility was now also on the map, thanks to information Johnny had pulled from Tsim Lui, the investor in Blue Downs. He'd called the place The Facility. He'd claimed to be in charge of shipping citric acid to them, but didn't know what it was for, and was unable to contact them directly. We'd had to believe him; the only other option was to kill him, which we weren't willing to do.

It was a necessary risk.

The Facility was relatively close to The Complex—separated by slightly more than a hundred kilometres—but neither of us had known the other was there.

We cut SCAV drive and switched to conventional screws. We had to be cautious, to infiltrate it quietly. If we gave our position away, it was all over.

Renée was at my back and staring at the screen. She pointed at the bathymetry of the area. "It's flat. There's no place to really hide our approach. We have to move in slowly."

"There's also no place to conceal a vessel, really, other than behind a few large boulders."

"Which is how they found Cliff's, no doubt."

I grunted. She was right.

"What are your thoughts?" she asked.

I looked at Johnny, still piloting and sitting beside me. "Johnny?"

He stared at the screen. "We could swim in. We don't have scooters."

I checked the depth. It was 1,618 metres. A deep dive, but possible. We'd have to decompress in an airlock after, though. The longer we stayed out, the longer the decompression, which meant more time for them to discover we were there. I said as much.

"So you want to get us as close as possible," Renée said.

"It's better."

"Unless they hear us."

I pointed at the nuclear reactor. "We could enter there. It's the farthest module from the plant. We could set down just outside of it, slowly. Then enter."

Johnny was staring at me. "And then what, Mac? That's a big plant. There are probably hundreds of people there."

The sonar was glowing from the noise. They were working with sheets of titanium, shipping them in and out, and coating them with layers of graphene. The process was not exactly quiet. "We go in and steal the secret."

"And what else?"

Renée was watching us. "What do you mean? What else is there to do?"

Johnny whispered, "He wants to expose The Shiv."

Renée's face paled. "Now? Here?"

I said, "This is where they've led us. They know we're coming. The trap is here." I hesitated, and then, "And this is where we're going to reveal everything. We're going to find out what's been going on, once and for all."

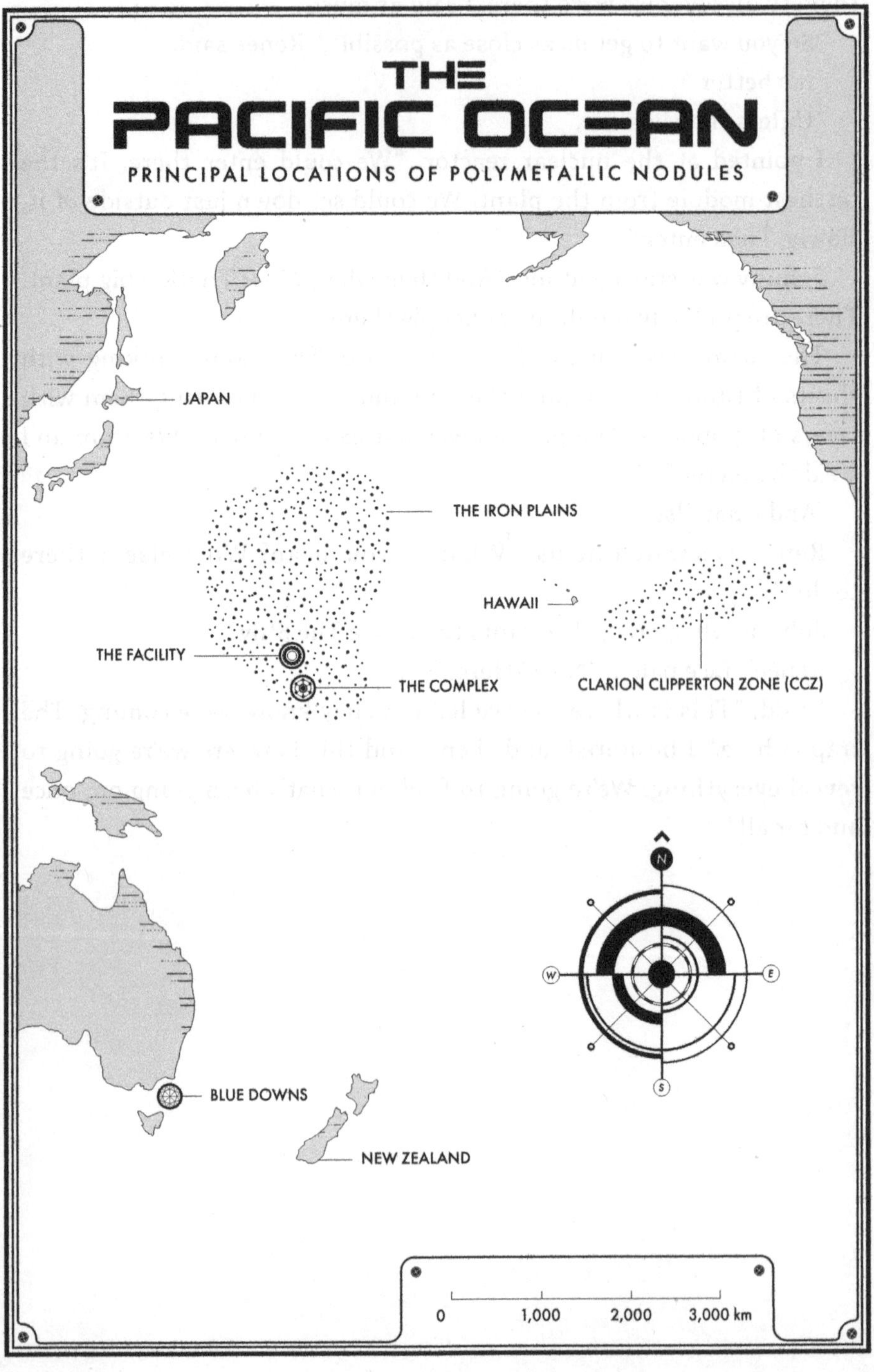
THE PACIFIC OCEAN
PRINCIPAL LOCATIONS OF POLYMETALLIC NODULES
JAPAN
THE IRON PLAINS
HAWAII
THE FACILITY
THE COMPLEX
CLARION CLIPPERTON ZONE (CCZ)
N
W
E
S
BLUE DOWNS
NEW ZEALAND
0
1,000
2,000
3,000 km

# Chapter Twenty-Three

THE FACILITY WAS HUGE. THE amount of noise coming from it vibrated every structure. Our sonar was absorbing an enormous amount of data. It only took moments to build a very detailed view of the compound. Most noise was coming from the largest module, which we decided was for the graphene-layering operations.

Johnny pointed at the attached sections, verbalizing what he felt each would be. "That's probably where they bring in the supplies. That's the airlock where they ship out the finished sheets of hull. There's the docking module—you can tell by the approach lights."

It was fairly expansive. The power plant was to the east. We switched course and slowly moved toward it, hugging the seafloor.

Fist-sized rocks lay scattered about the bottom. I knew what they were—the reason the superpowers were fighting for superiority in the oceans.

Polymetallic nodules.

Sometimes called manganese nodules, they were rocks that had grown in concentric spheres around a core, consisting of elements like iron, nickel, copper, manganese, and other metals. They were lying on the ocean floor in geologically active areas. The Pacific Ocean within the Ring of Fire is decidedly *active.* The nodules were just laying there for the taking.

No digging required.

No mines, no tunnels, no excavations.

Just scoop them off the seafloor.

They could be microscopic in size to a foot in diameter. Most were the size of gravel or fists. The abyssal plains were the wealthiest areas. The two richest were The Iron Plains and the Clarion Clipperton Fracture Zone. The superpowers were fighting for supremacy in every ocean in the world, but especially in the Pacific. And in the Pacific, those two regions were the most highly contested areas.

In some places, every square metre held seventy-five kilograms of ore.

Just scoop it up, and send for refining.

But of course, it wasn't quite that easy. The problem was getting to depth and using a vehicle of some sort to extract it. Once nations had achieved that, however, the rush had begun.

The Earth was seventy percent water, with more resources within than people could comprehend. Experts predicted there were over three trillion metric tons of such nodules on the ocean floors. This was the future of humanity, I knew. Survival started here, in the oceans.

The sonar pinged and I tore my eyes from the seafloor and studied the screen. There was a strong signal approaching from the north, hugging the bottom and making so much noise it was practically glowing angrily on the screen. On the VID display, projected on the canopy, the glow was also intense.

It was a vehicle used to scoop up the nodules. I'd never seen one before, but I'd read about them.

It was a *Loach*, which ocean dwellers and miners called a *Roach*.

A loach was an algae eater common in fish tanks. They scraped the bottoms, scooping algae into their mouths. They cleaned tank sides, bottoms, or any other features nearby. This did the same thing. Scaping bottoms, bringing rocks into their bellies for transport to the surface. They were huge vehicles, more than a hundred metres long, designed to travel seafloors. They could adjust ballast to move like a submarine, but once they started harvesting nodules, they grew so heavy that they were unable to lift off the ocean floor. Each had seven thresher pods, churning collectors which scraped the ocean floor. Similar to a wheat harvester topside, these threshers worked to scoop up rock, not vegetation. They scraped a 120-metre strip from the seafloor, traveled at a max speed of eight kph while harvesting, and could work at depths of 4,000 metres and sometimes slightly more. Fifty people or more worked on each one, and China, the US, and Russia were using them in The Iron Plains and the CCZ.

If these had graphene hulls, they would likely be able to descend to the abyssal plains themselves, to depths of eight to ten kilometres, opening up all the oceans to mining activities.

The *Roach* was approaching The Facility. I wondered if they were offloading ore for it, but likely not. There was probably a processing facility somewhere else for the ore, to refine and purify it, and eventually transform it into ingots of pure iron, copper, or nickel to combine with other elements and produce alloys like titanium.

It was producing a lot of noise as it moved, and Johnny looked at me. This was our chance. The *Roach* would mask our approach.

—••—

*SC-1* MOVED IN AT JUST a few km/hr. We were barely over the seafloor, and I struggled to make sure we didn't make contact and cause some unwanted noise. The sonar was glowing white—a diffused, scattered light over the entire display.

The whole team was in the living area. They were in dark wetsuits and prepared to infiltrate the Chinese base. I studied them and something occurred to me. We had a large group of people. I had multiple intentions here, but dying was the last thing I wanted.

"Sidra, Windsor, Min Lee, and I will infiltrate The Facility via the fusion plant. We'll set down near it and hotwire the airlock."

Meg frowned and studied the three agents. She'd realized I was bringing them all with me. "What about the rest of us?"

"The *Roach*."

"What about it? It's just passing by, but moving slowly."

"It's Chinese. It likely docks at Chinese bases. We can use it to our advantage."

"A distraction?" Johnny asked. He'd noticed that I hadn't given him a task. He was staring at Min Lee, then glanced back at me. He knew why I wanted her with me, and he was hesitant about it.

"The *Roach* is perfect for this. You, Meg, and Renée will infiltrate it. There won't be any resistance. Sahar will stay here and pilot *SC-1*. Rescue us if necessary."

"It holds fifty people—"

"They're miners. They're operating machinery and working in the hold. Some are off shift and sleeping. They won't know what's going on—unless you trigger an alarm, so don't do that! Get on board and get to the bridge. Turn the vehicle and dock at The Facility. Hold the bridge if they figure out what's going on."

Meg's face paled. "But Tru, that's insane. Why?"

"Because while you're doing that, the base personnel will focus on you. Meanwhile, the four of us will be in the structure stealing the secret to the graphene layering."

"But how?"

"In the factory. We've done this sort of thing before. There will be a computer running the show. We'll download its memory or just steal the entire CPU."

"You'll need the graphene nozzle," she said. "It sprays the graphene. Grab one if you can, so we can reverse engineer it."

I frowned. "You spoke to Max Hyland?"

"Of course, when you first mentioned graphene. I did my own research on it too."

"Anything else?"

"We'll need the carbon compound. The spray."

"It's a chemical vapour."

"It'll be in tanks of some sort. Find one."

So, we needed the computer, a nozzle, and a tank of the graphene in order for this mission to be a success.

But at the same time, of the three agents coming with me, one was likely going to try to kill me.

My PCD was blinking angrily; a message had come in from Kristen Canvel. She'd been researching the operatives. I glanced at her warning.

This was going to be the perfect opportunity to reveal the truth.

—••—

WE DEBARKED OUTSIDE THE POWER plant. The noise from the nearby *Roach* echoed through the airlock. Sidra, Min Lee, and Windsor faced me in the small chamber. They wore mission equipment: each of us had a gun and holster on our right thighs and a dagger on the left. My senses were on high alert; my heart was in my throat. The airlock was small and we were standing close together. My right hand was at my side, at the gun. If one of them made a move, I'd only have an instant to react.

The water flooded in slowly and moved upward. It was cold at this depth, though the wetsuit offered some protection. The faces before me were flat. No expression. No fear.

No remorse.

We were in mission mode now.

The pressure built suddenly and we had to equalize again and again. It was deep and the pressure enormous. Luckily, we'd only be out for a minute at most. We were beside the power plant, the dome that housed their fusion reactor a hundred metres to the east of the main base. We'd been right on the seafloor, basically, and noise from the *Roach* had hidden our approach.

I hoped.

The outer hatch opened.

We exited *SC-1*.

And entered a blackness that seemed to suck at our eyeballs. Disorientation in such conditions was common. Sometimes divers grew so confused that they lost all sense of up and down. They could end up swimming deeper than their mix would allow. The pressure would force more nitrogen into their tissues, and it was a narcotic.

Nitrogen narcosis would take over.

*Rapture of the deep.*

Consumed by euphoria, divers could end up dead, wounded, or crippled forever. Some had never returned from their dives, their bodies lost to the oceans. Others had swum—willingly—into the churning blades of warsub screws, without a care in the world.

We had red lights attached to our forearms, and we aimed them ahead. There was a structure just a few metres away.

The airlock was obvious. There were large yellow hatch marks around it. Sidra went to work on the controls and the outer hatch rumbled open. It was hard to hear with the mineral harvester so close. It was churning up the seafloor as it moved, its massive threshers spinning and sucking up rock. It was impossible to see it, but there was a lot of debris moving past us. Dust, sand, and small pebbles swirled around.

We entered together, the water lowered, and we began our decompression, which wouldn't last long.

We wouldn't open the inner hatch to the facility until the others had diverted the *Roach* and distracted The Facility's personnel.

I sat on the bench at the chamber's perimeter. The others did so as well, facing me.

The airlock started to bring the pressure down to four atms. We'd adjusted the speed of its simulated ascent based on the dive tables for our short excursion.

I stared at them in silence, and they all matched my gaze.

It was a waiting game now.

I drew my gun and aimed it at them.

"I know what you're planning," I said into the quiet. "I won't let it happen."

# Chapter Twenty-Four

THEIR FACES SHOWED SURPRISE.

They matched my gaze, locking eyes with me.

They knew I was serious.

"What do you mean, Mac?" Min Lee asked.

"One of you intends to kill me. It's not going to happen." I held my aim on them. "Don't move a muscle. Don't get up, and don't draw your weapon. I intend to figure this out, *now*."

"What the hell, Mac?" Sidra snapped. "Are you betraying us? We're here to get the graphene—"

"Shut up," I said. "And I'm not betraying you. One of you is planning to betray *me*." I keyed my comm and started to broadcast to the others. I knew they were listening, even while they were maneuvering close to the *Roach* to begin their infiltration and the attempt at distraction. They had their earpieces in; our words would be easy to hear.

They were probably staring at each other now, at that exact moment, in absolute shock.

"One of you is a foreign spy intent on killing me. Not only that, you're working for Russia."

"And you brought us here to face you? In a hostile base, during a mission?" Windsor said. "Are you mad?"

"The thing two of you don't know is the third has led us here. It's a ploy, a trap. One of you has been planting clues that you think we've been following mindlessly. But we know about it."

"But still," he said. "You continued to play along? What for?"

"For this." I gestured with my weapon. "To expose it. To *end* it. Because one of you is The Steel Shiv."

—••—

THE ANNOUNCEMENT DROPPED LIKE A bombshell. Their eyes were wide and collectively their jaws dropped.

"You're crazy," Sidra said. "We can't be." He stared at the others. "*None* of us can be."

"Isn't that what The Shiv would say, Sidra?"

"With logic like that, how can I prove it? It's impossible. But you sound deluded right now!"

"I'm not. I promise you."

Min Lee said, "But Mac, I'm not a threat. I want to live in Trieste with you and the team when this is all done." Her eyes were pleading.

"So you say. But you are my number one suspect, Min."

Surprise exploded across her features. "But why?"

I focused my attention—and my aim—on her. I offered her a slight smile. "You showed up at Trieste exactly as I made the announcement about independence. We still don't know how you knew, and you haven't shared that with us. You refused to answer when I asked you." I studied her expression as I spoke.

"I can't say what my bosses tell me or what they know."

"Your loyalty is not to Oceania?"

She snorted. "It's not that simple, Mac. I'm married to a Triestrian, so yes, it is, but I'm also a Sheng City Agent."

"They're also part of Oceania."

"I can't betray my sources or my superiors."

"Are they Russian?"

Her eyes went cold. "You have no right to say that!"

I knew Johnny was listening to all of this. He'd want proof. "There's more."

"I'm waiting then." Her tone was ice.

"Your arrival was mysterious. Your reasons for coming when you did were too. It also coincided with the bomb perfectly. You could easily have planted it before you docked. You cut power to Trieste effectively, and you were in the right place at the perfect time."

"No." She shook her head.

"There's another question too. Where were you before Trieste?"

"In the Pacific, on a mission."

"Doing what?"

"I told you, I can't say. It would break my oath, and they'd try me for treason."

"Sheng City? Or Russia?"

She leaned forward but I gestured with my gun. She snapped, "Don't say that again. I am losing my temper."

"One of you is The Shiv. I'm going to force it from you, Min."

"It's *not* me."

I leaned back and sighed. "The rumor is that The Shiv wears a black helmet and alters his voice. Is it because there's an accent?"

"It's possible," Sidra interjected. "Those are the myths, anyway."

"But it could be more than that."

"Such as?"

"What if The Shiv were actually a woman? The full helmet and voice distorter would make more sense, wouldn't it?"

He frowned. "That's correct, and there are theories like that already." He stared at Min Lee, clearly sizing her up. I knew what he was thinking: *Could this actually be The Shiv?*

Or . . .

Or, he was just trying to throw me off.

Min said, "You need more than this, Mac. Don't tell me that's all you've got." Her tone was still hard. She was angry now.

"We don't know where you were before arriving at Trieste. You could easily have been here."

"Here?"

"At this very facility. Killing Cliff Sim."

"That's outrageous."

"The Shiv laid a trap. It caught Cliff instead of me. You could have laid the trap and killed him."

"Absurd."

I shrugged. "It's why we're all here. We're in the trap now, together."

I paused and studied the airlock. "And we're not going anywhere." Suddenly, in a flash that turned my blood to ice, I realized that I recognized the deck. It had a distinctive pattern that I'd seen before.

It made me want to scream, but I had a job to do.

In time—only minutes now—I'd be able to unleash my anger.

I swallowed my rage and pressed on. "There's also been no sabotage at Trieste since we left. Since *you* left."

"Since nothing's happened, *I'm* guilty for it? Is that your twisted sense of logic?"

"There's also the matter of Grant Bell. Killed in Blue Downs."

The pressure was declining slowly. My ears kept popping, and it made me wince, but I had to keep my focus on what I was doing. I had to watch them closely, unveil the evidence carefully.

"You heard Grant say he was going to Blue Downs. In my office, when you arrived. You saw him with your own eyes, you knew what he looked like."

"But why would I want to kill him? I don't know him."

"Spoken like an innocent person, Min. But if you're The Shiv, you're working for Russia, and Ventinov wants to hurt me. To kill my team, to kill my friends. You knew Grant was in Blue Downs. You either killed him when Renée lost sight of you on the tour, or you told the Russian kill team to do it. He was the one who'd studied your course to Trieste. Maybe he was the one who could pin the explosion on you too, if you'd stopped to get out and plant a bomb before docking."

"No fucking way."

"Did I push the right button?"

She glared at me, and her muscles tensed. She seemed ready to leap at me. Physically, she looked formidable. Her toned arms, broad shoulders, athletic gait . . . she could very well be The Shiv.

I pressed on, "There's also the recent conflict with the *Sword* and the Russian kill team. You were arguing with Johnny to make contact first. You didn't want us to destroy them. Why?"

A perplexed look spread across her face. "You're crazy, Mac. I just wanted to make sure they really did intend on killing us."

"Their shutters were open. They'd been following us and were on an intercept. Of course they were hostile."

She shook her head. "I just wanted Johnny to make sure, that's all. It doesn't mean I'm The Steel Shiv!"

"Or maybe you wanted to conceal your involvement with Grant's death. Your orders to kill him in Blue Downs. You didn't want us to find them on board that vessel."

"That's insane."

"There's one more very, very important piece to the puzzle, Min."

The air was hissing around us and the counter ticking down. There were ten minutes left in our decompression, and I knew the others were also at that moment entering the *Roach* and making their way to the bridge to commandeer it.

"What is it this time?" she whispered, seemingly giving in to the inevitable perhaps. Or, just sick and tired of it all.

"Your arms, Min. The bruised arms."

She was staring at me now with hate in her eyes. "What are you—"

"When you arrived I noticed your arms almost immediately. I asked you later, and you said it was because of training. 'We don't pull punches' or something along those lines, correct?"

"It's true," she said. "But maybe it was from a mission I just can't talk about."

"Or maybe it's because you killed Cliff Sim, and that was the result. He put up a fight, which is reasonable."

The other two were staring at her now, in obvious shock. She was shaking her head and had locked her gaze on me. "It's a lie. I didn't fight your CSO."

"You arrived at the perfect time. It all makes sense."

Sidra's hand was on his gun, and I gestured for him to move it away. He said, "Is it true? Is this The Shiv? I noticed her bruised arms too."

I said, "Don't pull attention away from yourself, Sidra. If you do, I'm going to think it's you."

"Me?" His eyes were wide. "But I'm the one who told *you* The Shiv was after you!"

"At Sahar's orders. You were just letting me know."

"So *I'm* The Shiv now? Because of that?"

"There's also the accent. You're British. The helmet covers your identity and disguises the accent."

"But Mac, I can't kill for hire. My Muslim upbringing wouldn't let that happen. Not in a million years. Not even eternity!"

"True, although Sahar mentioned to me that sometimes you felt trapped between worlds. Your deep cultural beliefs contradicting western culture? Wasn't that what she meant?"

Shock appeared in his eyes, but only for an instant. "Does that mean accepting payment for murder? I would not do that! Straight and clear Mac—I *would not kill for hire*. It's against everything we stand for!"

If Min was angry before, Sidra was absolutely furious.

"You also claimed to be in the Atlantic Ocean, monitoring the coalition fleet buildup. It's where you supposedly heard about The Shiv."

"That's true."

"But maybe you were actually in the Pacific. Killing Cliff Sim."

"That's ridiculous. I followed orders. I was doing what Sahar sent me to do."

"Just assuming that's true, how did you know what Ventinov's communication said? How'd you know he had notified his other two dreadnoughts in the Atlantic about The Shiv, unless you yourself had killed Sim, taken the photos, and sent them yourself to Ventinov?"

The others were now staring at him. Min as well, and her eyes were hard. She realized that I might not actually think it was her, and that the person sitting right next to her could be the Russian assassin.

I continued, "So how'd you know, Sidra? How'd you know Ventinov had told his people in the Atlantic about The Shiv?"

"I was monitoring comms traffic. They were *all* talking about it. All the Russian crews, and between warsubs as well. There are multiple RSF ships there, and not just dreadnoughts. There are *Lenins, Vostoks, Leonovs, Kirovs*, and even an SSBN *Eliminator*! They mean war with Trieste, I'm here to help you, and you're accusing me of being a Russian!"

"Where were you as a child? England?"

"You know that! Sahar and I grew up—"

"I *don't* know that! I only know what you told me."

"Surely you've investigated this, before accusing us. You *know* where I grew up!"

It was correct, I had already looked into it. Kristen Canvel had told me via comm. "And you ran into the *Sword* against Sahar's wishes."

Absolute fury painted his features now. “To save you, Mac! To help you! What are you talking about?”

“Unless it was an attempt to kill me. Sahar ordered you to stay behind, but you didn’t. Since when do you disobey orders from your boss, your sister, and your Mayor?” I was repeating the exact words Sahar had said in *SC-1* earlier.

That stopped him. He blinked in surprise and his face flattened. “But I didn’t kill you.”

“You didn’t get a chance. I ended up saving your life, Sidra. You ended up needing me to survive, so you couldn’t take me out. Had you killed me, you’d be dead too.”

He shook his head. “Mac, I simply can’t believe you’d say this.”

I snorted. “I’m going to expose you now. I’m not stopping.”

And then I turned to William Windsor. “And now you, *Bill*.”

# Chapter Twenty-Five

HE'D FOCUSED HIS GAZE ON me, and his eyes were sharp. "My turn now, Mac?" Windsor's tone was proper and clipped. "Let me guess. The black helmet and voice distorter. It hides my strong British accent."

"Yes. And trust me when I say this, it's *very* British."

His eyes widened. "*Too* British? Is that it? Practiced?"

"Possibly. But you did grow up in Ripley, I checked that. You also knew that Grant Bell was going to Blue Downs. You could have killed him to hurt me."

"I was at Churchill Sands when you told us all that he was going. You said you needed all the help you could get, and he would be there too. But Sidra was also there."

"But you knew all about Cliff and his death. How?"

He didn't respond. He simply watched me.

I pressed on, "You showed me the photos. You said your network in the Pacific had obtained them."

"That's true."

"What network? Where?"

"I'd been working in this area. This is my theater of operation. I don't give up my fellow agents."

"Your comrades?"

He chuckled. "I didn't say that. *You* did. I don't give them up. I *can't*. It's not allowed, for the same reason that Min Lee can't tell you what mission she was on before arriving at Trieste."

"This isn't about Min. But how'd you get all the information about Cliff's death? How'd you know?"

"I can't reveal that. I report to Sahar, no one else."

"Do you recognize this airlock?" I stopped and stared at him, waiting.

"I don't understand."

"This is the one."

"Which?"

"Where Cliff died, Windsor. Look at the grating. Look at the drain in the center. It's the same."

He glanced down. "I wouldn't know." He hesitated. "Is this why you're doing it here? To avenge your friend?"

"It's fitting, wouldn't you say?"

"So this is a trap you've set for all of us?"

"Just one of you. Not all."

"Clever, Mac. Clever. You turned The Shiv's trap into your own." He stopped speaking and eyed me.

"Your life is on the line here."

"A threat?"

"It's death or life, right now. Not a threat. How'd you know about Cliff's death?" I asked again.

"Only Sahar can reveal that."

"She's not here. She's listening though. I know she'd give me the answer."

He sighed and watched me. He glanced at my gun; it was ramrod still and aimed directly at his heart. He knew I was telling the truth; I was deadly serious.

"My sources are monitoring all movements in The Iron Plains. They knew about this facility. They intercepted the comms traffic about the body that administrators here discovered. It surprised the personnel here. Chief Administrator Zhao Lin runs this place. She contacted Ventinov. My people intercepted the communication and sent it to me. I relayed it to Sahar, and she wanted me back home to inform you, so I went. It took me days to get back because I didn't have a SCAV vessel. As soon as I arrived, she called you."

"You also suggested this whole scenario was a trap."

He looked shocked. "But you yourself have said the very same thing!"

"Yes, because I'm right. But no one else thought so but you. Because maybe you *knew* it was a trap already. You were trying to throw the scent off yourself."

He snorted and laughed out loud. "You're accusing me of being a Russian agent because I'm as smart as you? That's rich!"

"You were trying to direct my attention elsewhere. Anyone but you. Assume it was a trap, and it couldn't be the person right next to me leading me there, right?"

"Ridiculous."

"But you were with us all along. You knew where we were going. You knew the clues were in Blue Downs, because you'd planted them. You knew that Tsim Lui was in Living Module E. You told Johnny when you went there with him. How'd you know?"

He paused. "I thought someone else had said that. Didn't they?"

"Bullshit."

"I'm being honest."

"But you just said it was 'ridiculous,' now you're saying it was a coincidence or that you can't remember!"

He suddenly looked flustered. "Mac, we went to find the investor in Blue Downs. Someone said he was in Living Module E. I told Johnny and we went. That's all there is to it." He paused and stared at me. "Do you *really* think I'm this great assassin? There are legends about The Shiv. Could I be him?"

"If you are, your disguise is marvelous."

"As an English prig. Your sister likes me, Mac."

I froze. "Don't say that."

"Do you really want to risk our relationship? I like Meg. It might turn into a lot more."

I knew she was listening to this broadcast. "Don't say that."

"But you need to know everything, Mac. You need to know the ramifications of what you're doing." He glanced at Min Lee. "What about them? The evidence against me is pretty light."

I cocked my head. "Blaming them now?"

"I know. But you suspect one of us as being The Shiv. I know it's not me. But if you're right, it has to be one of *them*. You haven't disarmed us yet. In fact, you let us equip ourselves with weapons for this mission and it makes sense why. You need the other two to help you when you finally reveal The Shiv. Right? You *need* us, Mac."

"You're the only one to try and pin the blame on the others to take the focus off you, Windsor."

"Sidra did too. He pointed out her bruises."

I considered that. He was correct.

"I just want the truth out," he continued. "Look," he sighed. "When the *Sword* attacked, Sahar ordered us to stay on *SC-1*. I'm the one who obeyed her! I could have gone in there. If I was a Russian agent, wouldn't I have gone after you then and killed you?"

I glanced at the airlock display. There were only three minutes remaining in the decompression. I had to hope that the others had infiltrated the *Roach* and were moving it closer to The Facility.

As if on cue, a PA announcement echoed through the corridor just outside. I couldn't make out what it said, even though I spoke Mandarin.

I held up my PCD. I'd received a message from my assistant just before we left *SC-1*. She had information for me. I was going to play it for them, and hopefully expose The Shiv.

"What's that?" Min Lee asked.

"Kristen at Trieste was investigating you three for me. So far she hadn't uncovered anything. But a message just came in before we left *SC-1*. Marked URGENT."

She stared at my PCD. "But you have no idea—"

I glanced around at our surroundings. "It's a perfect time to unveil the truth. In a perfect location too, wouldn't you say, Min?"

"I still don't know what you're talking about. I have secrets in my past. It's because I work in intelligence. Same as you Mac. There are things we can't discuss. It doesn't mean I'm The Steel Shiv."

I pressed play.

—••—

KRISTEN CANVEL'S VOICE RANG OUT into the small enclosure. "Mac. I've been looking into the three names you asked me about." I studied the eyes watching me.

Sidra swallowed.

Windsor shook his head as he stared at me, as if in pity.

Min Lee cursed under her breath.

Kristen continued, "Their governments have blocked their backgrounds, mostly. They're all spies. You know that. So I had to dig deeper."

There were more calls on the PA out in the corridor. The *Roach* had likely switched course and was headed for The Facility.

"I looked into their backgrounds. Where they attended school. Where they trained. Where they joined up with intelligence. But still, I couldn't find anything."

I exhaled. So, it was nothing after—

"I looked at their parents next, just to see if anything was amiss. Min Lee's immigrated to Sheng City shortly after China founded the colony. They brought her with them, and it's how she ended up working for the city. All of her early formative years were underwater. Her dad passed away, but her mom is still alive, still in the colony." She took a breath. "Sidra Noor was born into a large family in London, England. The star of the family is clearly Sahar, but the parents doted on all their kids. Each had a pathway to university, and Sidra followed his sister's journey and career to the oceans. He followed her to Churchill. The parents paid for his education and by every account they are hard-working, blue-collar people. They're still alive, still following Sahar and Sidra's lives. There has been no odd travel in his background, other than his work for Churchill Sands in their intelligence organization. We don't know what that involves, but I'm sure you can ask Sahar." Another pause. "As for Windsor, there is slightly more there. His parents have both passed from natural causes. I found medical records in their hometown of Ripley."

I eyed William Windsor. He was staring at the PCD in my hand.

"They spent a lot of money on fertility treatments shortly after they married. Seems they couldn't get pregnant. But then, it happened for them."

Windsor visibly exhaled.

He'd been nervous, perhaps scared that I would unfairly accuse him.

Kristen forged on. "But then I found something odd. One day, they didn't have a child but were undergoing fertility treatment at the local hospital. The next mention of them in any digital records is four years later. By then they had a child, William Windsor, whom they had to enroll in school."

I frowned. So what was she—

"But he was eight years old, Mac. He couldn't possibly be their child. They adopted him. There are no records at any agency of an adoption. I have our own intelligence people digging deeper into this, but it seems clear. I have no record of where he was actually born."

I shifted my aim to Windsor. "Don't move, or I shoot. I would love to kill The Shiv, here and now, in this place." His hands were in the air, as if warding me off. "Min Lee and Sidra. Draw your weapons and aim at Windsor. Slide slowly away from him."

They did as I asked. We now had three weapons on the man.

I said, "So, you claimed you were born in Ripley. But it was a lie."

He shrugged, "Adoption is not something many talk about."

"Bullshit."

"Maybe I didn't know it until now."

"Also bullshit. At eight years old, you'd remember. Where are you really from? Did you cultivate the accent to blend in better?"

He didn't reply to that.

"You killed Cliff Sim in this very chamber," I rasped. "Right here, on the deck. He was looking up at the steel ceiling above him as he died. Seems fitting that this is where we expose you."

His face shifted abruptly and waves of fear seemed to cross it. "But Mac, I'm helping you. I work for Sahar. Surely this isn't evidence that I'm The Shiv."

But his eyes gave him away.

I looked into them, ignoring his facial expression.

They were hard, uncaring.

Unfeeling.

Calculating.

He was figuring out how to get out of this.

There were three weapons trained on him.

"It's one of you three," I said. "But only you have the background of a double agent. I'm guessing you were born in Russia. Your parents taught you about the Motherland. About patriotism for Mother Russia, am I right? And someone got to them, convinced them to ship you to the West, where you infiltrated society and waited. You were an asset, placed somewhere for some distant future." I cocked my head. "How many more are there like you? How many children have they sent to other nations?"

"This is madness," he said in his cocky British diction. He was showing more courage now, more bravery, as if he didn't care what I was saying. "You're accusing an innocent man. Mac, what is Meg going to say when she hears this? She and I are closer than you know."

"She's been listening to everything. She knows what's happening."

His face flattened. "Is that true? Meg—I assure you, this is insane."

Meg's voice chimed in my ear. "*Mac.*" She was angry; her voice was stern. "Don't do anything rash. You know this might not be him. Even if he was born somewhere else, it doesn't mean he's a Russian agent."

"He's the only one, Meg," I whispered. "It's all come down to this."

"If you do it, our relationship is over."

I hesitated. "You don't mean—"

She shot back: "*I mean it!* If you kill him, we are no longer family."

"He killed Cliff. He is working to betray us. He's going to try to kill me tonight, Meg."

"He's not going to kill you. He's not The Shiv, dammit!"

Windsor was staring at me during the exchange. He knew he had Meg on his side now.

*Fuck.*

The airlock chimed and the hatch to the corridor sighed open.

And without warning, the power went out, plunging us into darkness.

A shot rang out, then another. I hesitated, Meg's words in my ears.

Something crushed against the side of my face, and a rush of air passed by me.

He'd run into The Facility.

# Interlude

## In The Iron Plains; "The Facility"

| | |
|---|---|
| Location: | Latitude: 12º 27′ 19″ N<br>Longitude: 183º 24′ 3″ W<br>On the seafloor in The Iron Plains; Chinese Manufacturing Plant—*The Facility* |
| Depth: | 1,618 metres |
| Date: | 13 June 2131 |
| Time: | 0038 hours |

CHIEF ADMINISTRATOR ZHAO LIN OF the Chinese Facility was in the Control Dome watching events unfold around her. It was after midnight on the thirteenth of June. Captain Ventinov had told her that more strangers would be arriving, and she was to allow them entry, and then wait.

Just let things unfold, and not worry about it.

Chinese officials had backed him up, including CSF military, and she was to do what they asked.

The last time it had happened, however, ten days ago now, an American man had ended up dead and discarded in their airlock.

Killing Americans was the last thing she wanted. She had pioneered the graphene-layering process in that facility. She had persevered against all odds, directing scientists, engineers, and manufacturing specialists to develop the de Laval nozzles and the organic monomer to work in concert and create the stable atom-thick nanomaterial two-dimensional graphene, even overcoming the stacking obstacles to develop the strongest substance known to humankind. It was revolutionizing Chinese ocean exploration *and* exploitation, and she knew it would also allow them to press out farther into space. Her existence at that very facility was responsible for their achievements in graphene production.

Each week, sheets of titanium arrived. Her processing equipment and specialists coated the hull plates with thirty million layers of graphene, one centimetre of the miracle carbon honeycomb, stacked in an AB formation, and then shipped out on the completed plates.

Engineers at CSF naval facilities were using the plates for their new hulls. They welded the titanium from the inside, but on the outer hull, the graphene chemical vapor bonded with the existing graphene, forming nearly unbreakable bonds naturally, sealing the plates and forming a single hull without any outer rivets, welds, seals, or seams.

And Zhao Lin had done it. Under her leadership, the teams had overcome engineering problems, solved manufacturing issues, and were now churning out product.

Everything was going smoothly, until this idiot Captain Ventinov had come into her life.

A dead American, in her facility.

Now another group had arrived, had accessed the fusion plant area through an airlock, and were currently decompressing. She had only a few minutes to decide on an action.

But she had already planned for it, with her Executive Assistant, Yan.

They were going to kill everyone, including the Russian operative.

Cut the power, seal the corridor, and flood it.

It might halt production for a few hours, but they'd prepared for an incursion at the power plant. The workers had sealed the corridor near the airlock and were waiting for further orders.

The decompression was nearly over.

Yan, standing next to her in the control center and staring at the schematic of The Facility, said, "We can just flood the airlock now."

"They've got wetsuits and scuba gear. Stick to the plan."

He turned to her. "Are you sure about this? Our superiors might be upset."

"This is Russia's business, not ours. They're putting the graphene production at risk. I can't allow that."

The sonar chimed and she glanced at the screen. The large mining vehicle that had passed by was turning back toward The Facility.

She frowned. That machine—a *Loach*—was supposed to pick up the layer of polymetallic nodules on the seafloor in a wide 120-metre swath. It was to scrape several kilometres of virgin seafloor before turning around, like mowing a massive lawn. For some reason, it was swinging around in a wide arc, as if they had an emergency.

*Surely they didn't mean to dock with them?*

It was headed directly for The Facility—for the airlock at the storage sector on the west side.

*What the hell?*

The countdown hit zero. The airlock on the schematic turned green. There was no time to think about the mining vehicle. She pressed a button and the airlock inner hatch opened, allowing the intruders entrance into The Facility.

Then she nodded to Yan, and he slammed his hand on a control, cutting power to that section.

They had already ordered all workers to return to their quarters and seal hatches.

"Get ready to flood the corridor," she said.

| | |
|---|---|
| Location: | Latitude: 12º 27′ 19″ N<br>Longitude: 183º 24′ 3″ W<br>On the seafloor in The Iron Plains; Chinese Manufacturing Plant—*The Facility* |
| Depth: | 1,618 metres |
| Date: | 13 June 2131 |
| Time: | 0041 hours |

HIS BIRTH NAME WAS VASILY Kinzhal Stali.

Kinzhal—*Dagger.*

Stali—*Steel.*

He didn't decide on his name, his parents had awarded him with it. He'd been born and raised in the rural wilderness of northern Russia. There he learned to forage, hunt, fish, and most important, *survive*. His parents had taught him. But more important, they'd told him stories about history, famous patriots, and the ongoing fight for survival in a world ravaged by ecological and climate catastrophe, caused mostly by the industrial West. The scorching heat would eventually kill the very forest in which they lived, his parents whispered at night to him. The forest which provided for them and kept them alive would soon die, and it was *their* fault. The stories of patriotism often turned to tales of horror, about the evil West.

The anger had burned within him from a young age, from the second he could understand his parents' words. As the years passed, they continued to stoke the flames. And then, when he was five, they told him what they planned for him. What the government had asked of them, and as great patriots, they had agreed.

They would send him overseas. Adopted to another family, where he would learn about the West and decide for himself the best way to hurt them. He would still be their son—still a *Stali*—but he would infiltrate and destroy the West.

*Somehow.*

At first his path scared him. He didn't know if he could do it. But as he approached his eighth birthday, he had come to accept his mission.

He was going to follow in the footsteps of the other great patriots.

He would work from within the weak superpowers, eroding them slowly and surely, without them even knowing.

He even decided *how* he was going to do it, before his eighth birthday even.

His name gave him a direction, a path, a goal.

A steel dagger.

That's what he was. His parents had started him on the path, and the government had taken him and sent him further down it. He would cultivate his name and become a steel weapon. He knew eventually his name would make his enemies tremble before they even knew who had come for them.

But he knew his name would eventually have to die. He would no longer be able to use *Stali*. It made him sad, but his new identity could compensate.

At eight years old, he moved to the new location and worked hard to fit in. He pretended to be happy, to be a loving son. He learned the language and perfected the accent. He trained hard. But through it all, he *remembered*. He knew the stories of the patriots, and he was one now.

He studied history and current events. He knew the best path for him to make a difference was in the oceans, where the current cold war was escalating. That's where he could make the most impact. Sometimes he'd sell his services to the highest bidder, but he worked for Russia, and he cultivated his reputation carefully, and kept his identity a secret.

His adoptive parents had suspected, so he'd had to deal with them, and he did so without feeling, without caring.

Russia first.

Kinzhal Stali—the Steel Dagger—became The Steel Shiv. His name would terrify his victims.

Now, however, he found himself in an odd predicament.

Ventinov had warned him about this man, about this Mayor Truman McClusky. He'd gone on for a while about how clever he was, how difficult to defeat. So, Ventinov and Stali had arranged a path for him, laid the clues, and waited to snare him, rather than just defeat him in outright battle.

And it had worked!

He thought.

Until that very minute. Now he was in an airlock facing three weapons, all aimed at him.

McClusky was clever indeed.

But it wasn't over yet.

Then the airlock hatch opened, and the power went out.

Not even the emergency lights activated, and Stali knew it was his chance.

He bolted to his feet, darted sideways, and struck at McClusky.

Shots rang out, missing him, and he connected once with the Mayor. He knew another round of bullets was imminent, so he ducked, fell backwards out into the corridor, turned, and ran.

They would follow.

And he would kill them, one at a time, ending with Truman McClusky.

# Part Six:
## The Facility

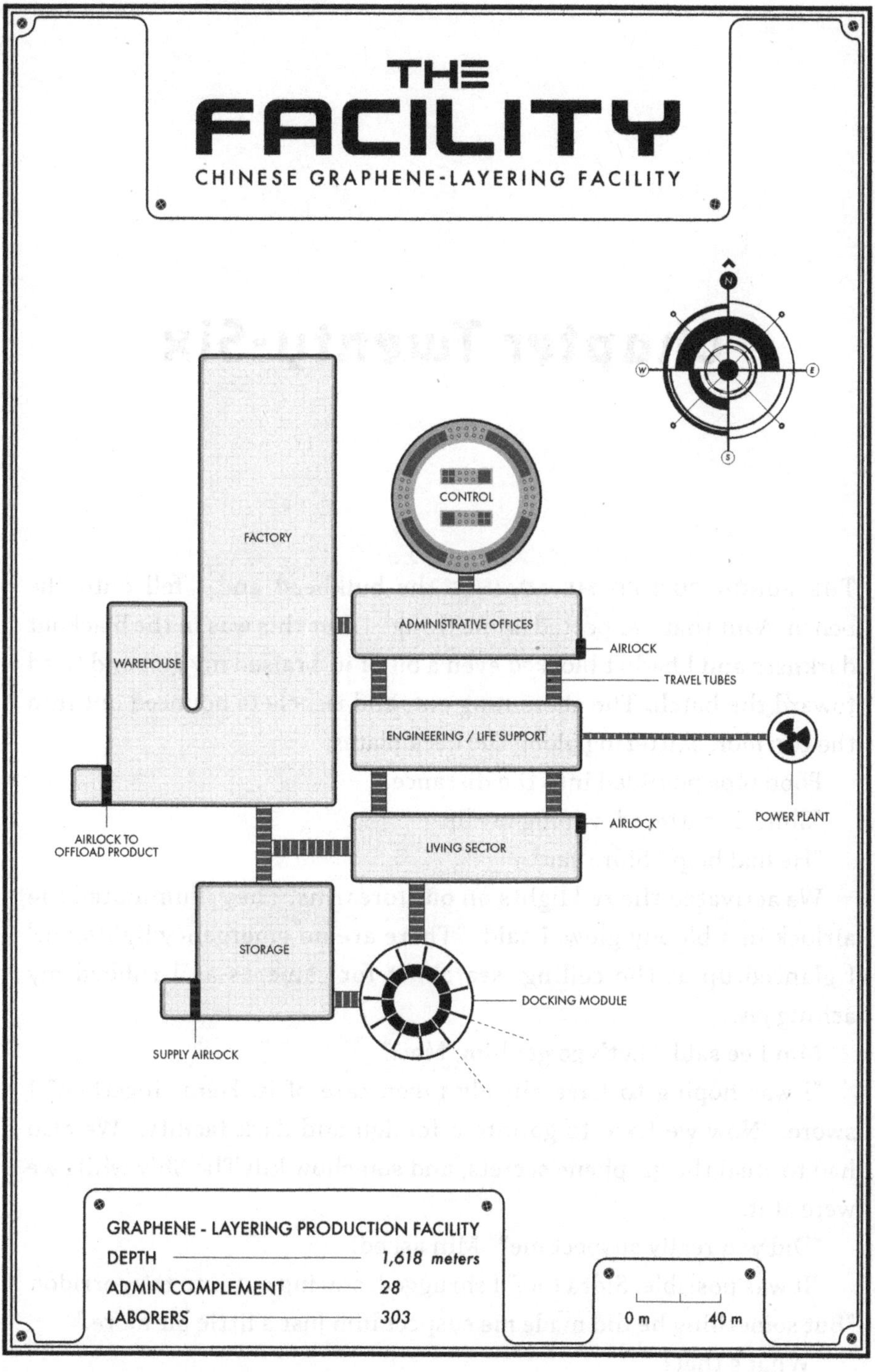
THE FACILITY
CHINESE GRAPHENE-LAYERING FACILITY
N
W
E
S
CONTROL
FACTORY
ADMINISTRATIVE OFFICES
AIRLOCK
WAREHOUSE
TRAVEL TUBES
ENGINEERING / LIFE SUPPORT
AIRLOCK
POWER PLANT
AIRLOCK TO OFFLOAD PRODUCT
LIVING SECTOR
STORAGE
DOCKING MODULE
SUPPLY AIRLOCK
GRAPHENE - LAYERING PRODUCTION FACILITY
DEPTH 1,618 meters
ADMIN COMPLEMENT 28
LABORERS 303
0 m 40 m

# Chapter Twenty-Six

THE PUNCH PUSHED ME AGAINST the bulkhead and I fell onto the bench. A hit that's expected is one thing . . . but this was in the blackout darkness and I hadn't blocked even a bit of it. I raised my gun and fired toward the hatch. The shots rang out, and ricochets bounced out into the corridor, skittering along the deck plates.

Footsteps pounded into the distance.

"Shit," I muttered, wiping my lip.

"He had help," Sidra said.

We activated the red lights on our forearms. They illuminated the airlock in a bloody glow. I said, "There are no emergency lights on." I glanced up at the ceiling, searching for cameras as I rubbed my aching jaw.

Min Lee said, "Let's go get him, Mac."

"I was hoping to have already taken care of it. Here. Together." I swore. "Now we have to go into a foreign and dark facility." We also had to steal the graphene secrets, and somehow kill The Shiv while we were at it.

"Did you really suspect me?" Min asked.

"It was possible. Sidra too." I shrugged, staring out into the corridor. "But something he did made me suspect him just a little bit more."

"What's that?"

"He went for Meg. He formed a relationship there, to throw me off.

And it worked."

"But you let him have a weapon."

I stared at the two in the airlock with me. "I wasn't sure. It could have been you, Min, or Sidra. I had to be sure."

Meg had been listening in. "He can't be The Shiv," she whispered in my ear. "Tell me he's not."

I hesitated. "He's not dead, Meg. He got away. But he's going to be coming after us—*all of us*—in a few short minutes."

Complete silence met my statement. Then, "You can't kill him," she said. "You just . . . *can't*."

My heart pounded. "Meg. If he's going to kill me, what do you expect me to do?"

Johnny said, "You kill him. You skin him alive if possible. Look, I'm sorry Meg, but it's him or us now. He *used* you."

"That's easy for you to say, now that we've proven Min Lee is innocent!"

"I'm sorry," he replied. "But it's not our fault. He's a weapon, Meg, that Russia aimed at us. Don't be fooled."

Renée said, "Mac, we're in the *Roach* and headed for The Facility. Someone there is calling us. We're ignoring it."

"Any resistance?"

"There were two people at the controls. We neutralized them."

I didn't press her about what she meant by that. Sahar was with us on the mission, listening in via comms, and I knew she wouldn't endorse killing anyone. "Dock at the supply airlock. Use an umbilical." I paused. "Sahar."

She'd been waiting for me to ask her. "You have to protect yourself, Mac. Do whatever you need to do. Stay alive for the movement. We have to get back to the Atlantic. The attack is only two days away."

I exhaled. "Thank you, Sahar."

She actually laughed. "You're about to face the fight of your life, Mac. I don't know what you're thanking me for."

"Where are you right now?"

"On the seafloor, about a hundred metres south of the base. Waiting."

I didn't know if the *Roach* had actually worked and caused a distraction. I didn't care too much at that moment. The Shiv was the person I had to worry about.

Min and Sidra were in the hall, each looking in opposite directions. The red glow from their lights surrounded them in a bloody cloud. I took a step toward them, then stopped.

I glanced back at the scuba gear we'd left in the airlock.

"What is it?" Min hissed.

"I have a feeling . . . " I muttered. "Cover me." Grabbing the tanks, I hauled three out into the corridor, along with the masks and regulators. Then I stepped out of the airlock entirely.

And it slammed shut.

Sidra's face was a mask of horror. "How'd you know?"

"Someone's watching us," I whispered. "They know we're here . . . and they want to kill us." The emergency lights should have been on in the case of an actual power failure, but they weren't. The airlock hatch had opened without a command. It had also just shut without warning.

Someone was manipulating the situation. I didn't know if it was The Shiv or not, but we had to figure a way out.

"What do we do?" Sidra whispered. "Worry about The Shiv, or go for the factory?"

I thought about it for only a heartbeat. "The factory. He'll find us. We just have to be ready. Stay on the lookout."

Turning toward the west, we began the trek through the long travel tube, away from the fusion plant. It was still black as night, and it made me swallow nervously.

We were sitting ducks. This was the way Windsor had run, and it was our only possible choice of travel. We had our tanks on our backs, just in case. The ceiling was low. Pipes and cables lined it as well as the bulkhead. Our red glow gave us some light, but we couldn't see far down the tube.

There was a distant *clunk* and the rattle of a hatch.

Something didn't feel right.

There was a sudden shift in air pressure, and a distant rumble.

I swore. "Get your masks on, now!"

There was a river of water headed for us.

There was nowhere to go. The airlock was well behind us, and there were no other hatches nearby. Our only chance was to wait for the tube to fill, but the water would hit with a force that could break limbs. The pressure of entry was extreme.

We collectively dove to the deck and grabbed deck plates to keep us down. Linking arms could work too, and beside me, Min thrust her arm under mine and hooked us down. She did the same with Sidra, on the other side. She grabbed a deck plate and glanced at me. Her face was calm and serene; there was no fear there at all.

The water hit. It was like being in a rapidly moving river; it didn't flow upward slowly and serenely like in an airlock. It was cascading around us as it ripped down the tube toward the power plant. I glanced back and saw the churning maelstrom coursing toward the way we'd come. It was not moving upward quickly, but once it reached the hatch on the far side, it would start to fill the tube.

Then, the pressure would build until it matched the outside, and once that happened, we were in serious trouble. We would have to leave the facility and find an airlock where we could decompress safely.

"We have to move!" I growled. "Get up!"

We rose to our feet and leaned into the current. Sidra's tank was gone; the force of the impact had ripped it from his back.

We took one step, then another.

Then another.

It took everything we had. Even with our weight leaning forward, it was fighting us. It was like leaning into a hurricane, and struggling for every step.

The tube disappeared into the fog of darkness ahead; I had no idea how far we had to go.

One step.

Another.

A voice called out from the PA: "You are not welcome—you'll die for coming here. All of you."

We could barely hear it over the sound of the crashing waves.

There was a thud behind us, and I turned to look. The water had finally reached the other end of the tube—at the power plant.

"Shit," I ground out. "Move!"

We continued to press forward, and the water was rising up our bodies. It was at our hips, and then seconds later at our kidneys, but it was also *slowing* as it grew deeper.

Our steps grew quicker.

The end of the tube was ahead. There was a hatch that in my heart I knew would not open. There was no hope, unless we could blow it, and then flood the entire facility.

But we had no explosives, no grenades. We only had the weapons in our holsters.

We were growing tired. Gasping for air. Fighting for every bit of movement with our very lives.

"*Move, move, move,*" Sidra was chanting.

In my ears, I could hear Meg, Renée, and Johnny crying for us. *Encouraging* us. They knew what was happening.

"Try to get into The Facility," I said to them over the comm. "Stop this. They know we're here, they're trying to kill us. But they don't know about *you* yet. We can be a distraction for you."

Situation reversed.

Now, our people in the *Roach* would use *us*.

Finally, we reached the hatch. Beside it, a large section of the tube was open to the outside. Water was flooding in, and it was up to our necks now.

"We have to go out there, find an airlock and get back in. Hopefully it's close."

I thought back to the schematic I'd seen only a few minutes ago. There were three large structures just on the other side of this tube. Each one likely had an airlock for safety reasons—for emergency escapes—and we'd just have to find one to hotwire.

The water was *pouring* into the tube and we couldn't just swim out. It was too difficult. It wasn't a hatch; it was more like a panel that someone had deliberately ripped off the tube to flood it.

The water was nearly at the ceiling. Thankfully, we had our scuba gear, but decompression was on my mind.

We didn't have time for this!

Finally, the water was nearly at the top and we squeezed out through the panel. The pressure was now at max for the depth, and I had to quickly equalize or my ears would implode; the pressure would crush them like a pancake and I'd never hear correctly again. It stunned me for a moment and I hesitated, using the Valsalva Maneuver to force air into my eardrums and increase pressure in them.

Then he attacked.

He'd picked the perfect moment to strike—right as the pressure spiked and disoriented us.

William Windsor had been outside, waiting.

The flooding tube had trapped him too, only he didn't have a tank or a mask.

He was outside, at 1,600 metres down, without any equipment and without a hope in hell.

He was desperate and dangerous, and only had a minute or two left.

It was our chance to kill him.

Maybe now our only one.

# Chapter Twenty-Seven

He grabbed my mask and tore it from my face. The water flooded in with incredible force, like a punch of solid ice. My eyes closed in reflex, but I pulled my knife and slashed across me without looking. Then I twisted my hips, angled downward, and slashed again.

Forcing my eyes open, I looked around. It was still dark, but his shape was visible just out of arm's reach. He was on Min Lee, and he was struggling with her, trying to grab her tank and mask. Sidra went at him in a flash, even though he didn't have a tank either. He was thrashing with the man, bubbles churning out from his nostrils and mouth as they struggled.

I reached out for my mask, dangling loose on the regulator hose. Putting it over my face, I purged the water and cleared it.

Then I pushed forward and prepared for The Shiv . . .

The knife was in my hand—

And he turned to face me, thrust Sidra off with an elbow, and backed off, staring at me.

He was struggling to keep from floating upward; he had no tank or belt to weigh him down.

I gestured with the knife.

He was going to die.

He looked around frantically. He needed a way back into The Facility if he was going to make it through this.

He could take a tank and mask from us, but there were three of us he'd have to get through.

He turned and swam away, disappearing into the murky blackness.

Sidra started to go after him and I grabbed him and held him back. I gestured to him to come with me, to find an airlock.

We couldn't risk staying out any longer.

The structure was close to us, and I pointed. They nodded and we swam toward it. There was a hull stretching from the seafloor upward; it was roughly four metres tall. It was hard to see anything else; the red lights only illuminated a very small sphere.

Prickles rose from the back of my neck. The Shiv was somewhere nearby. He could be right behind me, waiting to slit my throat and strip the tank from my convulsing body.

We moved southward, along the hull.

Finally, clearly painted yellow hatch marks appeared. An airlock. Sidra was buddy breathing with Min Lee and did not have a mask. I turned to the panel and studied it. The OPEN button wouldn't work.

Someone had locked it out.

It was a basic control panel though, and I removed a tool from my belt to unscrew it. I had it off in seconds and stared at the wires. The red glow had changed all the colours; yellow looked green, blue looked purple, green looked brown. I studied them, then snipped two and cross wired them quickly.

The hatch ground open.

We were back in.

—••—

"DO YOU THINK HE SURVIVED?" Sidra gasped.

We were in the airlock, dripping water and shedding equipment. We had a short decompression to endure, then we could move back into The Facility, though the staff knew we were here. "We have to assume he did. In which case, he'll be inside soon too, though he'll have to go through a decompression too."

"He'll try to stop us."

"There's a chance he'll just run," Min said.

"There's not. He's going to try to take us out."

"How do you know? If he survives, he may just—"

"Min, we know what he looks like. We know his identity. We're maybe the only ones on the planet who know, and he won't let us go." A shock rippled through my body. "The same goes for Sahar, Renée, Meg, and Johnny. They know too, and he'll have to kill us all. He's going to try. This is the only place where we're all together. He'll take us all out, now, or die trying." I adjusted my earpiece. "Did you hear that? He's going to take us all down."

Renée said in my piece, "We heard. We'll be careful."

"Where are you now?"

"In The Facility. It's dark, but there are emergency lights on. The workers have left the area; they must be hiding somewhere."

I considered that. The pressure in the airlock was dropping, air hissing out as it did so. It was bringing us back to four atms so we could re-enter the base. The personnel were likely in hiding, waiting for this to pass. "The people in control tried to kill us. They'll try again." I paused. "Where are you?"

"Storage. There are supplies here. Sheets of titanium, but untreated."

We were close to them. "We're in the airlock in the Living Sector." I studied the readout. "We have three minutes of decompression left."

"We can meet you there."

"No. Go for the Control Dome. See if you can distract the people here. We'll go for the graphene. But remember this—"

I glanced around at the others in the lock with me. "*Watch your back.* The Steel Shiv is here, and his only escape is to kill us all."

Silence met my statement.

I said, "Meg, did you hear me?"

"He won't kill me," she said.

I shook my head savagely. "You don't understand. *He has to.* It's the only way for him to continue his regular life. It's him or us now."

"He won't do it."

"And what if he kills everyone around you? Johnny, Renée, Sahar. Are you okay with that?"

"He won't do it," she said again.

I shook my head. She had a strong emotional connection to him, regardless of the truth. I knew she couldn't just shut down her feelings, or forget everything that had transpired between them. They'd been so happy on *SC-1* earlier; she'd seemed happier than I'd ever seen her. Even if he'd been acting—manipulating her—her feelings were *real.* She was a human being, and he'd twisted her emotions just to weaponize her against me. It made me furious, but she was my sister. "Just watch your back, Meg. Get to the Control Dome and try to enter. We'll go for the graphene."

The airlock chimed. The hatch wouldn't open, however, so Sidra ripped the panel off the bulkhead and stared at the wires. He cut a few and then reconnected them and it slid aside.

Things were dark, though here the emergency lights were on. We crouched in the corridor and glanced around. There were signs on the bulkheads identifying this area as quarters for the crews and workers.

"This way," Min Lee snapped. She rose to her feet and started down the corridor to the west. Sidra and I followed, our heads on swivels.

More announcements echoed from the comm system, directing crews to isolate in collection zones, cabins, and so on. Then a call turned my blood to ice. "Repel intruder alert. Military response in the factory. Repeat, go to the factory."

In a few seconds, we were going to be in a firefight.

There was a hatch ahead and I slammed a fist on the control panel.

This one would not open. There was no panel to access. It was a containment hatch, meant to keep emergency flooding at bay. There was a card scanner though, to bypass security, but we didn't have such a thing. "Uh, Johnny," I muttered. "We need your help."

"We're at the Control Dome," he whispered.

"We need this hatch opened."

"Give me a minute on it." I could hear him doing something. "We came across some people. They have cards around their necks."

I stared around me. The corridor was dim. It disappeared into blackness in the distance, though the emergency lights did provide some light. Red warning lights were also flashing, due to the intruder alert.

Footsteps echoed in the distance. They rang along deck plates as someone sprinted somewhere nearby.

Were the steps closing on us?

Was it the military response?

Or The Shiv?

Then there was another voice on the PA, directing security to the engineering sector. I frowned. We were nowhere near there. There was something off about it . . .

"That was Johnny's voice," Min Lee snapped. "He just made that announcement."

He'd said it in Mandarin. Perfect. "They're in the Control Dome," I said. "They surprised them."

It had worked. We'd ended up as the distraction for them now, and the administrators had been too focused on us.

The hatch slid aside.

The factory was on the other side, and it was massive.

The ceiling was high over our heads. There were conveyers and assembly line equipment ringing the huge area, sheets of titanium on forklifts, shelves with tools and equipment, and robotic-controlled devices moving about a grid system of rods suspended from the ceiling.

The workers had departed abruptly, leaving everything in mid-production.

The graphene secret was in this area.

"You're not going to get it," a voice called out.

I stopped and stared at the figure approaching from the bowels of the factory.

It was The Steel Shiv, William Windsor.

He was marching toward me. There was something different about him now. It was in the way he held himself. His gait. His stature.

He was menacing.

His musculature was obvious under the skin-tight wetsuit.

He was coming for me.

"Johnny," I muttered. "He's here. In the factory."

"Got it," came the crisp reply.

I hoped he could restrain the leadership there and get back to us in time to help.

I stepped toward him. "You killed Cliff. You brought us all here, for your hero, Captain Ventinov."

"He's not my hero." The accent was still utterly British. It was a contradiction; this man was a Russian spy, but he'd spent a good part of childhood and education in England.

"And yet you follow his orders."

"I don't follow anyone's orders, Mac."

"So you work strictly for money? You're a mercenary, is that it?"

"When I want to be. But I do what's best for Russia. To reclaim past glory."

I snorted. "That's Ventinov's goal too, but he's a pathetic loser. Just like you."

"Hardly. You're about to die. Do you know that?"

"You sound like a Brit, not a Russian. You've lost sense of who you are. You're nothing, caught between nations, cast aside. Your own parents gave you up. They don't care about you, and they never did. *No one* cares about you, Windsor."

"I said, call me Bill." He had stopped advancing and was staring at me. "Your attempt at psychology is useless. You can't survive this."

"I'm going to try my best, *William*." I said to the others, "Find the computer control system, a nozzle, and a tank of the vapor. I'll take care of this."

Sidra faced me slowly. Horror laced his features. "Mac. Are you sure? You want to do this on your own?"

Windsor was smiling. He knew that his chances of survival had just increased a hundredfold.

But he'd killed Cliff Sim and left his body here, in this facility, for them to later dump out into the ocean. Cliff hadn't deserved that.

And I was going to make The Shiv pay.

# Chapter Twenty-Eight

He was standing right in front of me. For days he had been the source of the mystery and the focus of my anger. Trying to figure out who he was, dragging him here with me, allowing him to think that he was leading us there when in fact it had been the reverse.

Now I had my chance.

I took a deep breath.

Sahar had said earlier that this would be the fight of my life.

It was not an understatement.

I took another deep breath and stepped toward him. The gun was at my side, in my holster, but I wanted to break this man, the way he'd broken Cliff.

He had a cocky grin on his face, tilting his head slightly to the side as he watched me. "You think you can survive?" he said.

"Where's your helmet now? You can't disguise yourself. I know who you are. You're just a silly English school boy."

"I'm Russian. Don't forget it."

"You don't sound Russian."

I feinted with a right and leveled a series of strikes at his head. It was a boxing combination and he bobbed and ducked and blocked every single punch. I matched his movements and we fell into fighting stances, circling, watching, studying each other.

He tagged me with a punch a moment later, and it rang my bell. I saw stars. It had been the hardest hit I'd ever taken; his knuckles felt like iron. I stepped back, shaking my head.

"How'd you like that?" he chuckled.

"Not bad," I said. I stepped forward and launched another attack, which he defended easily.

But I saw my opening a second later. When I punched with a left, he blocked with his right, but his left elbow dropped just a bit.

I swung an immense right roundhouse kick and powered through his block.

It worked.

I connected with his jaw and continued the kick, spinning as it landed, and then immediately swept his legs out from under him.

But he saw that move coming, and he hopped back and over my sweep.

Still, the kick had dazed him.

"How'd you like that?" I said.

He was shaking his head and rubbing his jaw.

I said, "Too bad you're not wearing your helmet. That kick hurt, no?"

He stepped back again, staring at me.

"I've taken worse. Your man Cliff was a tough fight."

We advanced again, toward each other, and continued the war.

He was smaller than I was. I considered getting him in a grapple and ending up on the deck, perhaps choking him out and breaking an arm or two. But despite the temptation, I didn't want to try it. Surely Cliff had, and something must have worked against him.

I remembered the series of knife wounds in Cliff's side.

The Steel Shiv had struck there.

I didn't want it to come to that with this man.

He was fast, he was agile. There was real power to his strikes. He wasn't wearing down, and he wasn't tired. He'd trained for fights like this, I knew. He was ready.

But I was too.

And I was highly motivated to avenge Cliff.

I tried an elbow and he blocked it. Another and he blocked that too. Then I threw one and at the same time kneed him in the gut.

That worked. He took the hit, hunching forward and absorbing it, but then he swung a right that hit me hard in the temple.

It staggered me.

He saw an opening and punched again and again. I tried to block them, but a series got through and dazed me again.

I stumbled back.

He advanced, and I slumped downward before him. He swung an enormous kick at the side of my head—

And I shot up, blocked it, grabbed his leg, and lashed out with my own kick at his face.

Connecting squarely with his nose, there was an explosion of blood which splattered my face. He fell back, gurgling, as blood spilled down his lips and chin.

He was off balance and struggling now, but so was I.

He pulled his blade and held it up. He gasped for air as he stared at me. Blood continued to pour from his nose, and he spit some at me, splattering my face.

He wanted to use his knife now.

Shit.

It was a curved dagger, and the hilt had a ring that surrounded his knuckles. He could slice and punch at the same time with this weapon.

It was a combination brass knuckles and homemade shiv.

My heart pounded. I didn't much want to get in a knife fight with this man.

With an assassin whose very name glorified his skills with a blade.

I crouched and pulled my own dagger. I was not great with knives, though. It was stupid to play his game and I knew I should just pull my gun.

But I matched his actions.

He smiled, an evil cockeyed grin.

We sliced and blocked and parried and sparks flew where the blades collided. The flashes reflected in his eyes as he studied me; he almost wasn't even watching the knives. He was staring into my eyes, and his seemed so cold, so hard, without an ounce of emotion inside. He didn't care about anything. I knew in that moment that he cared nothing for Meg; he'd only used her to weaken me and my family. To erode my resolve and instill hesitation.

I screamed as I struck again and again, but each one he blocked and countered easily. He swung after each and his shiv *whooshed* past, cutting my flesh as it cut the air.

My forearms were dripping blood. They were throbbing and within a minute were crimson slick. He moved forward and forced me back, on my heels. I stumbled.

A voice called, "Mac! Use your gun!"

It was Sidra. He could see I was failing.

The Shiv's nose was still bleeding, but there was a snarl on his face now. His lips were curled upward, and he was moving forward mercilessly, pushing me backward.

Backward.

Backward.

My arms could barely function.

I reached down to my right side, for my gun, but my arm would barely move.

He swung at my right side—my arm was down and could not block—and his knuckles cracked against my face. Solid steel.

Teeth rattled in my mouth, and I spit them out.

I fell to my knees, dazed.

He had me.

I was gone.

*Cliff, Meg, Renée, Johnny . . . I'm sorry.*

*I tried, I really did.*

My vision was so dark, I could barely see what was happening. The Shiv was advancing toward me.

William Windsor? Was that his name?

Or was it something else?

Did he still go by a Russian name?

He approached, his blade at my throat.

He was laughing.

I could only exhale, and there were gurgles of blood in my breath.

A figure exploded into my consciousness, hurtling at the Russian. It caught him off guard and he stumbled sideways. His dagger fell and skittered across the deck. There were a flurry of punches and kicks—

It was Sidra and Min. Both at once. They were on the man and fighting with everything they had.

I was on my stomach, arms stretched out. Blood covered me. My arms were useless and my face was one, giant bruise. Before me, I knew the three were engaged in bloody battle, but I couldn't make out what was happening. I reached down for my gun again.

Stretching out on the cold deck plates, I finally pulled the gun out and held it before me. It was trembling and shaking—I could barely hold it straight. The three before me were a blur. Just shadows. My vision was dim. I was not thinking clearly.

Who was I supposed to shoot?

I couldn't remember.

All three of the people before me looked terrible. Blood everywhere. All were beaten and bruised. I couldn't make anyone out, or, I couldn't tell who was the enemy. I couldn't remember. My head hurt too much. My vision was quivering, trembling.

I aimed upward, over all their heads, and fired.

The shot rang out, and all three stopped suddenly, turned and faced me slowly.

Arms were in the air.

"Stop," I rasped through shattered teeth. I could barely sound the words out properly. "Move and die."

My eyesight was still blurry, and I didn't exactly know what I was doing anymore. I only knew that I had to stop this before people died. Well, one death was okay.

I just couldn't remember which one.

"Don't move" I said again.

"Mac, fire at The Shiv!" one of them yelled. Sidra? "Not us! Kill *him!*"

The barrel was shaking too much.

And then he swung again. I couldn't do anything. Dazed, concussed, dizzy—I couldn't think clearly.

There were a barrage of punches and then pounding footsteps receding on the deck.

# Chapter Twenty-Nine

I COULDN'T DO IT.

Couldn't beat The Shiv, one on one. He'd been too good. I'd wanted to avenge Cliff in hand-to-hand combat, and defeat the man who'd killed my friend. To show him that he'd messed with the wrong person.

But I'd failed.

As my senses returned, as I spit out bits of teeth and wiped blood from my face and as Meg and Johnny wrapped my arms with gauze from a first aid kit to staunch the bleeding, I knew we were in grave danger.

"You'll need stitches, Mac," Johnny was saying. "They're deep. You're damn lucky to still be with us."

I shook my head and stared at my surroundings. We were in the Control Dome. It wasn't large—maybe fifty metres in diameter—but it looked much like any control center in an underwater colony. There were consoles to monitor pressure, life support, power generation and usage, recycling, and sonar stations to study the surroundings. But there were also large banks of consoles for the factory, to monitor output and power and the speed of the assembly line.

Dimly, I realized slowly that someone had carried—*dragged*—me there, and there were others with us, too.

There were two officers wearing uniforms, staring at me. They weren't military uniforms, but they were industrial supervisors of some sort. Their features clearly showed disgust and horror as they stared at my face and my injuries. I muttered, "Sorry to interfere with your operations."

"You will leave, *now*," the woman said.

I glanced at Johnny. "Status?"

"We've sealed the military squad in one of the sectors. They're trying to get out. They'll figure a way, soon. She's right. We have to leave." His voice was urgent as he continued wrapping my arm.

I turned back to the woman. "Name?"

"Administrator Zhao Lin. You will get out, immediately."

"I'm only here because you led me here."

She appeared confused for a moment. "I did no such thing. We are a Chinese manufacturing plant. You infiltrated and attacked us."

I shook my head. "You killed my Chief Security Officer here. Ten days ago. Do you deny that?"

That stopped her. She looked taken aback and she glanced at her assistant.

I continued, "I saw the photos. You either did it, or you assisted the murderer."

"You're here to kill us? It was Russia. We only gave them a place to conduct an operation, and it was out of our hands. Orders, from my superiors. We did nothing."

"Exactly. *Nothing*, as a Russian agent slaughtered my man. He almost killed us, too."

She had nothing to say to that; she only stared at me, her expression hard. Then, "Get out," she said again.

I turned to Meg. "He is still here. He's working for Ventinov. He has to finish his job. He used you to get to me."

She continued wrapping my arm, but her movements were sudden, sharp, and rougher.

Zhao reacted strongly to my mention of Ventinov. She'd flinched and her eyes had grown even harder. I said, "You know him. The Russian Captain."

"Yes," she said angrily. "He is responsible for this."

"He threw you to the wolves," I said. It didn't translate well into Mandarin, however; I wished I knew a proper colloquial phrase for her in her language, but couldn't come up with one.

She shook her head and looked around at us. Me, Min, and Sidra were a wreck, all bloody and bruised. Johnny, Meg, and Renée were tending to our injuries. Sahar was still in *SC-1*, waiting, but listening.

Zhao said, "You are clearly a team of spies who failed at . . . at *whatever* you were attempting. All of you look like operatives. Three of you are badly injured. One of you—a white American—speaks and understands Mandarin, which is rare. This is clearly something that is out of my experience. I am asking you to leave, and this is my final warning. If you don't, when my security squad escapes, I'll order them to kill you all. I'll dump you out the airlock."

"Like you did my CSO?" I snapped.

"I didn't kill him. *We* didn't. The Russian left the body and we had to deal with it."

"So you're innocent in this?"

"Yes."

I exhaled and shook my head. Then I examined my bandages. Grabbing Johnny and Meg for support, I hauled myself to my feet. "You have your wish," I said to Zhao. "We're leaving." I adjusted my PCD settings and said, "Sahar, can you dock with The Facility via umbilical? The Administrator will allow us to leave."

There was no response.

"Sahar?" I said again. Sidra snapped his gaze at me, concerned. I tried again, "Are you there?"

Johnny marched to the sonar screen. He pointed. "I don't see anything moving out there, Mac."

The seacar had settled down on the seafloor when we'd debarked, and was still quiet.

Could The Shiv have made it out there? And gotten on board?

If so, he was likely decompressing in the airlock. But why wouldn't Sahar respond?

I stared at the schematic of the station, in the center of the sonar display. We had two options, and one was on the west side, attached to the umbilical.

"Let's go," I said. "We have to get out."

"Where?" Meg asked. She was staring at the sonar, hoping against hope that *SC-1* would appear and that Sahar would speak and everything would be fine.

I pointed at Zhao and her assistant. "Bring them."

We marched through the darkened facility. There was still noise coming from the factory as machinery continued to operate, as hoists dragged sections of hull and moved from station to station, but there were no personnel around to monitor the production.

Sidra was nearly frantic. "We have to get to *SC-1*. What is going on out there? Why isn't she responding?"

"*He's* there," I whispered. "He's on board."

His face was pale. "We have to go save her."

I stopped and faced him. "Don't worry. *He'll* come to us. He wants us. He won't hurt her. *Yet*."

He hesitated. "Do you have a plan, Mac?"

"Not really. I only suspect what he's going to do. That might help us." Then I turned to Zhao. "Do you have a seacar here? A transport?"

Zhao said, in a huff, "Nothing at present. The last supply vessel was two days ago. The pickup for our product is in three days."

"No emergency vessels? How are you to escape in a catastrophe?"

"I'm afraid the mainland doesn't care about things like that."

I swore. "Fantastic." I turned to Min Lee. "Is this true?"

"It's very possible." Her lips were swollen. She was slurring her words. "The CSF likely visits on occasion to keep people in order. They rule by fear, and keep people working because there's simply no place for anyone to go."

Zhao said, "It's hardly like that here! We take good care of our—"

"Shut up," I said. I thought for a second more. So, the Docking Module was pointless. "We're going to the supply airlock."

She was surprised. "What for? I want you *out*. Now."

"We're leaving. You're going to order everyone out of the *Roach*. And then we're going to get on board and leave. You have your wish."

—••—

THERE WERE SLIGHTLY MORE THAN fifty people on board the mining vehicle. No one really knew what was going on as they filed off the vessel and entered the manufacturing base. They stared at us as they passed through the umbilical in a single line and marched deeper into the base. We stood behind Zhao and her assistant, a man named Yan, with guns in their backs.

Eventually, the *Roach* was empty. Johnny carried a small duffle that he'd found from somewhere; he'd shoved a tank of carbon vapor, a computer, and a nozzle from the factory floor into it.

Zhao did not suspect us of taking anything, but I knew when they reviewed the video footage of the entire incident, they'd figure out that we'd been there for more than just revenge.

I said to her, "You better hope we can kill The Shiv."

She blinked. "What are you talking about?"

"The Russian assassin. If he thinks you'll spill his secret, he'll come for you next."

"I hope he kills you, McClusky."

"If he does, you're next. Remember that."

We stepped through the airlock and began down the umbilical, into the *Roach*.

"You deserve to die for this!" she screamed at my back.

"The day's not done yet," I muttered. "It's only just started, in fact."

# Interlude

## In The Iron Plains

DATA PROCESSING

| | |
|---|---|
| Location: | Latitude: 12º 27′ 28″ N<br>Longitude: 182º 46′ 32″ W<br>On the seafloor in The Iron Plains; aboard SC-1 |
| Depth: | 1,693 metres |
| Date: | 13 June 2131 |
| Time: | 0318 hours |

VASILY KINZHAL STALI WAS IN *SC-1*. He'd faced Truman McClusky and had won. He hadn't doubted the outcome, but still, he had to admit to having a few nerves. Vengeance tended to make people stronger, more vicious, more willing to risk it all on one sudden strike or attack. Sometimes it worked, but sometimes it didn't.

Mac had been a tough opponent.

But The Steel Shiv had beaten him.

But then the others had jumped into the fight to save him. Sidra Noor and Min Lee. *Shit!* he thought. *Those two prevented me from killing my target!*

And not only that, now they all knew his identity.

They'd all been listening in during Mac's great reveal. He couldn't believe that the man had actually done that to him. He'd deciphered the mystery and unveiled it all in a secure, confined location while Vasily couldn't act.

Vasily shook his head. Mac was clever indeed.

But all was not lost, and the day was still young. It was only three in the morning, and he hadn't achieved his mission, but things were still progressing. Ventinov would be pissed, of that there was no doubt. The Chinese would be pissed. The team had damaged the facility, spies had infiltrated it, and during his fight with McClusky, Vasily had noted that the other two were stealing the factory's secrets.

No matter.

When he killed the group of Triestrians, protecting his identity, he would take the graphene and sell that to the highest bidder.

Before he could do that, however, he'd have to return to the factory and kill everyone there, too.

They knew who he was, now. At the very least, they had video of his face. He hadn't had his helmet with him.

But he'd run from the fight. There'd been no choice. He'd left via an airlock, and with scuba equipment from the lockers, had swum to *SC-1*. He'd entered its airlock, decompressed, and now he had possession of the great seacar.

*Mac's seacar.*

*SC-1.*

And, he thought, he even had a hostage.

He stared at Sahar Noor, sitting serenely on the couch in the seacar's living area. She was wearing a black hijab and a black scarf.

Black, to denote death, he thought.

Fitting.

She would make an exceptional prisoner.

"Leave at once," she said. "You betrayed me. You betrayed Oceania and all of us." And then, even more stern, "You betrayed Britain."

"What do you care for Britain, Mayor? You just declared independence from them!"

"I didn't declare war. We're still allies with economic treaties."

He snorted. "Right. They're just going to let you walk away."

"It's different. Climate change means they're looking for hope. We have that for them. And independently, we have more to offer the topside nations than as colonies." She stared at him for a long moment, and he just waited. "Why even debate with you?" she continued. "You're a traitor. Get off this ship."

"I have a job to do first."

She blinked. "You failed. You couldn't do it. Mac beat you."

He felt his skin tingle. "No. He didn't beat me. I beat him."

"Your face looks terrible. He's still alive. He won."

"He *didn't* win."

"You didn't beat him. You couldn't kill him. That means you lost."

"No, it doesn't!" He felt the heat rising within him. He didn't want to lose control, but she was pushing his buttons.

And it was working.

"We're in his seacar now. His precious vehicle." He pointed out a viewport. "They're in the *Roach*. Don't you think we can destroy them easily?"

She couldn't respond to that. She simply watched him.

He turned and marched to the pilot cabin. So be it. He'd just *show* her what he was going to do with the power at his fingertips.

He didn't fail.

He never would.

And he had *never* failed a mission.

—••—

SAHAR NOOR STARED AT WINDSOR'S back as he marched away. He seemed like a different person. His demeanor, expression, speech, and tone had all changed. He was still speaking with a British accent, but he'd morphed into something . . . *different*.

Fear washed through her as she realized what was happening. The end seemed inevitable. She knew he would never let any of them survive.

He'd arrived at *SC-1* fifteen minutes earlier. It had been a strange situation. She'd been waiting on the seafloor for Mac and the team to return. She'd been listening in on the comms and knew everything that had transpired. She'd heard about Windsor's real identity, and it had floored her. She was his boss and had directed him in Churchill Intelligence for many years, and he'd pulled the wool over everyone's eyes. He was skilled, trained, and an expert at subterfuge and disguise. This was final proof.

But then she'd heard someone *outside* the seacar. Tinkering with something, knocking or clanging something. She'd immediately tried to call Mac, but nothing. The comms had failed.

It was Windsor.

It had to be.

The Steel Shiv.

Her skull prickled.

*He'd* done it from the outside.

*How?*

She slammed her hand on the airlock hatch control and locked it out. She could not allow him to enter.

Then the outer airlock hatch slid open anyway. He'd bypassed the control pad.

He was in the airlock and depressurizing.

Panic rose in Sahar but she clamped down on it. She had won her spot as Mayor by staying in control. By being calm in the toughest situations. By managing her normal fears and emotions and anxieties.

She stared at the console in *SC-1*.

There were a few things she had to do, immediately, or the others would be in serious trouble.

Then . . .

The Shiv would kill her.

The weapons controls were the first. The Chinese Facility was directly before her, only a hundred metres away, and a torpedo would implode it. She'd couldn't allow that to happen.

She quickly brought the weapon systems up on the main screen and locked them out. She instructed the computer to request a code upon weapon activation. Countermeasures *or* torpedoes.

She pushed the final button.

*Done.*

She stared at the navigation console. That was next. Keep him wondering where the hell he was. Turn off the sonar and nav system.

Something happened at that point which startled Sahar. The pressure started to build in the ship. Air was hissing in. A coffee cup with a lid next to her in the pilot cabin suddenly squashed flat.

She gasped.

Windsor had accessed the seacar's environmental controls *from inside the airlock.*

He was increasing air pressure so he could get out of the airlock faster, then decompress inside the vessel without fear of decompression sickness and death.

She swallowed.

She'd have to work faster.

Soon she'd locked out the sonar system too.

Those were the two systems he'd need to destroy anything: weapons and sonar.

The pressure continued to build. Sahar's eardrums were in agony.

A headache had spiked and she could now barely focus on the panels.

The inner airlock hatch sighed open behind her, and she turned to see who it was.

But she already knew.

William Windsor.

The Steel Shiv.

She'd never cursed in her life. Her parents had taught her that there were better ways to express oneself. There was always a way out of tough situations, and bad words wouldn't solve anything, they'd say. *Focus on the problem, Sahar. You're brave and intelligent, you can get out of any tough predicament. Just think it through and a solution will appear. Allah will show the way.*

But Windsor was snarling as he focused his steely gaze on her.

He advanced quickly, and she rose to her feet and put her hands in the air.

—••—

NOW HE WAS AT THE controls and trying to activate *SC-1*'s systems. He hadn't killed her or restrained her, but she knew it was inevitable, after what Mac had said. After the truths he'd brought to light.

She swallowed the nerves away and continued to watch him.

He flipped some switches and stared at the screen.

Then he turned to stare at her; she was behind the control cabin, in the living area, on the couch.

"What did you do, Sahar?" he growled.

"Locked out the weapons. You can't use this vessel to kill. Not with me on it."

"Unlock the systems."

"No."

"I will slit your throat, Sahar, and watch you die."

"I won't do it. And something tells me you're going to kill us all anyway, so I'm not going to make this easier on you." She thought of her brother and his strength. He'd always fought hard. All of his training during school. Part time jobs. Getting good grades during it all. His university education. Then the training in Churchill Intelligence. He was strong too. He would be able to resist this monster, even if it meant his death. And her parents dealt with ignorance every day. Racist stares and outright words. They'd endured it for *decades* but it had not broken them. Instead, her parents had taught their children peace and coexistence. She'd used that in her politics, and it was why people embraced her so. They loved her, and she could draw from that too. She would draw from her brother's strength, from her parents', from her people at Churchill, and from her own constitution. She was strong. She'd get through this, even if she died, for there would be a place for her if that happened, she knew.

She was at peace with herself.

She took a deep breath and locked eyes with Windsor. "Bill."

"What?" he snapped.

"You're fired."

# Part Seven

## The Roach

# THE ROACH

NODULE HARVESTER | MINING VESSEL

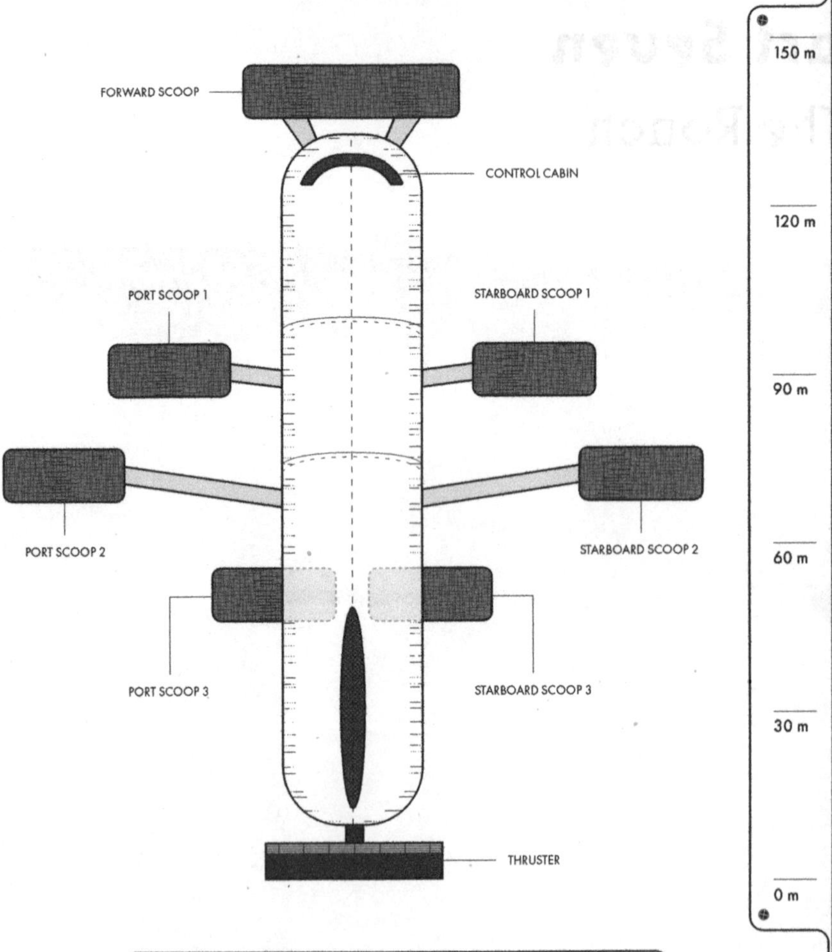


FUNCTION: Harvest nodules from seafloor; Minimal navigation abilities
BUOYANCY: Negative when in operation
HARVESTING STRIP MAXIMUM ———— 120 m
HULL DIMENSIONS ———— 30 m x 145 m
CREW ———— 53
MAX VELOCITY: 8 km/hr during harvesting; 40 km/hr when empty

# Chapter Thirty

We were on the *Roach*. It was a massive, crawling, mining machine. The scoop harvesters spun several inches down into the surface, churning up gravel and rock, swallowing it into the massive vessel's belly. There, along conveyers, the system sorted and dumped out the sand and pea-sized rocks. It was the potato-sized rocks that they wanted, the polymetallic nodules that refineries could process into ingots of pure iron, nickel, copper, and manganese.

I stared at the controls. We were in the large control cabin, which was twenty metres across. There was a curving viewport at the bow, though it was too dark to see outside without the lights. At the rear of the chamber was a ladder that led down into the bowls of the vessel, toward the mining collectors and rock-sorting conveyers. There was a lot of noise coming from the open hatch; a rattling and crashing as rocks churned into the beast.

Johnny flicked a switch and the seafloor before us lit. We didn't need the thresher scoops on, so I pulled the throttles for all seven toward me, to zero. Then I pushed the throttle for the main thruster forward.

"How fast can this go?" Renée said, at my side.

"Not fast while harvesting. But we're going to shed load and move as quickly as we can." I glanced at her. "Can you find out how to dump the nodules? There's a belly cargo offload hatch control somewhere." There were currently hundreds of tons of rock in the holds. If we dumped them, we'd be able to achieve positive buoyancy, ascend, and navigate more like a submarine.

It would be hard to handle, unstable and slow, but we could do it.

"On it," she said as she moved to a different console.

I continued to push the throttle forward. The vibration in the deck increased, and the seafloor outside began to crawl by.

The threshers weren't turning, however, and we rode on those much like tires. They were supposed to dig into the floor *and* help us move forward, albeit slowly.

Our speed was only five kilometres per hour. At that rate, it would take twenty hours. Too long. By then we'd likely all be dead, at The Shiv's hands.

"Where are we going, Tru?" Meg asked.

She'd been quiet since discovering what Windsor had done to us in the fight. She was processing the information, which would take time to fully understand, but I was okay with that. "The Complex."

"Why?"

"Johnny and Min Lee left their *Sword* there. It's the only option right now. We have to defeat Windsor."

Meg looked angry for a second, but clamped down on her response.

Min said, "I still can't believe you thought I was The Shiv."

"We've been over this already. I didn't know."

"But really? *Me?*"

"The helmet and voice distorter. There was a reason for it. And the bruises on your arms and the timing of your arrival. It all fit." I shrugged. "But there was good evidence for all three of you. I needed to confront you to find out once and for all."

"And you did it *here*, at the Chinese Facility?" Sidra asked.

"Confined in an airlock during decompression. It was the only place. Had I done it on *SC-1*, it would have put everyone at risk. Meg, Renée, Sahar."

"Really," he said. "We're in a predicament now, man."

"If I hadn't revealed him, he would have killed us all in there, *during* the mission. Do you realize that? It was his plan."

His face went blank. "I—I'm not thinking clearly right now. I'm worried about Sahar and what's happening to her. But you might be right."

"He's right," Renée said from the other side of the cabin. She was pushing buttons and the vessel seemed to be bouncing as she did. "He would have stolen the graphene secret and sold it to the highest bidder. He would have killed us all to maintain his identity. He's still going to try, too."

I ran my tongue across my broken teeth. They hurt like hell, my lips were swollen, and I was still slurring my words. I had double vision as well. The controls at my fingers were hazy and indistinct. I said to Meg, "Maybe you can talk to him. Communicate and see if he'll answer."

She was staring at me. Hesitating. In a flash of understanding, it came to me: *She was worried that it would confirm the truth.*

She didn't want it, just yet.

Then she nodded. "I'll try."

The ship bounced some more and the vibrations slowed. A cloud of dust and debris swirled around the *Roach* now as we moved forward. Our speed was increasing, and we weren't digging into the bottom so much. We'd dumped the entire load of nodules.

The ballast controls were next to the thresher scoop throttles. I shifted them to positive. There was a sigh of water through pipes, then a hissing scream, and the digital display showed the ballast tanks emptying.

We began to rise slightly, and lift off the bottom.

I waited until we were five hundred metres off the ocean floor before starting to navigate. The vessel was 120 metres from port to starboard. One sharp bank could result in a scoop scraping the bottom and tearing the vessel apart in an instant.

Implosion.

The vertical stabilizer's rudder allowed me to shift course, and I pushed the thruster to max.

Forty kph.

*Much better.* We'd arrive at The Complex in about two hours.

"Johnny."

He was nearby, and he approached. "Are you okay? I can find some pain killers in the clinic down below."

"That would be great actually, but I can go." I paused. "Windsor is going to be on us soon. He'll be firing torpedoes."

"Seems likely."

"We need to do something to protect ourselves."

—••—

MEG SAT AT THE COMM console. She was breathing hard and staring at the panel before her. Her arms were at her sides; she was still. I put my hand on her shoulder. "Are you okay, Sis?"

"No."

"I'm sorry about this."

"Don't treat me like a child."

"I'm your older brother."

"By only a few seconds." She snorted. "I really like that guy, Tru." She shot a look at my face then turned away. "But what he did to you . . . "

I understood her pain. For years, we'd had no family. Mom and Dad, both dead. Me in Trieste, and Meg in Blue Downs. We'd only reconnected two years earlier, but I had Renée now, and she had . . . nobody, really. Then Windsor came along, and suddenly she was smiling again and there was more there than simple emotions. I recalled the noises I'd heard from her bunk . . .

And now, *this.*

Betrayed by not just a man, but by an assassin who now wanted to kill her and everyone around her.

She raised her hands to the console and keyed a button, selected a frequency, and grabbed the mic. "Bill. Are you there?"

I left her to the attempts and studied the nav panel. We were on our way to The Complex. I knew The Shiv would follow. He had to. I could only hope that Sahar had somehow prevented him from leaving, but I knew it would only be temporary.

Johnny's vessel at The Complex was our *only* option, because we needed it to get back to the Gulf before the battle.

The *Roach* around me vibrated madly. It was not exactly hydrodynamic. The water was hitting the scoops, which were like giant anchors holding us back. Currents were pushing the vessel to and fro, we were dipping to the port and the starboard. Engineers had designed these vehicles to drive *on* the ocean floor for days or weeks at a time, not forge through heavy currents like a submarine.

The sonar chimed and I shot a look at the display.

There was a white light on it now, behind us and closing.

*SC-1*.

It was in SCAV drive, and it was coming fast.

"I'm guessing we don't have any weapons?" I said to Johnny.

He offered me a dry chuckle. "Mac, we've got *nothing*."

Min Lee was standing beside him, staring out the port. Our forward spotlights were on, and the odd fish or creature flashed by, but otherwise the only thing visible was swirls of plankton and green water.

I said, "I'm sorry your reunion wasn't better."

"We've had a good time, actually," Min responded. "The voyage from Trieste gave us privacy." She glanced at Johnny. "We'll get through this, Mac."

"I don't know about that."

"I'm sure you have some tricks up your sleeve."

I shrugged. "My seacar has SCAV drive and can go more than ten times our current speed. She has SCAV torpedoes as well." I shook my head. "Independence might die here, right now."

A silence fell over us. We were standing on the bridge, staring at the giant viewport, and the white glare from the sonar shone upward at us. It was a warning of what was coming.

The Shiv was on his way.

Sidra was staring at it. "Sahar will help us. I'm sure she can."

"She'll do her best," I agreed. "But in the end . . . "

"How much time until The Complex?" Renée asked.

"An hour."

Another minute passed. Meg continued trying to reach Windsor, with no effect.

Sidra pointed at the sonar. "There's something odd there, Mac."

"What?"

"His course. It's not an intercept."

I studied it. He was correct. It was slightly off. He was heading in the general direction of The Complex, but could miss it entirely. In fact—

In fact, he might not even know where *we* were.

If Sahar had disabled the sonar on *SC-1* . . .

I slammed the throttle back. "Johnny, turn off the forward lights."

He did so and the view instantly switched to black.

I kept some throttle on, for I knew his SCAV would keep him

from hearing even loud sounds, and we had to keep moving. I couldn't stop completely.

We stared at the light on the sonar as it continued to shoot across the screen.

He was going to miss us.

Then the speaker crackled. Meg's eyes went wide. "Bill, is that you? Do you hear me?"

"You can't win this, Meg. Let me end it for you quickly. It won't hurt."

Her eyes narrowed and she hunched forward, closer to the mic. "Tell me this isn't true. You're not a double agent."

"I'm not a double agent." The response had been immediate, and his British accent precise, clipped, and clean.

"Then why hurt others who are on your side?"

"They're not on my side, Meg. I'm an agent for Russia, no one else."

Meg blinked. She glanced at me. "But what about Churchill? What about your allegiance to—"

"I have *never* worked for them. I pretended to. I was good at that. Falsifying reports, making claims that no one could substantiate. But all this time, since I was eight years old, it's been Russia. *For* Russia. And you're going to die for my country, today, Meg."

She stared at the comm, her jaw hanging open and her eyes wide.

There was a long pause.

"Where's Sahar?" she finally asked, her voice a husk.

There was no response.

Sidra's face was white. Shock painted his features. "It can't be," he said. "She can't be gone."

I said, "Have faith. We need to get to The Complex. We'll figure out more there."

Then *SC-1* heeled to the side and changed course. The sonar system beeped angrily.

*Collison alert.*

He was headed directly for us.

# Chapter Thirty-One

The contact on the sonar glowed angrily and obscured all other sounds in the region as it approached. *SCAV-1*'s drive was *loud*. Powering toward us at 450 kph, it was a missile that could destroy us as easily as a torpedo. Even though our mining machine, the *Roach*, was a hundred metres long, all Windsor had to do was target the bridge and he'd wipe us all out in an instant. The vessel was likely large enough to withstand such a strike and maintain buoyancy, but it would kill us all.

But that didn't make sense. He'd kill himself and end his chances at maintaining his identity if he did that. The people at The Facility would expose him, eventually, once they watched the video surveillance recordings.

Something else was going on here.

I adjusted course and made us positively buoyant again. We began to rise and banked slightly to port as we did so. Then I leveled us out again and stared at the sonar. He hadn't changed his depth. He was going to pass by below us.

He still didn't know where we were.

He'd been guessing.

There was less than an hour now to The Complex, but *SC-1* continued to cut past us again and again. He was still using the SCAV drive, and hadn't figured out that if he wanted to identify us, he should run silent and listen carefully.

Still . . . it was obvious that his sonar and weapons were not functional.

Johnny said, "He's trying to intimidate us? He's sending us a message?"

"He's telling us to stop and let him board?" Renée added.

"No," Sidra said, emphatic. "Sahar would have locked him out of the systems."

Meg frowned. "Really?"

"Consider the events," he continued. "We fought him in the factory. He eventually ran. He knew there were three of us against one—"

"Although I was out of it," I muttered.

"And he had no choice. There was also a military squad in that base, somewhere. He did the only thing he could. He swam out to *SC-1*, boarded, and then—"

"He had to decompress," Renée interjected. "In the airlock."

"That would have given Sahar some time. She realized what was going on."

"But she didn't contact us."

"He must have locked out the comms from the outside. Maybe damaged the antenna. Then he's in the airlock going through a short decompression. She had a few minutes and did the only thing she could."

I sighed. "It makes sense."

Sidra gestured out the viewport. "And now he's just zigzagging across our path, hoping to connect with us or to make visual contact, which isn't likely at this depth and with our lights off. He's just trying to find us before we get to The Complex and Johnny's seacar."

So. Sahar once again figured out a way to salvage everything.

But she was on board my seacar with a maniac.

"Meg," I said. "Imagine Sahar *has* locked out the sonar and weapons, and she doesn't give up the code. *Could* he figure out a way to fire?"

She stared at me. I could see the conflict roiling through her mind. Then she nodded imperceptibly. "He could go into the weapons bay and bypass the computer entirely. Load a weapon manually and fire without any electronics."

"And the sonar?"

She considered that. "No. That's entirely computer controlled. He can't get that to operate manually."

I sat in a chair with the controls. "Then that's what he's going to do. He'll figure it out any minute, if he hasn't already." I turned back to

Johnny. "Have you prepared the broadcast?"

"Yes."

Meg stared at him. "What do you mean?"

I said, "In case he fires. We need a way to avoid the torpedoes." I pointed at the nav system. "We're still thirty minutes from The Complex."

And then, ten minutes later, The Shiv finally managed to fire a weapon.

The sonar shrieked. There was a red line on the screen. It had originated from *SC-1*—from the glowing star on the display—and arrowed out to the west. Then, it slowly turned to the south, and locked to us.

It was now headed directly for us, and its speed ramped up quickly. The callout label next to it reported its velocity: 1020 kph. Even the letters seemed angry—red and flashing for attention.

The collision alert sounded.

Only seconds left.

"Johnny," I muttered.

At my side, he pressed a button on the comms console, and then he nodded to me. "Done."

I slammed our ballast to negative and stared at the depth display. We had over eight hundred metres below us to spare, and we began to descend. The ballast was flooding in. The sound of water churning into the large tanks was thunderous; it was crashing into the baffles meant to keep it from sloshing around a large space, which would cause instability.

Meanwhile the sonar was *crying* for attention.

I wondered absently what the computer would be thinking. *Did it know its existence was about to end?*

*Was it actually pleading with me to do something?*

But we already had.

The signal transmitted outward in all directions, in a sphere a thousand metres in diameter. Its message was simple and clear.

The Shiv had managed to fire a weapon. It was a devastating torpedo: cutting through the water at a thousand kph, surrounded by a bubble of air, it was a supercavitating weapon and hardly silent—it *screamed* its intentions to everyone and inflicted fear and terror in its targets. It was a Trumpet of Jericho some two hundred years after WWII, but its purpose and effect was the same.

The missile was telling us we were about to die.

The sonar was interpreting it and also telling us to just drop everything and *move*.

Our depth continued to plummet. I increased our speed, hoping to reach The Complex slightly faster.

Meg stared at me. "Mac, you're making us even louder now."

"I know." I gestured at the sonar. "Look."

The weapon was still on its previous course.

It was going to pass by overhead.

"What the hell happened?"

I offered her a sly smile. "Johnny broadcast our identity: *SC-1*."

She frowned as she processed that. "The weapon thinks we're *your seacar*? But we don't sound anything like—" Then she stopped suddenly as she realized. "The friendly fire transmission?"

Every one of our vessels had a signal which notified Triestrian weapons that we were friendly. *Do not destroy*, basically. During large battles, it kept torpedoes from locking onto the wrong targets. There were often so many vessels in the theater, along with screw noise, explosions, countermeasures, mines, secondary implosions from Crush Depth, that weapons could grow confused and detonate on the wrong targets. This signal prevented that.

The weapon continued on its course for a few seconds, then began to circle.

Its sound was distinctive—a whine, a shriek, as it soared by and began to patrol, searching for another target.

"Will Windsor know that it didn't work?" Renée asked.

"He'll figure it out eventually, but his sonar isn't going to tell him, and his SCAV drive is too loud. It'll drown out any other sounds. He might not realize for a while."

Which meant he would either go back to The Facility, or stop at The Complex first.

I pushed the throttle to max.

We were nearly there.

—••—

"McClusky?" Windsor's voice called from the comm. "Are you there?"

It made me smile.

Barely.

My teeth were a wreck and my face was *throbbing.*

I'd survived—for the moment—but it was only because of Min Lee and Sidra Noor. They'd saved my life, and I owed them for that.

Now he was calling to confirm whether I was dead or not. "Don't answer," I said. "If he thinks we're gone, he'll leave."

His SCAV was a telltale sign of his intentions.

I stared at it to see what he was doing.

"Are you there?" he called again.

We were collectively holding our breath. Then, his vessel peeled off to the port and went back toward The Facility and Administrator Zhao. She was going to have to deal with him.

"Are you going to let him kill them?" Renée said.

"It's more important that we get to Johnny's *Sword.*"

"But he'll fire at the base. Implode it."

I stared at Renée. "What we're doing is important. We can't get pulled away from it. Besides . . . " I trailed off, hesitant to say what I'd been thinking.

Her eyes flashed. "They allowed Cliff to die, is that it? You think they deserve death at Windsor's hands?" I couldn't respond to that, and she said, "There are over three hundred people there, Mac!"

I sighed and considered her words.

She was right.

Then I thought of Sahar. What would she do in this situation?

She'd never let him kill that many people. If she were in my shoes, she would do something.

Anything.

"Okay," I muttered. "You're right."

Meg was sitting at the comms console, staring ahead morosely. She wasn't saying anything. Confusion glazed her eyes, her thoughts a million miles away.

"Meg?" I asked.

She turned to me.

"I'm sorry," I said.

"He tried to kill us. He fired a torpedo."

"He did. He's going to destroy the Chinese graphene facility now. Sahar might try to stop him. If she does, he'll kill her."

Sidra interjected, "She's dead anyway, Mac, if we don't do something. He can't leave her alive. She might already be—" He choked off his last words, unable to say them. His arms were tense at his sides, and there was a trickle of sweat on his temple.

I considered the situation. What could we possibly do here? I had to get Windsor to turn back, come after us again. And then somehow save Sahar and take The Shiv out.

"Johnny, is your *Sword* fully armed?"

"Ten torpedoes. Half are SCAVs."

"So we just have to get in it and then it's a battle." I shrugged. With the friendly fire code, it should be straightforward. He wouldn't be able to shoot at us. Still . . .

He was smart. He'd figure it out. He'd change the friendly fire settings as soon as he realized we were still alive. After all, the *Roach* was loud, massive, and slow moving. There's no way his SCAV torpedo wouldn't have killed us.

But I realized that it couldn't come to a battle. We couldn't risk it. The larger conflict—the one back in the Gulf and Atlantic—was brewing, and we needed to focus on that one. *Not* on one tiny seacar here in the Pacific. I had to send the others home to Trieste. I'd stay and face The Shiv. It was the only way now.

I waited until Windsor was nearly halfway back to the Chinese base. Then I picked up the mic. "Hey, Windsor. You called?"

There was no response.

"It's McClusky here. Still alive and well, sad to say. You wanted something?"

On the sonar display, his vessel's white glow abruptly changed course and began to circle back toward us.

# Chapter Thirty-Two

"What's the plan, Mac?" Johnny asked, eyeing me. *SC-1* was on a direct course and closing fast.

"We'll drop you off at your seacar. You take the others back to the Gulf. To Trieste. I'll stay."

He stared at me in horror. The others were dead silent too. They couldn't believe what I'd ordered. Johnny couldn't even speak.

I said, "Look, some of us have to get back. *The battle is happening in less than forty-eight hours*. We have to have some leadership back at Trieste." I shook my head. "I know it's difficult to accept, but this is the only way. I'll stay."

"And do what?" Renée snapped. "Fight him again? Take him on, beat him this time?"

Sidra said, "She's right, Mac. I have to save Sahar. She's my sister. I won't leave. You can't order me to leave, either."

I stared at them, considering it. "Renée. You're in charge of Triestrian defences. You have to be there. Meg. You're in charge of the *Swords*. Our fleet. Repairs. You have to keep the vessels functioning. You also have to get the graphene secret back home. Johnny—one of us has to lead the battle. I *have* to stay here and deal with The Shiv." I'd faced each one of them as I spoke. I thought it made sense.

"Why? What's so important?" Renée snapped. "Revenge?"

"He killed Cliff. We have to end him." I paused suddenly, cutting off my thoughts. I'd just confirmed her statement, though not intentionally. I took a breath and exhaled. "Maybe it's revenge. But Renée, if we don't stop him, he's going to kill everyone here, at The Complex *and* The Facility. Then he'll go to Trieste to get the rest of us. He's not going to stop. He *has* to maintain his secret. It's the only life he knows." I looked away and considered the situation. "There's also Ventinov. He's *out* there, right now. In The Iron Plains. He wants me dead. I have to deal with him too. But there are currently *two* other dreadnoughts preparing to attack Trieste, as well as a fleet of over a thousand warsubs. Some of us *have* to get back and protect the city."

Renée said, "We can all go. You don't have to stay!"

"He'll kill everyone here," I repeated. I glanced at the sonar, then I pointed at it. "We don't have time. You have to get into Johnny's seacar and get out of here. *Now.*"

—••—

SIDRA ENDED UP STAYING WITH me. I understood his motivations. I wasn't his boss—Sahar was. She was also his family. He wouldn't listen to me, and I could see it in his face. His features were hard, determined.

He knew this might kill him, but he couldn't abandon Sahar.

The others listened to me. Johnny, Meg, Renée, Min Lee. They marched through the umbilical into Johnny's vessel, carrying the duffel with the graphene secrets. Their eyes were hard too. They were upset. Renée gave me a hug and a kiss and whispered in my ear, "Come back to me. But . . . but I'm *so angry* at you."

Meg was downcast. "I—I—"

"You don't have to say it."

"He made me feel something I haven't felt in years."

"I'm sorry, Meg." I gave her a lopsided smile—which must have looked odd with my missing teeth—and hugged her. "You can save Trieste. Give the people what they want. You might be the last McClusky. You have to be there for them. In the future, too."

She stared at me for a long moment.

In the corridors of the *Roach*, alarms pierced the dusty air. Pebbles and debris covered the deck grating and there were footprints from the crew still there. I looked into her eyes. "I love you, Meg. I'm glad we got to achieve Dad's dream together. At least for a while. Make sure it continues, and win the battle." Then I hugged her and she turned and left.

—••—

SIDRA STOOD WITH ME ON the bridge of the *Roach*. It was quiet now. We'd silenced all the warnings and all the lights were off. The ship was dark.

Dead.

"What now?" he muttered.

*SC-1* was nearly on us. She couldn't fire at us easily though, which gave me some options.

"Take us there." I pointed out into the distance, to the north of The Complex. "Set us down. He'll come to us."

He peered past my outstretched finger. Then he shrugged. "It's as good a place as any, I guess."

"He'll come on board to kill us."

"He might just hotwire a torpedo and fire at point blank range."

"It's possible." He'd likely do that to the two bases, should he escape from us. But I knew his mentality. I knew what type of person he was.

I grabbed the comm and spoke into it as Sidra maneuvered the enormous vessel and brought us down to the seafloor. He purged the air from the ballast and we sunk into the soft sand; it billowed around us in a small mushroom cloud that enclosed and surrounded the giant mining machine.

"Windsor," I said. "I'm here. In the *Roach*. Waiting."

"Do you think he'll come?" Sidra asked.

"Yes."

He stared at me. "He's that easy to manipulate?"

I shrugged. We were sitting in the *Roach*'s control cabin. Waiting. We'd powered down all systems, including ventilation. "In a way. His disguise was brilliant. He's a perfect operative and a deadly assassin. But he's also vain. Arrogant. Maybe due to his upbringing, maybe due to his extreme patriotism for Russia. He's also used to winning. With me . . . " I trailed off.

"He won though." Sidra looked abashed as he studied my bruised face. "Sorry."

"No, it's true. He did win. He beat me." I rubbed my tongue over my teeth. "I tried everything I could. I couldn't overcome him."

"But you think this will work?"

"I escaped from him. I'm the *only one* who has ever gotten away from him. He'll have to finish me. I do understand revenge, trust me. Better than most others." I paused as I thought about the man who had killed Dad, and how Meg and I had harbored a need for vengeance that no one else could really understand. She had ended up acting on it, killing Admiral Benning in cold blood one night in her cubicle at Trieste. That act had started a chain of events that led to enormous death and destruction. It had affected Meg's mental health, and she had still not fully recovered.

I pulled myself from the reverie and pointed out the starboard viewport. *SC-1* had appeared. The landing skids descended with a distant whine and the seacar settled to the soft sandy bottom.

"And he's coming right now. As expected."

I took a breath and my heart began to pound.

It was time.

—••—

THE COMM CRACKLED TO LIFE. The voice sounded official and commanding. "Attention mining vessel that has just set down north of our complex. This space is off limits. Trieste claims these mineral rights. You have no—"

"It's us, Coda," I said into the mic, cutting him off. "McClusky."

There was a long pause. Sidra flashed me a half smile. "We're quite a surprise for them, I'd imagine."

The *Roach* was so large it could crawl over The Complex and crush it beneath our scoop threshers. And we had set it down just to the north of them. Coda Rose and Melinda Sinora must have been crapping their pants, to put it mildly. I flashed a glance at the sonar; sure enough, alarms were ringing in The Complex and there was *a lot* of noise coming from the base.

"Mac?" Coda said. "Why didn't you warn us?"

"Sorry. There have been some major developments."

"Are you all here? Someone took the *Sword* a few minutes ago and left to the south."

"Those were our people. No worries." I frowned and considered what to say next. I gripped the handle of the mic; my hand was sweaty. "Look, Coda. The man who was with us when we visited. William Windsor."

"What about him?"

"He's a Russian agent. And he's in the seacar that just set down next to the *Roach*."

I stared out the viewport. *SC-1*'s umbilical was stretching outward, toward the *Roach*'s docking airlock. "I don't have time to explain everything, but whatever happens in the next few minutes, *do not let him into your base*." I paused and swallowed past a dry throat. A figure was moving through the umbilical now. I could see the silhouette march toward the *Roach*'s airlock. "The problem is that he has access to my seacar, which has torpedoes."

Sidra said, while staring at a console, "He's bypassed the airlock. The outer hatch is open now."

I continued into the mic, "The Shiv is holding Sahar Noor on board my ship. Get some miners together, arm them, and send them out to get her. Bring her back to The Complex."

"Wait, The Shiv? What?"

"No time—"

Sidra said, "Hatch just closed. Inner hatch open."

"We'll try to take care of The Shiv. Just protect Sahar. And be careful. If we can't beat Windsor, do not underestimate him. Shoot to kill, and don't negotiate. *Just kill him*."

I snapped the toggle, turning the mic off. It had cut off a splutter of protests and questions. Then I turned to Sidra. "Are you ready?"

"Do you think they can save her?"

"It depends on what we can do in the next few minutes."

I marched to the vessel navigation controls and began to power the ship up. Motors whined and a rumble reverberated through the deck and bulkheads. The *Roach* quaked under my feet. The main thruster was next, and I pushed the throttle to forward. Then I activated the thresher scoops.

The seafloor under us suddenly grew unstable as the seven scoops begin to spin, churning sand and gravel and large rocks and hurling it all into chutes that led into the mining vessel's sorting channels. A cloud of debris rose from the bottom and encircled the entire vessel. In the viewport, the ocean grew foggy from sand. Our lights were on again, but the debris blocked any view of our surroundings.

The vessel began to crawl forward. I stared at the navigation map and tweaked the course slightly.

The comm sprang to life again and it sounded angry.

I ignored it. I knew it was Coda, warning us.

In the control cabin, near the rear of the chamber, there was a ladder leading downward. "I'm going below. Watch your back."

Sidra said, "Mac."

I turned to him.

He continued, "It's been a pleasure working with you."

"It's not over yet, Sidra."

His face was pale. His gun was now in his hand. "I feel like death just boarded this vessel."

"It did. But we've set something in motion here." I pointed at the nav screen. "Whatever happens, *keep us on this course.*"

On the digital map, the large Roach was slowly crawling to the north, moving away from The Complex. A few hundred metres ahead, the unexploded Chinese mine sat half-embedded in the ocean floor. Our forward scoop was going to collide with it, yank it violently from the seafloor, and hurl it into the belly of this mining machine.

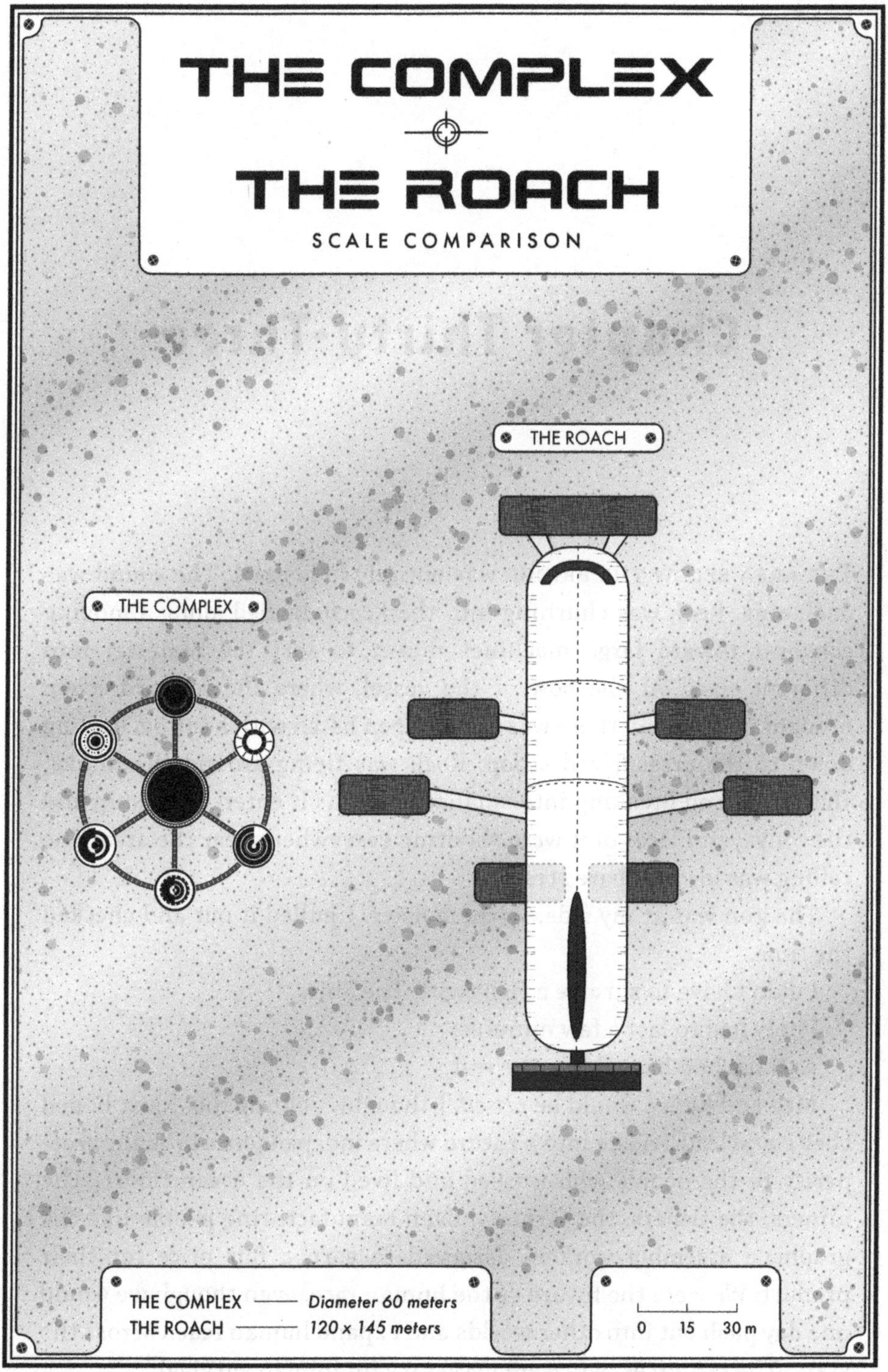
THE COMPLEX
THE ROACH
SCALE COMPARISON
THE ROACH
THE COMPLEX
THE COMPLEX — Diameter 60 meters
THE ROACH — 120 x 145 meters
0 15 30 m

# Chapter Thirty-Three

THE AREA BELOW THE BRIDGE was entirely industrial. The sound was deafening. Rock was churning into the *Roach*, hauled along a moving conveyer toward large machines meant to sort the material into different sizes. At the bow of the vessel, where the forward scoop brought in material, there was a large open hatch with a tunnel leading down to the pressurized scoop. Rock was flying around the intake, shattering and breaking into smaller pieces as it entered the ship and the conveyer. Pieces of it were shooting everywhere near the area. The ceiling was low and bare steel.

The gun was at my side, in the holster. I pulled it out and checked the time.

I didn't have to survive a fight with The Shiv.

I only had to last a few minutes.

And the bomb would do the rest.

Meg and Renée would be *pissed*, I thought. Johnny too. I just hoped they could lead Trieste into a future where independence brought prosperity to the people who worked and lived on the ocean floors. The miners, the fishers, the farmers. Even manufacturing people like the graphene assembly workers deserved to earn a fair price for their product. We were the future of the human race, even though we would one day push out into other worlds and expand human reach across the stars. The resources here were necessary for human survival.

I snorted as I thought it. It was a vicious counterpoint to what was about to happen.

"Mac," a voice said.

He was standing at the end of the bow collection compartment, about thirty metres away from me. He had no weapons, he was wearing black, and he began to stalk toward me.

"Don't call me that. You don't have the right."

"I've been telling you to call me Bill. But you won't."

"It's not your name." I paused. "In fact, I don't know your real name."

"Vasily Kinzhal Stali."

I frowned. "Seems to fit. But it doesn't match your accent."

"It's my true self."

"Russian." He was getting closer by the second. I kept the forward scoop collection hatch at my back. There was a cloud of dust behind me, and I resisted the urge to cough. "You must be so confused."

"I'm not," he said. "And don't try any pitiful psychology on me. I have a job to finish."

"You're not going to be taking photos of me."

"We'll see." He paused for a minute. His nose was swollen and bruised. "Where are the others?"

"I sent them back."

A series of emotions flashed across his features. He'd stopped a few metres from me and watched my face. "That was a mistake."

"They're not going to stay to face you. They've gone home."

He shook his head. "Now I'm going to have to find them. Track each one down maybe."

"Your secret is going to get out. There's no stopping it now."

His face hardened at that. He didn't respond.

I pressed on, "Everyone is going to know that this great Russian operative is actually a pompous Brit."

"I'm not British."

"You sound like it."

"I'm from the Urals in Northern Russia. Born to hardworking Russians. We worked in the forests. Survived off the land. Chiseled an existence—"

"They sent you away as a child. They gave you up. They didn't care about you."

He cocked his head. "I told you, the psychology won't work. I'm Russia's servant. A weapon."

"Why do you care about people who only use you? You're a tool for them, nothing more. They never cared about you. I think the Brits cared more for you. Sahar certainly did."

"Don't talk about British people to me. They're so weak, it's pathetic."

The *Roach* bounced slightly over some heavy rock, perhaps a ridge of solid basalt. I reached out to grab a railing next to the machinery to maintain my balance. I hoped Sidra could keep the vessel on the seafloor, and keep the ballast at fully negative.

"They took you in. Raised you."

"They didn't raise me. They didn't tell me about the great people of history. My *real* parents did that."

"Maybe, but how did you repay your British family? You *killed* them, didn't you? Wiped them out."

He hesitated and I resisted the temptation to check the time. "They were suspicious."

"So, like anyone else who knows the truth, you kill them."

"Like you, I guess." He sneered as he said it.

"There are too many who know you, Windsor. You can't kill everyone."

"We'll see. I can still finish you here and try to catch up to them."

"With a slower seacar and a disabled navigation system."

"Sahar will talk. I just need some time to peel it out of her."

So, she was still alive. I hoped Coda Rose was rescuing her as we spoke.

The *Roach* bounced again. There was a loud clang behind me and the scoop thresher seemed to pound against something immobile. Something that was harder than the gravel around it . . .

Windsor and I both reached to the railing beside us.

He glanced at the conveyer behind me, clearly wondering what was coming up from the seafloor.

His eyes instantly widened, and his face dissolved into shock. "What the—"

The mine was a large sphere, painted red and black and bristling with protrusions meant to trigger the explosion. Some of the spring mounts were clearly out of commission—bent and flattened and stripped away—but I hoped that some could still work.

He continued to stare at the mine as the thresher scoop pulled it from the ocean floor and hurled it into the *Roach*. It was now on the conveyer, headed toward us.

I raised my gun and fired.

—••—

HE SENSED WHAT I WAS doing before I acted. He darted to the right, then to the left, and jumped toward me. The bullet ricocheted off some equipment somewhere, and then he was on me. I blocked his tackle but his hand had pushed my gun aside. I threw a quick elbow with my left, which he blocked, but I had managed to maintain the grip on the gun. I pulled it back, aimed directly at his chest, and fired three times.

The force of the impact shoved his body away. He took three steps backward, then was on me again.

There was something under his shirt. The sound had been clear. A *clang* as the bullets made impact. He was wearing something thin but able to resist a bullet. He grinned as he struck my hand. The gun skittered away. Then there were blocks, strikes, counters. It was a flurry of angry blows. I was tired though. The earlier fight had nearly ended me. I had only one hope here, but fully expected this to end in only seconds.

The mine was on the conveyer now, rocking back and forth on a bed of gravel. It was rolling slightly. There were more plungers on the sphere, and as the conveyer moved, the mine shifted with it.

It was passing by us as we fought.

And then another bullet exploded nearby.

I ducked as pieces of rock flashed up and struck the side of my face. It felt like sandpaper peeling my skin.

Sidra was standing on the ladder leading from the control cabin and was shooting at The Shiv. Bullets hit his side but didn't have the expected result. Others hit rock on the conveyer, which shattered and sent sharp shrapnel flying.

Windsor grinned again. "So, not everyone is gone, Mac? You lied? Surprise, surprise."

He was staring at Sidra, and his attention, for an instant, was not on me.

I leapt forward and hit him with a front kick to the face.

He gasped and fell back. It was the same place I'd hit him before. I kept on him, hitting again and again with elbows and fists to his face and nose. It had staggered him. Grabbing his left arm, I locked it in my own grip, turned my hip and hurled him in a judo throw onto the conveyer.

He was on his back, lying on the rock, and I slammed my elbow on his forehead, dazing him.

The conveyer carried him now, toward the sorting machine.

The mine was just in front of him.

It disappeared through the large hatch into the sorter, and I jumped to my feet and ran for the ladder. "Run!" I bellowed.

I hit the ladder and followed Sidra up to the control cabin.

"McClusky!" I heard from below.

Now The Shiv was in the sorter, where it dumped sand and gravel out the ship and metal prods *shoved* larger rocks onto a different conveyer, leading to the large cargo hold in the *Roach*'s belly. It hurled anything that entered it around violently.

On the bridge, I grabbed the yoke and turned the vessel toward the cliff.

Toward The Drop, that sheer wall that led to the abyssal plain.

Our zircon mine was down there.

The *Roach* was now crawling toward the abyss, where earlier Johnny and I had dangled from an ore collector on a steel wire that The Shiv had remotely severed.

Now he was heading straight for a drop into hell.

And then the mine exploded, inside the *Roach*.

# Chapter Thirty-Four

THE SHIV HAD BEEN ON the conveyer, next to the Chinese bomb, sucked into the sorter when the explosive finally detonated. The *Roach* lurched to the side, jumped slightly up off the seafloor, then settled back down before it dug back into the rock and sand bottom. Alarms were screaming and blue pressure warnings flashed in the control cabin. The main power had flickered and the emergency lights were on. Strobing lights flashed across us as we pulled ourselves from the deck.

Sidra and I were still alive.

The concussion had dazed us, but we were breathing.

There was a distinct pressure change in the bridge though.

And the smell of rock dust, smoke, and . . . seawater.

The sound of it crashing through the mining vessel was clear. It was a dull roar, and a cascading surge as it tore equipment from bulkheads and picked up anything from the decks and hurled it along with the crashing waves as it churned through corridors and cabins.

I grabbed a console and pulled myself to my feet. The viewport across the entire area was cracked, and the spiderweb was growing as I watched. I could hear the transparent material splintering as outside pressure worked its inexorable force on it.

Water began to spray in from some of the cracks.

The control console was directly in front of the viewport. I stumbled to it and pushed the thruster to max power. The detonation had mortally wounded the *Roach*—killed it, in fact, only it just didn't realize it yet—and it was taking on water. But the giant stern screw was still turning.

*Somehow.*

The *Roach* vibrated and seemed to scream in agony as the power ramped up.

But it was still moving.

*Grinding* along the seafloor.

And The Drop was just ahead.

"Mac!" a voice cried from the comm. It was Commander Coda Rose. "Get off that thing! It's heading for the abyss!"

"I know," I said to myself. I glanced back at Sidra, who was pushing himself off the deck. The vessel lurched to the side and he fell into a console. Grabbing him, I whispered, "Come on, we have to get out."

"Where? We're going over the edge."

"We still have some time."

He stared at the nav display in horror. The abyss was only a few metres away.

I hauled him to his feet and pushed him in front of me, toward the hatch at the back of the control cabin. Lights were flashing and blue light bathed his face. He seemed to only just realize it.

"Mac, it's blue."

"I know."

"It means there's a pressure—"

"I know."

"Water is flooding into—"

"Yeah, I got it, Sidra. Let's get out."

We stumbled along the deck toward the nearest airlock. Water was rising through the lower levels, but had yet to reach the command deck at the top. Watertight hatches had slammed shut everywhere, but still ocean pressure was forcing water into the ship's interior. The explosive must have destroyed compartmentalization somewhere in the core of the vehicle.

"Is The Shiv . . . "

"He's gone," I said.

And then the *Roach* seemed to moan in agony. Metal wrenched under tremendous stress and it lurched to a sudden stop, throwing Sidra and me to the deck.

Then it began to tilt.

We were over the edge now.

The thruster was on full, pushing us out into open space and a five-kilometre drop to the bottom far, far below. To Crush Depth.

The gigantic ship was heavy now, laden with water and rock, and it seemingly creaked in pain as the stresses overcame its structure. Metal beams on board began to warp and crack from the sheer mass as it dangled over the edge. Sirens were *tearing* out now, warning the crew of imminent death.

The ship continued to tilt downward.

Large *booms* echoed through the vessel. The structure was giving way.

The weight of the water and the ballast, pulling us down.

The ship dangling over a sharp rock edge.

The weakened core from the detonation and pressure wave.

The shattered interior meant a brittle and fragile structure—

And then it fell over the edge, into The Drop.

—••—

THE AIRLOCK WAS RIGHT NEXT to us. *SC-1* was nowhere near; we had torn away from it earlier, shredding the umbilical and leaving the vessel behind, presumably with Sahar still alive inside.

I hoped.

The *Roach* tilting downward meant we could no longer stand upright. I clung to the airlock hatch, my legs dangling down a long corridor. Sidra grabbed the hatch frame and stared down, horror on his face. If we dropped at that moment, we'd die at the end of a long fall. I took several deep breaths, trying to pull myself up over the frame and into the small chamber. I was too tired. I just couldn't do it. The fights with Windsor had tired me to the point of utter exhaustion. I could barely hang on let alone do a pull-up.

Below us, water was churning upward. It was in the corridor and rising quickly, green and frothing. The *Roach* was now totally vertical, plunging straight down into The Drop.

Sidra clenched his teeth and hauled himself up into the airlock. The noise below was thunderous. He reached down, grabbed my wrist, and said, "Come on, Mac. We have to get out."

"We're too deep," I said.

He pulled me up into the airlock. I fell on my back—on the bulkhead, for the deck was now a vertical wall—and stared up at the steel over my head. I was huffing like I'd just run a marathon. I couldn't do much else.

"There's a tank here," he snapped. "In the corner. We'll have to buddy breathe."

"The mix isn't right."

"We'll have to swim up as soon as we get out. *Now let's go!*" He'd bellowed into the small chamber. He slammed his hand on the CYCLE button.

Nothing happened.

The inner hatch didn't close.

Alarm lights were strobing and the blue pressure warning light bathed us in its glow. Our skin looked blue from it. The sound of rushing water roared from the corridor; it was almost at the airlock.

"Can you open the outer hatch without cycling the lock?" I said.

He knelt and scrabbled at the plate. "Have to," he said.

The water was about to hit us. When it did, the pressure would rise until it matched the exterior.

And we were plummeting downward.

The outer hatch ground open, but halted about halfway aside. Water hammered in against the bulkhead. I threw myself to the side to avoid it as best as possible and held my arms over my head. Then the water churning up the vertical corridor beside us reached the lip of the airlock and flooded in. It was a wall hitting us from both sides, colliding directly over us. It hurled us against the metal bulkhead, stunning us with its impact. Sidra pushed a mask over my face, and his iron grip latched onto my biceps. He pulled me with everything we had, and we fell out of the airlock, into open water.

Beside us, the immense mining vessel was scraping past the cliff, peeling chunks of rock with it as it plummeted down. Gravel, sand, and boulders fell in a shower with the metal carcass. Bubbles soared upward. It was a remarkable sight. The shell of a ship surging downward, carrying the broken remains of The Shiv with it.

Into the depths.

My lungs were pounding, and Sidra pushed the air hose to my mask. It was half full of water, and I purged it before taking several deep breaths. Then I passed the hose back to Sidra. There was still air in my mask—it covered my entire face—and I pulled my gaze from the dead vessel and stared at Sidra. We were floating over the immense canyon, and as the ship disappeared from sight, the area around us fell into total blackness.

"Thanks for saving my life," I said.

Sidra had a light and he flicked it on. Above us, the cliff towered upward like a skyscraper disappearing into a black cloud. It was impossible to say how far we'd descended, but the pressure peeled at my skull like a hydraulic press. We began to swim upward.

Within seconds a feeling of intense joy washed over me. I stopped swimming. Floating felt so serene. So peaceful.

Nothing mattered.

The pressure was over, I thought. The Shiv was gone. Johnny could lead the fight. I'd achieved my Dad's dreams, and Meg would be happy. She'd find someone, eventually, and live a good life in Trieste. My death would crush Renée. She'd come to the colony to be with me. She'd made it a home, but she'd be lonely without me.

Sidra and I were close to the cliff face, and I put my feet against it and kicked out. I put my back to the drop below and floated there, breathing steadily.

The sky was so far above. It was black, but it was up there, I knew.

The topside.

The surface and its people, struggling so mightily against the inevitable.

Climate change was inexorable. There was no stopping it. There was no changing it. Not the way things had happened, with every country working for themselves, unable or unwilling to act for the common good. Not when some were rich and some were poor.

I took a large breath and exhaled. It seemed hot and stale.

Who had I been with? Who was swimming with me? Why was it so dark?

Another breath. Hot and stuffy.

My lungs started to pound.

The nitrogen from a few breaths had made me feel euphoric. Ecstatic. But now that was wearing off.

Hypoxia was setting in quickly.

Sidra!

I'd been with Sidra Noor!

But where was he? He had the tank . . . he was breathing the mix, but it was wrong for that depth. There was too much nitrogen in it.

Looking right and left, up and down, I failed to see him.

My eyes were fluttering, and a massive headache quickly took hold.

I distantly realized that bubbles were churning around me, rising from below, from the *Roach*'s death throes. That vessel had served its purpose, and it was now dead and gone, falling to the distant rock seafloor, so far below.

I closed my eyes.

# Interlude

## In The Iron Plains; The Drop

DATA PROCESSING

| | |
|---|---|
| Location: | Latitude: 12° 27′ 20″ N<br>Longitude: 183° 24′ 3″ W<br>On the seafloor in The Iron Plains |
| Depth: | 1,270 metres |
| Date: | 13 June 2131 |
| Time: | 0613 hours |

VASILY STALI / THE SHIV / William Windsor stared out *SC-1*'s viewport at the scene before them. The Complex, its six domes surrounding a larger, central one, was just at the lip of The Drop. The three winches with ore collectors moving up and down the sheer cliff were obvious, although it seemed people were scrambling to get back to the security and safety of the main outpost. There were divers swimming toward it from the mine, as well as people clinging to scooters and other smaller "people-movers" just over the ocean floor, and all headed toward the docking dome. The reason might have been the presence of the *Roach*, the gigantic nodule harvester that was just to the north of the facility. It was dark, not moving, and seemed empty.

But he knew it was not.

His targets were there.

Behind him, in the seacar's living area, he'd restrained his boss, Sahar Noor. She led Churchill Intelligence, and McClusky had revealed him as a Russian asset, an assassin for hire, and the man who had murdered the Triestrian CSO.

And that was only part of it. There had been so many other jobs and victims that she knew nothing of. The New Zealander, the previous year. The Australian military envoy to Blue Downs, only a few weeks earlier. The English politician at Churchill, two years before that. The German advisor to the Chancellor. *That* one had been tough, for he'd had to decompress for over a hundred hours to complete the job, on land.

That job had bothered him immensely, for Stali had gotten a close view of topside after so many years of living underwater in the colonies. The refugees, the lack of resources, the empty grocery stores, the constant anger that people carried around with them. The uncertain future and the dry land and the hot sun. It had been almost too much to bear, and Stali could not wait to get back to the seas, where people were happier and more optimistic.

Unless they were one of the names on his list, that is.

Stali piloted the seacar toward the *Roach*, and set down on the seafloor just to its port, by the airlock.

He pressed a button and extended the umbilical, to connect airlocks.

The comm squawked, and the base's commander, Coda Rose, warned them of approaching their base. He was very nervous of the sudden appearance of the Chinese mining vessel.

Stali ignored them.

To Sahar, he said, "I have to go kill your friends now. I wish I could say I'm sorry, but I can't."

Her eyes were hard, but there was more there than that. There was . . . pity, he thought. Sadness.

She said, "You will regret doing such a thing."

"Don't feel sorry for me. People are paying me well."

"To be a traitor to your people. How do you sleep at night?"

"My people are Russian, not British. Not Churchillians."

"You have no honour. You are pathetic." Then she looked away, as if she would not speak again.

Stali stared at her. He needed her to reactivate the systems on board this seacar. He was going to enjoy ripping the information from her when he returned.

—••—

ON BOARD THE CHINESE VESSEL, he found his target at the bow scoop intake. He'd entered easily, and as he made his way forward, the vessel had started moving. He wasn't sure where McClusky was taking them, but it did not matter. Mac wouldn't be around to make decisions for much longer.

And then, it had all fallen apart.

The Chinese explosive.

It must have been on the seafloor, and the harvesting machine had sucked it up into its inner machinery and mining system. Then Mac hit him with a lucky kick, and threw him onto the conveyer, and before he knew it, he was lying on a pile of rock, next to the bomb and moving into a giant machine sorting the rock into different sizes.

He screamed at Mac once and then jerked his gaze around to search a way out. The noise was maddening. Metal prods were pushing larger rocks onto a channel that presumably led to the cargo hold. The sand was falling through a grate to a different conveyer below him. Prods were shoving giant boulders, too large for processing and not polymetallic, onto yet a different chute, and the red and black explosive sphere rocked back and forth as steel poles pushed it savagely over into—

Stali leapt off the conveyer to the sand sorter below. It was moving quickly toward a hold, dumped in from the ceiling. When the hold was full, the inner hatch would seal and the outer one would open, depositing the useless sand and smaller rocks back to the ocean floor, underneath the Chinese harvesting vessel.

Stali took a breath and prepared to jump—

And the bomb detonated.

—••—

SAHAR WAS BREATHING CALMLY. SHE knew she had to remain calm. The Russian agent had left the seacar to confront the others—Mac, she assumed—and there was still a chance.

He'd tied her hands and ankles, and as soon as he'd left, she'd begun to figure a way out. The comm was in the pilot cabin. If she could get there, she might be able to call the mining base for help. They must have recognized Mac's seacar and realized that something was up.

Then the Chinese *Roach* started to move forward. The deck under her began to vibrate and the viewports showed rocks and sand and dust floating by and clouding the view.

The umbilical connecting *SC-1* and the *Roach* stretched—

And Sahar gasped. The mining vessel was pulling away.

*But it was attached to the seacar!*

*SC-1* heeled to the side, throwing Sahar down. The ship spun, tilting and hurling interior contents everywhere.

Including Sahar.

She ended up on her back, alarms ringing in her ears. Smoke filled the cabin from an electrical short somewhere. In the pilot cabin, console lights were flashing angrily. The *Roach* was moving away, having pulled the umbilical apart, yanking *SC-1* around ninety degrees and nearly rolling it onto its side.

Thankfully, the inner airlock was closed tight. Water had flooded the umbilical as it ripped, and it thundered into the tight chamber—a white and green froth—but the hatch had held.

She leaned back and exhaled. She was pretty sure the violent event had bruised her side from ribs to ankle. She'd tumbled around the seacar, restrained and unable to cushion her falls. The bulkhead walls were steel, covered with pipes and vents and wiring.

Unforgiving.

She breathed again and again, trying to gather her senses and develop a plan.

She coughed from the acrid smoke.

Then the airlock cycled.

She snapped her gaze to it.

"Oh no," she said. It had only just been full of water—

Then it opened, and it was now dry inside.

A large man entered. He was enormous, with a bushy beard, dark eyebrows, and thick forearms. He looked around at the mess within and then set his gaze on her.

"Are you okay, Sahar?" he bellowed.

She smiled at the Triestrian miner, instantly relieved. "Hi, Vinnie. We could use your help."

Then, a distant *thud* caught their attention. It was a distinct explosion, followed by a concussion wave blast.

DATA PROCESSING

| | |
|---|---|
| Vessel: | Russian Submarine Fleet |
| | *Dreadnought* Class *Voskhod–The Rise* |
| Location: | Latitude: Unknown |
| | Longitude: Unknown |
| | In The Iron Plains |
| Depth: | 550 metres |
| Date: | 13 June 2131 |
| Time: | 0615 hours |

CAPTAIN IVAN ARKADY VENTINOV WAS furious. He'd followed The Shiv's movements over the past few hours, tracking him through the Pacific waters, and was growing more nervous by the minute. First the failed attempt at the mine, when the kill team had successfully severed the wire while McClusky was over the abyss in the ore collector. Then the failed attempt on his life by the hired killer in the Agricultural Dome. That attempt had been unplanned and against Ventinov's wishes, but the kill team had tried anyway.

Then, they'd tried to sink Mac while in his seacar, and that too had failed!

The Russian team—who had stolen a Triestrian vessel that had once belonged to The Steel Shiv's previous victim—had all died.

Sunk, following a torpedo strike.

He clenched a fist.

The man had more than nine lives. He seemed impossible to kill.

But finally, when he'd entered The Facility, and Ventinov knew The Shiv would finally make his move, there had been silence.

Just silence.

There was no way for him to contact The Shiv. He didn't know what was happening, if McClusky was finally gone.

His XO, Mila Sidorov, had repeatedly tried to speak to him about leaving the area and going to where the other dreadnoughts awaited them, in the Atlantic. The strike force was preparing, she'd said.

But Ventinov had told her to wait.

She had pressed, more than once now, and he had finally exploded.

He *needed* to know that McClusky was dead. That Ventinov had achieved vengeance over the Triestrian.

He wanted photographic proof—video would be preferable—of the man after life had left his body. He wanted more, in fact, and he'd even screamed this at her while the crew had watched.

*He wanted video evidence of the actual killing.*

Perhaps slicing his throat. Or stabbing him in the heart. Or shooting him in the head.

Sidorov had watched him in silence, stunned and terrified, he thought.

But her job was to follow.

His job was to lead.

And this was his mission.

His superiors knew that he meant to kill the Mayor of Trieste. They *wanted* him to do it, so they could defeat the city in battle.

He just needed proof, that was all.

He just needed to know that the man was gone. Then—*and only then*—could they leave for the gathering forces to destroy the underwater American city.

But then, and to his immense horror, something happened at the Chinese Facility.

Ventinov could only see on his sonar what the computers interpreted. But there had been a power outage. Some flooding and alarms. And then a mining vessel had departed the area . . .

*Along with the seacar, SC-1.*

And it was headed back to the Triestrian mine, The Complex.

Ventinov fumed. He had no idea what was going on. He was pacing the bridge and swearing repeatedly. The surrounding crew was watching with alarm, and he knew that they were wondering about his sanity.

It didn't bother him.

He just wanted McClusky dead, then they could continue with the mission.

Then he felt a presence at his back, and he whirled around.

It was Sidorov. Again.

—••—

Lieutenant Mila Sidorov had watched the rapid decline in the Captain's faculties. He also appeared disheveled. His hair and uniform were unkempt. Now, however, over the past two days, he had descended into what someone would describe as *obsessed*. At the start of this campaign to kill the Triestrian, he'd planned the events, *calculated* them precisely. He'd even said earlier that he didn't want to go blasting in like a crazy person, hoping to kill with sheer force.

But now . . . now there was something different. Circumstances were pushing him over the edge. The more McClusky eluded him, the more unbalanced he seemed.

And even worse—she could see the worry in the crew's eyes. They knew he was growing *foggy*. Unsure.

The Captain was supposed to be a picture of competence, the *one* person on board who knew what to do, who knew how to solve problems, who knew what was needed to survive any particular issue or dilemma.

Instead, he was *scaring* the crew.

She was on the bridge, watching him pace, and she moved toward him.

He turned on her, and his eyes were wide.

"Sir," she said. "It's time to go. There is nothing to do here."

He glared at her for a long moment, then visibly tried to collect himself. He pointed at the sonar. "They are on the mining vehicle. It's moving."

She shook her head. "It doesn't matter. Trieste is more important. The other dreadnoughts are waiting." In fact, she thought, the Captains of both the warsubs had contacted her, concerned about Ventinov's well-being. She'd assured them that everything was fine, they were on a separate mission for Russia, but they hadn't believed her. They knew about The Shiv, because the Captain himself had told them all about it.

They were now wondering what was going on, and why *Voskhod* was not with them, preparing for war.

"Sir," she said again, calmly. "Our mission is in the Atlantic. I implore you to please set course immediately."

The sonar suddenly chimed, and Ventinov sprang to it and stooped over the screen. Its light shone up at his wild eyes. He said, "There's been an explosion. In the mining vehicle."

Sidorov sighed. "And?"

"It's moving toward the cliff."

"Then they will all die. Let's be done with this and leave."

He peered at her. "Are you a traitor, Sidorov?"

"What?" she snapped, suddenly angry. "I'm a loyal sailor in the RSF. I'm your Executive Officer. I'm here to follow. But the crew is questioning your actions."

"The crew?" he bellowed, staring around him. Faces suddenly ducked behind consoles.

She lowered her voice, "Captain. You are . . . unwell. You need to go shower. Sleep. Clean up. We'll gather with the coalition forces."

His eyes hardened and he leveled a look at her that could melt lead. "Are you insane?" he screamed. "Look at that sonar! He's about to die! I'm not going to miss this!"

She took a deep breath and watched him. He was losing it. "And after? What's next?" She peered at the screen. "The vessel is going over the edge. What happens when it's all over?"

He straightened and seemed to compose himself. "Then we will depart immediately."

"For?"

He turned to her as if he'd only just noticed her presence. "We go to the Atlantic, of course! As I ordered!"

She nodded and sighed, then turned smartly to leave.

The crew was watching her silently, and she noticed the looks in their eyes.

They were scared.

# Part Eight

## The Puerto Rico Trench

# Chapter Thirty-Five

LIGHT BATHED ME.

My first glimpse as I opened my eyes was my shadow on the cliff face. I was drifting face up, limbs splayed out. I stared at it for a long moment. I'd stopped breathing. I was just staring.

It took me a moment to realize that it was actually *me*.

*My* shadow.

I looked dead.

A current shoved me to the side. I couldn't move a finger or even twitch a toe. I just lay there, floating, uncaring, unfeeling.

Something was rising below me, some sort of steel creature, moving up from the depths. Was it the *Roach*? Had it somehow achieved buoyancy? Or was it some debris from its death spiral into the deeps?

Then I heard it.

A whine. From thrusters.

And it seemed very familiar.

A *Sword*.

Johnny's seacar.

I turned my head and stared at it. There was an intense spotlight right on me. There were figures in the control cabin, staring out the canopy.

One was pointing at me, gesturing wildly.

I recognized the short black hair, the broad shoulders. I could almost hear the French accent.

My eyes shut.

Somehow they got me in the airlock. I'm not sure how. It began to cycle, and I fell to the deck, limbs lying haphazardly, and the water lowered toward the drain. Someone pulled my mask off and slapped me. I gasped and choked and tried desperately to breathe. Then I passed out again. When I next awoke, I was underwater again. There was another person entering, and then the lock cycled once again. The water lowered and drained completely, and someone fell next to me, coughing and hacking and puking into the metal grate and the drain below.

I passed out again.

The decompression lasted an hour. The airlock hissed and whined the entire time as it lowered the pressure and brought us back down to four atms. My headache cleared slowly, and eventually I could open my eyes and study my surroundings. It still hurt like hell; it was a spike into my brain. Breathing deeply helped somewhat, but I would need pain relievers to feel somewhat human again.

Morphine would be nice, I thought.

Sidra was next to me, breathing steadily, but his eyes were still closed.

Then I noticed the person who had brought us in.

Meg.

I smiled at her. "You saved us."

"Yes." Her eyes were sad though.

"I'm sorry about Windsor."

"It doesn't matter, Mac."

"It does. He meant something to you."

"He tried to kill you. All of us."

"It doesn't make things easier." I turned my head toward Sidra. "Is he okay?"

"He's like you. Barely breathing but he's here. Nitrogen narcosis got you both, but he had it worse. He had the tank and the air. You had it, but only for a bit. Then you ran out of air, so we had to grab you first."

"You didn't leave."

She sighed. "How could we? We couldn't leave you to die."

"You put the movement at risk. Independence."

"We've already achieved it, Mac."

"But the battle. It's coming."

"We need *you* for that." Then she patted my chest. "Now, stop talking. We have to go to The Complex and get Sahar. And your seacar."

She still looked sad. Or was it . . . *anger*?

—••—

THE VESSEL ASCENDED FROM THE Drop, the thruster whining as it pushed us toward the mining outpost. It was not far, and Renée called into the airlock to tell us what was happening. I could hear the joy in her voice; we'd killed Windsor and survived to tell the tale. Meg whispered to me, "Frenchie is happy you're still with us."

"I can tell."

"You're going to have to put a ring on that."

I stared at her. "Really?"

She shrugged. "Don't you think it's time?"

I didn't have an answer to that. Beside me, Sidra had opened his eyes. Meg filled him in and he smiled. "Sahar's alive? She made it?"

"The miners have her. Mac's friend went out to get her, apparently."

I frowned. "My 'friend'?"

"Vinnie. The big guy. You were in the ore collector—"

"I remember." It had seemed so long ago, now. The descent into The Drop. The winch and wire that The Shiv had sabotaged with help from the Russian kill team. "He has Sahar?"

"He got your seacar, with Sahar, and it's docked at The Complex."

Sidra said, "Is she okay?"

"She's fine." Meg grabbed his hand. "She locked out the sonar and weapons. Then Bill—Windsor, I mean—got in. He was going to force her to unlock the systems if he managed to kill you and Mac. You saved her."

"*She* saved *us*, actually."

He sighed and closed his eyes again, and fell into a deep sleep.

Within an hour, we'd reunited on board *SC-1*. Sidra and I felt terrible, but a medic from The Complex gave us a shot that perked us up. It wasn't morphine, but it was close.

Vinnie was grinning from ear to ear. I had to smile as I shook his hand, and he bundled me up into a bear hug. "I'm glad to help!" he boomed.

"You did more than help."

"Just protecting my paycheck, boss."

That took me aback, and I blinked. The only person to have called me that was Cliff.

"Everything okay?" Renée asked, noticing my expression.

"Yes," I said. "I'm great. Really." I hugged her tightly. I didn't want to let go. "Things aren't over yet. There's still the coalition force."

"I know."

I looked at Sahar. She and Sidra were sitting on the couch, and she was bandaging a cut on his arm. They were all over him, I realized, when I looked closer. Then I studied myself. I was a wreck. Bandages still covered my arms from the earlier knife fight with Windsor, but they were now wet and ripped, exposing my scabbed and stitched arms. There were bruises and welts all over my body from the *Roach*'s flooding and sinking. The explosion and plummet into The Drop had been violent, to say the least. Our bodies had taken a pounding.

"I'm afraid we have to leave now, Vinnie," I said.

Coda Rose and Melinda Sinora were also on board *SC-1*. They were asking questions in a staccato stream, not fully understanding what had transpired since we'd left The Complex the previous day. Johnny was filling them in about William Windsor, Blue Downs, the Russian kill squad, and the fight with the *Sword*. Min Lee was standing with them, and she was also providing pieces of the puzzle as Johnny spoke.

I noticed Meg, standing to the side, watching the reunion. Her expression was somber.

She saw me watching her, and moved toward me. "I'm so glad you're still with us."

I said, "It's been the toughest mission of my life."

"There's still one more to come. Then we can relax."

I exhaled. She was right. Time was ticking and we needed to get moving back to Trieste. "How's the storm back home?"

"It's dying out."

"And the relief efforts on the shore?"

"Progressing." She shrugged. "It happened last year and it'll happen next year too. The superpowers know that they need the oceans to supply resources. But they want us under their thumbs."

"Sahar is right. We need to prove that we can provide more resources as an independent nation rather than a colony. If we can do that, maybe they'll let us be."

She stared at me, confused. "You know they won't do that, Mac. The coalition force is proof."

I thought about the collection of warsubs gathering in the Atlantic. Kristen had told me there were over a thousand now, including two dreadnoughts. I wondered—

Then I thought of Ventinov, and his dreadnought in the Pacific. He'd sent Windsor to kill me.

I needed to talk to him.

—••—

I WAS IN THE CONTROL cabin, with the hatch shut behind me. I keyed the comm and sent a broadcast out along the fiber optic network. I knew generally where Ventinov and his dreadnought were . . . I just hoped he'd respond.

Eventually, a Russian officer appeared on the screen. Her name was Mila Sidorov, a Lieutenant in the RSF. The Executive Officer of *Voskhod*. Her hair was pulled back and there were lines in her face. They weren't from worry or stress, though; they looked more like sun and wind damage, as if she had once been a sailor on the surface. On second glance, however, I noted that there were some dark shadows under her eyes. Her expression was stern as she stared at me. She studied my face, noticing my bruises and broken teeth.

"I'm Truman McClusky," I said.

"I recognize you." Then she remained silent, waiting.

*Interesting*, I thought. She wasn't rushing to get Ventinov. "I survived your assassination attempts. Your kill squad is dead."

"I'm not sure what you're—"

"The Shiv is dead too. I killed him."

That stopped her. She stared at me, and her eyes widened slightly.

*So, she knew about this.* "He was good. He was *very* good. His disguise was exceptional, but we exposed him then killed him. He was posing as a British operative of Churchill Sands."

"I don't know what you're—"

"Bullshit. Let me talk to Ventinov." She hesitated at that, not knowing what to do. I felt immediately that she wanted to know more before she called the Captain. Maybe she didn't agree with his tactics, I thought. I made a sudden decision and pressed on. "Ventinov is obsessed. He's not thinking clearly. He will do anything to make me pay. Even sacrifice his own crew. He'll do anything to reclaim his reputation."

She remained silent, staring at me.

I said, "He'll put you all in great danger. Right now, in the Atlantic, there's a coalition force gathering. I'm going back there now. We're going to end this. I'm warning you now, if you go, if your dreadnoughts participate, they will go down. We'll destroy them, the same way we destroyed the other one—*Drakon*."

That had an effect. She snorted. "You are very sure of yourself, McClusky. Too arrogant and vain for your own good. I've heard that about you."

"Maybe there's a reason for that. Maybe people hear it and then they underestimate me. I surprise them, in the end. The Shiv was certainly shocked. It's also what Ventinov thinks. But look what happens when people assume. I destroyed a French and USSF fleet eighteen months ago. They thought I was overconfident too. I took down *Drakon* last year. I just killed The Shiv. Next will be your three dreadnoughts." I didn't say anything about how I was going to do it, but in my mind I pictured the Neutral Particle Beam around Trieste carving their boats to pieces.

She scowled at me and said, "I will relay your message to the Captain. But know this: If you face our ships in battle, we will bury you at sea. In your wreckage."

Then she snapped off the comm and the image turned blue.

I swore. It was time to get home and end this.

# Chapter Thirty-Six

WE WERE SHOOTING BACK TO the Gulf of Mexico as fast as the SCAV drive could push us. Steam erupted from the stern thruster, and the fusion reactor flash-boiling seawater rumbled through the seacar. The deck vibrated, the roar settled over us like a warm blanket, and turbulence rocked us back and forth. We had to be careful walking around; *SCAV legs*, people might call it one day, when the drive was commonplace around the world.

Talia Tahnee came to mind. The steam propulsion was *loud*. The seacar cutting through the ocean, generating a bubble of supercavitation around it, created enough noise to affect marine life. She wanted to change that. To make the ships quieter.

"What are you thinking?" Renée asked, from my side.

"About the noise we're making." I was in the pilot chair, holding the yoke, and keeping us steady en route to the Panama Passthrough. Johnny and Min Lee were in *Destiny*, traveling at our side to the Gulf; Sahar, Sidra, and Meg were with us on *SC-1*.

"It doesn't matter if people hear us. The world is focused on the upcoming battle."

I nodded but didn't respond.

"What's wrong?"

"I'm worried about Meg. I killed her boyfriend."

Renée looked shocked. "They only knew each other for a few days, Mac. And he tried to kill you! Hell, he killed Cliff!"

"I know, but still. She was happy."

"He was only acting. He took advantage of her."

"Still," I repeated. Since leaving The Complex after killing Windsor, Meg had been remote. "I need to speak to her, I think."

Renée sat back and processed what I'd said. "The Shiv would have killed all of us. Surely she understands that."

"Emotions are more difficult than that," I said. And I knew Meg very, very well. She was my twin sister, after all. Even after she'd murdered Admiral Benning, I'd stood by her. She was my flesh and blood, the only family I had left, and I loved her.

"She'll understand."

"Oh, I know she will. But it doesn't take away the hurt, Renée. And hurt builds up over time."

"I know that too."

Something about the way she said it caught my attention. "Are you hurting, Renée?"

"No." She shook her head. "I love my life in Trieste. With you."

I stared at her. I loved it too. I told her, and she smiled.

"I know, actually," she said. Then she cocked her head to the side. "Tell me, you weren't planning on killing yourself, were you? To take The Shiv down with you?"

"If need be."

She looked shocked. "But Mac, after what I've done to be with you? You'd throw that aside?"

"Hardly. I would have done it to *protect* you, Renée. To save you."

"By killing yourself?"

"No. By killing *him*. Windsor."

She shook her head. "At some point you have to stop this, Mac. Give up. Let someone else worry about this."

I sighed and stared at her for a long moment. We'd had a tumultuous beginning, without much question. At our first meeting, I'd fired on her vessel. One man had died. Her superiors had punished her, and she'd spent the rest of her FSF career hunting me.

But now we were a couple, in love, and anxious for a future together. She'd given up everything for me, and I'd never forget that.

But had I really been trying to kill myself?

Not a chance.

But to protect the people around me, including the only family I had left, then I would not have hesitated taking The Shiv out with me.

I studied her silently, for a long series of heartbeats, while we sat in *SC-1*'s pilot cabin. Her hair was short and dark, her nose small and upturned, crow's feet at her eyes, and a deadly serious expression on her face as she stared at the churning and blurred cavitation bubble out the canopy surrounding the seacar.

I considered what she'd just said, about letting someone else worry about things for a change. "I've been thinking about that, actually."

—••—

MEG WAS IN THE LIVING area, sitting with Sahar, and when they saw me, Sahar rose to her feet and retreated to the ship's engineering area.

I said, "Wait, Sahar. I wanted to see if you're okay."

She turned to me. "A few bruises. No worse than what anyone else has experienced on this trip." Then she glanced at Meg. "Some wounds are not visible." Then she spun and disappeared through the hatch.

I sat next to Meg. "I'm so, so sorry."

She sighed as she stared at the deck. "It's not just him. It's this crazy life we live, Truman. The uncertainty. The constant missions. The battles. The pain."

"Dad started the path years ago. For a long time I wanted nothing to do with it." Dad's vision had torn our family apart. But despite my misgivings, I'd ended up back in TCI, fighting for independence, and had finally made the Oceania announcement a week earlier.

We'd been through a lot, and Meg was suffering, even though she'd joined willingly two years earlier.

She said, "I didn't want it either. We both agreed on that. But then . . ." She sighed and threw her arms up. "Here we are. On a seacar headed to war."

There were a thousand warsubs or more waiting for us in the Atlantic. We would have no time to rest. As soon as we arrived, it would start.

"There's only one more fight, Meg."

"And then what? Only one more mission? Only one more invention to steal? How many missions until we die, Tru? First it was the SCAV drive. Then the syntactic foam. Then the Acoustic Pulse Drive. Then the mission to sink the dreadnought. Then the Isomer Bomb. Then the Neutral Beam. Now it's the graphene process and . . . and The Shiv." She swore. "It *never* ends."

"It's getting us to the end, Meg. And we invented the SCAV, the APD, and the Isomer Bomb. We didn't have to steal those."

"It's all put us in great danger! And Bill—" she choked off, and tears started to come.

"Go on," I whispered.

"He actually made me feel something other than fear or tension or drama. I know that I didn't know him for long, but it was something I hadn't expected."

"He made you feel like nothing else mattered." I understood it. Renée had done that for me, after all.

"And then what happened? He fucking turned out to be a Russian spy! And not only that, *the most notorious spy in oceanic history!*"

I almost laughed at that, but held it in. She was correct. We were in a black hole of danger and spycraft that never seemed to end, and it seemed to suck everyone we knew or worked with into its embrace.

"Meg, you're right. It's been a ridiculous life. We haven't been able to settle down. Renée has been upset with me before because of that too. Because I can't focus on anything else."

"At least you have her."

"*You* have her too. She'll be part of our family if she's not already. But there will be other guys in your life. I promise."

"This is *never* going to end. *One* more battle. *One* more mission. *One* more fight." Her expression had gone flat, and she was staring into nothingness.

"What are you saying?"

"Maybe I should leave, Tru." She sighed. "Maybe Trieste isn't for me, after all."

She'd lived in Blue Downs for many years, after Dad had died, and I knew she loved the city. Being back there must have brought back many memories. I asked if that's where she wanted to go.

She glanced at me, guilt on her features. "I don't know. All I know is that maybe I should leave Trieste and try to start a life. Try to be happy."

I sighed. I understood what she was saying and what she was feeling. I felt it too. "I think this is the final mission, Meg. I agree with you. This has to be the end."

She stared at me for a long minute. The sound of the thruster echoed around us. It was comforting, in a way. It spoke of power and a technology that few nations had. "What does that mean? Are you planning something I don't know about?"

"No. I just mean we have to win, or it's all over."

"Until it's not."

"What do you—"

"Just that if we fail, the USSF will occupy us again. Then you'll work to free Trieste from them and proclaim Oceania two years from now. Then it'll all happen again, with people around us dying and more battles and death. I can't go through that anymore."

Her face was set and her eyes were firm.

"I promise this is it, Meg. We've been planning this for months. We're *ready*. But if you decide to leave after, I'll understand."

She didn't respond.

—••—

THE PUERTO RICO TRENCH IS the deepest area of the Atlantic Ocean, reaching depths of over eight kilometres, farther below the surface than any fleet warsubs could reach. A battle in that trench would be a do-or-die scenario for any fleet. Take any damage, take on water and start an uncontrolled descent, and it was game over.

And the Trench was where we were planning to make our final stand.

They were gathering to the east, in the Atlantic. Over a thousand warsubs, of every host or mother nation to an ocean colony in The Fifteen's orbit, including some nations whose cities had not yet joined with us. They were worried they'd lose their colonies, so they were preemptively joining the fight to prevent the inevitable. The major players were America, Britain, Germany, Russia, France, China, and Australia. But also, I noted, New Zealand, the Philippines, Spain, and South Africa were present in the coalition fleet. Perhaps some others that I wasn't aware of.

In the trench, our opposing force consisted entirely of Oceania's seacars. We had fleets from Trieste, the six Chinese cities, Churchill Sands, Blue Downs, the three French cities, Seascape, Ballard, and New Berlin.

Our ships were technologically superior to every other nation's vessels, with the exception of the USSF and the CSF, who also now possessed the SCAV drive. The RSF was a danger as well, for their three dreadnoughts were going to prove an immense challenge. Just sinking one of them had taken all of our energy and efforts and weeks of planning and preparation, culminating in a mission to infiltrate and destroy the warsub from within. This was not going to be a similar situation.

We had to take the three dreadnoughts down with sheer force.

Our seacars was gathering secretly in the Puerto Rico Trench. My task now was to lure the coalition force there. If any split off and went to Trieste to invade and occupy, we'd have to deal with them with our defensive technologies and a small force of weaponized seacars.

And, of course, our Neutral Particle Beam—the energy beam designed to fire underwater and tear apart warsub hulls until the surrounding water pressure broke containment and flooded the vessel.

My heart was pounding.

We hadn't been through any battle like this, ever.

If we failed, Oceania would end almost before it had begun.

# Chapter Thirty-Seven

JOHNNY'S *SWORD, DESTINY*, WAS WITH us on the journey to the trench. He and Min Lee were piloting, and we made the uneventful journey quickly. As we approached Trieste, we slowed, turned off the SCAV and the fusion reactor, and, hugging the seafloor, began a slower journey to the Puerto Rico Trench.

Quietly.

The others had been moving forces there during the past month, even before I'd made the proclamation.

We knew this would be the play.

We'd predicted that a force of warsubs would first gather in the Atlantic before attacking Trieste.

We had a collection of small but fast, heavily armed seacars. All had the SCAV drive and could reach velocities of at least 450 kph. Many had the Acoustic Pulse Drive as well, which allowed them to descend to six kilometres, and perhaps more. With the APD, we could sail below the fleets of warsubs and shoot upward at them, from below their Crush Depths of 3,000 to 4,000 metres. It was ocean superiority, much like air superiority on the surface.

It was almost ocean *supremacy*.

Their mines and torpedoes could not go deeper than five kilometres.

And we had something the opposing forces didn't: the Isomer Bomb.

It occurred to me that if the battle was going poorly for China or the US or Russia, they might consider using a nuke. If that happened, we would have to be ready.

*SC-1* pulled quietly into the trench at a very low velocity. The Gulf had just endured one of the worst hurricanes in recorded history. Shore defences in Texas and Louisiana and Florida had all failed in places, which was a first for the nation. Usually severe damage might affect one or two states at landfall. In this case, the hurricane had pummeled three states and the storm surge—the largest in history—had shattered shore walls in all three. Aid efforts were underway topside, but it was a brutal environmental disaster—and one in just a series. These events were wearing the nation down. The US was dealing with not only shoreline wall failures and a serious refugee issue, but at the same time famine and drought in other areas of the United States. There was also the usual threat from rising waters, which were frequently breaking through seawalls around major cities like New York.

The States also seemed to be at a breaking point, and a lot of Triestrians wondered how much more they could take before they just gave up trying to keep us in their sphere.

We arrived at the trench and stared at the sonar display in wonder. There were hundreds of seacars on the image, arranged in clusters according to city allegiance. It was easier to coordinate them that way, even though we were all fighting for each other.

I pressed the comm button on the yoke trigger, and said, "Hello, people of Oceania. It's Mac."

The comm practically exploded with messages in response.

"Mac is here!"

"I told you all that Mac wouldn't let us down!"

"Now we've got them beat!"

"Oceania forever!"

"Let's hit them hard *now*, Mac!"

"Where have you been, Mac?"

I let the comments wash over me for a long minute. Renée was grinning. Meg, Sahar, and Sidra were behind me, watching over my shoulder, and they were smiling too.

I leaned forward and spoke again: "I've been in The Iron Plains. Sorry I'm late." I glanced at Renée and then behind me, at Meg. "While you've been gathering here, preparing for battle to protect our nation,

Oceania, I've been investigating a threat against myself and other Triestrians. A Russian agent, The Steel Shiv, was attempting to kill me. He successfully killed our Chief Security Officer, Cliff Sim, and used it to draw me into the same trap. Some of you may have known Cliff and I'm sorry to give you this news. But, I have to tell you that we fought The Shiv in The Iron Plains."

The fleet's silence was deafening. They couldn't believe it.

I continued, "The Shiv was hiding in plain sight. He was a British spy, born in Russia but raised from the age of eight in England. His name was William Windsor. He's dead."

Now there was an absolute uproar. People couldn't believe that we'd uncovered his identity, and not only that, had managed to kill the spy.

"We'd heard about The Shiv being involved in this, Mac," a familiar voice echoed from the speaker.

I frowned. "Francois? Piette? Is that you?" It was the Mayor of Cousteau, in charge of his fleet of seacars.

"*Bonjour.*"

"How'd you know?"

"The Russians are making a stink of it. You probably haven't been following the news, since you've likely been fighting for your life, which you seemingly have to do every day. But the RSF are speaking openly of The Shiv's involvement in this. It's been a morale boost for them."

"Not anymore," I said. I glanced back at Meg, and her face was frozen.

But she touched my shoulder and squeezed. The message was clear. *I'll be fine, Tru.*

"What's next for us, Mac?" Piette asked.

I exhaled. "We have to draw the coalition fleet here. To the trench. Then we'll begin. But first—" I turned to Sahar. "Sahar Noor is with me. She'd like to speak to you all."

A silence fell over the comm.

Around us, seacars drifted in the deep expanse of warm water.

Below, the seafloor was kilometres away, a maelstrom of tectonic activity, hidden by pressure and darkness and dense waters.

Above, thousands of metres up, the sky was clearing and finally turning blue after more than seven days of storm, clouds, rain, and churning waves.

I held the mic out and she took it from me. She cleared her throat.

"This is Sahar Noor. You might know me. If you don't, hear me now. This is what we've been working for, for many years now. It's all come to this. We've declared Oceania, and now we'll work for ourselves. We'll forge economic partnerships with the colonizing nations, and we'll work hard to make these countries *more* successful through our efforts, not less successful. We'll make them see that the best thing for them is to set us loose, to let go of our leashes and see what we can do as a free nation, fighting hard underwater to extract and produce and process resources to sell. They'll pay a fair market price, but in the end, they'll receive *more* than they would have otherwise. But before that happens, we have to get through this last hurdle."

She took a breath and glanced at me. "I only ask this. You know my culture forbids killing. It's simply wrong. I will extend this same plea to the other side, as well. What I ask is that if you're forced to fire, you do so only as a last resort. You *wait* until they fire first, and if you fire back, you shoot to *disable* warsubs, not sink them. That's all I ask. We must have clear consciences when this is all over. We can't exist with guilt hanging over us for the next decades as we try to celebrate free lives. Freedom, yes, but at what cost? How many families won't see their mothers and fathers return because of our actions today?" She took another deep breath.

Inside, I was quaking. She knew how many warsubs I'd sunk, how many crews I'd killed. I'd had nightmares for many years. In them, sailors screamed my name as their cabins filled with water. The last breaths they took as the green water rose over their heads and enclosed them forever were to scream in hate. All to secure the freedom of my people in Trieste.

I wondered what impact her words would have. Would we be able to disable rather than destroy?

At least she was still with us, still leading, and present in the battle.

She passed the mic back to me. We were on video as well, and I hoped my thoughts—my inner demons—were not obvious.

I said, "Prepare the floats. Ready the crews. I'll go and bring the enemy to you. And when I do, this day will be one to remember."

# Chapter Thirty-Eight

THE COALITION FLEET OF OVER a thousand vessels was in the Atlantic, at roughly the same latitude as Puerto Rico.

*SC-1* was the lead seacar in our fleet. I rose from the trench and, as we cleared the lip of the tectonic feature that tore the ocean floor for hundreds of kilometres from northwest to southeast, I set course due east. The rest of the Triestrian vessels were with us—238 of them.

It was our largest fleet ever; our secret facility in the Mid-Atlantic Ridge had been producing *Swords* as fast as we could deliver the parts and components.

To Sahar, still behind me, I said, "How many seacars from Churchill are here?"

"Eighty-seven at last count."

The Chinese cities—there were six of them, including Sheng City—had sent over three hundred. Collectively, we had a huge fleet, though our vessels were tiny. Each only about twenty to thirty metres long. The coalition fleet facing us had warsubs hundreds of metres long, some with nuclear ballistic missiles. We were insects in comparison, but we were *powerful*, and we were fast.

I activated the SCAV drive and accelerated quickly. It was more to show them where we were hiding. Our location would appear as a cluster of flares on their sonar screens.

"Well, they know where we are now," I muttered.

Johnny's *Sword*, *Destiny*, was next to me, on the screen. I keyed for his frequency and said, "Are you ready, partner?"

His response was immediate. "We've been preparing for this for years, Mac. Hard to believe we're here." Min Lee was next to him, reviewing information on a computer pad on her lap.

"We're only a few minutes from engaging them." I checked the navigation map and began to slow. I didn't want to get too close.

Johnny glanced behind him, off camera, and his face screwed up in confusion.

"What's wrong?" I asked. I hoped his vessel hadn't suffered a fault of some sort.

"A noise, that's all."

"I'll check," Min Lee said. She rose and disappeared to the back.

My comm buzzed. It was the flagship of the coalition fleet, approaching rapidly. I brought our velocity to zero and stared at the sonar in horror.

There were too many signals to comprehend. The entire screen glowed with contacts. The passive range was thirty kilometres, and the entire area was crowded with bright, glittering lights.

*Thirty kilometres in radius, and full of warsubs.*

*And they all want to kill you, Mac.*

The largest three signals were next to each other, keeping a comfortable distance from the surrounding vessels. They were the Russian dreadnoughts, and they worried me the most. To prevent them from killing people and to disable them at the same time would simply not be possible.

Still, we had planned for this.

"Attention Truman McClusky of Trieste City."

"Go ahead," I said.

"This is Admiral Kenley."

I blinked. She commanded a USSF *Terminator* Class ballistic missile boat: *Infiltrator.* It was the largest warsub in the fleet. It made sense that she would be in charge of the coalition fleet. People respected her immensely. The warsub was 261 metres from bow to stern. Still small, compared to the dreadnoughts, but it was a scary presence here. It had thirty-six torpedo tubes, nuclear ballistic missiles, and a crew of 210.

I located her boat on the sonar; the callout display contained the ship's relevant stats. "Hello."

"Stand down. Surrender immediately. We intend to dock at Trieste and occupy the colony. The city council will also stand down. Our forces will from this point on take over your resource production."

"I don't think so. We're an independent nation consisting of fifteen cities. And I have to warn you—if you attack Trieste, then you attack *all* members of Oceania."

"We're only concerned with Trieste, Ballard, and Seascape. I don't care about the other cities."

"Really? Then why are you leading warsubs from other nations? There are German and Russian ships behind you right now."

I turned *SC-1* back, westward. Slowly but surely.

"Halt your progress," she said, after an instant. Someone had informed her of our course change.

"Listen to me, Rebecca Kenley."

"It's *Admiral*." The anger in her tone was clear.

"Kenley, we're an independent nation. If you persist in this action, you will suffer. Already the USSF has faced the destruction of three bases. Are you sure you want to risk more losses?"

"I'm ordering you to stop. Do not continue on that course."

Renée, at my side, pointed at the screen. The Russian dreadnoughts were approaching.

I said, "You're working with the Russians now. They destroyed Norfolk and San Diego. Really?"

"We have a common threat, you could say."

"Our desire to work independently in the oceans is a threat?"

There was a long pause. "Look, McClusky. I'm not here to debate with you. I'm following orders. And I'm passing them on to you. Stop your vessel, *now*."

She was *commanding*, I had to give her that.

I switched the broadcast to a common frequency so every ship could hear me. "This is McClusky. If you persist in this action, you'll die. Today will be your last day on Earth."

Behind me, I could sense Sahar growing nervous.

I continued, "Captain Ventinov failed in his attempt to kill me. His weapon, The Steel Shiv, is dead. Do you hear me, Ventinov?"

On the screen, the three dreadnoughts continued their approach. I knew those three had the SCAV drive. I pushed the throttle higher, and kept my eyes on the RSF vessels.

"You failed," I said. "It was a pitiful attempt, and your most elite assassin is dead. I killed him in the Iron Plains."

The response, for the moment, was only silence. Then, his voice stabbed at me. "So be it. Today we will use force. My blade didn't work against you. But this is your end."

"We have weapons that you have never faced. I sunk *Drakon*. I'll sink *Voskhod* too."

I could hear the joy in the man's voice. He thought he knew. "I don't think so."

It made me smile. We were going to lead him to his death. His speed continued to increase, with the other two dreadnoughts matching his actions. I punched the SCAV button and brought the reactor back online.

I cut the call and turned to Renée. She said, "He knows we're trying to lead him somewhere. Probably to the trench, and try the same thing we did to *Drakon* over the Kermadec."

"He has suspicions. But those three vessels are the biggest challenge." I stared at them. They were a separate threat from the others. We had to deal with them before facing the rest of the coalition.

What the hell was I doing here?

"Don't hesitate," Renée said, sensing my doubts. "We've planned for this. Lead them to the trench."

"Got it." I pushed the throttle the rest of the way forward and the supercavitation began. Our reactor began flash-boiling seawater, and at the bow, air began to emerge, surrounding us in a frictionless bubble.

Our velocity increased.

"McClusky," Admiral Kenley broke in. "Do not do this. Surrender now. You're making a decision that will affect more than just you."

I ignored her and continued back, toward the Puerto Rico Trench.

Behind us, the three RSF dreadnoughts were entering SCAV drive, thrusting through the ocean, hammering ahead, their own frictionless bubbles beginning to form.

The sonar alarm chimed in anger.

*Multiple torpedo shutters open.*

"Johnny," I said, on the frequency for *Destiny*. "They're getting ready to fire. Are you ready?"

He was with me, on the same course, along with the other Triestrian *Swords*.

The three dreadnoughts were preparing to fire. Together, there was more firepower there than we could comprehend.

But there was no answer from my Deputy Mayor.

"Johnny?" I asked again, frowning.

Still nothing.

I recalled how Min Lee had earlier reacted to some kind of malfunction or noise on their *Sword*.

Then, he replied, and his face appeared on my comm screen. He was in the pilot chair, and kept glancing over his shoulder, studying something behind him. "Mac, I have a problem here. A *very big* problem."

"What is—"

"Min Lee is in the back. There's someone on board with us."

A prickle worked its way up my scalp.

My guts twisted.

"Someone? How could that be? We've come here straight from—"

"She's fighting with someone back there, Mac. It's—it's William Windsor, Mac! The Steel Shiv. He's on board my *Sword*. *He's not dead*."

# Interlude

## In the Atlantic Ocean

DATA PROCESSING

| | |
|---|---|
| Vessel: | *Sword* Class Triestrian Vessel, *Destiny* |
| Location: | Latitude: 18º 45' N |
| | Longitude: 60º 19' W |
| | The Atlantic Ocean, east of the Puerto Rico Trench |
| Depth: | 200 metres |
| Date: | 15 June 2131 |
| Time: | 1917 hours |

VASILY STALI / WILLIAM WINDSOR / The Steel Shiv had hid in the *Sword*'s cargo hold since The Complex.

He'd noted, with some hint of irony, that the vessel's name was actually *Destiny*.

Yes.

Destiny.

McClusky's destiny.

This would be the vessel that finally brought him a painful end.

The Mayor had set a trap for Stali on board the *Roach*. One second, they'd faced each other as opponents were meant to—in hand-to-hand combat, without weapons, testing one man's steel against another's. Then, to his horror, the mining thresher scoop had pulled something totally unexpected from the ocean floor. A large metal sphere, painted red and black.

An explosive mine.

*What the hell?*

It had distracted him. Then Mac landed a lucky kick, a judo throw, and Stali found himself in sudden and immediate danger.

He'd been on the rock conveyer, trying to catch his breath, his back pressing against wet fragments of sharp rock, *next to an unexploded Chinese bomb*.

And then, in the large sorting machine, he'd jumped away at the last possible moment into the sand hold. The explosive concussion had forced the outer hatch open, flooding the hold, and he'd had to swim out into the deep ocean, without gear, without a tank, without anything.

He'd nearly drowned swimming to The Complex, but he'd managed to find an airlock and enter before blackness took hold.

He'd waited there, shivering from cold and nearly dead from hypoxia, until the two small seacars had docked at the mining base.

Then, he'd snuck into the one with the fewest number of people.

*Destiny.*

He'd spent the rest of the time recovering, resting, healing, and preparing.

He no longer cared about Russian goals, or the upcoming battle.

He didn't care about Ivan Ventinov or his obsession with Trieste and McClusky.

The cargo hatch slid aside, rattling as it did so.

He stepped out, after more than a day of hiding in the cramped, cold, steel space.

Time to end this.

He would take his destiny back. Take it into his own hands, and end McClusky once and for all.

# Part Nine

## The Final Battle

# Chapter Thirty-Nine

My blood turned to ice. Renée was speechless.

Then the sonar screamed a warning.

*Torpedo in the water.*

*Torpedo in the water.*

*Torpedo in the water.*

There were multiple weapons heading for us.

Johnny was at the controls of *Destiny*. Somehow, he was going to have to avoid the torpedoes while also fighting The Shiv.

If Min Lee failed, that is.

She was fighting for her life somewhere back in the engineering compartment.

"You have to seal the hatch," I snapped. "Lock him out. Pilot the vessel. The torpedoes first, Johnny. We have to survive in order to beat this bastard."

His face was flat. "Min Lee is back there. By herself."

"Listen to me. If you go back there to help her, you're doomed. Even if you win the fight, the torpedoes will hit by then. I can't save us both!"

The sonar system was booming a warning to us. Renée flipped the switch that controlled the alarms. She said, "They're approaching at eighty kph."

"Prepare countermeasures." I stared at the screen. Johnny's ship was next to us, still accelerating as the frictionless bubble formed around *Destiny* and *SC-1*.

"The speed is now . . . " Her face exploded into shock. "Two hundred and climbing." She turned to me. "They're SCAV torpedoes, Mac. Top speed is more than double ours."

Sahar was behind us, watching the entire scene unfold. She remained silent; her fingertips on my headrest were white.

Sidra was with us too, his face tight.

"How much farther to the trench?"

"Twenty-nine kilometres!"

Too far. We'd have to deal with this now.

"Johnny, these are SCAV torpedoes. You have to avoid them first."

His face was set like stone. "I can hear the fighting, Mac. The sounds . . . "

Johnny's vessel was still accelerating, but it remained on course. I stared at his face on the screen, waiting for a response. But I had to act any second; the torpedoes were closing.

Then he bolted from his chair with a single, blurted statement. "Good luck, Mac. I have to help her. Win for Trieste."

The screen went black.

I swore.

"How many missiles are heading for us?" I asked Renée.

"Ten."

"Prepare countermeasures. We have to somehow lead them away from *Destiny*."

"Ready."

I decelerated slightly and brought us *behind* Johnny's seacar. The wake from his supercavitating drive tossed *SC-1* like a tin can. "Better sit down and strap in," I said to Meg, Sahar, and Sidra.

The torpedoes were closing.

There were ten angry red lines on the sonar screen, heading straight for the green triangle in the center.

*SC-1*.

And I was slowing down.

The yoke jerked in my grip; my palms were sweaty.

I continued to slow.

Then I blurted, "Countermeasures!"

Renée pressed the button, and the *clunk* of ejecting countermeasures echoed through the vessel. Then I peeled away, to the port, and accelerated.

I watched the missiles on the screen.

If any made it through the cloud of churning bubbles and noise, then Johnny might be finished before this had even started. But I was hoping they'd follow us, and not *Destiny*.

On a comm all-broadcast to my own people, I said, "Everyone engage SCAV and help me get these torpedoes—converge on this location, *now!*"

The sound generated by over two hundred seacars simultaneously closing on the same location was simply *enormous*.

Each missile's computer was searching for sound to lock to, to track and destroy.

And now, a flood of sound overwhelmed each. A roaring, cascading, churning, *maelstrom* of cacophonous thunder.

At the same time, they entered the zone of countermeasures we'd dropped—

And they decided to explode, hoping to take the enemy out with them.

A gargantuan explosion ripped outward in a sphere of vaporized water. The surrounding water crashed back into the void, causing secondary concussions that echoed outward, rippling pressure waves flooding and radiating in all directions.

They'd failed.

Johnny's seacar continued to power toward the trench, to the west.

I watched it on the screen as it grew more distant.

And came to a sudden decision.

I couldn't leave him.

The three RSF dreadnoughts were hot on our tail. Their SCAVs were still ramping up—the sheer size of each vessel meant it took longer for the bubbles to form—and they were leaving the rest of the coalition fleet behind. I assumed Kenley did not want to barrel into a situation they weren't fully prepared for, and were allowing the three RSF warsubs to be the point of the spear. The Russians were more than a kilometre behind us now, but accelerating past 250 kph in pursuit.

*Voskhod*. The Rise.

*Vechno Medved*. Forever Bear.

*Soprotivlenive*. Resistance.

Each had the Tsunami Plow weapon, capable of generating a concussion pressure wave that on the surface could overwhelm sea walls, and underwater, could *shove* ships aside as a giant might sweep aside toys. Hurled against the seafloor, or against each other, this could achieve Crush Depth instantly.

And Johnny was fighting The Shiv, on board *Destiny*.

Renée touched my arm. "You can't go after him. You have to stay and fight *them*." She nodded at the dreadnoughts.

I was about to object, when the image of the three dreadnoughts pursuing our *Swords* caught my eye. We were leading them to the trench and the rest of our hidden forces.

"But Johnny and Min Lee—"

"They'll have to do their best against him. He's likely hurt and tired, after what he's been through. They have a good chance. Besides, *Destiny*'s not going anywhere."

"What are you saying? Leave him on his own?" I snapped, perhaps a bit out of frustration, and not meant to be rude. "They're—" I cut off my words. The seacar was now in a wide circle, just over the trench ahead. Johnny must have switched on the autopilot before leaving his chair.

Renée said, "He'll be there for a bit. Now, let's take on these dreadnoughts."

—••—

"Attention Triestrian fleet," I said. "The plan remains in play. Proceed to the Trench. And wait."

We were an incredible sight. Over two hundred *Swords*, including *SC-1*, all in SCAV drive and powering toward the lip that led to the abyss, over 8,000 metres down, on the east side of the Greater Antilles Island chain.

There, we had thrown all our eggs into one basket.

*Almost* all our eggs, that is. We still had one surprise left.

We stopped at the edge of the trench, maintained neutral buoyancy, and turned to face the oncoming dreadnoughts.

Below us, the rest of our fleet rose behind us. *Hundreds* of seacars, all heavily armed and equipped with the newest technologies, emerged from the trench to make a stand against the coalition force.

Our torpedoes would have minimal effect. We'd tried it before, against *Drakon*. Puncturing its outer hull only flooded exterior compartments. The warsubs were so large that the inner compartmentalization maintained a positive buoyancy. The ships had backup reactors, too.

A nuclear blast would work, but we didn't have a nuke, and besides, that would signal an escalation that no one was comfortable with. The other side might use one on us—that possibility had occurred to all of us while planning this.

But we did have the Isomer Bomb.

It released an enormous concussion of gamma rays, which were neither fission- nor fusion-generated. It was *non-nuclear*, but a similar-sized blast. And because of this, it skirted the non-proliferation treaties.

We had finally proved the Isomer Bomb worked by detonating it at Seascape, in the Gulf of Mexico off the coast of Texas. The superpowers of the world had suspected Germany of detonating the bomb and ushering in the Isomer Age, but *they* had not.

Trieste was to blame.

*I* was to blame.

And I was about to detonate one again.

"Max, are you there?"

"I'm here," came the immediate response over the comm. Max Hyland, creator of the bomb, was in our fleet, in one of the *Swords*. Within, he had an armory of several Isomer Bomb torpedoes.

My heart was pounding.

*This* was going to be an escalation that the RSF would feel for generations.

I glanced at Sahar, behind me.

She was watching, and I knew she didn't want to kill needlessly.

"We'll detonate the bomb *behind* the warsubs. Remove their propulsion capabilities, leaving them stranded here."

Max replied, "Got it. They're so close out there, one should do the trick."

"Does it need to actually *hit* the hull? Or can you—"

"I can program a destination detonation."

"Okay. Use the nav console to choose the location." The pilot of his seacar, Chanta Newel, our new CSO, would show him how to do so. "Fire when ready."

Our fleet of seacars was floating above the trench.

Then one torpedo shutter opened, on one of the *Swords*.

I was sure the dreadnoughts noted it.

Then the rest of the seacars also opened shutters and locked onto the targets.

We fired together.

It was dramatic, loud, and spoke clearly of our intentions to not give in to the superpowers.

Each torpedo churned toward the dreadnoughts. They were not quiet.

The *real* weapon, however, was slow and stealthy. It hugged the bottom.

Above it, the storm of steel collided with countermeasures and hulls and exploded remotely. The concussion waves churned through the water and tossed us like insects above the giant abyss.

I watched the lone torpedo moving across my sonar screen. The rest of the noise obscured the device; my computer predicted its location based on programming along its predetermined path.

I held my breath.

The dreadnoughts weathered the wave of torpedoes easily. Little damage. No real effect.

The warsubs were so massive that conventional weapons would simply not work. It's why, one year ago, we'd had to infiltrate *Drakon* and cause a China Syndrome meltdown in its reactor to bring it down into the Kermadec Trench. It had been the only way, and Ventinov had never expected it.

I didn't think he'd expect this, either.

—••—

THE ISOMER BOMB MOVED AT barely ten kph. Previously, it had consisted of two torpedoes—a trigger and the actual device. Now, the entire mechanism was in a single cylinder. It crawled only a metre over the ocean floor, as above, the battle raged. Countermeasures churned, torpedoes launched and detonated, and explosions vaporized tons of seawater at a time. Concussion blasts echoed in the theater of war.

At the predetermined location, the weapon left the seafloor and its aft planes angled the cylindrical bomb upward. It was *behind* the RSF warsubs now, and it reached the location undamaged.

*No one* in the RSF control cabins had noted its approach.

It detonated.

# Chapter Forty

An enormous sphere of gamma radiation bathed the sterns of all three dreadnoughts in a blinding flare of light.

Ventinov had been stupid to keep his warsubs in such close proximity.

Still, I understood why. He'd been born and raised to believe they were unstoppable. It didn't matter that he'd failed before. He was too cocky and arrogant about his vessels, because that was what his history had taught him. Russia is always better.

Bigger is better.

The bigger the warsub, the more devastation it could cause.

He had been expecting something else from me, but not *this*.

*Not* an Isomer Bomb.

Sahar had been over my shoulder, peering out the canopy. Renée was at my side. Meg was with Sidra, looking out the viewports in the living area. Sudden waves of light flooded the interior. We shielded our eyes with outstretched hands and squinted against the agony. The three warsubs instantly appeared as silhouettes in front of the expanding ball of energy, which was shifting through all colours in the spectrum. It hurt my eyeballs—a deep hurt that penetrated far up my optic nerves—and I squeezed my eyes shut and screamed into the comm, "Everyone, descend into the trench, *NOW!*"

The concussion blast would destroy us all if we were in the open and unprotected.

As one, our seacars flooded ballast tanks and descended below the lip of the abyss.

My heart was in my throat.

If the concussion damaged any of the *Swords*, they could take on too much water and descend to Crush Depth.

The ships plunged below the edge of the sheer drop into the abyss.

Ten metres.

Fifty.

A hundred.

And then the water concussion hit.

It flooded over the Puerto Rico Trench and moved westward, toward the Antilles island chain. The water currents were strong and they tossed us about madly. The stabilizing engines whined to keep us in place, with limited success. Luckily, we were far from the other vessels, and no one collided.

I released my breath.

The sonar screen had flared white and remained that way.

The system was rebooting; the blast had overwhelmed the algorithms to monitor sound in the passive range of thirty kilometres. The dreadnoughts had been only hundreds of metres from us when the Isomer Bomb blew.

Shifting to positive buoyancy, I brought *SC-1* back up over the edge of the trench.

The scene before us was something nearly impossible to describe.

Two of the dreadnoughts were shedding hull plates and chunks of metal superstructure from their stern compartments. Gouts of bubbles were rising to the surface, and the warsubs were listing badly to the seafloor. The water around the warsubs was still—

*Glittering?*

The Isomer Bomb's radiation dissipated rapidly—one of the strengths of this new classification of weapon—and the glow was fading but still present. Each dreadnought had two massive thruster pods; the screws were bent to oblivion, the structures were shattered as if exploded from the inside out, perhaps due to concussion blasts passing within the warsub and twisting and winding their way out into the ocean. There was a rumble echoing in the waters, transmitted through *SC-1* by its hull, bulkheads, deck plating—anything metal—and it surrounded us in a deathly embrace.

Sparks arced into the water from the warsubs' aft sections. Minor explosions continued to light the sea, possibly from the arsenal inside each RSF vessel. Torpedoes and mines exploded. Above, pressure waves continued radiating outward, toward the surface three kilometres away. The ocean above was no doubt undulating madly from the isomer explosion.

Two of the vessels hit the bottom and sand churned upward and surrounded the hulls like mushroom clouds. The impacts registered on the sonar, which was now coming back online. There were implosion events occurring within each dreadnought as well and water churned through the corridors, breaking containment and shattering watertight hatches.

Sahar's face was ashen. She was staring at the destruction before us, horrified.

"We did what we could," I said. "We targeted the aft sections. People died, but many in the forward compartments are likely still alive, Sahar. And the ocean is not beyond Crush Depth here. We detonated the bomb before the dreadnoughts were over the abyss."

She attempted a nod. "I understand. But still . . . it's enormous destruction."

"There are still over a thousand vessels arrayed against us, just a few kilometres to the east."

"I know."

I pointed at one of the dreadnoughts. It remained seaworthy, not sinking, but it was still and quiet. The sonar indicated that alarms were ringing inside, as well as screams, pipe breaks, and some minor flooding. "One of them survived the blast." I shook my head. "Incredible. Somehow it absorbed the concussion and didn't sink."

Calls started to ring out over the comm.

"Mac, we did it!"

"The bomb worked!"

"They walked right into it!"

"They're gonna be shitting right about now! Imagine what the coalition fleet is thinking!"

"Two down, and no damage on our side."

"How many more of those do we have?"

I didn't answer the last question. Instead I stared at the sonar, trying to locate *Destiny* and Johnny Chang, who was likely in a fight for his life against William Windsor.

*Destiny* was moving in a circle around the arena of battle. It was in SCAV drive, a white flare on the sonar display. There were no communications from her. No navigation. No calls for help.

We had to get to her and find out what was going on.

Meg was at my back, also staring at the screen.

I said, "The coalition fleet doesn't realize how powerful we really are. Now they know."

"They might use nukes in retaliation, Mac."

I hesitated. She was correct. Not against Trieste, however. There were too many civilians there. But here, in the open, over a massive trench?

It was very possible.

But I knew they'd have to get permission, and *that* would take time. It gave us a buffer.

I squeezed the yoke comm trigger. "Attention Oceania fleet. It's time to engage the enemy. Lead them back here, over the trench, and use your deep diving technology." With the Acoustic Pulse Drive, our ships could descend over five kilometres, out of the coalition fleet's weapons' range.

Meg said, "What are we going to do, Mac?"

"I have to go there. Confront him."

"I know." Her voice was soft.

"What about the rest of our people?" Renée said. "There's a battle—"

I said, "They'll fight, and they'll do well."

On the sonar screen, the coalition fleet was now advancing.

I pushed the throttle forward, activated the SCAV drive, and turned toward Johnny's seacar.

"How are we going to get aboard?" Sidra said.

"There's only one choice. We'll have to dock with an umbilical."

"While at SCAV drive? At 450 kilometres per hour?" Sidra looked terrified. "With the cavitation bubbles around us!?"

"There's no other way aboard. Our umbilical is gone. Destroyed. But *Destiny* still has one. We'll use that." I matched the seacar's course, ahead of it, and slowed *SC-1* slightly. "It's going to be tricky."

Understatement of the century.

But Johnny was aboard that ship, likely in a hand-to-hand fight with William Windsor.

And, I noted, my insides twisting, our circular course took us directly through where the coalition force was currently headed.

We were going to cut right through the looming battle.

As I thought it, the sonar screamed. Torpedoes were launching *everywhere.*

*Holy shit.*

I said, "We'll get over into their airlock, Renée. Detach immediately and get out of the way."

Sidra said, "I'll go with you."

I nodded and grabbed his arm. "Thank you, Sidra. I need all the help I can get." I looked at Sahar. "Can you stay here with Renée and assist the fleet?"

"Yes," she said, determination now on her features. "I want this to end today. No more fighting after this. No more cold wars, no more battles, no more death. Today is the end."

I got to my feet. "Then let's get over there and deal with this."

"Wait."

I stopped suddenly and turned to Meg. Her face was set like stone. Her blue eyes were glowing with an intensity I'd never seen. "Meg?"

"I'm coming too."

An explosion larger than the one that had just taken out *two dreadnoughts* coursed through my body. "Meg. I don't know what's happening on that seacar." I pointed out the canopy. It was next to us now, on a remote, preprogrammed course, and there seemed to be no life on board. I knew something was still occurring, otherwise an occupant would have brought *Destiny* to a stop.

The fight was still on.

Johnny was still alive.

She said, "I know. I have to see him again. Bill. The Shiv. Confront him."

"Are you sure? You know what he did to us. What he's trying to do."

Her face was determined, her expression grim. "I know. I have to speak to him, one last time."

I watched her for several heartbeats. The sound of the SCAV echoed around us. Johnny's seacar was beside us, also in SCAV, and its roar added to the cacophony. Renée was pulling us closer, and beginning the delicate process to link the two vessels.

The bubbles had combined around both ships, and the buffeting was enormous.

Meg was absolutely set on going over there. There would be no changing her mind.

I sighed. "Okay. Let's go. We have to finish this."

# Chapter Forty-One

BOTH SEACARS MAINTAINED A PRESSURE of four atm. The umbilical was trembling as if in a hurricane, and I worried about the structure tearing due to the buffeting of supercavitation. The bubble surrounded both ships, the vehicles were traveling at 450 kph, and Renée was struggling with the controls to keep the seacars close enough for us to transfer over.

She was yelling over the comm. "Get over there now!"

We stumbled through the umbilical, rocking from side to side, and made it to the airlock as quickly as possibly. The outer hull was cold and wet. There were puddles of seawater on the umbilical's flexible deck. We entered, shut the outer airlock hatch, and I whispered into the PCD, "We're here. Detach, but try to stay close, if possible."

The relief was clear in her voice. "I'll try, but Mac, your course is going to carry you right through the battle! There are torpedoes, countermeasures—"

"It is what it is. We have to do this."

"Just be careful. Get that ship under control if possible."

"I will. Mac out." I pocketed the device and stared at the inner airlock hatch. I withdrew my gun. Sidra had his out as well, as did Meg. "Are you ready?" I asked them.

Our fingers were tight on the grips.

"Do it," Sidra said.

Meg remained silent. Her face was drawn. I couldn't imagine the emotions going through her. She remained focused on the hatch.

It slid open.

Inside, it was dim and cloudy.

Alarms were ringing from the pilot cabin.

They were sonar alarms: torpedo shutters open, weapons in the water, collision course, and so on. There was a haze in the air from an electrical short or fire of some sort, and I suppressed a cough.

Emergency lights cast a pale glow over the deck.

The vessel was small, like *SC-1*, which our designers had modeled it after. At the bow, the pilot cabin hatch was open. I peered up the corridor and could see out the canopy. Renée and *SC-1* had detached and were moving away. The bubble around us made the scene foggy and indistinct; but we were also too deep for light to penetrate the water—we were at a depth of roughly 3,000 metres, just above the lip of the canyon to the abyss below. The circular course took us over the trench, but for a quarter of the route we were over the shallower lip at the east side.

We were currently above the abyss, far from the battle, but we were approaching it quickly.

There were noises from the aft, from beyond the living area and into the engineering compartments, which housed the ballast pumps, batteries, air circulation, SCAV equipment and the reactor. We advanced toward the compartment, passing over the moonpool hatch. We marched past the lavatory.

We entered engineering.

Inside, Min Lee was lying on the deck, bloody and battered.

I swore inwardly.

Johnny was on his knees, staring at me. He looked horrible. The Shiv had beaten him too.

Behind him, William Windsor stood with a gun at Johnny's head.

"Hello, Mac," he said.

The distant sound of detonations reverberated the seacar. There were torpedoes exploding and countermeasures churning in open water, attempting to distract weapons. High-pitched screws passed by *Destiny*, making me cringe in horror. My skin tingled, the hair on the back of my neck stood on end. At any moment, a torpedo could hit us.

Windsor looked like a wreck. He did not appear the same person I'd known earlier, when he was masquerading as a British spy. That man had been calm, confident, and arrogant. He'd held himself with more than a hint of superiority and swagger. The man before me seemed weaker. There were bruises on his face, and blood on his right forearm. There was a cut on his forehead. The gun in his hand was trembling slightly. His left eye was swollen shut.

Johnny and Min had hurt him.

"You've led us on quite the chase," I said.

"It worked. We got you to The Facility."

"But I already knew about you by then. You failed. And you couldn't kill me."

His face hardened and his grip on the gun tightened. "Don't tempt me, Mac. I can shoot your partner here *right now*."

"My name is McClusky. You don't get to call me Mac." I glanced at Johnny. He was staring at me through his bruised face. I said, "You don't look so good, Johnny."

"I look about as good as you, now."

I realized my teeth were broken and my face looked much like his: black and blue. "Maybe half as good," I joked.

"Right."

I turned my gaze back to Windsor. "I've ruined your identity now. Everyone knows. I announced it to the entire coalition force."

"I expected as much from you."

"And yet you want something from me now. What?" I cocked my head. "What could you possibly want from me?"

Sidra was to my left, Meg on my right. Windsor glanced at each, then back to me. His gaze had lingered on Meg, though.

"You want to speak to my sister?" I asked.

He snorted. "What I want is slightly more important than that."

I considered that. He could have already killed Johnny and just shot at us when we entered. Instead, he'd led us into that engineering compartment to talk.

It came to me in a flash. "You want your identity back. You want me to . . . recant? Lie?"

Waves of anger and rage passed across his face. "I will shoot right now and kill your best friend. But you have power over me at the moment. You can tell the fleet that you were wrong. You can announce that The Shiv framed me. I'm innocent."

I hesitated. "I could, you're right."

"You can do it from the pilot cabin of this vessel." His gun was trembling even more now. His breathing was heavy and his face flushed. There was blood dripping from his forehead, trickling onto his face.

To Johnny: "You beat him pretty good. You got a lot of hits in."

"He hurt Min."

"Is she okay?"

"Unconscious. Sorry, Mac. I couldn't focus on the battle."

"You did the right thing. Don't doubt it. Everything is fine."

"I heard a detonation. Massive. Then a concussion wave shorted some systems here."

"An Isomer Bomb. Disabled two of the dreadnoughts."

"And the third?"

I shrugged. "Still have to deal with it. In time." I smiled at Windsor, but it was fake, forced. I wanted him to think I didn't have a care in the world. Could I just fire at him and be done with it?

Possibly.

Sidra stood next to me, also with a gun. The two of us could finish this.

But Johnny would end up dead, too.

Meg had been quiet. I said to her, "What do you think, Meg? Should I broadcast to everyone that Windsor is not really The Shiv?"

She was staring at him, her eyes pleading. "I'm—I'm not sure."

He said, "But Meagan, after everything we went through? I thought I meant something to you." His voice was courting pity from her.

"You did."

"We'd talked about living together when this was done. That can still happen."

"It can?"

"Of course."

I stared at Meg. I was sure the horror on my expression was clear. "What are you saying, Meg?"

"We'd spoken about a life together, after this battle. Living in Oceania as free people."

"He doesn't care about that. He never did. He only wants to continue his life as The Shiv. Listen to what he's saying."

"I *am*."

"He wants his previous life back. That doesn't involve you." I paused before, "I'm sorry, Meg."

"It *can* involve me though!" she snapped back. "And don't dictate what my life will be like. I'll make my own decisions!"

"I know that. You're your own person. I want you to be happy. But Meg, he wants to kill me. That's his mission. And he's going to have to kill all of us, after I make the announcement he wants."

I glanced at Johnny. He was staring at me. He signaled me, silently.

Meg said, "Not necessarily." Then to Windsor, she said, "What will you do?"

"You can all continue your lives too. Just keep my identity to yourselves."

"He's lying," I said. "Don't believe it."

Johnny was still eyeing me.

I said, "Meg."

"What?" she said, tight and angry.

"I'm sorry."

"For what?"

"For this."

In the blink of an eye, Johnny jerked sideways.

I fired the gun.

It happened in a microsecond.

Sidra fired as well.

The sounds of the gunshots exploded in the cabin.

Windsor's chest shuddered from the impacts. The force threw him backward, into a bulkhead, and he collapsed with a thud, his breath wheezing from his lungs.

"Mac!" Meg yelled. "What did you just do?"

I stalked forward. "Check Min Lee." I crouched over Johnny. "You okay?"

"Don't worry about—"

And then Windsor rolled to his side and his arm flashed forward. There was a blur of steel in the air—

And the shiv he carried buried itself in my gut, right to the hilt. The agony speared through my body and I fell to my knees. He spun faster than seemed possible, raising himself from the deck, and slid behind me, using me as a shield. Sidra had his gun pointing at him, but I was now in the way.

I clutched the blade in my hand. The pain as I wrenched it out was excruciating.

Windsor said, "Don't even think about it. Drop it." He shoved the gun into my skull. I dropped the knife on the deck; it rattled as it fell.

"Do it, Sidra," I whispered between my broken teeth. "Shoot."

"If you do, you all die," Windsor said. "You can't beat me, you can't win."

He was pressed to my back. I could feel his torso against my shoulder. I swore. "You're not just wearing armor."

"Surprise, surprise."

Sidra frowned. "What?"

It had suddenly occurred to me. "It's graphene. Super strong. Super thin. Like fabric. Thinner than silk, even. It's why we couldn't beat him. The bullets won't penetrate. It cushioned punches and kicks. And it's lighter than clothing, so he's still fast and agile."

Windsor snorted. "A gift from Administrator Zhao at the Chinese Facility. Ventinov arranged it. Took you long enough to realize it."

*Only a bullet to the head was going to work here*, I thought. Meg was staring at Windsor. I leveled my eyes on her and tried to communicate what I wanted her to do.

*Fire.*

Kill him.

*It doesn't matter if I die.*

Do it.

Windsor said, "What about it, Meg? You can make the announcement too. They'll believe you. You're a McClusky. We can say Mac died in the battle."

"And you'll come with me when this is over?" she asked, her voice soft.

"Yes. Together. You're tough. We can work together."

"For whom?"

"For whoever pays."

"Where can we go?"

"Any city you want. I know you like Blue Downs. It's beautiful there. We can go there."

"Meg," I said. "Don't believe him. Don't—"

"Shut up!" she snapped.

I glanced at Sidra. "Do it, Sidra. Fire."

His expression was pure shock. He couldn't believe what was happening.

Meg said, "Don't. If you shoot, I'll kill you too."

"How can you say that!?" I bellowed. "You're my sister, Meg. We've been in this together since the beginning. Dad's dream—"

"Don't tell me about him! I don't want to hear about him anymore!" She dissolved into rage and hate. Her freckled face was flushed, and it was vicious counterpoint to her blond hair. "He *destroyed* our family! He ruined it. What do we have as a result? We've lost everything. Our lives, our parents. We spent two decades apart after they killed him. And now this quest for independence is going to ruin us again!" Concussions pounded the ship as it speared through the battle. Collision alarms were ringing from the control cabin. "Listen to that! People are *dying* out there. It's because of us."

"You wanted this too," I said. "You were with us on it. Oceania. It's been your dream too."

She shook her head savagely. "No. I don't want it anymore. I want a *normal* life! I want peace. I want to go to work and be in love. I want a family."

I couldn't believe what she was saying.

"But I—"

"But nothing!" she screamed. "You've ruined everything for me!" She looked at Windsor. "If I make the announcement, can we leave immediately?"

"Of course." His voice was calm and he smiled as he said it.

Horror coursed through me. My blood was ice. I couldn't comprehend her words.

She said, "Then put these four out the airlock, with scuba gear. I'll tell the fleet you're not The Shiv."

He paused. "I can't do that, Meg. I have to kill them."

She titled her head. "But I thought you wanted me to make the announcement? We could start our lives?"

"We can. But they'll still know the truth." He gestured at the rest of us with his gun.

Meg nodded. "That's what I thought."

Then, without warning, she raised the gun and fired.

# Chapter Forty-Two

THE BULLET HIT VASILY STALI / William Windsor / The Shiv in the center of the forehead.

She had aimed perfectly.

He fell to the deck behind me with a thud.

I stared at the man, wondering if he had actually died this time. His face looked serene, peaceful.

But the back of his head was a gory mess. The bullet had exploded.

Meg was staring at him. Then she looked at me. "Was I believable?"

I nearly vomited from the stress. My breath blew out in a rush. "Shit Meg, I thought you were a hundred percent truthful." I shook my head. "Did you mean any of that?"

She flashed me a grin. "Not a bit, Tru. I want a normal life, for sure, but I wouldn't give this up for anything." She pointed out past the bulkheads, at some undetermined place underwater, but nearby. "This is the last battle. I can feel it. After this, we're free. It's going on without us right now. Let's win it."

"I'm sorry about this," I said. I looked at Windsor. "I know you liked him. I didn't mean—"

"He was full of shit. I'm not dumb, Mac. We had fun, but he didn't mean a word he was saying. I realized it when I stepped in this cabin and saw him. He would have killed us all, stolen this ship and dumped us out the airlock." A shrug. "I had to make him think I was with him."

Sidra made a noise similar to a growl. "You scared me."

Johnny crouched over Min. I said, "How is she?"

"Breathing, at least." He turned her over, revealing a badly beaten face. "Shit."

Alarms from the control cabin were still piercing the seacar. A new one had started, and it was *screaming* for attention.

We'd been circling the battle blind, cutting right through it, on a preprogrammed autopilot course. Explosions rang out all around us, along with the sound of SCAV drives and torpedo screws. I couldn't believe that nothing had hit us yet.

"Better get her to her feet," I grunted as I pulled myself up. The stab wound in my abdomen oozed blood. I put pressure on it as I stumbled forward, toward the hatch to the living space. I had made sure to grab the shiv from the deck.

We had just passed through the hatch and were next to the airlock when I peered up the corridor to the pilot cabin. The canopy was fuzzy and partly obscured because of the SCAV bubble, but the ringing alarm was now shredding my eardrums.

The sonar was flashing red.

The dreadnought *Voskhod* was directly before us.

*Collision alert.*

*Collision alert.*

*Collision alert.*

*COLLISION—*

Our course had taken us in a wide arc, through the battle multiple times, but our luck had run out.

We were only eight seconds from impact.

Before us, the giant RSF warsub—Ventinov's ship—loomed in our view. It had regained some functions; it was launching torpedoes and countermeasures.

There was no time to think, no time to do anything else.

We were next to the airlock, and I wrapped my arms around the four people with me and shoved them through the hatch. "Out now!" I blurted. They stumbled into the lock, not fully understanding.

"Mac, what—?" Johnny blurted.

I slammed my fist on the CYCLE button. "No time!"

"But we don't have gear!"

Water flooded up our legs. It was cold.

There'd been no chance to alter course. I would have had to run up the aisle, into the pilot cabin, deactivate autopilot and skew the course to the side to avoid the immense warsub. It simply wasn't possible in the time remaining, and the dreadnought was just too large. I made an instinctive, sudden decision.

Min Lee was unconscious.

There was no scuba gear for us. No tanks or masks.

Nothing.

Water flooded over our heads, but not before we gulped in a huge breath of air. All but Min, that is. Johnny was staring at her, suddenly scared.

The outer hatch opened and I pushed the group out, into the air bubble and the ocean beyond.

*Destiny* tore through the ocean like a missile, a hundred times larger than a torpedo and traveling at five times the speed. It hit the dreadnought directly at its bow, piercing its hull instantly, and plunged deep into the vessel like a hot needle through cold flesh. It obliterated and vaporized hull plates at the point of impact. People in the compartments where the seacar penetrated exploded into bits of blood and tissue and turned into rapidly expanding clouds of hot, red moisture—an ichor that did not resemble anything remotely organic.

Johnny's seacar ripped through the dreadnought, making it to the very center of the warsub. It further devastated the vessel's superstructure, and ocean flooded in along its path, damaging electronics, shattering bulkheads, flooding cabins, and further destroying compartmentalization.

And then Destiny's armaments exploded.

There was a white-hot flare of fire and power as the explosion ripped out. Anyone in the vessel's path or the immediate vicinity of the explosion died instantly. Water flooded in after, but not before shrapnel had penetrated the warsub's armory.

It ricocheted through the massive vault, piercing multiple weapons.

Conveyers had been busy transporting torpedoes to the many torpedo tube cabins throughout the ship. Storing the weapons deep in the ship's core had been a smart decision. The RSF engineers had not wanted an errant weapon to reach a torpedo, resulting in an explosion and fire on board *Voskhod*. No one had expected a kamikaze attack of a vessel at SCAV speeds penetrating this deep into the warsub.

A torpedo suffered a shrapnel impact, deep in its fuel store.

A spark arrowed up—

And the fuel exploded in a sudden blast of fire and energy.

Then the torpedoes next to it also went up.

Then more.

The explosion was thunderous, and it *pulverized* the interior of *Voskhod*.

An expanding blast of energy and expanding gases and steam lashed outward and tore hull plates from the dreadnought. Pieces speared out in all directions and surges of bubbles soared upward from the hulk. Large areas of its structure were now visible, after shedding much of its skin. Its superstructure—beams crisscrossing the huge fuselage—thrust through its dead shell and protruded in multiple places.

We'd jumped from *Destiny* only seconds before the impact.

While hurtling through the ocean at 125 metres per second. We'd left the seacar maybe two seconds before it hit. The forces on our bodies whipped us around like rag dolls. I pulled my arms in and formed a ball to prevent breaking an arm or leg. The ocean spun in a whirlwind around us as we came to a stop.

And then the concussion waves washed over us.

Around the battle, at that depth, it should have been pitch black. Instead, it looked like the middle of a thunderstorm. Flashes, some blinding but some distant, illuminated the scene in all directions. *Booms* echoed in my ears.

Holy shit.

We were right in the middle of the battle.

We were floating, thousands of metres down, as explosions and torpedoes and countermeasures churned. Dead vessels plunged to the bottom of the trench, so far below.

The dreadnought, 250 metres away, listed to the starboard and fell toward the ocean floor. It was right on the lip of the abyss though, and would not hit Crush Depth. It appeared as though the vessel were dead already. Hit by an Isomer Bomb near its stern, and then an explosion within, it didn't seem like it could continue.

A whine came to me, and I spun frantically to seek it out.

*SC-1.*

Renée.

Looking for us.

She was visible through the canopy, searching frantically. She had seen the impact, and didn't know if we'd been on the seacar.

I pulled my PCD—thankfully it was still there, in my pocket—and pushed a button. The response was instant; Renée's gaze snapped down to her lap, and she pulled the throttle back and stopped the vehicle.

I swam to it, with the others next to me.

We pulled Min Lee's motionless body with us.

—••—

BACK INSIDE, WE GASPED FOR breath and swore repeatedly.

I wondered absently where Ventinov had been. He was likely dead, but I didn't want to count him out just yet. That class of RSF vessel had backup after backup after backup for all systems.

"*Mac!? Mac!?*" a voice was screaming from the speaker in the airlock.

"I'm here, Renée."

"I can't believe what just happened! Is everyone okay?"

Min was lying on the deck; Johnny was administering CPR. We'd been outside for maybe a minute. She was unconscious, and there was a strong possibility that there was water in her lungs.

"Hold on," I whispered.

There were defibrillation paddles on a latch in the bulkhead. Sidra pulled them out, along with a mask to help with the breaths, and a suction tube to remove water from the airway. They administered a shock quickly—

Then another.

Min took a massive breath, arching her back upward as she did so.

Johnny fell back on his knees and gasped with her. His face was ashen, but now a smile tugged at the corners of his lips. "Min? Can you hear me?"

"Johnny . . . " Her voice was a husk, dry, rattling. "The Shiv, he's here. On the seacar. We have to kill him."

He put his face next to hers and said, "We got him. He's gone. You're going to be safe now."

He hugged her, and then looked up at us. "She hurt Windsor. In their fight. He landed a lucky kick and knocked her out, but she hurt him before it. But we had no idea he'd been wearing graphene." He shook his head. "Bastard." Then he glanced at Meg. "Sorry, Meg! I didn't mean—"

"It's okay. I'm over it." She turned to me. "We have to get back to the battle, Tru."

Chanta Newel, from security, was piloting a *Sword* and had been in charge while I was absent. Max Hyland and the Isomer Bombs were on the same vessel.

"Let's find out how things are going without us," I said.

Back in the pilot cabin, I slid into the chair next to Renée. The others were in the back, looking after Min Lee. Sidra and Sahar were helping keep her comfortable.

The battle raged around us. The entire coalition fleet had joined the fight and our Oceanic fleet was in the canyon, shooting up at the warsubs. All three RSF dreadnoughts were on the bottom near the edge of the Puerto Rico Trench.

"Chanta," I said into the comm.

"Mac!" came the instant response. "Where have you been?"

The sonar indicated which vessel the transmission had come from.

"I've been dealing with some issues. How are things going?"

"They have held their own, for the most part. They also have some of their own SCAV ships! They're causing issues. The SCAV torpedoes too."

On the sonar, there were red markings sweeping through the theater. They were Hunter-Killers, USSF small and vicious vessels, called *Houston* Class. They were going nearly 500 kph.

The CSF *Mao* Class were also tearing through the area at similar velocities.

I swore. Both fleets had the SCAV. I'd known it for months, but seeing the ships in battle was something we hadn't dealt with before.

"So," I said. "They've adapted the new drive system to their fleet."

"Yes. Very fast. Very agile."

"Just like ours," I said. "But they can't go as deep." I watched explosions light the battlefield. "Are the floats ready?"

"Yes."

"Let's go lower and wait for the fleets to follow. Then we'll launch them."

Our entire fleet began to descend into the canyon, the bottom eight kilometres deep or more in some places. It was tectonically active; there had been frequent quakes in the region. As our ships plunged lower, orange blobs appeared on the sonar display.

*The floats.*

They were rising from the deeps.

I adjusted course and navigated around them.

Then I paused, changed ballast to neutral, and watched the weapons on the sonar as they rose higher, toward the coalition fleet.

They were visible on my screen because the computer *knew* about them. But they were utterly silent, not under any power, and rising due to positive buoyancy.

There were hundreds of them, rising toward the fleet above, which was pursuing us.

They were mines, but instead of falling and impacting vessels, these were *rising.*

They would detonate in proximity to any foreign, enemy vessels.

Chanta's voice floated to me. "They're on the way."

"Stop at this depth," I said. We were close to four kilometres deep. We couldn't go much deeper unless we used the Acoustic Pulse Drive—the APD—which used sound waves to push the ocean back onto itself. Not quiet, but it gave us water superiority.

The floats soared upward quickly now. Over the canyon, their vessels had appeared. USSF *Typhoon, Matrix, Neptune, Trident*, and *Reaper* Classes. *Houston* Hunter-Killers as well.

Admiral Kenley's *Terminator.* The two-hundred-metre missile boat, *Infiltrator.* British *Spitfires* and *Victories.* German *Attentäter, Morder*, and *Jagers.* Chinese *Han, Shang, Yuan, Soong*, and *Ming* Classes.

*Hundreds* of vessels pursued us into the canyon.

The floats rose silently.

Then the detonations began.

We'd planned this for many months.

We'd predicted the most likely location of the superpowers' attack—from the Atlantic direction—and we'd decided to use the Puerto Rico Trench as the site of the battle.

The floats were easy to build and plant in the trench.

They were quiet. No splash, no cavitation as from a mine dropped by a surface vessel. They were large frames of lightweight plastic, loaded with explosives. They drifted up, positively buoyant and driven by currents.

It was a decidedly low-tech approach, but sometimes that was the best defense.

Now we'd see whether they worked.

The explosions flared across the screen. In the canopy, looking up, distant strikes flashed across the ocean. It was a lightning storm.

The sonar screen was flashing; the interior of the pilot cabin strobed with the white lights as each explosion rocked out. The distant booms echoed from the ocean, reverberated the hull, and vibrated the deck plates at my feet.

Massive warsubs suffered immense concussion blasts. Flooding alerts rang out in the ocean, and multiple contacts on the sonar screen switched colours, indicating alarms, damage, flooding, and even implosion events.

It worked.

Then Renée pointed out the canopy.

There were a cluster of SCAV vessels approaching from the north. They hadn't been near the fleet and the floating bombs that had just detonated.

They were *Houston* and *Mao* class. USSF and CSF, acting together, against us.

"Everyone get ready," I snapped into the comm. "Bearing 290. Approaching SCAV ships." I stared at the sonar; the callout displays showed a velocity of 490 kph.

*Oh, no.*

"Here they come!" I bellowed.

Around us, massive warsubs plunged toward Crush Depth and the trench floor, so far below, shedding debris and bodies.

We pushed our SCAV to max and prepared to take on the faster enemy vessels.

# Interlude

## At The Puerto Rico Trench

| | |
|---|---|
| Vessel: | Russian Submarine Fleet |
| | *Dreadnought* Class *Voskhod—The Rise* |
| Location: | Latitude: 18º 53' N |
| | Longitude: 61º 03' W |
| | The Puerto Rico Trench |
| Depth: | 3,313 metres |
| Date: | 15 June 2131 |
| Time: | 1933 hours |

CAPTAIN IVAN ARKADY VENTINOV SCREAMED in fury.

A massive detonation had damaged the three RSF dreadnoughts, and he watched in horror as the other two sunk to the ocean floor. Plumes of sand rose from the impacts, obscuring the view, but not before he saw their rear compartments. The boats were both out of commission. They might never function again. Air gushed from the hulls, oil, debris, and bodies rose from the disaster site. The concussion from the blast had sheared both thruster pods, from *both* vessels. They were gone, likely lost over the edge and into the trench.

The explosion shook *Voskhod*, and Ventinov grabbed the edge of a console to maintain his footing. The ship vibrated massively. Alarms were screaming and sparks and flame flew from some of the systems on the bridge.

"Pressure alerts!" Sidorov cried, staring at readouts. "Our rear compartments."

Ventinov stared in horror at the light radiating through the water around them. "McClusky just detonated a nuclear bomb!"

A thunderous concussion shook the warsub, and the noise was absolutely deafening.

The ocean seemed to be *glowing*. He stared above him, out the large viewport canopy, as the light faded. Churning sand and debris floated past *Voskhod*. The ship continued to shudder as secondary explosions—*implosions!*—cavitated through the vessel.

A crewman yelled, "Multiple reports of flooding in the stern compartments! Watertight hatches closing! Some are malfunctioning though!"

"Do we still have compartmentalization? Neutral buoyancy?" Sidorov asked in a calm voice.

"Checking now," came the response. He stared at the computer readout, its light casting a glow on his horrified face. "I think so. Many ruined compartments though." He pointed at the schematic; much of the rear of the dreadnought was red. "We're lucky we didn't sink."

"Was it nuclear?" she asked.

"Of course it was!" Ventinov screamed.

Another voice spoke up. "Strong gamma radiation detected. We might all develop cancer eventually. But . . . "

"But what?"

"But it's fading quickly. The explosion was . . . *different*." The crewwoman shook her head in confusion. "I've never witnessed anything like it."

Ventinov fumed. He couldn't believe what was happening. McClusky was *still alive!* He'd made an earlier announcement to the entire fleet. He'd also stated that The Shiv was dead, ruining all of his plans from the past year.

McClusky.

Still alive.

"We're still in this battle," Sidorov said. "We can still take them down." She pointed at the fleet, rising from the Puerto Rico Trench beside them. "We have torpedoes. SCAV torpedoes too. We're still seaworthy."

"I want McClusky!" he grated between clenched teeth.

She approached him and said in a quiet voice, so no crew could hear, "Sir. We need to focus on the immediate threat. The ships approaching from the trench. It's a fleet. There are hundreds of them. *Now*."

Ventinov straightened and stared at his XO's face. "But I want—"

"Listen to me," she hissed. Her face was growing red, and there were veins at her temples. "We have to salvage this and engage that fleet. We can't worry about one seacar in a mass of seven hundred of them." She straightened, took a breath, and seemed to compose herself. "Defend this ship against that fleet, or I will assume command and do it for you!"

"You wouldn't dare."

"I will. And the crew will back me. Now, what do you want to do?"

He stared into her eyes. She was determined. He couldn't risk the crew seeing them divided. And perhaps, maybe she was correct. He deflated and said, "You're right. But I won't forget this insubordination, Sidorov."

"Just don't lose." She walked away, toward the damage control team collecting nearby. Clouds of smoke partly obscured her; alarms continued to pierce the bridge.

Long minutes passed.

Then an hour.

The dreadnought regained some control and power. Repair teams managed to get some torpedo tubes operating, and they began launching weapons at the Oceania fleet. Meanwhile, the rest of the coalition had joined them, over the trench, and there was now a full-fledged battle raging around them.

The coalition fleet began to inflict some damage. Multiple enemy seacars suffered devastating impacts and plunged down into the trench. SCAV torpedoes crisscrossed the theater of battle and countermeasures and detonations further obscured the view. The sonar screen was aflame with activity. There were glowing clouds *everywhere* on the screen. The sonar operator was having difficulty tracking all the activity.

Sidorov returned and he faced her. She said, "Crews have contained the flooding. We have neutral buoyancy. They don't think we can achieve positive buoyancy though; you'll need to use bow planes for that. We have several torpedo tube cabins up and running. We should be able to continue the battle."

"Good." He stared at her. He was still angry at her insubordination earlier, but she had led efforts to get their warsub back in action. But after this was over, he would demote her. He'd already made that decision. The crew had seen her yelling at him, even if they hadn't heard what she was saying. They knew she was upset. They likely assumed she thought he was incompetent. He couldn't allow that.

She was staring out the canopy.

"Continue to bring tubes into the battle. We need all the firepower we can get."

She didn't respond.

"What are you doing?" he snapped. "Did you hear me?"

She was still staring out into the ocean. Then she pointed. "What's that?"

He turned to stare past her outstretched finger. There was a cloud of white in the distance, but it was growing quickly.

Bubbles rose from it, trailing behind. They floated upward.

It was a wake.

It was a vessel in SCAV drive.

Headed directly for them.

*Surely they'd veer off?*

The seacar was headed directly for *Voskhod*, which was too large—and too damaged—to move away quickly.

Ventinov eyed the emergency hatch and sprinted for it. He'd done this once before, too, when he'd Captained *Drakon*.

He ran for the emergency bridge.

Behind him, people were screaming.

The seacar slammed into *Voskhod*'s bridge.

# Part Ten

## Trieste

# Chapter Forty-Three

I STARED IN HORROR AT the USSF and CSF SCAV vessels as they cut through our forces. They were highly maneuverable, and they were firing multiple weapons as they arrowed toward us.

*Hundreds* of them.

Chanta Newel was calling out orders, directing our forces. We were doing exceedingly well against the larger warsubs in the coalition fleet, but these two classes of ship were a different beast entirely.

"SCAV torpedoes everyone," I said into the comm. "Lock onto those quick little bastards."

The sonar lit with the launches. Multiple torpedoes appeared in the water, all accelerating at the tip of burning oxygen-rich rocket fuel. The bubble of supercavitation quickly surrounded them, and they began to shoot for the Hunter-Killers, homing on the tremendous noise.

There were *clouds* of torpedoes in the water.

An enemy SCAV torpedo fell on our tail and I pushed the yoke down and *SC-1* plunged into the deeps. Growling under my breath, I struggled to keep control of the seacar as we veered from side to side to keep the weapon slower than its top speed of over 1,000 kph. It could double our own velocity, and if I couldn't get it to lock onto something else, implosion would be imminent.

Deep.

Deeper.

*Deeper still.*

The hull began to creak.

Meg cried from behind me, "Tru! We're too far down! You're at 4,500 metres!"

"Shit!" I blurted, pulling the yoke toward me. Traveling at such speeds meant a slight change in direction resulted in a rapid change in depth. Even though there was a bubble of air around us, it was at the same pressure as the exterior environment.

We rocketed up from the depths. Before us, I spotted Kenley's *Terminator* Class vessel, and Renée launched multiple torpedoes at it as we rocketed past. It looked damaged already; listing and chugging through the water slowly. The supercavitating drive was the future of travel and warfare in the oceans, and we were leaving these lumbering beasts behind in every way.

The concussions echoed through *SC-1* as we continued upward.

"Countermeasures," I gasped to Renée.

She dropped the devices as we peeled past a cluster of German Submarine Fleet vessels.

The SCAV on our tail followed—

And impacted on the screw blades of the *Attentäter*—or *Assassin* Class—vessel.

The detonation vaporized thousands of tons of seawater instantly. The ship shuddered and the screw blades vanished in the destruction, torn to shreds and hurled aside in the blast of energy. Then the water stormed back into the void, causing secondary impacts, and stern sections of the sub began to implode. The chaos outside almost overwhelmed our sonar, but it did detect the sounds of pressure loss alarms.

I exhaled in relief. The missiles were *fast*. They were difficult to avoid, but they were having an effect in the battle.

Multiple armed Oceania seacars were plummeting downward, trailing bubbles and oil.

There were a flurry of overlapping voices on our common channel:

"Get that *Houston*—I wounded him!"

"He's listing already. Hit the starboard."

"That *Han* is trying to track me—someone hit him with a SCAV!"

"There are two on my tail—need help."

"Take them through the cloud of countermeasures. You'll see them at one o'clock, three hundred metres above you."

"I'm hit, the ballast won't purge."

"Get over the lip, onto the shallower seafloor, *now!*"

The last had been Chanta Newel, yelling an order.

Most of the voices had been in English, though some had been blurted in Mandarin. The Chinese cities were very much in this fight. Their seacars were performing amazingly well against their CSF counterparts, but we were still taking damage.

"They're hurting us," Meg whispered.

"They're hurt too," Johnny said. "Look." He was pointing out the canopy. Two GSF warsubs, a BSF warsub, and three CSF vessels were plummeting into the deeps. They were no match for superfast SCAV enemies and torpedoes.

The Chinese colonies had lost a dozen or more seacars. We'd lost at least twenty. Blue Downs had sent us a minimal fleet, due to their fledgeling status in the oceans, and they were nearly gone. Eleven of their fifteen vessels were nowhere in sight. And the French colonies, with Piette leading them, had lost nearly thirty. We couldn't afford to lose more.

We had only one choice.

"Go deep," I rasped. "Everyone. APD to six thousand metres. Do it, *now.*"

I arrowed at a forty-five-degree angle down into the trench. At 4,000 metres, I deactivated the SCAV fusion reactor and pulled the throttle back. Making our speed fifty kph, the Acoustic Pulse Drive ramped up.

The sound pulses radiated outward from the seacar, and *shoved* the water back on itself, forming a tunnel in front of the vessel. We moved into the low-pressure zone as it closed behind us, and the next pulse pounded out, lengthening the channel before us.

It was hardly quiet, though; the sound pulses echoed in the trench, white flares on sonar screens, broadcasting our exact locations to everyone in the arena.

But it didn't matter, because we were *deep.*

Their mines and torpedoes couldn't make it much past five kilometres.

I held my breath as we retreated to the deep trench.

Then we began to fire upward at the enemy.

We darted up to shallower depths, fired weapons, then reactivated the APD and dove below their attempts at retaliation.

Even their *Houston* and *Mao* vessels could not touch us.

They were churning back and forth at high velocities, trying their best to disrupt our homing weapons' abilities to lock onto targets, but having little luck.

Bit by bit, the battle began turning back to our side.

They'd inflicted large damage, but now their losses began to pile up.

A *Typhoon* plunged past us, *screaming* pressure alert alarms into the water. Our sonar detected implosion sounds from the warsub.

A *Yuan* and *Ming*, somehow intertwined and locked in a deadly embrace, spiraled downward, trailing bubbles. They must have collided in the battle, before a SCAV missile had taken both out, simultaneously. One dragged the other into the depths, where death awaited, always hungry for sailors who dared descend too far.

A BSF *Victory*, blown in half, fell into the trench.

Sahar's face was pale as she watched. She didn't want to see death on this scale. I'd warned her, months ago, about this probability. She'd been ready for it, and had hoped for more damage and less death, but this had been inevitable.

She whispered, "People are dying, Mac."

"On both sides, yes."

"We have to stop this."

I gripped the yoke. I didn't know how to do that.

"You have to stop it," she said.

"Admiral Kenley is leading this attack. Maybe we can ask her?"

She nodded. "Try it."

"Admiral," I said into the mic. "This is McClusky. We have water superiority. You can't win like this. Your people are dying. Please, stop the attack, now."

A minute later, her voice echoed from the speaker. Klaxons from her vessel's command deck—emergency alarms—accompanied her angry response. "You are guilty of war crimes!" she cried. "You fired on this vessel!"

"We are an independent nation. You have attacked *us*, not the other way around. For a week you've built up this force to intimidate and threaten us. You're down by more than fifty percent. And the losses are going to continue."

"You can't operate on your own. You are a US colony!"

"We want to forge treaties with you. We'll supply everything you need. But you have to pay fair market prices for them. I said this in our proclamation."

"The president doesn't care about your statement."

"You have to know when to cut your losses, Kenley."

The APD continued to send its pulses out—*thrum, thrum thrum*—and we powered under conventional thrusters at a depth of just over 6,100 metres. The comm fell silent.

Nothing.

"Admiral," I said again. "The USSF is losing. We've sunk hundreds of boats. The Russians destroyed Norfolk and San Diego last year. You lost Seascape too. You can't afford this."

"Are you trying to help us now, McClusky? We don't need your—"

"It seems like you do."

There was a long pause. And then she said something that sent shudders through me. My heart started pounding and I felt instantly sick.

She said, "If we can't beat you, we'll just take out the colony."

"What does that mean?" I snapped. "There are thousands of innocent people there. Families!"

"They voted you in. They knew what they were doing. They're part of this. They'll have to pay for it."

"So if *I can't have you, then no one can?* Is that the USSF philosophy now?"

"Enough talk, McClusky. We end this, now."

And the USSF forces began to blow ballast, ascend to 200 metres, and change course to the west.

Toward Trieste.

# Chapter Forty-Four

"CHANTA!" I CRIED ON OUR dedicated frequency. "We can't let those SCAV vessels get to Trieste." We could deal with the slow-moving ones—I had a plan, for them—but the *Houston* and *Mao* were warsubs that we had to deal with, *now.*

"They're faster than we are, Mac."

"I know. Pursue them and let them know we mean to fight. Leave the slower warsubs behind."

Hyland's voice floated to me. He was with Chanta, in the same seacar. "Mac! We still have more Isomer Bombs. We can use one here."

I considered that. Then I glanced at Sahar. "No. We used one against the RSF dreadnoughts. I don't think we need to use any more."

"Are you sure?"

"Yes. We need to win, but not obliterate them. We can't leave them licking their wounds. They have to feel like they lost, on *their own terms*, if that makes sense."

"Not really, no."

I exhaled. "Look. If we leave them hurting and angry, they'll just try again. They have to come to this decision on their own."

"A bomb will do that."

"They might eventually use a nuke. They're on their way to Trieste. We can't let them destroy the city."

"Once again, a bomb will—"

"There's a psychology that you have to understand, Max. Maybe it's partly political. But if we make those bombs the norm, then all bets are off for us. We have to get them to retreat, accept defeat, and do it without too many dead. Sahar is totally right about that. Treaties are the solution. They won't negotiate if we humiliate them. Using a bomb against Russian warsubs is acceptable, in a way. Especially after what the RSF did to the US and China last year. But if we use one against the USSF . . . they'll interpret it differently."

He remained silent, but I inferred it as acceptance.

"Do you understand? Chanta?" I asked.

"Acknowledged." Her response had been curt. Then the comm cut out.

Maybe she thought I was sentencing them to death, and maybe I was. But there was no other choice.

I hoped they'd understand, in the end.

I glanced at Renée, Johnny, and Meg. "We have to leave them to it. Get back to Trieste, and prepare for the next phase."

*SC-1* began to soar upward from the trench, and I pushed the SCAV to full.

Meg said, "Max might be right. We can't let them destroy the city, Tru. And I know you want to avoid needless death, but you're leaving our forces against those SCAV enemies, and they're superior."

"I agree in part. We can go deeper, and we have that. Don't count out Chanta and our *Swords*. But we have one more card to play too, back at Trieste. And if I'm right, it'll have a massive impact. Bigger than any Isomer Bomb."

As we powered back toward Trieste, I studied the sonar recording. Our initial force of Triestrian seacars had been 238. It was down to 135.

That made me gulp. Each vessel had had two pilots and two crew to handle torpedoes and engineering.

As for the other forces, we'd had a total of over 700 vessels. We were down to just over 400.

The coalition fleet had suffered similar losses though. They'd had over a thousand large warsubs. Many were on the bottom, at the lip of the trench. They'd settled on the sandy seafloor, waiting for repairs or rescue. Others, however, had endured massive damage and flooding, and had sunk below Crush Depth, into the Puerto Rico Trench.

Now their fleet had largely given up on defeating us; they were en route to Trieste.

Admiral Kenley had decided to just finish this, once and for all.

Either they were going to threaten to destroy city modules, and hope for us to surrender . . .

Or, they were just going to do it. Fire at the modules and watch them implode under ocean pressure.

We'd spent the last year building shelters beneath the modules, carved into the bedrock of ocean basalt. Our people had places to survive, but I wanted to save the city infrastructure as much as possible.

Around me, the others were silent as *SC-1* forged toward our city.

Toward home.

Eventually, I turned to Johnny. "How's Min Lee?"

He'd been with her in the living area for much of the battle. "Injured from the fight with Windsor, but she's resting now. She told a joke, which is a good sign."

I frowned. "What was it?"

"She said that now she can brag that she survived a fight with The Steel Shiv, which makes her the greatest operative in the world."

"She did, didn't she?" I muttered.

"So did you."

"And you."

Meg whispered, "I survived too." Then she shrugged. "It's not all bad, Tru. I used that against him, in the end."

I turned back to the controls. I clutched the yoke and suppressed my worries about what was coming.

Behind, we'd left the remainder of our forces to engage the SCAV vessels and take them out. There were roughly 180 *Houston* and *Mao* Class vessels left. While the Oceania forces had double the number, they were up against much better warsubs.

It made me worry for another reason, too. For years we'd always had the superior technology. We'd fought hard for that. But now, suddenly, the USSF and CSF had a class of vessel better than our *Swords*.

Luckily, we'd taken down the RSF dreadnoughts. Those had caused a lot of consternation over the past year.

We had to end this here.

At Trieste.

—••—

THE PUERTO RICO TRENCH WAS 2,100 kilometres from Trieste. It took us four and a half hours. I stopped about ten kilometres from the city, and turned the seacar to the east, facing the oncoming warsubs. They were large and slow moving, and would take thirty-five hours or more to arrive, depending on the vessel. During that time, they would undoubtedly make repairs, assess their losses, and communicate with their governments.

"Kristen," I said into the comm. "It's Mac."

"Mac!" she practically shouted. "We've been following the battle over the news. *Riveting* is an understatement. Work has completely stopped; people are glued to the news."

I blinked. "You're watching it from Trieste?" I activated the visual, so I could see her as we spoke.

Her features showed her glee. "Yes! It's on all the channels. Over the entire world. Everyone is watching and debating. Governments everywhere are talking about it."

"What are they saying?"

"There are international discussions about why exactly it's happening. Why the cities are angry, why shouldn't they be an independent nation, what it would mean for others, and so on. Sahar Noor is a big topic of discussion."

I felt Sahar appear over my shoulder.

Kristen continued, "Apparently Sahar has been speaking about this with the other governments and the media in those countries too. They're on our side, and criticizing this battle. Saying it's unnecessary."

Sahar was smiling. "It's working," she said. "The seeds are growing."

"If we have the world on our side . . . " I trailed off.

"The superpowers might stop this."

I checked my PCD. "We have a bit of time. Is everything ready here?"

Kristen replied, "The shelters are prepped. The people are overjoyed. If any danger appears, they'll get down there quickly."

"And the surface monitors?"

She shook her head. "No surface ships of any note. They've thrown everything into the coalition force. They thought it would work."

They hadn't been prepared for our combined fleet to be there, ready and waiting. But I'd warned them. I'd told them an attack against one was an attack against *all*. When they gathered to destroy Trieste, The Fifteen had been waiting for them.

"Okay Kristen. Good luck there. I'll stay in touch."

She cut the feed and I leaned back, thinking about what she'd said. Behind me, Sahar exhaled.

"Good work," I said. "Public opinion is on our side. That's more important than any weapon."

"I've been trying to tell you that," she replied with a smile.

"And I believed it. But you're the better messenger. I'm famous, and people recognize me, but they associate me with rebellion and my dad, the great Frank McClusky. They associate you, on the other hand, with peace and prosperity. I think you're a better spokesperson than I am."

She shrugged. "We'll see." She hesitated and then, "What are you planning now?"

"We'll let the world debate. Maybe you can do some interviews, if you're willing. And in—" I checked the time "—less than two days, we'll end this, once and for all."

# Chapter Forty-Five

SAHAR SPENT THE NEXT SEVERAL hours in constant interviews with major networks around the world. She made the argument over and over that we could be more of a help to the surface nations as independent cities than as colonies. We could expand faster, exploit more, produce more, and ship more in a free market where people could earn more than what the mother nations were paying. It was persuasive, I had to give her that.

*She* was persuasive.

The interviewers ate it up. They *loved* her. People around the world knew of her struggle underwater, and her desire to help bring independence to the people of the underwater cities and their struggle for seafloor colonization.

It seemed that public pressure was totally on our side. It had given people something to be optimistic about, after all the suffering on the surface due to climate change. Displaced by rising waters, hungry due to famine, and thirsty from drought, they were finally watching people not just survive and persist, but *succeed* and *prosper* somewhere on Earth. Our success motivated them to call for our freedom.

And maybe, just maybe, one day they could join us.

I watched one such interview. After Sahar had finished, speaking from the living area in *SC-1*, sitting on a chair with a viewport behind her, the viewers knew that she was in the middle of a fight for our very survival. Even though she was a pacifist, she had sacrificed everything for this. The news station interviewed people in the street outside of the station, in Toronto, Canada, and their words made me blink in shock.

"They're doing the right thing! They're defending our future on this planet. Sahar knows the best way to help us out."

"The oceans have resources that they want to produce for us. But the colonists are not our slaves."

"They're trying to *help* us, not hurt us. And look what happens! A fleet of warsubs goes to take them out."

"Sahar Noor wouldn't kill people. She wants a future for people, *underwater.*"

"Truman McClusky is working for the future of the underwater colonies. He cares about the human race."

It was a collection of interviews with a random group of people. It was quite convincing.

Public opinion *was* more important than an Isomer Bomb.

Well, maybe that was overstating things. Public opinion wouldn't have stopped the three RSF dreadnoughts.

Then the sonar chimed, and I stared at it in horror.

It was a warsub, in SCAV drive, heading toward us from the east.

Four hundred and fourteen metres from bow to stern.

An RSF dreadnought.

It was *Voskhod. The Rise.*

"Ventinov's not dead. His dreadnought is still seaworthy."

The others approached from behind, doubt clear in their features. "But the hafnium bomb . . . the *Sword* . . . " Meg trailed off.

There was a cavity at the dreadnought's bow, penetrating deep into the vessel. Hull plates puckered *inward*, marking the impact wound. Warped and twisted girders protruded from the stern sections. Hull plates were missing. Even badly damaged, *Voskhod* was still powering through the water at SCAV velocity.

"There are backups on these dreadnoughts," I muttered, recalling the last time we'd tried to defeat one. There'd been a backup reactor, a backup command deck, backup drive intakes, and more. Still, this made me shake my head. I couldn't believe the warsub was still seaworthy, after the explosion in its core.

It was approaching fast.

Without a sign of stopping.

It was at the same depth as us—about 200 metres. On the surface, it displaced water upward in a giant wake; had someone seen this from the sky above, it might have appeared as a giant sea creature.

Johnny said, "Uh, Mac. I don't know what—"

"He's going to use the Tsunami Plow!" I bellowed, realizing in sudden fear what was happening. "Everyone grab hold of something!"

The vessel tore through the water just off the coast of Florida. It was approaching at over 240 kph. The damage prevented it from going faster; it was hammering through the ocean, hardly hydrodynamic, *pushing* water aside rather than slipping through it.

At its bow, the plow opened like two giant flower petals. Hydraulic rods angled them out until the ocean took hold and slammed them fully open. The warsub stopped moving forward due to incredible friction with water, and the plow—now locked in place—*shoved* the water forward. The vessel's incredible momentum had translated into a sudden surge of water.

It slammed into *SC-1*.

The seacar shuddered from the impact. Water started to spray from the canopy. In the living area, those who had not had time to strap in flew through the narrow space and collided with bulkheads and the ceiling. Skin tore, blood flowed, and bones broke.

The wave thrust us to the seafloor, held us there, and pressed downward with tremendous force. The hull creaked as pressure spiked.

Our max depth was 4,000 metres, with a built-in safety factor of perhaps ten percent. Over the years, we'd suffered a great deal of damage, stresses, and detonation impacts. The APD was not currently on, and the water pressure began to worm its way in.

The impact had cracked the canopy. Seawater sprayed my face. Renée was unconscious next to me, slumped against the bulkhead. Alarms were screaming, and most of the console was blinking red or completely black.

Blue lights flashed and the emergency lighting system flicked on.

Water flooded into the ballast system; the pumps could not clear it. They were either shorted out, or the impact had sheared the power lines leading to them. We quickly lost buoyancy in the tanks.

*SC-1* listed to port, descended quickly, and hit the ocean floor. Bubbles churned upward.

The seacar—*my* seacar—settled into the soft sand.

Dead.

Unbuckling the safety straps, I pushed myself to my feet. My body was now one giant bruise. The fights with The Steel Shiv, the fall outside a ship while at SCAV, the Tsunami Plow impact.

I was limping badly and pain radiated from every joint, every nerve, every muscle, and almost every bone. I had taped my torso to staunch the stab wound, but it was oozing. Water sprayed into my face, and it was rising rapidly on the deck. It was at my ankles.

Gathering Renée in my arms, I stumbled back through the hatch and into the living area. The others were lying on the steel deck, limbs intertwined, moaning in pain and barely moving. Min Lee was unconscious again, but she was still strapped to the couch, which may have saved her life. Johnny clutched his arm; there was a compound fracture just above his wrist. His expression radiated agony.

I set Renée on the other couch and, dragging myself back to the control cabin, hit the hatch's EMERGENCY CLOSE button. It ground shut, and I caught a last look at the pilot controls. This ship had been with us from the beginning, from the start of my attempt to bring independence to Trieste. There was an emotional connection to *SC-1*, not the least of which was the fact that my girlfriend, Katherine Wells, had invented it, built it, and died in it during battle.

I turned to the others, who were pulling themselves up and coughing from the curls of smoke drifting in from engineering. The water on the deck had stopped rising, but it had shaken the others awake, startling them with its sudden cold shock.

The PCD was in my pocket, and I pulled it out. "Kristen, are you there?"

"Here, Mac. We detected the dreadnought coming in. It seems to be drifting, dead. *SC-1* isn't on the screen anymore though."

"We're on the bottom. Systems down." I paused, casting my eyes on the airlock. "How close is *Voskhod* to the defense line?"

"Three hundred metres."

I muttered under my breath. Damn. It needed to be closer. "Watch the dreadnought closely. Wait for our command." I turned back to the others. Sahar was drifting in and out of consciousness, on the couch next to Renée. Sidra was seeing to her, and Johnny was trying to help, but having minimal effect due to his own injury. Renée and Min Lee were still unconscious. Meg was sitting on the deck in three inches of water.

"I'm going over there. To *Voskhod*," I said.

"Are you sure?" Her face showed surprise. "We might be able to fire a torpedo from here."

"It won't be enough. The sudden stop disabled them, but they might get back up and running any minute. This is our only shot. If they start moving again, they'll do the same thing to Trieste."

"Then I'm coming with you."

"We have to swim over there. Find a way in. Get to the backup command cabin."

"Sounds easy," she joked. She splashed through the water toward the airlock. "Let's suit up."

Johnny said, "Mac, are you sure?"

"Get ready here, if you can. Watch us closely, and coordinate with Kristen. You know what to do."

# Interlude

## Ten Kilometres South of Trieste

| | |
|---|---|
| Vessel: | Russian Submarine Fleet *Dreadnought* Class *Voskhod–The Rise* |
| Location: | 30 kilometres west of Florida; 10 kilometres south of underwater colony, Trieste |
| Depth: | 185 metres |
| Date: | 15 June 2131 |
| Time: | 1848 hours |

IVAN ARKADY VENTINOV STOOD IN *Voskhod*'s auxiliary command center. There was chaos around him. Systems were down, alarms pierced the entire boat, smoke hung in the air, blue lights bathed him and a large portion of the ship was destroyed, flooded, disabled, or simply impossible to reach due to watertight hatches. One of the armories had exploded, following an impact with a *Sword*, but the backup reactor and SCAV had still functioned.

Barely.

They'd managed a Tsunami Plow attack against McClusky's seacar, *SC-1*, and had destroyed it. Repair crews were bringing the dreadnought's systems back online, and their next target would suffer a similar fate.

He felt emotion surge through him. He'd wanted so badly to kill the Mayor, ever since the death of *Drakon*. He'd thought of nothing else but killing the man responsible.

And yet, as the emotion drained away, there was still a void. He realized that he hadn't finished the job.

Trieste.

He still had to destroy the underwater city.

"Bring the conventional thrusters online," he snapped. The crewman was scrabbling at the controls. There were only three other people in the cabin with him, keeping the ship stable and seaworthy. Computers were mostly down, and two of the crew were fully engaged in shifting ballast to keep the ship from capsizing. It was a daunting task; some cabins were full, others partly full, and the vessel's center of balance was changing second by second as flooding continued.

"They're not responding," the man said.

"Then bring them *back online!*"

"Repair crews are working on keeping the ship from sinking, sir."

"I don't care. Redirect them."

His XO, Mila Sidorov, had been on the bridge during the *Sword* impact. Ventinov had left her behind at the last second. He didn't need her for this last attack, and besides, she'd been showing signs of insubordination.

She'd died in the line of duty, and there was no point now dwelling on her poor qualities as an executive officer. He would waste no more time thinking about her.

A voice said from behind him, "Ventinov."

He turned.

There were two divers there, dressed in black. One male and one female. Members of the repair crew? He frowned. He noted that they'd locked the hatch behind them with the emergency close function.

"You failed again," the man said, in English.

Ventinov gasped. It was Truman McClusky.

The Captain realized belatedly that they clutched weapons at their sides. The other crew were hard at work completing his orders, but they were not armed. They continued at their consoles, attempting to keep *Voskhod* seaworthy.

Something told him, it would not matter.

# Part Eleven

## The End

# Chapter Forty-Six

I STARED AT THE CAPTAIN. He looked nearly as bad as I. Bruised, battered, and beaten.

"You survived," he said in English. "How did you get in?"

I aimed my weapon at him, and glanced at Meg. "Find the thruster controls. Give us velocity." To Ventinov I replied, "Your ship is full of holes. It was easy to swim in."

Meg moved to a console, where a man was pushing buttons furiously and staring at a power schematic of the dreadnought. Large sections were red, others blue, and some were white.

The man looked up at the Captain and blurted something. He was grinning, oblivious to what was happening around him. He'd managed to get some power to the conventional thrusters.

Meg pointed her gun at his face, and nodded to him. "Five percent thrust, please." He looked confused, and she gestured with her weapon. He glanced at Ventinov, his face pale, but turned back to his console and completed the order. It was the same thing his Captain wanted anyway, so why resist?

He didn't understand what was about to happen.

I removed the PCD. "Tell me when, Johnny."

The dreadnought was vibrating in apparent agony. The deck was *howling* from the stresses.

But we were moving forward, slowly.

I stared at Ventinov. "The Shiv failed. Your plan failed. *You* failed."

"Oceania will never exist. Russia is the dominant power in the seas."

"No, it's not. Russia failed as well. All three of your dreadnoughts are gone, now. It'll leave a void in the oceans, and the other superpowers, including us, will fill that void. Your time here is done." I shrugged. "For now, anyway."

Anger flooded his face. "What do you mean? This dreadnought is still here! This dreadnought will destroy Trieste."

"Not going to happen."

The ship continued to shudder around us. More alarms were sounding, but we were indeed moving forward.

Johnny's voice fluttered to me. "In range."

I said to Meg, "Stop us here, Meg."

She pulled the throttle back and the ship stopped vibrating. Friction brought us to a halt and we remained, neutrally buoyant, in place. Two of the crewmen were working on the ballast, paying us no attention.

Ventinov looked confused. "What are you doing?"

I ignored him. To Johnny I quietly said, "Fire."

—••—

THE NEUTRAL PARTICLE BEAM, HOUSED in a transparent and pressurized tube on the shallow ocean floor, moved along a nearly frictionless rail. It positioned itself directly underneath the dreadnought *Voskhod*. We'd placed the firing tube here, anticipating an attack from this direction and an incoming fleet from the Atlantic. The tube was fifty kilometres in length, covering a large angular bearing from which an attack force heading for Trieste might approach.

The beam consisted of two weapons. The first, a ten-terawatt laser, vaporized seawater and created a vacuum channel to the target hull. The range was short—less than 200 metres—but shooting upward at attacking vessels was something no one could anticipate.

Through the vacuum channel, the *real* weapon fired. It was a stream of neutral particles—deuterium, a form of hydrogen, made up of neutrons and protons. They fired at nearly the speed of light, slammed into the underside of the dreadnought, penetrated several inches, and disassociated atoms and pulled apart hull molecules. The titanium shell at point of impact began to weaken at the molecular level.

And ocean pressure began to take hold.

It was only a matter of minutes—or *seconds*—before the beam cut this warsub in two.

The sonar was blaring.

Ventinov frowned. "What is that?"

"Fish farms," I said. The bubbles churning upward from the vaporizing laser produced a wall of bubbles, enveloping the warsub, churning toward the surface. Outside, through the viewport, it looked like an upward-moving waterfall. Bubbles streamed past us.

We were so close to it; well within range.

It sliced deep into Ventinov's ship.

Only a few more seconds . . .

Realization flashed across his features. "The neutron beam? But it's not located here! It's still five kilometres—"

"That's what I led you to believe. I knew where you were getting your information. I leaked the fact that we were building the beam at a distance of five kilometres." I shrugged. "We lied. We'd always planned it for this location. And now, this vessel is directly over it."

Meg said, "It's hitting the hull." She stared at a readout. "Sonar is signaling a fish farms alert."

"It's confused," I said to Ventinov. "The computer doesn't know what the bubbles are. It's guessing." I'd been through this before, while first learning about the weapon and then stealing it from the BSF research base in the Indian Ocean.

"You will never defeat me."

"I already have. It's over." Then to Meg I said, "Do it."

She raised her gun and began firing into the control console. The gunshots rang out loudly and people covered their ears, shocked and stunned and lurching from the destruction. Sparks flew and more smoke billowed out. The ventilation units were quiet, however.

The ship was dying.

And soon it would be in two halves, fully flooded, on the seafloor.

Ventinov's face was white.

I said, "You came after me this time. Remember that. You killed my friends. It's over now."

New pressure alarms were blaring. Sections were flooding, and the neutral beam was cutting through the inner bulkheads easily. Anyone in the area would die swiftly as the laser and neutral beam easily cut through flesh. It would slough off bodies, puddling on the deck around them in a gory, bubbling ichor.

There was a high-pitched whine droning over everything, punctuated by thunderous creaks as steel beams succumbed to stress.

There were screams in the corridors.

The deck under us shuddered and seemed to fall several metres. I reached out to steady myself. "We better leave, Meg."

We backed toward the hatch, guns held outward.

Ventinov's face was full of rage. It was flushed now.

"Should we shoot him?" Meg asked.

An image of Sahar came to me. I couldn't kill the man in cold blood, despite what he'd done to me. I replied, "The Neutral Beam will take care of it."

*Voskhod* was trembling from the incoming water and the continuing destruction of its superstructure. The sonar was shrieking its alarms.

Meg said, "Then allow me to do this." She aimed at his legs and fired multiple shots. He crumpled to the deck, screaming. He clutched his wounds. The other crewmen were watching, but no one leapt to his defence.

The hatch closed behind us, and we sprinted for the airlock.

# Chapter Forty-Seven

THE DREADNOUGHT HOVERED OVER THE neutral beam weapon for several minutes as the stream of neutrons carved the beast to bits.

I watched from the living area of *SC-1*. Our seacar was out of commission—dead—but we controlled the weapon through contact with Trieste and Kristen Canvel. The beam was arrow straight, vaporizing seawater, and bubbles churned upward, slightly obscuring the view of the bright light slicing into the dreadnought's hull. The neutral beam, within the vacuum channel, was *obliterating* the molecular cohesion of the titanium hull, the inner bulkheads, and any equipment it touched. The ship fell apart under the onslaught. Maneuvering controls would not work. The backup bridge controls were no longer functioning, and Ventinov had likely watched the ship crumble around him.

It plunged to the seafloor in its final death throes, gouts of air billowing out and soaring upward. An immense oil slick on the surface marked the grave.

We watched in silence.

Ventinov was gone.

—••—

KRISTEN CALLED A MINUTE LATER. "We've shut the beam off, Mac, but sonar indicates that another vessel is approaching from the Puerto Rico Trench. It'll take hours to get to you though."

"Acknowledged," I whispered, still staring at the destruction outside. The scene was unimaginable. The warsub was four football fields long. It was now in two pieces. We were shallow enough here to watch the unfolding events without computer-enhanced imaging. "What ships?"

"*Infiltrator*. It's Admiral Kenley's vessel."

"Is that the only one?"

"Yes."

"What about our *Swords* and the rest of the fleet?"

"They're still engaged in the fight, but the Hunter-Killers in the Puerto Rico Trench are mostly gone."

"And the other warsubs?"

There was a long pause.

"They're moving to the east."

*What the hell?*

She continued, "Mac—reports are that the coalition fleet has broken. They're retreating."

Meg and Johnny shouted in joy. Sahar and Renée had both regained awareness of the events going on around them, and they managed smiles. Then Sidra joined in and I moved to hug them. We embraced and howled in victory.

Then I hugged Meg, and we stood like that, ankle deep in water, and cried, standing in my dead seacar. We couldn't believe it. The last two years had been tumultuous, but we'd finally achieved our father's dreams.

—••—

TWO DAYS LATER, *INFILTRATOR* FINALLY reached our position. It stopped near the *Voskhod* wreck. They had no idea what had happened, but the sight of a Russian dreadnought sheered in two would have given anyone pause.

Kenley signalled. Inside, I was nervous. We'd brought some systems back online in *SC-1*, but we were hardly seaworthy. But the Neutral Beam was ready, and the *Terminator* Class warsub was in range. Our remaining vessels were nearby, hiding in case we needed their assistance.

But I wasn't too concerned. I only had to give the signal, and the

Neutral Particle Beam would cut the ship in two.

"Go ahead," I said into the comm.

"McClusky," her voice was strong and resilient. "I have a message from the USSF. And, a directive from even higher up than that."

I glanced at the others. *Higher.* It meant the president. "Go ahead."

"Your request is granted."

The others looked genuinely confused. "What does that mean?" Johnny asked. Min Lee was up and watching, and she was curious too.

I said into the PCD, "You mean—"

"We are granting the American colonies their independence. There will have to be economic treaties established, but . . . but it's something we can work with." She sounded resigned to the fact, ordered by her superiors.

I said to Sahar. "Your media interviews worked."

"The pen is mightier than the sword," she replied with a smile.

"Sometimes a Neutral Particle Beam helps too."

"And an Isomer Bomb," Renée added.

And then we cheered again. We even cried some more.

We'd won.

# Epilogue

## Trieste City

# Epilogue

A WEEK PASSED, AND WE watched the superpowers closely to see if their actions matched their words. They'd agreed to let us forge our own paths underwater, and all members of The Fifteen received the same message from their colonial mother nations. The desire for war had diminished, especially after global protests by citizens intent on helping our plight, together with the extreme impacts of rapid climate change.

The rising water was inexorable. Nations could fight it with massive engineering projects. Famine and drought were also something that couldn't change. Instead, agricultural land migrated north, meaning expensive infrastructure additions and large-scale fertilization projects. Water needed to be diverted south from freshwater supplies in the higher latitudes, and this also required large infrastructure investments.

Climate change was *expensive*.

They couldn't waste more money fighting underwater. In the past few years, the USSF had lost multiple bases and hundreds of warsubs in the fighting. They were done. They'd lost the cold war, which kept flaring hot. They'd lost those intense flareups as well. In the final confrontation, we'd been ready for them. They hadn't expected the weapons in our arsenal, and it had shocked them.

Perhaps, one day, they'd try to control us again, but, I thought, not for many, many years. There was too much to do on the surface, if they were going to live in a much hotter and more violent world. Deadlier storms, more intense hurricanes, more frequent tornadoes, shattered shore defenses—that was their future. They were throwing themselves into the challenge, and it made me happy. It meant they would leave us on our own. We just had to continue to succeed underwater, and prove to our own people that we could keep them happy and supplied with necessary resources for survival.

Meg was in the Repair Module, in her office, still catching up on work she'd missed during the mission to kill The Shiv and then the fighting in the Puerto Rico Trench. She looked up and smiled as I entered. It was a genuine smile; she had pulled herself out of the depression following Windsor's betrayal and attempts on our lives. She was wearing overalls with grease across the front. "Hiya, Truman."

I sat before her and returned the smile. "I just wanted to check in with you. See how you've been doing."

"You've been busy dealing with the fallout. Making treaties with The Fifteen. And I see you got your teeth fixed. It's a good look for you."

I shrugged. "Thanks. Sahar has been doing the negotiating, mostly. I'm just there as an advisor." I paused and stared at the office. There were seacar blueprints on a large bench, tools on the bulkheads, and even a model on a mount in the corner. It was a seacar I didn't recognize, and I frowned. It was like our *Swords*, but it was longer, sleeker. It seemed deadlier. "What's that?"

"Our new warsub. We have to replace the lost fleet. We're upgrading our *Swords*."

"But I haven't signed off on a new design."

"It's just a prototype."

I stared at it for several heartbeats. It was stunning. It seemed beautiful and dangerous. "I love it. It doesn't seem heavily armored though. Can it go deep?"

"Graphene."

She said the single word, and it made me catch my breath. "You've figured out the process?"

"Hyland did. He studied the de Laval nozzle we took from The Facility, along with the graphene in the tank. He used citric acid as the substrate." She flashed me another smile. "It worked. Now we're going to start production on these vessels, once you agree."

"I'll have to look at the specs," I mumbled. "But it looks impressive." I turned back to her. She was in her element, once again. Thrilled to be working in aquanautic engineering, with new challenges and a new goal.

"How's my seacar?" I asked.

"We're still working on her. I assume you'll want a graphene coating?"

"Absolutely."

"These new seacars will be better."

"Than *SC-1*? She's been with me since the start. I couldn't give her up. Ever."

"I figured." She paused. "We're also going to design our own version of the *Roach*. For mining in The Iron Plains and the CCZ. Using the graphene, it'll go deeper and can haul more nodules."

"Makes sense." I shifted in the chair. "I wanted to talk to you about the things you said. About our family, needing someone, and thinking about leaving."

She stared at me, her eyes blank. Then she smiled again. "Come on, Tru. I'm not going anywhere. This is my home. I have to help my city survive and prosper."

I frowned. "But you seemed so upset, just a week ago."

"And I was. But Windsor tapped into my inner pain and used that against me. You have the same pain, because of Dad and what happened to him. But you're doing fine. And I am too." She tilted her head. "Besides, I'm going on a few dates this week. To see if anything develops."

"Really? You? Dating?"

"I know, it's not like me. But if Windsor taught me anything, it's that I need to share this life with someone. Like how you and Renée are doing this together, in Trieste. I would like that too. I know it's out there for me, somewhere."

I studied the surroundings, at the tools and grease and blueprints. At her freckles, blue eyes, and blond hair. "Something tells me you're not going to have much of a problem, Meg. You just have to be open to it." Something would happen for her, very soon. I had no doubt. "I'm thrilled that you're staying in Trieste. I was scared."

"I spent too many years in Blue Downs. I want to be with you and

Renée. You're the only family I have."

We stood and hugged. I thought about the tears we'd both shed after Admiral Kenley had accepted our demands. Dad's death and the following breakup of our family had caused years and years of trauma. Time to focus on this now, I thought. On family. On moving forward, together. Trieste would be fine. Family was more important.

—••—

BACK IN MY OFFICE, I sat behind the desk and stared at the device before me. It was a PCD.

*Cliff's PCD.*

I had retrieved it from his *Sword* minutes before it sank. The Russian kill team had failed, and Sidra and I had gone over to the seacar to investigate, and I'd found it then. Our computer specialist had finally had time to repair it, and I switched it on. The memory was intact, and his files were all there.

In the messaging folder, there was one for me, unsent.

The date on it was 3 June.

My breath caught in my throat.

I'd sent Cliff on the mission to retrieve the graphene, and it had killed him.

I wondered for a moment if I should listen to the message. I don't think I could have handled more guilt at that particular moment. There had been too much death over the past two years. Too much fighting. Too many battles.

Too many nightmares.

But I pressed play, and hunched over the device as he spoke.

He was sitting in the pilot cabin of his *Sword*. He wasn't looking at the camera, he was staring out the viewport. The seacar was under power; the engine thrummed in the background.

"Mac," he said. "I've located the graphene facility. I had to follow the trail. It led to Blue Downs and an agricultural dome. There is an intermediary there, named Tsim Lui, running the operation. He's producing citric acid and shipping it to the plant. It's needed for the production, for some reason." He paused and took a breath. "But I'm skeptical. It seemed almost as if . . . almost as if someone left these clues for me. But I'm going in anyway, to see if I can get anything. I'll be careful." He adjusted course slightly. He pushed the ballast levers and began to descend. "I wanted to let you know something before I go in there. I know I'm not an emotional man. I don't express myself well. I make one of these messages before every single mission, just in case I don't get back. This is probably the tenth one I've made, so it's getting routine. I set it to transmit to you unless I get back in time to stop it. I have always succeeded at my missions, but you never know." He took another breath as he continued to pilot.

So, it was a failsafe in case he died, and he did it before every mission. But why didn't this final message send? Then I realized. It was likely because the Russian kill team—or The Shiv—got on board his *Sword* and destroyed the PCD before it could.

He continued, "So my message is this: I have loved working with you at Trieste. It's given me a purpose in life again, after so many years of monotony. The fight for independence, working in intelligence for you. It's been so rewarding. If we do achieve freedom from the superpowers, I have no idea what I'll do with myself. But I wanted you to know how great these last two years have been. I was in the USSF, many years ago. I was in the Gulf during the action that killed your dad. I've always lived with regret for that, even though I wasn't part of it. I hope I've redeemed myself, in your eyes. If I don't get back from this mission, I just wanted you to know how grateful I am."

By then I'd dissolved into tears, and could barely hear his words.

"There's something else. I've uncovered a mystery back at Trieste. I'm going to look into it more when I return, but I wanted to tell you about it here, in case I don't come back."

He continued to speak for a minute, and I stared at the device in horror.

I would never forget the man, nor his contribution to my family's incredible journey.

—••—

JOHNNY WAS IN A RECREATION lounge with Min Lee. They were having a drink together, relaxing, after the events of the past week.

The bruises were fading—as mine were—and the two were smiling and laughing. Others were in the bar, still celebrating, drinking, and cheering. Someone was singing karaoke and music was blasting.

People in the lounge saw me enter and swarmed me, shaking my hand and hugging me. I shared many smiles and laughs with them. This was what I had been fighting for: people's happiness and joy. The need to work for ourselves and determine our own paths underwater. I hoped the celebrating would continue for many more weeks.

Finally, I made my way to Johnny and Min. They'd seen me enter and had been watching me interact with Triestrians, who no doubt were pleased to be socializing and celebrating with both the Mayor and Deputy Mayor.

I sat before them and ordered a kelp beer. I winced as I took a gulp.

"Still hate the taste?" he asked, smiling.

"I never hated it. I just endure it. It's better than importing stuff."

We drank together and shared laughs and stories about what we'd just been through. We also spoke of the past two years, how Johnny had come back into my life just as the struggle for independence flared up again, and I took over as Mayor of Trieste, and he as deputy shortly after. And then I said, "Look, I've been meaning to talk to you, Johnny."

His face grew serious. "I know that look. What's up?"

"Nothing major."

"No new mission?"

"No. Nothing. Things are actually going to be boring around here for now. Mining, farming, developing our exploitation settlements and shipping produce to the mainland. Economic agreements with The Fifteen."

"Which is soon to include a lot more colonies, from what I understand."

He was correct. Already the Japanese and Canadian cities were clamoring to join our alliance. "Yes. But the thing is—"

"Yes?"

Min Lee was watching, wondering exactly where I was going with this.

I said, "Are you two staying here? In Trieste?"

He looked at Min. "That's the plan, Mac. We need a home. This is the place."

That made me happy. His past had been traumatic too. We'd been through a lot together.

"Good," I said. Then I blurted it out. "The thing is, I'm resigning."

—••—

"WHAT?" JOHNNY ASKED, HIS FACE blank.

I shrugged. "I'm done. I've achieved what I wanted. I don't need to be Mayor anymore. I don't need to be the director of TCI. I can rest easy. And Renée . . . " I stopped and considered what to say.

But I didn't have to. Johnny interjected, "Are you leaving Trieste?"

"No way." I said it with finality. "Never. I'll work for the city. Somewhere. I'm a good kelp farmer. I've done it before. Or I'll help Meg. She's working on a new seacar for our military."

The two sitting across from me grinned. "That's great news," Min said.

"I was hoping you'd take over as Mayor, Johnny. Until the next election, that is, but I think you'll do just fine. The voters are happy right now." I gestured over my shoulder, at the continuing celebrations.

He looked shocked. Min smiled and nodded at him. Then he raised his glass. He took a swig of beer and said, "Absolutely. I would love to. But only if you stay on in case an emergency develops."

"For sure."

We continued to drink and celebrate. It made me feel better, knowing that Trieste would be in good hands. Chanta Newel had taken over as Chief Security Officer, and now Johnny Chang would be Mayor.

After a few more drinks, Johnny excused himself and wandered over to the washroom. A swarm of partygoers stopped him on the way, to chat with him about the recent battle and about fighting The Shiv, which *everyone* knew about now. It was just going to add to the legend and mystique surrounding us. We'd fought the greatest spy in the world and had survived.

I turned to Min. "So, when were you going to tell me about the bomb you planted?"

Her face immediately fell. Waves of despair seemed to cross her features. "You know." It was a statement.

She'd planted the bomb at the start of all of this, severing the power to the city. We'd never identified the culprit nor found evidence of the device, because of the hurricane, which had swept the destroyed components away. "I do." I watched her carefully.

She sighed. "They were orders. I carried them out. But I did so in order to deflect suspicion."

"Go on."

She stared at Johnny, who was far enough away that he couldn't hear. He was still talking to other Triestrians about recent events, laughing and explaining what he'd been through. She said, "An order came through to Sheng City Intelligence. To kill you, Mac."

I raised my eyebrows at that. "Who wants me dead now?"

"I looked into it for a while. Mainland China. But the original order came from Russia."

"Russia." I said it, finally understanding.

"Yes. I think Ventinov. It was part of his plan to get you. One part consisted of planting clues to get you to The Facility. Administrator Zhao reluctantly played her part, but really wanted nothing to do with it. They were orders from her superiors. I had similar orders."

"From the CSF?"

"Yes. But my Sheng bosses told me to do it, but not succeed, if you get me. They wanted it to look like they were following orders, but failed. They didn't want to damage their treaty with you and Trieste. So I planted the bomb where it would make news but not actually hurt anybody, especially not you. But it kept the CSF off our backs, and no one got hurt. Now Ventinov and The Shiv are gone, no one wants you dead anymore, so there's no need for anyone to follow up." She shrugged. "It put me in a dilemma. I wanted to be here with Johnny. I didn't want to kill any Triestrian—definitely not you!—but China was determined to make Ventinov happy."

"To maintain good relations with Russia, I guess."

"That's my thinking."

And she'd come up with a bomb where no one would get hurt, but it would make the news broadcasts. "I think I understand."

Her eyes looked remorseful. "I'm sorry I didn't tell you earlier."

"Were you going to?"

"Yes. I think so." Then she paused. "I don't know, to be honest. I just want to start a new life here, away from the craziness."

That, at least, I understood. Meg and Renée felt the same way.

*Renée.* I needed to speak with her, too.

"Are you going to tell anybody?" she asked me.

I stared at her. "There's no need, Min Lee. You did what you had to."

"How'd you find out?"

"Cliff Sim."

She blinked. "Your CSO? He told you before he died?"

"In a way. He uncovered the plot. He knew you were on the way to do something. He warned me to keep my eyes on you." I shrugged. "The rest, I guessed."

She shook her head. "You forced me to confess by pretending you already knew."

I smiled. "Yes."

She stared at Johnny. "I want to stay here now, Mac. With Johnny. Make a new life for ourselves."

"I won't tell him," I assured her. "I believe you." I hesitated, then, "But you have to separate yourself from Sheng. No more orders from them, no more contact with your superiors."

"I'm working for Trieste City Intelligence now, Mac."

I hesitated, wondering if we even needed the organization anymore.

But that was silly. I knew that there would always be enemies out there, competing with us for dominance in the oceans.

—••—

SAHAR AND SIDRA HAD SPENT a week recovering in Trieste. They'd been through an ordeal. To compound the issues, while recovering after her injuries sustained during the battle, Sahar had been answering constant interview requests. She needed to keep public opinion on our side, so continued to speak to the world about the needs for an independent nation underwater, to develop the resources peacefully and safely, with minimal environmental damage. Talia Tahnee, the Mayor of Blue Downs, had joined with Sahar in helping make that happen as much as possible.

But now Sahar was leaving for Churchill Sands, and Sidra was going with her. The brother and sister team were going back to their city to lead their people into this new frontier, together. It made me smile.

It seemed familiar.

We were in the Docking Module, where they were boarding a seacar to take them back to their home. Standing on the dock beside the vehicle, I said, "I haven't told you something, Sahar."

She stared at me, waiting.

I continued, "I'm quitting as Mayor. Johnny is taking over."

She frowned. "But you're the leader of Oceania. How can you lead The Fifteen if you're not Mayor?"

"I'm not leading The Fifteen."

"You're not? But we're all under that belief."

"A false one." I sighed and looked at the module around us. At the open water, the moored seacars, the waves splashing the docks. "Look, Sahar. I was good as the leader of a revolution. Pushing people to fight. Planning battles. Fighting seacars, launching torpedoes. Fighting hand-to-hand." I shrugged. "But that's over now. It's done."

"But people respect you, Mac. They need you. Without you, Oceania—"

"Will be fine. They'll prosper and continue to exploit the oceans. Hopefully peacefully. I'm a wartime leader, you could say. The war is over. They don't need me anymore."

She frowned, and Sidra approached from the seacar to see what was happening.

I continued, "What I wanted to say is that *you're* the future of Oceania. Not me, not Meg. You're the person to lead The Fifteen and grow the nation and do this peacefully. Work with the others, keep us on an even keel, which is why you came with us on the mission in the first place. You know I'm right, Sahar. You're the future of colonization. I'll be here, if you need me. I'm not going anywhere. But I have to move on, now. I'm forty-six years old." I grinned. "I'm too old to keep up the fight. And the thing is, the fight is over. I'm not the best at diplomacy and treaties and economic agreements."

"And I am?" she asked.

"You're better at it than I am. But more important is that the people love you. All the people all over the world. That's what Oceania needs. Not me."

She stared at me for a long moment. "Are you sure?"

"I made my mind up a while ago. I knew this was my decision. Besides," I said with another grin, "I have something else more important to do now."

I shook Sidra's hand and hugged Sahar. They were smiling.

"It's been an adventure, Mac," she said.

"I wouldn't change anything for the world," I replied.

—••—

RENÉE WAS IN MY OFFICE, waiting for me. Sahar and Sidra had just departed, and I was sad to see them leave, but we would always have fond memories of our adventures and what had occurred during the past few months. For her, the struggle was only just beginning. She was going to continue bringing colonies into Oceania, and making the nation stronger and better than ever. I knew, and I was more sure of it than of anything else in my life, that Sahar Noor was the best person to lead Oceania into the future.

Renée smiled as I entered, and I hugged her hard.

She pulled back and stared at me. "What's that for? Is everything okay?"

"I resigned as Mayor."

She blinked. "I beg your—"

"And I quit as leader of Oceania."

Now she stepped backward. "Are you joking right now?"

"Not at all." I smiled and looked around. This office had been my home for far too long. Cramped, bare, sparse. Barely any decoration, and a small viewport.

Steel all around me.

"I'm moving on, Renée."

Now she looked truly horrified. "Mac, what are you saying?"

"I'm moving on, *with you*. If you'll have me, that is." I paused and then, "Will you marry me? Stay here in Trieste with me, and start a family?"

It stunned her. She couldn't speak.

I continued, "I'll find work here. But I want to have kids with you. Teach them how to live in the oceans, how to colonize the ocean floor. It's a new world for us down here, and the fight is done."

"For now."

"What do you mean?"

She sighed. "Mac, it's not over. Someone will always be there to threaten us. Another nation, underwater. Another country. Russia will return. Or China. It'll never end."

"It's over. For me, it's done. I told you, I quit. I want us to be together, officially. Stay here with me and start a family." I paused again, and then, "I'll get you a ring soon. I promise. It'll be graphene."

Now she laughed, realizing that I was actually serious. "Why graphene?"

"It'll never get damaged. The pressure will never affect it. It'll never go dull, and never scratch."

She cocked her head. "Symbolism, Mac?"

"What's your answer, Renée?"

She stepped toward me and we kissed, long and hard. "My answer is yes."

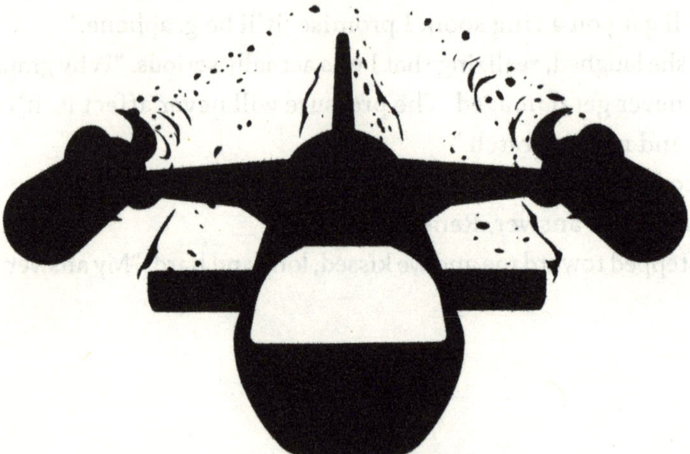

# A Note from the Author

Any errors in regards to the physics of cavitation and supercavitation, the effects of water pressure, graphene and its manufacture, sound propagation underwater, sonar systems and SCUBA diving are mine alone.

Thank you to artist Nelson Housden for creating the images of *SC-1* on the cover, spine, and its silhouettes in the interior of this book.

Thank you to Cheyney Steadman for once again creating the schematics and maps. She created the graphics from *Fatal Depth* and onward, and her images have contributed to the overall aesthetic of Oceania. Fitzhenry & Whiteside, when releasing new versions of the eBooks for *The War Beneath* and *The Savage Deeps*, even included her images (of Trieste and The Ridge) in those editions as well.

I put William Windsor's home in Ripley, Surrey. I actually lived there for a year, in 1978/79. It seemed familiar enough to me to use it, although it was a *long* time ago, but I thought it would be a nice note to the town. I remember playing in backyard bomb shelters, a remnant of World War II and the London Blitz. In fact, the war was still important to so many Brits at the time. As an 8-year-old, the comics we read and the toys we played with were mostly related to the war in some way. The school I attended practiced corporal punishment, and it scared me into good behaviour. I never got sent to the headmaster, but the fear was always there. Not finishing the hot lunch provided was reason for getting strapped, or "the slipper." That was traumatic. The fish and chips were no problem . . . the dish was a huge staple in our diet, and I still love salt and vinegar. The steak and kidney pie was slightly more of a challenge. The mushy peas and custard were things I had to keep down, and I never got used to eating them.

I had known, ever since writing *The War Beneath*, that Mac would eventually declare independence. The timing of the event had always been amorphous in my mind, though I knew it would be *somewhere* in the final book. Would it happen at the very end of *A Blanket of Steel*, to cap the entire series? Or would it happen earlier? I eventually decided to do it much earlier, at the beginning of the book, and then have the climax involve the resulting battle. I designed the cat and mouse game with the notorious spy, and thus *The Steel Shiv* was born. This tied in nicely with events from *Fatal Depth*, providing an important thread of continuity and drama, and I decided to make the final book a revenge thriller. I made the assassin's identity a mystery, to keep the reader engaged. I hope it worked. I truly enjoyed writing the tense reveal that took place in the airlock at the end of Part Five in this book.

*The Rise of Oceania* originated during my studies of physical geography, geology, geophysics, and environmental systems at Western University (the University of Western Ontario) in the late 1980s and early 1990s. Every class seemed to involve discussions and studies on the Greenhouse Effect, rising water, flooding, shore defenses, famine, greenhouse gases, and more. I quickly realized that nations would have to locate new resources for Earth's exploding populations. We are not going to stop climate change. Any thoughts along these lines are a pipe dream, a fantasy. The developed nations of the world can try, but the truth is that the less developed nations will continue to burn cheap coal and fossil fuels. It's akin to one person trying to clean a lake while neighbors continue to dump their sewage into it. Not that we shouldn't try—we should always make steps toward being more environmentally conscious—but we need to be prepared to adapt and change as quickly as the environment. So where can we get new food, minerals, and resources? The oceans seem the likely location, and more realistic than outer space. The oceans are more immense than people can truly understand. Seventy percent of the world is covered by water. The world's largest mountain range is underwater—the Mid-Oceanic

Ridge, which is nearly 65,000 km long. The deep abyssal plains contain polymetallic nodules, and the stats provided in this book are accurate. I set on the idea of colonization / exploitation of the ocean floors, and the idea of a new Cold War flaring up wasn't far behind. The world of spycraft, espionage, subterfuge and outright fighting was obvious, but I didn't actually write *The War Beneath* until 2008. I finally secured a deal for its publication in 2016, and the rest is history. Since 2018 (or thereabouts) I have written one thriller in the series each year, give or take. I have designed them to tell the arc of Oceania and the McClusky family, but each is a standalone featuring a different genre. They are:

| | |
|---|---|
| *The War Beneath* | Spy vs. spy chase thriller |
| *The Savage Deeps* | Military thriller |
| *Fatal Depth* | A 'do or die' mission |
| *An Island of Light* | Prison break |
| *The Shadow of War* | Heist |
| *A Blanket of Steel* | Revenge thriller; also a combination of all of the above genres |

I did this so readers would not grow bored by the books. I didn't want them to feel that they were constantly reading the same type of story. I wanted each to feature the familiar setting and characters, but to be different and always keep readers entertained. I hope I succeeded.

Each book also involves a unique technology that future ocean colonists will need to descend deeper, travel faster, and defend against their enemies. Some are purely fictional, like the Acoustic Pulse Drive. Others already exist, like supercavitation, invented in the 1970s, though not yet used in crewed vehicles. Some of the other technologies you might learn about in these books include: syntactic foam, anechoic tiles, underwater drones, fusion, fission, graphene, neutral particle beams, lasers, isomer bombs, virtual imaging displays, screw blade designs, and more.

The history of graphene in this book is real. The notion of a 2D substance and its applications are astonishing. Engineers are creating graphene tubes to transmit power and communications. I focused on compressive strength for exploration in the ocean deeps. The story about the scotch tape and graphite did really occur. One day graphene will be commonplace as we push deeper into oceans and farther into the solar system.

Thank you for joining me on this journey into the oceans and following the McClusky siblings on their paths to their ultimate destinies. If you've only read just this book, and no other books in the series, I hope you consider picking up the others or borrowing one from a library near you. I will continue writing thrillers, and I have books already completed and ready to put out into the world. I hope you look for my writing and stay with me on my creative journey. You can learn more about me on my blog and website, so please consider joining me at www.timothysjohnston.com/blog.

I'd like to thank Sharon Fitzhenry of Fitzhenry & Whiteside for acquiring the series. Also, Holly Doll and Peter Doll for publishing and marketing the books. Ken Geniza designed the interiors and the covers of *Fatal Depth, An Island of Light, The Shadow of War,* and *A Blanket of Steel.* The entire team at Fitzhenry has been incredibly receptive and open to my creativity and my stories. From the bottom of my heart, thank you, all.

Finally, I'd like to thank my family for their unending support and encouragement. They come with me to signings and other public appearances, they beta read my work, and they provide feedback on story ideas and on my writing. They put up with me when I'm writing, editing, and spending countless hours on these books. They have supported me from the very beginning.

My futuristic murder mysteries include *The Furnace* (2013), *The Freezer* (2014), and *The Void* (2015), all published by Carina Press.

Please visit me at Facebook, Instagram, and X (Twitter) @TSJ_Author. Also visit www.timothysjohnston.com to receive updates and learn about new and upcoming thrillers, and also to register for news alerts.

Thanks again for investing your time in this novel. Do let me know what you think of my thrillers.

Timothy S. Johnston
tsj@timothysjohnston.com
24 September, 2023

Timothy S. Johnston has won the GLOBAL THRILLER Award, the CYGNUS Award, the EPIC Award, the CLUE Award, and has been finalist in the SILVER FALCHION Award (Best Action Adventure)—*three times*. His newest technothriller, *A Blanket of Steel*, is the sixth and final book in his underwater colonization series, *The Rise of Oceania*, published by Fitzhenry & Whiteside Limited. Timothy S. Johnston is a Canadian writer who lives in London, Ontario. He has been an educator for over twenty-five years and writes thrillers in pursuit of a radical dream: to give back to the genres that have inspired him over the past five decades, and to thank the creative minds who provide much-needed escapist entertainment in times of need. Timothy is a firm believer that a good story has the potential to heal the world. His favourite movie is *Planet of the Apes* (1968), his favourite director is John Carpenter, and his favourite writers are Michael Crichton, Isaac Asimov, Agatha Christie, and fellow Canadian, Robert J. Sawyer. Timothy has spent the past six years underwater (metaphorically) writing about a new Cold War, espionage, colonization, and gripping action. Previous books include *The War Beneath, The Savage Deeps, Fatal Depth, An Island of Light*, and *The Shadow of War.* After finishing the sixth and final book in *The Rise of Oceania* saga, *A Blanket of Steel*, he can finally take a deep breath and decompress . . . until adventure calls again, of course.

***Experience the gripping adventure of underwater colonization in the midst of a cold war rapidly turning hot.***

# THE RISE OF OCEANIA

**from Timothy S. Johnston and Fitzhenry & Whiteside, Ltd.**